Praise for *Armor of God*

"This religious thriller alternates briskly between present-day New York and Jerusalem and scenes set in the time of the Crusades in France. . . . The authors show a good grasp of the variety of various religious traditions and histories that underpin the series." —*Publishers Weekly*

"Fans will relish the sequel to *The Masada Scroll* . . . in which a gospel of peace and harmony is unacceptable to the powerful who need the masses conflicted."
—*Genre Go Round Reviews*

Praise for *The Masada Scroll*

"This is a book that delivers in every way: a great concept, a fascinating journey, and high-class storytelling. *The Masada Scroll* will take you to new places and open your mind to new ways to look at the world. It is the right book at the right time for those of us who seek the ultimate answers to the world's many troubles. I enjoyed *The Masada Scroll* as I have enjoyed few other contemporary novels."
—Greg Tobin, author of *Conclave* and *Selecting the Pope*

"A Catholic priest, an American scholar, and a nice Jewish girl mull over the significance of an ancient document unearthed at the site of Israel's to-the-last-man stand against the Romans. . . . [Block and Vaughan] include a great deal of arcane knowledge, perhaps even enough to satisfy *Da Vinci Code* fans." —*Booklist*

"*The Masada Scroll* is an interesting mix of subgenres. It has the miraculous events that you would expect from religious fiction and the historical technology that has become a mainstay of popular action / adventures. . . . A unique and fun story." —*Midwest Book Review*

ARMOR

OF

GOD

PAUL BLOCK
AND
ROBERT VAUGHAN

A TOM DOHERTY ASSOCIATES BOOK
NEW YORK

This is a work of fiction. All of the characters, organizations, and events portrayed in this novel are either products of the authors' imaginations or are used fictitiously.

ARMOR OF GOD

Copyright © 2008 by Paul Block and Robert Vaughan

A Tor Book
Published by Tom Doherty Associates, LLC
175 Fifth Avenue
New York, NY 10010

www.tor-forge.com

Tor® is a registered trademark of Tom Doherty Associates, LLC.

ISBN 978-0-7653-5185-2

First Edition: January 2009
First Mass Market Edition: September 2009

Printed in the United States of America

0 9 8 7 6 5 4 3 2 1

To Paul's grandsons,
Jonas Martin Block and Evan Garrett Block,
and Robert's grandchildren,
Lauren Elaine Vaughan
and Ryan Kyle Jack,
who, with their new generation,
are the true armor of God

ARMOR
OF
GOD

CHAPTER 1

Three initiates, bare from the waist up, lay facedown on the marble floor. At the head of each stood a disciple wielding a flagellum bearing nine cords embedded with bits of sharpened bone.

"Renounce your own will for the salvation of your soul," the Grand Master intoned from his place in the outer circle of two dozen followers. Emblazoned in blood-red on the breasts of their brown hooded cassocks was the symbol of the Sacred Order of Via Dei: a T-shaped cross topped by a circle, within which a blazing sun shot two beams downward to form a pyramid superimposed against the cross.

Grand Master Jean Fournier continued his recitation from *The Order of Sanctity,* by which all members of Via Dei—the Disciples of the Way—were to conduct their lives.

"Strive everywhere with pure desire to serve the Holy Trinity of Via Dei, the Catholic Church, and Jesus Christ. Feel now the pain of the scourging received by our Lord."

The disciples whipped their flagella against the bare backs of the initiates, leaving red stripes.

"This I will do, so help me God," the initiates responded, their voices strained with pain as they fixed their gaze on the floor, not daring to look up into the eyes of the Grand Master.

"It is a dangerous thing to gaze too long upon the face of a woman," the Grand Master proclaimed. "Avoid the kiss or embrace of a woman lest you be contaminated by the sin of lust. Remain eternally before the face of God with a pure conscience and a sure life."

Again the disciples snapped their whips down hard. The red marks became welts.

"This I will do, so help me God," the initiates repeated as they fought to calm their shuddering bodies.

"Avoid idle words and laughter. There is much sin in any conversation that is not for the glory of the Lord."

The sharpened bone in the flagellum cords tore into flesh, spraying blood on the cassocks of the disciples.

"This I will do, so help me God," the initiates cried out.

"In order to fulfill your holy duties, so that you may gain the glory of the Lord's mercy and escape the torments of hellfire, you must obey the Grand Master of our Sacred Order of Via Dei. Do you swear now, so to do?"

Another brutal lashing punctuated the initiates' response: "I swear always to obey our Grand Master."

"The Sacred Order of Via Dei, the Catholic Church, and our blessed Lord are the trinity that guides our lives, symbolic of the Holy Trinity of Father, Son, and Holy Spirit. You will protect the sanctity of Via Dei by whatever means necessary. There is only one path to salvation, and it is the mission of Via Dei to protect that path. Destroying an enemy of Via Dei is doing the work of the Lord. Do you accept our doctrine?"

Once more the whips flailed, and the initiates cried out, "I accept the doctrine."

"Rise now, Disciples of the Way. Clothe yourselves in the garment of the Sacred Order of Via Dei and greet one another in brotherhood."

The three men struggled to their feet. Despite the pain they were enduring, they appeared rapturous as their sponsors— the very men who had wielded the whips—presented them with the brown cassock of membership.

The circle of disciples broke up and the members began

to mingle and congratulate their new brethren, each remembering the joyous day of his own initiation.

As a disciple in his early thirties was embracing one of the new members, he was interrupted by a gruff voice calling his name.

"Philippe Guischard . . ."

Turning, the disciple felt a knot of nervousness at seeing the Grand Master looking up at him. Philippe was a tall, muscular fellow, standing a good six inches above the compact and slightly hunched Jean Fournier, yet he felt inconsequential in the older man's presence. His anxiety lessened, however, when he saw the Grand Master's expression was serious but not severe.

"I have a mission for you, Philippe." Fournier grasped the younger man's elbow and led him away from the others, to one of the marble columns that encircled the sanctuary.

"I will obey your instructions with joy in my heart," Philippe answered, his voice a monotone that hid a renewed sense of unease.

"You have shown great promise, Philippe. Because of that, and because of the importance of your family's ties in Rome, we have asked you to serve as our envoy to the Holy See. But now I must ask you to put aside, for a time, that lofty office and undertake a mission of the utmost importance."

Fournier looked around to confirm they were alone, then continued in a hushed voice.

"You will return to Castile, there to deliver a letter. The letter will contain further instructions for you and for the person to whom you shall present it."

"And who is to receive this letter, Grand Master?"

"Tobias Garlande."

"My former teacher?" Philippe said in surprise. "But he's a heretic—you told me so when I arrived four years ago from Toledo. It is because of his heresy that you urged me not to return to his service."

"Four years is a long time. It is now the year of our Lord

one thousand ninety-five, almost the second century of the second millennium. During your time with us, you have made great progress and shown great inner strength; I no longer fear your becoming contaminated with his heresy."

"Thank you, Grand Master," Philippe said with a slight bow of the head.

"Yes, Tobias Garlande stands with those who believe Trevia Dei refers to three paths to God," Fournier said, adding in a derisive tone, "as if Christian, Jew, and Infidel could ever walk the same path or share the Lord's graces." He shuddered as though he were shaking off evil. "He doesn't accept what we have received through divine revelation—that Trevia Dei is the Holy Trinity and that there is only one path to God and salvation—Via Dei."

"Our new chosen name, so that we may suppress the false doctrine of the Trevia Dei heretics," Philippe replied, and Fournier smiled in approval. "So, the letter is a chastisement?" Philippe asked.

"No," the Grand Master replied. "I believe this letter to be the means by which Brother Tobias can save his eternal soul."

CHAPTER 2

MID-ATLANTIC, PRESENT DAY

F r. Michael Flannery jerked awake and shook his head to clear the imagery. *A dream or a vision?* he wondered as he rubbed his eyes and blinked against the sunlight streaming through the airplane window. He had been having both in increasing numbers and strength, and usually he could tell them apart. This one seemed unreal—almost surreal— with its circle of hooded men and bloody, knotted flagella cords flaying the skin of the initiates' backs. Surely it had been a dream, colored by his ongoing and intensive research of the early days of Via Dei.

"Jean Fournier," he whispered, recalling the name given the grand master. He'd have to look it up when he returned to Rome after his stay in New York. *And who is Philippe Guischard?* he wondered, not remembering anyone by that name or description in the archives of the Vatican, where he served as a historian and archaeologist.

"You're awake," a voice said, and Flannery turned to the young man in the next seat.

"Why, yes. How long was I out?"

"Ten, fifteen minutes or so."

"Really? It seemed longer."

"Dream time," the young man said cryptically.

Flannery's seat companion was a bespectacled American named David Meyers. They had struck up a conversation in the Rome airport, and by coincidence they wound up together in business class. David had his laptop open and was surfing the Web via the new in-flight portal provided by the airline.

David glanced over at the priest. "It's a lot more comfortable up here than in economy, especially for someone as tall as you, don't you think?"

"Yes, though I do feel guilty about it."

"Guilt? That's very Catholic of you," David joked. "However, we Jews wrote the book on guilt, though I confess that particular gene seems to have bypassed me."

"I just hope I didn't put anyone out. I booked economy, but somehow it got changed. When I asked, the gate attendant said, 'Perhaps somebody up there likes you.'"

"Divine intervention, eh?" David grinned as he shook his head. "Nothing so supernatural, I'm afraid. Just a few well-placed keystrokes . . ." He moved his fingers as if typing on the laptop.

Flannery looked at him curiously.

"I confess my sins, Father. I was enjoying our conversation at the terminal, so I figured why not continue on the plane."

"You did this?" Flannery said incredulously.

"Don't feel guilty; no one was put out. There were still open seats in business, so I gave you an upgrade."

"That explains it," Flannery said, looking a bit relieved. "I didn't realize you work for the airlines."

"I don't. I work off the grid, so to speak." Seeing the priest's look of confusion, he gestured at his laptop. "I'm what some folks call a hacker, Father Flannery. I hacked into their system and issued an upgrade . . . the same way I got my round-trip tickets to Europe. I could've flown first class but didn't want to push my luck. Here in business no one pays me any mind."

Flannery couldn't help but be impressed by the younger man's skills. At forty-seven, Flannery was perhaps twenty years older than David, but he felt ancient when it came to the gap in their computer skills. Still, arranging a free upgrade broke at least the seventh commandment and possibly the eighth, and he felt compelled to offer some advice on morality. But seeing David's sincere, almost innocent expression, he found himself smiling in spite of himself and said only, "I can't offer absolution for a confession like that."

David laughed. "I'm not confessing—I'm bragging. After all, what's the fun of being a Good Samaritan if you can't boast a little?"

"So long as it's just a little," Flannery replied. "You know what they say about pride going before a fall."

"Yes, well, I pride myself on my ability to fall and get back up—" He halted in midsentence, his eyes narrowing as he stared at the laptop screen. "Talk about falling . . ."

"What is it?" Flannery asked, seeing the genuine concern in his companion's expression.

"A plane." David angled the computer toward Flannery, revealing that he had accessed a private Web page of the Federal Aviation Administration. Lowering his voice, he said, "It went down over the Atlantic a short while ago."

Flannery read a bulletin that gave a sketchy account of an American Global flight that went off radar and was seen plunging into the ocean by a ship in the vicinity.

"No report of trouble, no Mayday, no explosion or flames; it just went down," Flannery said after reading the notice. Running a hand through his thick dark-brown hair, he shook his head. "It doesn't sound like an accident."

"It probably wasn't."

"And bound for New York, like us."

David nodded glumly. "I'd feel a lot better if we were heading somewhere—anywhere—else."

As if in reply, the cabin speaker crackled to life and the captain said in a calm voice, "Ladies and gentlemen, I know how patient you were during our departure delay, which makes it even more difficult to tell you that we've been called back. We are returning to Rome."

There were some gasps of surprise, followed by annoyed murmurs and a few obscenities throughout the cabin.

"I don't know how long we'll be on the ground in Rome," the captain continued. "But as soon as we get everything sorted out, we'll be able to resume our trip. I apologize for this further delay."

"Ah, someone up there heard me," David said.

Flannery tilted his head slightly, taking in the younger man. "You didn't have anything to do with—I mean, the plane returning to Rome . . ."

"Me?" David chuckled. "Book a free ticket, upgrade a seat, sure. But issue new flight directives? No way. That's more your guy's department." He nodded toward the heavens.

"Nothing so mysterious, I daresay. It's probably because of that downed plane. I wonder if all flights are being grounded or just those bound for New York."

As the plane banked to the right, a message alert popped up on the laptop, and David muttered, "Oh, no."

"What do you mean, 'Oh, no'?"

"I think someone's hacked into the plane's computer."

"How do you know?"

"I'm on the network; I can see incoming traffic." David shook his head. "This can't be good."

SHELLY PAIGE CARRIED a tray onto the flight deck, and the reserve pilot closed the reinforced cockpit door behind her. The spread of digital readouts across the panel and above the two pilots was both familiar and unfathomable to Shelly, who had been a flight attendant for fifteen years.

"Coffee for Ted and Jerry, tan-colored milk for the captain," she teased, making fun of his affinity for coffee heavily laced with cream and sugar.

Capt. Wayne Poppell glanced over his shoulder. "Any delicacies from first class?"

"I brought cheese Danish."

Poppell smiled. "You really know how to treat the flight-deck crew. Give me an older flight attendant over those young ones anytime."

Shelly gasped. "I'm only thirty-seven!"

Copilot Ted Friedman laughed and jabbed the captain's shoulder. "You're so full of couth."

"I didn't mean 'old,' I meant—"

"Best keep quiet, Captain," Friedman cut him off. "You'll only dig yourself deeper. Better safe than sorry."

"Speaking of safe," Shelly interjected, "we have special protection on this flight."

"What kind?" the captain asked.

"Seated three abreast in coach—and this isn't the opening line of a joke—there's a Catholic priest, a Jewish rabbi, and a Muslim imam."

"Side by side and not at each other's throats?" Friedman asked.

"They're quite friendly. I heard them mention some sort of ecumenical conference in New York."

"Christians, Jews, and Muslims . . ." the captain mused as he took a swallow of his coffee. "That would be great, but I'm gonna have to see it to believe it."

"I don't know, Captain, look at us," Friedman said. "I'm Jewish, you're a Baptist, and he's . . ." He turned to Jerry O'Hearn. "Are you Catholic, Jerry?"

"I'm a Republican," the reserve pilot quipped.

The copilot grinned. "See, and we get along."

"Were they upset that we turned back?" Poppell asked.

"No. Some folks were annoyed, but they settled down. Are you gonna tell them about that American Global flight?"

"Not unless I'm told to by ground control."

"Any more word on what happened?" Shelly asked.

"A ship saw the plane go down. No explosion or sign of distress; it just plunged into the ocean."

"Could someone else have gotten onto the flight deck?"

"Seems unlikely. But it might be wise to take a look at all

the passengers. Call if you see anyone suspicious." He turned back to the controls, then added, "And Shelly, I'm not opening the door again, for any reason."

She nodded. "I understand."

Shelly and the other flight attendants walked the length of the plane, taking in the passengers: a young boy in a St. Louis Rams shirt, a young woman refreshing her makeup, two uniformed soldiers in animated conversation, newlyweds on their honeymoon, an elderly couple returning from their first visit to Tuscany, a number of clerics, perhaps all bound for the same ecumenical conference.

After the other flight attendants reported back, Shelly picked up the cabin phone and informed the captain that no one aroused suspicion. Poppell thanked her, then told the crew, "Shelly says all is copacetic."

"The panel looks good," Ted Friedman said.

Poppell stroked his chin. "Yeah, no need to worry."

Suddenly all the LEDs blinked several times and the panel went black. The left wing dipped, and Poppell put his hands on the wheel to override the autopilot. The wing dipped deeper.

"Kill the autopilot," he said in a calm voice.

Friedman attempted to disengage. "I can't," he said, shaking his head in surprise.

"Either of you have any idea what's going on?" Poppell asked.

"No, sir, not a clue," the copilot replied.

"Captain, what about Satcon?" O'Hearn asked.

"Good idea. Disengage."

"I can't!" Friedman blurted. "It won't disengage."

"Reboot, then," O'Hearn suggested.

"Negative. The computer is locked up. I can't make it do anything."

"What the hell?" Poppell muttered as he worked the controls but didn't get any response. His voice was taut with fear now. "Put out a Mayday! I can't—"

A violent shudder threw the flight crew against the seatbacks, then jerked them forward against their straps. Suddenly the airplane did a complete wingover and plummeted straight down, gaining speed as it plunged into the ocean and disintegrated on impact.

FR. MICHAEL FLANNERY felt a violent shudder as all the cabin TV monitors went blank and the overhead lights went out. A moment later the engines shut down, and the plane banked hard and steep to the right and began spiraling downward. There was a moment of silence before people realized that something was terribly wrong. A few cried out in fear, some could be heard praying, but most were rigid in their seats, petrified with fear.

As the airplane continued losing altitude, descending in wide spirals, Flannery also began to pray. From the corner of his eye he noticed that David was typing frantically, the laptop screen aglow under battery power.

Flannery was about to accuse him of interfering with the onboard systems and causing the catastrophe, when David shouted, "There it is!" and gestured excitedly at the screen, which was filling with gibberish code. David resumed typing, and suddenly the stream of numbers and symbols shut down.

"I-I blocked it!" David exclaimed.

"What?"

"Someone was hacking into the airplane's computer, some sort of denial-of-service attack."

Flannery had no idea what he was talking about but realized it wasn't good.

"Now, if the pilots are paying attention . . ."

Before David could finish his comment, the airplane leveled its wings and stopped the spiral. Then one of the engines fired up, followed by the second.

The lights came back on, and the passengers cheered and

applauded in relief. The speaker system clicked on, and after a moment of crackling silence, the captain's voice filled the cabin.

"Ladies and gentlemen—uh—this is the captain. I won't lie to you. I have no idea what just happened, but we seem to have things back under control now. I'm declaring an emergency so we can expedite our return to Rome. You have my sincere apologies for any discomfort this may have caused."

"David!" Flannery said, gripping the young man's forearm. "You did it!"

David's almost perpetual grin was a lot less assured but somehow seemed more genuine. "I . . . I did, didn't I?"

"I'll say a special blessing for you."

"Will it work for a Jew?"

"Absolutely, my friend. Absolutely," Flannery declared.

Just then a flight attendant came by, reassuring passengers that the danger was over. Seeing that David's computer was running, she stopped and said, "I'm sorry sir, but you need to turn that off."

"I can't," he replied a bit cryptically.

"Until we know what caused our problem—"

"Someone on the ground hacked into the Satcon system."

The woman's eyes narrowed. "Satcon? I don't know what you're talking about."

"Call the captain, he'll understand," David said. "Tell him someone hacked into Satcon but I blocked their access. But the block is effective only as long as I keep my program running."

"Really, sir, I don't—"

"Please do as he asks," Flannery insisted. "I saw him do it. As soon as he did, the pilot regained control."

"And tell him that if he checks with ground control, he'll see that at least two other planes have gone down—"

"Two?" Flannery interrupted.

David nodded. "Just before all hell broke loose, I saw

that a second flight was reported missing." He turned back to the flight attendant. "Please, do as I ask."

"I . . . all right. I'll call."

She walked to the nearest bulkhead and picked up the phone. After a moment she returned to David's seat with a strange expression on her face. "The captain said whatever you do, don't shut down your computer. And he wants to talk to you after we land."

David grinned at Flannery. "Maybe they'll bump us to first class for the flight to New York."

"Don't worry, young man," the flight attendant said. "If you did what you say, I'll personally get you upgraded, even if I have to pay for it myself."

"There you go, Father," David said as the woman walked away. "We're both going first class. You scratch my back, I scratch yours."

"I'm afraid you've been doing all the scratching," Flannery said.

"Weren't you praying?"

"Yes, plenty of that."

"Like I said, you scratch my back . . ."

CHAPTER 3

TOLEDO, 1096

La Casa de Biblioteca, or Library House, was solidly constructed of fitted and mortared stone and had stood for nearly a hundred years on Calle del Angel. Although the building was ample in size to entertain scores of guests, its current occupant, the quiet and unassuming Tobias Garlande, personally used only three of its many rooms. The first floor was largely reserved for the kitchen and cook, Sansoles de Rojas, and also held sleeping quarters for the household staff. At one time they might have numbered a dozen, but Tobias employed only the cook and a young Jewish woman, Rachel Benyuli, who served as his assistant.

Tobias confined his own activities to the second-floor dining room and his bedroom and library on the third floor. While the dining room held a table long enough to seat twenty, Tobias generally ate alone. His bedroom was modestly furnished with a hard bed and a trunk for his few clothes. The library was the most comfortably furnished of the rooms he used. At its center stood a large desk with a high stool, where he spent long hours painstakingly transcribing ancient Greek, Hebrew, and Arabic texts. Beside it was a squat chest of drawers that held inks, parchment, and other supplies. An oversized table, which dominated the left side of the room, was covered with dozens of scrolls and documents awaiting examination. On the right-hand wall, a wide fireplace with a facing bench provided a warm place to sit on cold days. The room was illuminated in the daytime by a trio of tall windows in the far wall, at night by an oil lamp and a half-dozen fat, guttering candles.

This morning, Tobias was seated at the library desk, but he had pushed aside the Missal of Silos he had been transcribing onto rare sheets of imported hemp paper. In its place sat a shallow bowl of scented liquid on which floated a single lighted candle. Although he was staring intently into the bowl, he no longer was aware of the flame.

AN ENORMOUS SILVER eagle stands frozen in a barren field on carriage wheels as tall as a man, its featherless wings outspread as if in flight. The statue seems molded of burnished silver, sleek and polished brighter than any warrior's shield. Strangely dressed men and women approach two by two in a winding column and, like beasts entering the ark, ascend a narrow stairway into the belly of the bird. When all are aboard, the stairway rolls away, and the opening in the bird's belly slides closed, leaving no hint a doorway had ever existed.

A great rush of wind and thunder shakes the ground, as flames shoot backwards from the eagle's wings. For an instant the apparition shimmers and fades like a desert mirage, and in its place Tobias sees the flickering tip of the candlelight. But he calms his breath, relaxes his gaze, and watches in wonder as the colossus begins to roll across the field, gathering speed as it lifts into flight.

From off to the right, a phalanx of bowmen comes rushing into Tobias's field of view, each soldier bearing a heavy crossbow pressed against his shoulder. In what seems a futile effort, they release their tiny bolts at the great eagle, which is circling ever higher as it heads out over a great sea beyond.

In amazement, Tobias watches as the crossbow bolts veer off their straight path and follow the bird's circuitous flight. One by one they lodge themselves in the animal's metal

*skin, until it starts to crack and tear apart. As the eagle
breaks into pieces, men and women spill out of its shattered
belly and plummet amid the fiery wreckage into the roiling
waters below.*

THE VISION PASSED, replaced by bowl and candle, and
Tobias realized the little flame had been snuffed out in the
scented liquid, leaving a trailing wisp of smoke. He stroked
his full white beard as he tried to make sense of what he had
just seen. A message from the ancient myths, perhaps, or a
disquieting glimpse of a world yet to come?

As he shook his head to clear his thoughts, he suddenly
felt hungry and recalled that Rachel had gone to the market.
She would be back soon, he told himself. Until then, he had
best return to work.

RACHEL BENYULI WALKED briskly along the narrow lane
toward the market square. Thursday was one of the busiest
in Toledo, as it was the last business day before the worship
days of the three religions that coexisted in the Spanish city.
Friday marked *Youm al-Jum'a*, the day of assembly for the
Muslims. The Jews celebrated next, with their *Shabbat* from
sundown Friday until sundown Saturday. The Christian Sabbath came Sunday, marking the resurrection of Jesus.

Rachel found herself wondering why these great religions
that had grown on the same vine would practice their faiths
so very differently. Why, for instance, had Christians chosen a new day for worship? Didn't that break the commandment to remember the Sabbath and keep it holy? Her master,
Christian scholar Tobias Garlande, had explained that his
religion taught that Jesus' sacrifice on the Cross had fulfilled the commandment, and that Sunday was chosen as
the day of worship in honor of Christ's resurrection. But

Rachel's fellow Jews considered it further proof that Jesus was a false messiah, since God's commandments can neither be changed nor abrogated.

As for Islam's *Youm al-Jum'a*, Rachel was vaguely aware that the Qur'an called for a day of prayer but not of rest, and that for some reason it was the day before her people's *Shabbat*. And while followers were not prohibited from working on that day, commerce was limited by the long mosque services.

Rachel kept her eyes down as she moved through the jostling crowd, focusing instead on her empty basket and on the fish and other foods she needed to purchase. She knew the route by sound and smell—rhythmic tapping from a cobbler's stall, the perfume of spices from a warehouse tucked down an alley, the bleating of sheep and goats awaiting their turn under the butcher's knife—her senses attuned to each familiar landmark along the way.

When at last the dusty lane spilled into the market square, Rachel heard a new, disturbing sound. It wasn't the plaintive strumming of the oud but the lyrics of the troubadour's song that unsettled her. While voice and melody were pleasant enough, the sweetly sung words revealed a cruel intent:

> *"The pilgrimage of peasants,*
> *Who by divine grace and will*
> *Shall march to the Holy Lands,*
> *The infidels to kill,"*
> *Pope Urban prays, head bowed.*
> *"God wills it," shouts the crowd.*
>
> *"Let noblemen bring armies,*
> *Let peasants take up sword,*
> *Let thieves become knights*
> *And gain eternal reward,"*
> *Pope Urban vows, uncowed.*
> *"God wills it," shouts the crowd.*

"And battling the infidel
should you be well acquitted,
All penance for your sins
Shall wholly be remitted,"
Pope Urban cries aloud.
"God wills it," shouts the crowd.

As we take up our swords,
Barbarian blood to spill,
Vows the pope, "It is salvation,"
Shouts the crowd, "It is God's will,"
As we march to the Holy Lands,
The infidels to kill.

Rachel shuddered at the harshness of the lyrics, and she noticed that Muslims in the square seemed equally discomfited. But many of the Christians found the song to their liking, and the troubadour's inverted cap quickly filled with silver coins.

Putting aside the disquieting thoughts, Rachel turned her attention to the marketplace, selecting items for the midday dinner for Tobias and herself. The market was never a pleasant place to visit. Meat merchants killed livestock right on the spot, the terrified squealing and bleating cut short by the butcher's cleaver. Rachel had to pick her way through streets that ran red with fresh blood or were stained with the dried viscera of the slaughtered animals. Chickens and ducks, their legs bound, flapped their wings against the cobblestones, while shoppers poked and pinched at them. Everywhere, flies hovered around the freshly cut meat and piles of offal.

Rachel clutched her purse, lest it be snatched by one of the many thieves who preyed upon the shoppers. Spying a fishmonger and knowing Tobias's fondness for eel, she approached the woman and began haggling.

CHAPTER 4

JERUSALEM

Antonio Sangremano nodded as he spoke on the cell phone. *"Io capisco. Noi siamo riusciti con due, ma uno rimase a Roma. Professore Heber? Sì, grazie. Noi vedremo a lui."* He snapped the phone closed and smiled at his two companions. "It has begun."

"All three aircraft?" Benjamin Bishara asked.

Sangremano shook his head. *"Solo due*... only two. There's no word yet on the flight from Rome."

"Do not worry," Mehdi Jahmshidi assured them. "My man will succeed. Their fate is already sealed."

Sangremano drummed his fingers on the armrest of his chair and frowned. "We do have one problem, though."

"What is that?" Jahmshidi asked.

"At the last minute, Professor Heber canceled his flight. He's at his home, here in Jerusalem, suffering from a head cold."

"I'll take care of that," Bishara said, opening his own cell phone.

"Remember, we agreed to speak in English," Jahmshidi reminded the others. "We want no misunderstandings."

"You're right. Forgive my Italian on the phone," Sangremano apologized.

There could be no more unlikely a gathering anywhere in the world than these three men who sat like old but somewhat mistrustful relatives in the parlor of a suite in Jerusalem's David Citadel Hotel.

Fr. Antonio Sangremano, who had booked the suite using an Italian passport under the name Silvio Laurenzi, was a tall, athletic man in his mid-sixties who had been the former first secretary to the subprefect of the Prefettura dei Sacri Palazzi Apostolici, which served as the State Department of the Vatican. He had gone into hiding after engineering the theft of the Scroll of Dismas, a two-thousand-year-old Christian gospel that predated Matthew, Mark, Luke, and John and had been unearthed just over a year ago at the ruins of Masada. The gospel was considered the founding document of Sangremano's organization, Via Dei, or Way of God, which traced its roots to Dismas bar-Dismas, the son of the Good Thief who was crucified beside Jesus.

Via Dei was so deeply buried within the complex layers of Roman Catholic structure that even many church leaders were unaware of its existence, other than as an historical oddity, like the Knights Templar. To the few scholars who had heard of the society, it had been dissolved and condemned in 1890 by Pope Leo XIII, who proclaimed in a papal bull, *"Those who belong to Via Dei, though making claims to serve the Lord, are heretics who, in their secret initiations and meetings, use the holy name of Jesus to secure power within the Church. From this day and for all time, Via Dei is outside the protection of the Church."*

Benjamin Bishara, a slight man in his seventies with a bushy black beard, had dark, penetrating eyes that gazed suspiciously from above his wire-rim reading glasses and gave his scholarly appearance a menacing edge. He led the ultra-radical Jewish group Migdal Tzedek, or Tower of Justice. The elite and secretive organization traced its origins to the 1940s, when they fought for an independent Israel by carrying on a guerrilla war against the British and later the Palestinians. They considered Christianity a perversion of

Judaism and had no love for its adherents or for the Roman Catholic Church, which they considered complicit in the Holocaust.

Migdal Tzedek held Islam in even lower regard and opposed any rapprochement with the Palestinians. Several times over the last half century, the group had committed violent acts against Palestinians, and even against Jews they considered too liberal, to ensure that tensions remain high between Israel and its neighbors. Like Via Dei, Migdal Tzedek had been forced underground after the Israeli government outlawed it just before the 1967 war.

Mehdi Jahmshidi did not look the part of the leader of the militant Islamist organization Arkaan, or The Fundamentals. At forty-nine the youngest of the three men, he was clean-shaven and wore a well-tailored brown suit, lending him the air of a banker or businessman. It was a disguise born of necessity, for he graced every international most-wanted list and had eluded capture only because no intelligence agency knew precisely who he was or what he currently looked like.

Unlike the other two organizations, there was nothing secret about Jahmshidi's Arkaan, which even boasted its own Web site. More militant than the Taliban, al-Qaeda, Hezbollah, or Hamas, Arkaan was dedicated to establishing a pan-Islamic caliphate throughout the world and believed it a sacred duty to wage jihad against all non-Muslims—especially Jews and Americans—and to attack any ally of the United States.

"Professor Heber will be taken care of," Bishara said, closing his telephone.

"Good," Sangremano replied.

Sangremano looked at his two companions and suppressed a smile. Via Dei had issued a death warrant against both men, and he knew that their organizations had made similar decrees. Yet here they were, leaders of three enemy organizations, forming an unholy alliance to prevent the fledgling People of the Book, an assembly of prominent Christians, Muslims, and Jews, from achieving their goal of ecumenical concord among three great religions.

Sangremano had convinced his counterparts to work together against this common and potentially lethal threat. There would be time enough, once the People of the Book movement was quashed, for them to fight over the spoils. For now Sangremano would be guided by the old aphorism: Keep your friends close, and your enemies closer.

Sangremano's cell phone rang and he answered it in Italian. Seeing Jahmshidi's frown and remembering their pledge, he switched to English. "You are certain it was the flight from Rome? Good. Goodbye."

Snapping shut the phone, he grinned broadly at the others. "Gentlemen, we have first word that radio contact was lost to Michael Flannery's airplane. By now the good father has joined his friends. I think we can safely say the People of the Book movement has been buried at sea."

PROFESSOR EFRAIM HEBER was propped up on pillows in his bed, a reading desk straddling his legs. His left hand cradled a box of tissues, his right a pen with which he was jotting notes on a yellow lined tablet. A bad head cold had prevented him from attending the People of the Book symposium in New York, but he intended to write a few remarks, then have his assistant send them by e-mail so they could be read at the assembly.

A theology professor at Jerusalem's Hebrew University, Heber was one of the organizers of the symposium, which would bring together leaders of the three great monotheistic religions. Heber firmly believed that people of faith, character, resolve, and courage could find ways to unite the religions—if not in actual practice, then at least in their desire to coexist in peace. Because he was a best-selling author of seven books on theology, his early support of the symposium greatly increased its visibility and legitimacy and brought other prominent men and women of faith on board.

"Let us remember that we are all the children of Abraham," Heber read aloud from his notes, "and that we all worship the same God. I believe God's house is sufficiently large and inclusive for all His children to—"

"Professor?"

Heber looked up to see his research assistant, Moshe Goldman, standing in the doorway. "Ah, Moshe, you're done with your call. I'm afraid I've not quite finished this missive. I'll call downstairs when I'm ready for you to e-mail it to the conference chair."

Heber gave a dismissive wave of the hand and turned back to his tablet. But instead of withdrawing, the young man took a hesitant step forward and stood running his hand nervously through his curly black hair.

"Well, what is it, Moshe?" Heber said distractedly when he noticed his assistant still standing there.

"That phone call . . ."

Heber waited a moment, then said with a hint of annoyance, "What about it?"

"It was from a mutual friend . . . Benjamin Bishara."

The professor dropped the pencil on the writing tray. "Bishara is no friend of mine."

The nervousness seemed to fade from Moshe's expression, his voice growing more steady as he said, "Mr. Bishara has always held you in the highest regard. He has told me so on many occasions."

"Told *you*? What business have you with Bishara or his Tower of Justice hooligans?"

"Benjamin Bishara is my father, as he is father to all of us in Migdal Tzedek." He used the Hebrew name for the radical group.

Heber looked both surprised and angry. "You're far too smart to be spouting Bishara's babble. When did you fall in with that lot?"

"I have always been with Migdal Tzedek."

"Now I *am* surprised. And disappointed. You know how I feel about those people. I never would have hired someone from the Tower of Justice—*in*justice is more like it."

"Yes, I know how you feel," Moshe said, advancing closer to the bed. "And it is out of respect that I have told you all of this, so that you would know I am truly sorry it must end this way."

"Yes, it must," Heber agreed, again waving his hand to dismiss the young man. "I have no use for anyone who aligns himself with Migdal Tzedek or Benjamin Bishara."

"As Migdal Tzedek, I'm afraid, no longer has any use for you," Moshe replied, his words as cold as his expression.

Heber looked up to see that his assistant had reached into his pocket and was withdrawing a small pistol.

"Mr. Bishara sends his regards, and his farewell."

Heber raised a hand and started to cry out, when the pistol jerked and a bullet tore through the fleshy part of his palm and shattered his right temple, sending shards of bone deep into his brain. He neither heard nor felt the second bullet, which struck his lower abdomen, or the final shots to either side of his chest.

As Moshe Goldman returned the pistol to his pocket, he looked from one wound to the next. "Spectacles, testicles, wallet, watch," he intoned, admiring the symmetry of his handiwork and the subtle message it would send other Jews who dared serve as pawns of the Catholic-inspired People of the Book movement.

MID-ATLANTIC

Settling back in his seat, Michael Flannery closed his eyes and envisioned the airplane bathed in protective light as he prayed for their continued safe return to Rome. When he opened his eyes again, the golden glow remained before him, an egg-shaped aura surrounding an old white-bearded man. For a moment he thought it merely a passenger bathed in a shaft of light from one of the windows. But then he realized he was looking both at and through the man, who gazed back with familiarity, compassion, and concern.

The old man raised his right hand and brought the thumb, index, and middle fingers to a point, as if he were about to make the Sign of the Cross. But then he curled the three fingers into a circle and laid his hand upon his heart. Flannery smiled, secure in the knowledge that his prayer had been answered and the airplane would make it back safely. As he returned the Keeper's hand sign, the vision faded, the golden aura receding into a tiny spot of light until it was gone.

"You all right?" David asked, glancing at the priest.

Flannery realized his hand was still covering his heart, and he quickly lowered his arm. "I'm fine."

And he was fine, though it had not always been so. Such visions had come with increasing frequency, appearing at first in moments of weakened faith when he found himself doubting what he had experienced that day upon the mountain fortress of Masada. Could there really be a line of men and women known as Keepers of the Sign—Christian, Muslim, and Jew—beginning with Simon of Cyrene and stretching for fifty generations? More preposterous was the notion that an unassuming Palestinian woman, Azra Haddad, had been the most recent in that line and, in death, had chosen Flannery to be the next Keeper and to reveal to the world the secret symbol and message of Jesus.

But during the past year he had learned to trust these visions, to rely on them for guidance and understanding. The old man who appeared so fleetingly in the aisle was a stranger, but Flannery recognized him at once as a brother Keeper and knew that his visit was an affirmation that they were protected and there was still work for Flannery to do in this life.

The priest curled his thumb and two fingers into the hand

signal used among the Keepers. Touching it to his chest, he felt the exquisitely carved case that hung upon a silver chain beneath his clergy vest. The case was a gift from the Prophet Muhammad to the Keeper who influenced his conversion. But the greater gift lay within, a cloth given to Simon of Cyrene by the Master himself, stained with his own blood.

"*Sanguis Christi,*" Flannery whispered. And drawn in the blood of Christ upon that cloth was the symbol Trevia Dei, the three paths to God that are one.

CHAPTER 5

TOLEDO

Tobias Garlande pushed away his meditation bowl. The floating candle had long since gone out, but not the memory of what he had seen. His first vision had been of an enormous silver bird that exploded in flight, spilling scores of people from its twisted, gaping belly.

He had gone back into trance, this time discovering incredible wonders inside one of those bird machines. There were lights that glowed without flickering or any sign of flame, and moving pictures that hung on the backs of the long rows of seats. Curiously dressed men, women, and children sat in plush, high-backed chairs, and one in particular had caught his eye. The man wore a tight-fitting black outfit with a stiff white collar, and Tobias could see—no, perceive, for it was hidden beneath the vest cinched at the man's waist—the suspended silver case bearing the Trevia Dei cloth. It was the very case that hung beneath Tobias's own coarse woolen robe, and when he had placed his hand over it, the stranger had returned the Keeper's sign.

As Tobias sat alone at his library desk, he wondered about this vision he had been given. Did it carry a message from the future, some special understanding or mission he needed to accomplish? Or perhaps he had been brought there for the sake of his fellow Keeper, to strengthen the man's faith or provide affirmation for some crisis or challenge. Tobias nodded in acceptance, confident that in time he would understand all he had witnessed and what, if anything, he was meant to do.

As the vision receded from his thoughts, Tobias became aware again of his surroundings, the babble of street merchants and passersby outside his window, the sound of a cart rumbling down the cobbled street, the pungent aroma of freshly baked bread. Realizing he was hungry, he called out, "Rachel? Rachel, where are you, girl?"

Getting no answer, Tobias left his library and walked down the hall, peering into each of the other rooms on the floor. He again called her name, but got no response.

Tobias made his way to the second floor and found it empty, with no evidence of any preparations for the midday dinner in the dining room. Heading down to the kitchen, he saw the cook half asleep on a bench. Smelling the bread baking in the oven, he smiled and said, "Is dinner almost ready, Sansoles?"

The old Spanish woman jerked awake, looking quite flustered as she wiped her hands on her apron and said, "Dinner? Only the bread, I'm afraid. Rachel has not yet returned from market."

"That's odd." Tobias pulled at his beard, deep in thought. "She's been gone since morning. She should have returned long before now."

"I hope nothing has happened to her," the cook said. "The market is becoming no place for a young—"

"You mustn't even think such a thing," Tobias snapped, though the same fear was in his own mind. "Quickly, say a prayer," he added as he crossed himself.

"Yes, m'lord," Sansoles replied, giving a slight curtsy as she made the Sign of the Cross.

Tobias turned away and headed for the stairs. He was deeply troubled, first by the disconcerting vision and now by the absence of a young woman who had become increasingly important to his work—and to his heart. Some fellow scholars, as aged as he, had noticed the softness with which he spoke of Rachel and had encouraged him to take her as his wife. Certainly it was not unusual for a man of property to marry someone less than half his age. More problematic was that she was a Jewess, an obstacle easily overcome by compelling her to profess the true faith.

But Tobias was not interested in a wife, nor were his feelings for Rachel in any way amorous. He had come to think of her as a daughter, as someone whose own interest in the life of the spirit was not unlike his own. He had even begun to suspect she might be the one he awaited—the one destined to take up the Keeper's path when his own commission was fulfilled.

As for compelling a Jew to convert, this was a fate Tobias was not alone in fearing. During the past decade, since Alfonso VI of Castile had stormed Toledo and wrested control from the Moors, the city had indeed become a more dangerous place for young women of any faith and for all non-Christians. The city's golden age under the Caliphs of Córdoba was quickly fading from memory, and Tobias wondered how much time was left for La Convivencia—the centuries of coexistence of Jews, Christians, and Muslims. Indeed, the Reconquista by the Christian forces of Leon-Castile had begun, and it was only a matter of time before Toledo and indeed the entirety of Hispania would prove inhospitable for anyone who did not profess the one true Catholic faith. Or even for Christians like Tobias who dared believe that Christian, Muslim, and Jew could live in harmony as children of the same Father.

RACHEL BENYULI HAD often dealt with marketplace thieves who would try to snatch a young woman's purse and run off into the crowd. But today's confrontation was different, and far more frightening. While heading out of the market square, she had found her way blocked by three of the mercenary soldiers of Leon-Castile who composed the backbone of the forces that controlled Toledo in the name of Alfonso VI.

Two of the soldiers stood with their hands on their hips while the third drew his sword and held it toward Rachel, saying, "You, girl, is it the practice of your husband to allow you on the street without escort?"

"Please, sir, I am late in returning to my master's house and will soon be missed," Rachel said.

"Master, not husband?" the man said, grinning at his companions. "Then you are little more than a kitchenmaid?" He waggled the tip of the sword at the basket of food in her hands, then lowered it to the hem of her dress and lifted the material as high as her knees. "Not married. Then the fig, while ripe, has never been plucked?"

His comrades laughed, a rasping, lewd chortle.

Seeing Rachel's cheeks flame with blushing heat, the soldier said smugly, "So you *are* a virgin. Are you a slave?"

"I am no slave," Rachel declared. "I am employed by Tobias Garlande."

"Tobias el Transcriptor?" he said, using the title by which the transcriber was known. "The old man who lives in La Casa de Biblioteca?"

"Yes. Please let me by. I have food for the cook to prepare his dinner."

"I have seen this man Tobias. He is well-fed."

"He is fat," one of the other soldiers interjected, though in truth Tobias was solidly built but not at all overweight. "It will not harm him to miss a meal."

As the three soldiers laughed at their attempt at wit, Rachel grew increasingly uncomfortable. She tried to move past the trio but was stopped by the point of the sword against her neck.

"Do you know what a beautiful trophy your head would make?"

"Or your ripe fig," the second soldier added, his lewd grin widening.

"Have I displeased you in some way?" Rachel asked, trying to keep her voice calm.

The first soldier looked her up and down. "I am displeased because I fear the fig may grow old and fall from the tree, untasted and unwanted." He lowered the sword and again lifted the hem of her dress.

Rachel was on the verge of panic. She knew they would not rape her here, in the open, but she doubted anyone would intercede if they dragged her off.

As if in reply, an angry voice called out from behind her, "Sheathe your sword!"

The voice was so commanding that the soldiers instantly lost their smug, taunting expressions. Rachel spun around to see a man moving out of the shadows, and in surprise she realized he was a Muslim, dressed in the black flowing robe of his people. Gripped tightly in his hand was a gleaming, curved scimitar.

The soldiers now realized they were being confronted by a Moor, who had no authority in Toledo since their army took the city. The one with the sword stepped boldly forward and declared, "Who are you to speak so brazenly to a Christian soldier, one who serves at the will of Alfonso the Brave?"

The Moor grasped Rachel's arm and moved her to the side, away from danger. Taking her place in front of the soldiers, he declared, "I am al-Aarif of al-Andalus, nephew of the great al-Mamun of Toledo, whom Alfonso himself honored as *Caballero Aunque Moro*"—a knight although a Moor. "I ask you again to sheathe your sword or suffer the consequences." He spoke the language of Castile even better than they did, with no hint of an accent.

From nearby, Rachel saw the uncertainty in the eyes of the soldiers. They were clearly afraid of this leader among the Moors, though they tried to cover it with bravado. Everyone in Toledo had heard of al-Mamun, the former ruler of Toledo who had been an ally of Alfonso's before being poisoned in Córdoba twenty-one years ago. Many believed their friendship had led Alfonso to adopt a more tolerant attitude toward the Muslims and Jews of Toledo, a policy not mirrored in other regions he conquered.

Almost as well known was the young Moor, al-Aarif, who one day might have ruled Toledo had Alfonso not taken it ten years after al-Mamun's death. Al-Aarif had been barely in his teens at the time but had handled himself in battle with such bravery and compassion that Alfonso took to calling him "little Mamun" and saw to it that he and his family retained some measure of authority, if only over the Moorish population.

Rachel had never before seen al-Aarif, though she had heard many tales of his exploits. Looking at him now, she believed she had never seen a man so handsome. He was tall, olive complexioned, with strong yet smooth features and dark eyes—eyes that flashed now in anger.

"You are a Moor; you have no standing here," the lead soldier said a bit hesitantly as he raised his sword.

"And neither shall you be standing if you do not put away your sword and leave in peace."

One of the other soldiers came forward and started to draw his own weapon, but the leader reached over and grasped his wrist, staying his hand. "It's all right," he told his comrade with a nervous grin. "We have no dispute with our friend among the Moors. If he desires this young wench, certainly King Alfonso would not desire us to stand in the way."

Feigning a smile, he faced al-Aarif as he made a show of returning his sword to its sheath. Then he turned back to his companions.

"Let us leave them to their particular pleasures." With a slight flourish of the hand, he directed his comrades toward the nearby square. "Come, there are plenty of other ripe figs in the market."

Al-Aarif put away his own sword and watched the soldiers until they were gone. Then he turned to Rachel and asked, "Were you harmed?"

"No, I—I was frightened, but not harmed."

"There was a time when such behavior would have resulted in the most severe of punishments. But I am afraid it would have stirred up more harm than good to have given those . . . those creatures even a measure of what they deserve. I apologize for all the men of Toledo."

Rachel smiled. "You take on far more than required of any man. Indeed, you owe me no apology at all, whereas I owe you the deepest gratitude."

"Perhaps I should escort you to your home," al-Aarif offered, returning her smile.

"There is no need."

"But I insist."

She hesitated a moment, then nodded. "Very well, but I must tell you, it is not my home."

"I know. Your master is the transcriber, Tobias Garlande, who lives on Calle del Angel."

"How did you know this?" Rachel asked in surprise.

"I am al-Aarif," he said with an air of mystery and a hint of humor. "My people have known all the comings and goings in Toledo since long before Calle del Angel was given its new name. Before I was born, when my uncle ruled this region, Tobias and other Christians worked alongside our Moorish transcribers—as did your father and his fellow Jewish scholars."

"You know of—?" Rachel stopped herself, as if afraid to say her father's name aloud. She rarely spoke of her parents or of the tragic circumstances of their deaths three years ago, which had led Tobias to offer his colleague's daughter a livelihood and a place to live.

"Levi Benyuli was a great scholar and an even greater man," al-Aarif declared. "I own one of his translations, which I would be honored to present to his daughter."

"I . . . I don't know what to say."

"Say you will allow me to escort you to La Casa de Biblioteca."

Rachel blushed. "Very well, al-Aarif, I shall be honored to have you escort me home."

As he took the basket from her and led the way down the street, they fell into casual conversation.

"Do you realize, Rachel Benyuli, we share more than this walk and a love of scholarship . . . and fresh eels, I might add," he said, noticing the contents of the basket.

"How do you mean?"

"You are Jewish."

"And you are a Muslim."

"Ah, true, but my mother was a Jew, and my father could never convince her to recite the *Shahadah* and profess the faith of Islam." He gave an almost boyish grin. "He had to console himself with three other devout Muslim wives."

"With a Jewish mother, there are some who would consider you a Jew," Rachel said, referring to the *Halakha,* or Jewish Law, of matrilineal descent in determining if someone is a Jew.

"Indeed, I consider myself not only Muslim but Jew and even Christian. We are all People of the Book, are we not? We are all children of Abraham."

"Yes," Rachel said. "I believe that to be true."

They continued to discuss religion and philosophy as they turned onto Calle del Angel and approached the home of Tobias. Reaching the front door, al-Aarif halted and asked Rachel, "Does Tobias ever accept invitations for dinner or entertain guests at his table?"

"Never. He dines alone."

"You do not join him?"

"I've been invited, but I keep kosher and take my own meals."

"What a pity. I believe that you and Tobias and I, sharing the same dinner table, would make for a very pleasant evening."

At that moment a horse cart arrived, driven by a peasant wearing a homespun russet tunic and cap. Sitting on a bench at the back of the cart was a tall man of early middle age with an angular face and unkempt beard and hair. He was well dressed in wool trousers and a silk shirt, over which he wore a pallium, a narrow scarf of white lamb's wool emblazoned with crosses that was draped over his shoulders and hung to his hips in the front and back.

"Stop here, man," the passenger said in Castilian laced with a haughty French accent.

When the cart came to a halt, the driver unloaded the passenger's baggage, which consisted of a pair of wooden trunks. The Frenchman dropped to the ground and held forth a coin. It apparently was not enough, because the cart driver turned it over several times, then looked beseechingly at the passenger and said in a cautious tone, "Good sir, I brought you all the way from the river gate."

"Yes, and I have paid you. Now be gone, be gone." He gave a wave of his hand, then turned his back on the man and walked over to al-Aarif and Rachel.

The driver shrugged in resignation and climbed back onto his seat. He snapped the reins against the horse's back, and the cart clattered away down the street.

"You, girl," the man said to Rachel, who had just opened the door of the house. "I am Philippe Guischard. Tell your master that I have returned from France. He will want to be informed at once."

"She is not a servant," al-Aarif said, his voice edged with annoyance.

"It's all right," Rachel whispered, then turned to the visitor. "I shall inform Tobias that Philippe Guischard is here." She gave a perfunctory curtsy, then disappeared inside.

Philippe studied the Moor, as if wondering what business an infidel had at the home of Tobias Garlande. "Excuse me," he finally said, "if I look surprised to see someone of your . . . of your faith speaking with such familiarity to a young Christian woman."

Al-Aarif suppressed a grin. When he spoke, it was in

perfect French. "That young Christian is a Jew, a faith she and I hold in common through the great prophet Abraham." He paused for effect, then added, "As do you."

"We have nothing in common," Philippe snapped, reverting to his native French.

"Apparently we do," al-Aarif countered. "A knowledge of languages and business at the home of Tobias el Transcriptor. But as my business is finished, I shall leave you to yours."

He started to turn away, but Philippe called after him, "I believe I speak for Tobias in saying that you would do well not to return here."

Al-Aarif spun around, one hand on the hilt of his scimitar. "You speak boldly, for one who is unarmed."

"Do not provoke me, for I am armed with the sword of Holy Spirit and protected by the shield of Jesus Christ."

Al-Aarif stood rigid, fighting the urge to slice the arrogant Frenchman into tiny strips. But then his shoulders relaxed, and he lowered his hand from his sword. "I do not wish to offend one who follows the prophet Jesus. I will be on my way." Turning, he strode off down Calle del Angel.

As Philippe Guischard watched the Moor disappear into the afternoon shadows, he felt a swell of pride for having called upon the power of Jesus. His reverie was interrupted by a voice from behind him.

"Monsieur Guischard, Tobias will see you now."

He turned to see the young Jewess standing in the doorway. "Do you make a habit of calling your master by his Christian name?" he asked.

"I address Tobias as he wishes to be addressed."

"Really?" Philippe replied. "And how does he address you?"

"By my given name—Rachel."

"Apparently things have changed since my departure four years ago. Very well then, Rachel, if that is the way it is now done, you may address me as Philippe."

She didn't respond but waited for Philippe to bring his

travel cases into the entryway, then led him upstairs to Tobias's library.

"Brother Tobias," Philippe greeted as he entered the room.

"Brother Philippe, welcome back to my home," Tobias replied. He stood up from his desk and approached, clasping the younger man on the shoulders. "Rachel tells me that we are having eel. You must dine with me."

"I would be delighted," Philippe replied, turning and smiling at Rachel in a way that seemed calculated to make her uneasy.

"Tell Sansoles we have a guest," Tobias told Rachel, who nodded and headed away down the hall.

When they were alone, Philippe turned back to the older man and said appreciatively, "I must say, Tobias, you have taken a most beautiful servant girl. I would never have expected—"

"She is not my servant," Tobias interrupted. "She is quite learned and works as my assistant."

"Assistant?" Philippe said incredulously. "But I was your assistant."

"Was," Tobias said pointedly. "You sent word you would remain in France, and Rachel had all the qualifications."

"A woman? And a Jew?"

Tobias looked at him curiously. "You are well informed, as usual. Then you must realize she is not just any woman—or any Jew. She is the daughter of Levi Benyuli."

Philippe nodded with sudden recognition. "Rachel Benyuli. I recall hearing about her—I think we even met once, but she was but a child." His smile returned. "She has turned into quite a comely young woman, for a Jew."

"Here now, Philippe, you don't sound like yourself. Too much time among the fanatics, I'd say."

"The Grand Master is no fanatic."

"We both know what Jean Fournier is and is not," Tobias countered. "But enough of that for now. There will be plenty of time to debate theology in the days to come. I want to hear all about France and Fournier and your time among the Disciples of the Way. But first we must dine."

Philippe shook his head. "No, first I must fulfill my commission. I bring you secret instructions from Grand Master Fournier of Via Dei."

Tobias smiled, but without warmth. "Somehow that does not surprise me, Philippe. But I belong to Trevia Dei. I take no instructions from Via Dei or its Grand Master."

"Perhaps I misspoke. I come bearing a letter; I do not know what message it contains."

"Where is it?" Tobias asked.

Philippe reached into a hidden pocket in the tail of his pallium and removed the letter, tied with ribbon and sealed with wax. He handed it to Tobias.

"Come," Tobias said as he laid the letter unopened upon his desk, then headed toward the hall. "We will eat."

"But I've journeyed all the way from France. Are you not going to read the letter?"

"I have no desire to face Fournier's words on an empty stomach. There will be time enough for secret messages and Via Dei intrigues once we have dined."

CHAPTER 6

NEW YORK CITY

I'm expecting a pair of friends," Preston Lewkis told the waitress at Bernie's Deli as she showed him to a table in the back. "I'll have a glass of milk while I wait. And could you please add a teaspoon of vanilla extract?"

"Vanilla?" the waitress asked in surprise as he took the seat facing the front.

"Yes, please."

She gave a shrugging nod and headed to the kitchen.

Preston glanced up whenever the front door opened, looking to see if it was one of his dinner mates. He expected the punctual Fr. Michael Flannery to arrive first, and a quick look at his watch confirmed his friend still had a few minutes to spare.

Preston and Flannery had met a decade earlier when the Irish priest taught a semester course on Christian Artifacts in Israel at Brandeis University, where Preston was a professor of archaeology. They had renewed their friendship the previous year while working in Israel on an archaeological find, the discovery of a first-century scroll that contained a hitherto unknown gospel of Jesus.

The Gospel of Dismas bar-Dismas was purportedly written by the son of the "good thief" who was crucified beside Jesus. The ancient scroll had been discovered in a most unlikely place, sealed in an urn and buried in the ruins of Masada, a mountaintop fortress where, in AD 73, nearly a thousand Jewish Zealots sacrificed themselves rather than surrender to the Romans—a site with no known ties to Christianity.

The discovery of a gospel that predated Matthew, Mark, Luke, and John had immediate repercussions. Some Christian scholars and theologians embraced it fervently, believing this earliest account of Christ's Passion would convince even the most skeptical of the veracity of the New Testament. Even some Jewish scholars were enthusiastic in their belief that the scroll would create a new awareness of early Christianity as an essentially Jewish movement.

But there were skeptics, also. One had authenticated the ossuary of James, the brother of Jesus, only to see his reputation tarnished when it was unmasked as a fake. He and his colleagues would not accept the gospel's authenticity until it could be proved beyond a doubt. Unfortunately, before their work was completed, the scroll had been stolen by the secretive organization Via Dei, and all that remained were photographic scans of the document.

The waitress returned with the milk, and Preston added two packets of sweetener, then stirred it with a spoon. He had just taken his first swallow when he saw Michael Flannery enter the deli. Preston stood and waved at the priest, who gave a nod of recognition and weaved his way through the crowded room. He paused to say something to the waitress, then continued to the table.

The two men shook hands, and as they took their seats, Preston nodded toward the departing waitress and said, "Coffee, extra cream and sugar, I'll bet."

"Ah, you remember," Flannery said with a smile. "But this old dog has learned a new trick. I've managed to give up the sugar."

"Cold turkey? You used to take three, four spoons."

"The sugar was easy; it was the Baileys Irish Cream that proved a challenge."

"Well, you deserve some whiskey after that flight of yours the other day."

"I had something better than whiskey . . . my own personal computer geek."

"Yes, that young fellow who hacked the hackers," Preston commented.

"David Meyers. If not for him, we'd all be in the drink, and I don't mean the booze variety." Flannery shook his head in wonder. "I still can't fathom how he figured out so quickly it was a computer attack from the ground."

"I watched all the news accounts, but I still don't understand how a hacker could've taken over the controls and locked out the flight crew," Preston said.

"All thanks to a security system designed to protect us from a hijacker taking over the cockpit. I, for one, don't feel very reassured about these high-tech safety measures, especially after seeing David in action. I'd feel better if they'd found the hackers."

"I hear you," Preston agreed. "At least four Islamic extremist groups have taken credit for the downings. But nobody's heard of any of them, which makes it unlikely they had anything to do with it."

"I was told that six passengers on those downed airliners were en route to attend the symposium."

"Seven, actually," Preston said. "And you and I and Professor Heber would've made ten."

"Thank God he missed that American Global out of Jerusalem. Has he taken another flight?"

"I sent word for him to hold off. Given what happened to seven of our presenters, most of the other attendees were frightened away. It looks as if they're canceling the symposium."

"Cancelled?" Flannery said in alarm. "I thought it was just postponed."

"The final decision hasn't been made yet," Preston said.

"But the steering committee has scheduled a meeting, and chances are good that they'll cancel it."

Flannery shook his head. "They shouldn't. Given the political climate, a peaceful accord among the religions may well be the best hope for all of us."

"I'd like to think you're right, Michael. But I find myself wondering if such a thing is really possible."

AS THE TAXI headed north past the Flatiron Building toward the theater district, a cell phone rang and the woman in the backseat snapped it open and gave her name: "Sarah Arad."

"It's Schuler. Can you speak?"

Natan Schuler was Sarah's superior at Yechida Mishtartit Meyuchedet, better known as YAMAM, Israel's elite counterterrorism unit. Sarah checked the ID card on the dashboard, which identified the driver as Stefan Stocowiac, definitely not an Arab.

"We can speak in Hebrew," she said in that language.

"We have found the murderer of Professor Heber."

"Al-Qaeda? Hamas? Arkaan?"

"No," Schuler said. "His name is Moshe Goldman."

"A Jew? Heber was killed by a Jew?"

"Yes. He's been working the past few years as the professor's research assistant. He claims that Heber's book *The Sacrifice of Abraham* was largely his work but that he was neither credited nor properly compensated."

"Then you don't believe Heber's murder had anything to do with the People of the Book symposium?"

"It appears to be a coincidence," Schuler said. "*Abraham* is an international best-seller, which all but guarantees challengers will come crawling out of the woodwork. Remember the lawsuit over *Da Vinci Code*? At least these disputes rarely involve murder."

"What about the attacks on the airliners?"

"No, those were highly coordinated, and while we have no proof, you're probably right that they were designed to disrupt the gathering. Where are you now?"

"New York City, about to meet some colleagues connected to the symposium."

"Your boyfriend?"

"Professor Lewkis is a friend," Sarah said curtly.

"And a sandstorm on the Sahara is just a little dust in the air."

"All right, he's a good friend," Sarah replied.

Schuler chuckled. "Be careful over there. We don't know who these people are, but we know they're determined."

"I'll call in anything I find out." She said good-bye and closed the phone.

Sarah leaned back in the seat and smiled as she contemplated seeing Preston Lewkis again. They had met a year earlier during the Masada excavation. Though barely thirty at the time, she did not expect to be interested in anyone after the violent deaths of her husband, Maj. Ariel Arad, and her parents, the world-renowned archaeologists Saul and Nadia Yishar. But Preston had awakened feelings she thought dead. They had managed to get together a couple of times during the intervening year, once at a conference in London, the second time on a clandestine vacation in Paris. They had also kept in touch via e-mail and phone.

The cab pulled to a halt, and Sarah glanced outside at the neon Bernie's Deli sign. Reaching into her shoulder bag, she pushed aside the Beretta Model 71 pistol, which had recently replaced her old standby Glock, and drew a twenty-dollar bill from her wallet.

"Keep the change," she told the cabbie as she opened the door and stepped onto the curb.

As the cab pulled away, she turned and almost collided with a young man who looked a bit distracted as he strode down the street. "Sorry, ma'am," he muttered, not waiting for her reply as he hurried off.

She stared at him a moment, bemused at what an incongruous figure he appeared. The man was thin and blond, his bright blue Hawaiian shirt hanging over his cargo pants like a surfer from Malibu or Oahu. But what struck her as peculiar was the leather attaché case he clutched so tightly that it hung rigid at his side, barely swaying as he walked away. He seemed uncomfortable bearing something so conventional—as one would expect of any surfer suddenly encumbered with a businessman's briefcase.

"New York," she whispered with a smile. She looked forward to the next odd person she would encounter in the endless parade that was Midtown Manhattan.

CHAPTER 7

NEW YORK CITY

S arah, it's wonderful to see you again," Preston Lewkis said, and gave her a kiss on the cheek.

"I wouldn't have missed this for anything in the world," she replied.

As Sarah warmly greeted Farther Flannery, Preston pulled out a chair for her, but she eased around to the far side of the table so she would have an unobstructed view of the entire deli.

"How was your flight?" Flannery asked.

"A lot less exciting than yours, Father."

"Please, call me Michael."

"We were discussing that a few minutes ago," Preston said. "That young man who saved the plane said the attack was from a ground-based computer, and we were trying to figure out how that worked."

"Ah, you mean David Meyers, alias Scorpion, alias Nerd Power, alias Mongo," Sarah said.

"All those aliases?" Flannery said.

"Meyers is a hacker of some international repute. Or perhaps I should say infamy."

"He's one of those guys who create worms and viruses?" Preston asked.

Sarah shook her head. "Most of his hacking is benign and often beneficial, which is why he's avoided arrest. He prefers to hack into the most sophisticated systems in the world, negotiating around firewalls and security blocks. He usually leaves behind a message detailing the weaknesses he exploited and how to shore up security. As far as we know, the only way he's profited is the free travel he's booked himself, which we only learned about because of what happened the other day. But as you can imagine, the airlines don't want to prosecute a hero."

"They ought to hire him," Flannery said.

"I'm sure he's already had a lot of offers, with more to come," Sarah agreed.

"I heard that Trans-Atlantic has already given him a lifetime pass," Preston put in. "But what exactly did he do? I mean, how was the airliner under attack?"

"It was a coordinated attack by multiple computers on the Satcon system—something the IT folks call a denial-of-service attack. Somehow David Meyers discovered it and managed to block the incoming signals that were overloading Satcon."

"David mentioned Satcon," Flannery said. "What is it?"

"It's short for Satellite Control," Sarah explained. "After 9/11, all airplanes flying over U.S. airspace were required to install an improved satellite tracking device. What the government kept secret—" She looked around cautiously and lowered her voice. "Now, you're sworn to silence, mind you. If I worked for the U.S., I could get in big trouble talking about this. But I'm Israeli, and a lot of it is already being leaked onto the Internet."

"By David Meyers?"

"No, he's been entirely cooperative, from everything I've heard. But it didn't take long for other hackers to figure out what happened to those planes."

"All were taken down the same way?" Flannery asked.

Sarah nodded. "You see, what the government kept secret is that the upgraded Satcon system gave them a backdoor into the airplane's computer so they could take over the onboard controls should a hijacker seize the cockpit. They could actually shut down all manual controls and fly the plane remotely."

Preston shook his head in amazement. "Like a drone? They can actually do that?"

"With the newer planes they can, right down to landing on the runway."

"And older ones?"

"They wouldn't have that kind of control, but they could thwart a hijacker trying to hit a specific target."

"By forcing the plane to crash," Flannery said. "Not a very reassuring thought."

"No, but it could save thousands of lives on the ground."

"How exactly did David figure all that out so quickly?"

"Apparently, he already knew. In fact, he says he left one of his security warnings about a year ago when he stumbled on the Satcon system while hacking into one of the less-secure airline networks. And if he knew, you can be sure others did."

"Like whoever tried to bring down Michael's plane," Preston said.

"Are there any leads on who that might be? Another hacker, perhaps?" Flannery asked.

"Technically, yes, a hacker," Sarah replied. "But not like Meyers. It had to be someone with an agenda that includes terrorism."

"Political?" Preston asked.

"Or ideological."

Preston nodded eagerly at Flannery. "Then it could have been connected to the symposium."

"Yes," Sarah agreed. "U.S. officials are looking at the usual terror groups. And while there may be a connection, I'm convinced there's a link to the symposium. I don't trust coincidences, and the three targeted planes were the very three that were carrying some of the main speakers for the symposium."

The waitress stopped by the table, and Preston told her, "Give us a few more minutes." He tapped the menu in front of him but didn't pick it up or open it.

The woman frowned but said nothing as she walked toward the front door to seat the latest arrivals.

Preston folded his hands over the menu and turned to Flannery. "Well, thanks to your friend David—and to your God, no doubt—they failed to get you. Professor Heber is also safe, thanks to a bad cold that kept him at home."

The comment drew Sarah's attention away from the front door, where she had been watching the waitress greet the man with the Hawaiian shirt and briefcase who had almost barreled into her on the street.

"You haven't heard, have you?" she asked the two men.

"Heard what?" Flannery asked.

"Professor Heber . . . he's dead, murdered in his bedroom."

"My God!" Preston blurted.

Flannery crossed himself. "May his soul be with God."

"So, whoever brought down the planes decided to finish the job," Preston said.

"Israeli police have already made an arrest and have a confession. A disgruntled research assistant claims he had a personal motive."

"That's quite a convenient coincidence," Preston noted.

"And I hate coincidences, which is why I don't trust it." She turned to Flannery. "And why you won't be returning to your hotel but to a different one."

"You think they'll come for me?" The priest looked more than a bit skeptical.

"Better to err on the side of caution," Preston said, then turned to Sarah. "Where will you take him?"

She looked distracted as she stared beyond Flannery toward the front door, where she caught a glimpse of the man in the Hawaiian shirt moving quickly through the door and out to the sidewalk, apparently having changed his mind about dining there. But then she realized his arms were swinging freely, and she looked over at the nearby table where the waitress had seated him. There, tucked almost out of sight under the seat, was the leather attaché case.

Jumping to her feet, Sarah called out, "There's a bomb! Everyone out!"

"What?" her two companions said in unison, looking as surprised as the other patrons, who turned en masse toward what appeared to be a crazy woman at the back of the dining room. Some grinned nervously or frowned in irritation, others turned away and whispered to their companions.

"Everyone get out!" Sarah shouted as she snatched up her shoulder bag. "There's a bomb! Get out of here! *Now!*"

She punctuated the demand by jerking her Beretta from the purse and firing a single bullet into the base of the wall behind her.

"Everyone out, now!"

As she waved the pistol over her head, the patrons leaped from their seats, some shouting or crying as they scrambled to be first out the door. Sarah motioned for Preston and Flannery to follow the others, then hurried over to the kitchen to roust the staff.

Sarah was the last onto the sidewalk, where she waved her pistol at the milling crowd of patrons and passersby. "Away from the windows!" she ordered, herding them out down the sidewalk and away from the deli.

"She's got a gun!" someone shouted at a mounted policeman, who was approaching from up the street, drawn by the screaming and commotion.

Seeing a woman waving a pistol, the officer started to draw his own revolver, but before it cleared the holster, there was a thunderous boom. Two huge balls of fire exploded through the windows on either side of the door, spraying the street with jagged shards of glass and debris. There were screams of pain and shock as several people were cut by flying glass.

The policeman's horse reared up, and he struggled to

bring it under control. When the animal finally settled down, he dismounted to find Sarah Arad standing right next to him, the gun hanging loosely in her hand.

"Drop that gun, miss!" The officer drew his revolver. "You're under arrest."

Turning her pistol around, Sarah handed it to him, butt first.

"Don't arrest her!" said one of the diners who was standing nearby. "She saved our lives. If she hadn't ordered us out, we would've still been in there when the bomb went off."

"That's true, Officer," Michael Flannery said, coming over to them.

"Who are you?" the policeman asked Sarah.

"I'm Sarah Arad, with Interpol. May I take out my ID?" she asked, indicating it was in her shoulder bag.

The policeman motioned for her to proceed, and she withdrew her passport and Interpol ID. As a YAMAM agent, she had been given a collateral position in Interpol, which both protected her YAMAM identity and provided her with some police authority beyond Israel's borders. Attached to the ID was a special permit from the New York Police Department allowing her to carry a handgun in the city.

The policeman handed the gun, passport, and ID back to her. "How did you know about the bomb?"

"I had been watching someone who looked suspicious. When he left a briefcase behind in the restaurant, I suspected a bomb."

"Yeah, well, you Israelis are used to things like this. Lucky for us you saw the Arab when you did."

"He wasn't Arab. He looked more like a Californian."

"What?"

"A blond surfer-type, about twenty-four or so, thin, average height, with a blue-floral Hawaiian shirt and tan cargo pants. Last I saw, he was headed north." She gestured up the street.

"A blond surfer bomber, huh? Well, I'll be damned." He

glanced over at Flannery and quickly added, "Excuse me, Father."

"That's quite all right, Officer," Flannery assured him with a grin. "I was thinking that very thing, though with a word a lot harsher than *damn*."

Twenty blocks south of Bernie's Deli, on the seventh floor of the Marcel Hotel, Tim O'Leary turned on the shower. While he was letting the water warm, he began undressing, removing his pants and blue-floral shirt. His back was covered with raised, crisscrossed scars, the result of having been scourged. He stepped into the shower and let the stream of water cascade down his body.

O'Leary had heard the explosion as he circled the block and headed south toward the hotel. He wondered what his Uncle Paddy would think about what he had done. Padraic O'Leary had been with the Irish Republican Army, and Tim's family had often hidden him in a secret room behind their china cabinet. The Brits had come to the house dozens of times, but they never found him.

Now the younger O'Leary was carrying on the family tradition, despite an uneasy peace between the IRA and the Brits. But he had gone a step beyond Uncle Paddy, fighting not just for the Catholics of Northern Ireland but of the whole world.

When O'Leary had first been given the order to assassinate Fr. Michael Flannery, he had been confused.

"But, 'tis a Catholic you're asking me to kill," O'Leary had said. "Sure'n he's a priest besides."

"Do not concern yourself with that," Fr. Antonio Sangremano had told him. "I know Michael Flannery well, and he is a disgrace to the collar he wears. He is a heretic and a sworn enemy of Via Dei. Disciple O'Leary, when you joined The Way, you took an oath to always obey the Grand Master. Would you deny that oath now?"

"No, Grand Master, sure'n I would not."

"Then carry out your assignment."

After finishing his shower, O'Leary lay on his bed and waited patiently for the evening news. At one minute until six, he turned on the television.

"A bomb blast destroys a popular Manhattan eatery," said the opening tease. *"Threats of a transit strike, dry weather to continue, Yanks beat the BoSox and the Mets lose to the Cardinals. After this."*

O'Leary sat through commercials for a local car dealership, a parlor-style pizza chain, and an airline, and promos for the station's prime time lineup. Then the news began with an attractive black woman staring at the camera.

"Good evening, I'm Brennell Merritt. It wasn't Baghdad or Jerusalem or Madrid. It was right here in Midtown Manhattan at Bernie's Deli," she began.

A stock photo of the deli cross-faded into a live shot on the street outside the popular restaurant. The front of the building was blackened, and the windows and doors had been blown out. Yellow barrier tape circled the scene and kept the gawkers at bay. Several policemen patrolled the perimeter, with a white-clad forensics team moving in and out of the building.

"Miraculously, nobody was killed in the bomb blast, and there were only a few superficial cuts from flying glass," Brennell said in a voice-over.

"Impossible!" O'Leary blurted as he bolted upright on the bed. "'Tis a lie!"

As if answering him, Brennell's voice-over continued, "Witnesses say that a tragedy was averted by the quick action of a young woman later identified as an officer with Interpol, the international police organization. She spotted the bomb and shouted a warning, just in time to clear everyone out of the premises before the explosion."

The camera moved in on one of the blast victims, a

heavyset, middle-aged man with scratches on his cheek and a bandage across his forehead.

"Could we have your name, sir?" the street reporter asked, jabbing a microphone in front of the fellow.

"Hayes. My name is Bertram Hayes, and I'm from Piggot, Arkansas."

"Mr. Hayes, could you tell us what you saw?"

"Yes, sir. Well, me'n my wife was having our lunch, when all of a sudden this woman started yelling. Well, being as we're from Arkansas, we figured, I don't know, maybe this kind of thing happens all the time in New York. But the next thing you know, this woman was shooting her gun, so we and everyone else commenced to running. When the bomb went off, I got me a couple of scratches and this gash here." He gestured at his bandaged forehead. "My wife, she was even luckier, she didn't get nothing."

"Have you spoken to the woman who shouted the warning?"

"No, sir, I haven't, but I'd sure like to. Her shouting out like that saved our ass."

"Yes, uh, thank you," the reporter said as he quickly withdrew the microphone, then turned toward the camera to give his wrap-up. "The police have a description of the bomber, Brennell, and get this—they say he was a young man, thin, with blond hair and blue eyes. And dressed like a surfer. Not your typical Islamic terrorist."

"No, it is not, Peter," Brennell said. "Have you been able to interview the woman whose heroism saved so many lives today?"

"I'm afraid not, though every reporter is out looking for her. Either the police are keeping her under tight wraps, or she's as modest as she is brave."

"Yes, well, wherever she is, I hope she knows that the entire city of New York is grateful. And thank you, Peter, for your report." The image switched to Brennell Merritt at the anchor's desk. "We'll have more later on the Surfer Bomber, as he's being called. But now let's get a first look at the weather from meteorologist Todd Wolfe. . . ."

Tim O'Leary snatched up the remote and turned off the television, then dropped back onto the pillows and lay staring up at the ceiling. He had failed his assignment. The Grand Master was going to be very unhappy, indeed.

CHAPTER 8

TOLEDO

After Vespers, Tobias Garlande invited his guest, Philippe Guischard, to join him in the great hall. There was still some light filtering through the oriel windows, but it was dark enough that Tobias had the cook lower the large iron chandelier from a crossbeam in the vaulted ceiling so the candles could be lit.

Although it was late spring, the air had cooled considerably as the sun set, so a fire was laid in the large stone fireplace to push away the chill. Tobias and Philippe sat in facing chairs in front of the fireplace, their skin gleaming gold in the dancing firelight.

Tobias held up the letter, which was still sealed with wax and did not appear to have been opened. "You have no idea what this is about?" he asked.

Philippe shook his head. "Grand Master said only that it would involve me."

Tobias broke the seal and unfolded the letter. He read in silence for a moment, then put it down and sighed. "Jean Fournier wants us to go to Constantinople."

"Constantinople? Such a long journey. Does he say why?"

"Shall I read it to you?"

Philippe nodded, and the older man lifted the letter and began to read:

I bring greetings to Brother Tobias, who though he has abandoned Christ has not been abandoned by Him.

At the Council of Clermont, the Holy Father called upon all Christians to cease our quarrels and turn our energies to God's own service. Pope Urban promised that in so doing, we shall obtain a rich reward on Earth and everlasting Glory in Heaven.

The pope has asked us to take up the Cross and mount a mighty crusade to wrest the Holy Sepulcher from the foul hands of the infidels, and to take back the holy city of Jerusalem.

The Holy Father has offered indulgence, total remission of all sins, and remission of Purgatory after death to all who would take part in this glorious crusade. This should be of particular interest to you, Brother Tobias, as you are badly in need of forgiveness for your sin of heresy.

Brother Tobias, you have falsely interpreted the intent of Dismas, the founder of our order. You have made it evident by word and deed that you have placed your trust in the literal translation of Trevia Dei, that it refers to three roads to God. In fact, divine interpretation informs us that Trevia Dei is the Holy Trinity of Father, Son, and Holy Spirit and is exemplified by our own sacred trinity of Via Dei, Catholic Church, and Jesus Christ.

As long as you continue to espouse the false doctrine that Trevia Dei represents a sacred unity between the one true path to God and the false teachings of the Jews and the Moorish infidels, you are placing your soul in danger of eternal damnation.

By these words, I command Philippe Guischard to travel to Constantinople to meet with our esteemed brother disciple, Peter the Hermit, who is gloriously exhorting the Christian masses to take up this great battle in the name of our Lord.

Brother Tobias, as you no longer consider yourself

bound by the oath you took to obey the Grand Master, I can but ask you to accompany Philippe, and pray that you will see fit to do so, for the salvation of your immortal soul.

Tobias lowered the letter and looked at Philippe. "That's the end."

"Well, then, surely we must go," Philippe said. "We must make preparations at once."

"I want to think on it tonight," Tobias said. "I will let you know tomorrow."

"But Brother Tobias, you heard the Grand Master. Surely you will not reject this opportunity to save your soul from eternal damnation?"

"I will give you my decision in the morning," he said. "There are many sleeping chambers in this house. I will have Sansoles de Rojas show you to one you may use."

IN HIS OWN bedroom later that night, Tobias removed his necklace, then opened the silver case that it bore and took out a folded piece of cloth. Though over one thousand years old, the cloth was as white and fresh as when it was woven. As he gazed upon the cloth, he remembered with vivid clarity the day in 1053 when he had been chosen to be Keeper of the Sign and given the awesome responsibility of caring for the cloth and all it embodied.

At a very early age Tobias had shown a remarkable talent for languages and, because of that, often served as an intermediary between the churches in Constantinople and Rome. Communications from the Western Church were in Latin, while those from the Eastern Church were in Greek. Even though each side employed competent interpreters, suspicion grew between the two factions until, in 1053, Caerularius, Patriarch of the Eastern Church, unleashed a series of unfounded accusations against Rome, declaring war and striking the pope's name from the diptychs of the churches in the East.

Tobias recognized that the broadening schism was based on the jealousies of men rather than on doctrinal differences, and he tried to bring about a rapprochement between the two parties. His attempts met not only with failure, but also with the enmity of both sides. After one meeting in which he preached reconciliation to a bishop of the Eastern Church, he was arrested, charged with heresy, and thrown into irons. It was while in prison in Antioch that he met Hermitimos. The old prisoner was dying, and Tobias cared for him as he would his own father.

It soon became obvious to Tobias that Hermitimos was not only a good man but a holy man, holier than anyone Tobias had ever encountered. Just being around him, even in his weakened state, Tobias could sense the man's deep spiritual power. In the short time they were together, Tobias realized that Hermitimos had affected him more deeply than anyone he had ever met.

Hermitimos could not possibly be guilty of any crime, so one night Tobias summoned the courage to ask the question that had been troubling him. "Why, Brother Hermitimos, are you in prison?"

"To meet you," the old man replied.

"To meet me? I don't understand."

"I heard you speak once in Constantinople, when you challenged the Patriarch himself to examine his own heart. You were a bit foolhardy but exceptionally brave for one so young. Then later, I saw you in a vision and knew you were the one to carry on—to be the next Keeper."

"Keeper? The keeper of what?"

Hermitimos lifted his frail arm and touched Tobias, first on the forehead, then on his chest over the heart. At that moment a wondrous thing happened. The stone walls of the prison fell away, and Tobias found himself standing on a road, watching as a tall black man trudged toward him. He did not have to wonder who the dark stranger was, because suddenly he became that man, he became Simon of Cyrene.

AS SIMON BEGINS the long return journey to Cyrene, he cannot get the events in Jerusalem out of his mind. It wasn't just the brutal scourging and execution of a good, gentle man that had so moved him, but the strange sensation he experienced under Jesus' gaze as he took on the burden of the cross. It was as if he had been shown the future—not just his own but that of mankind as well. In what must have been only an instant, he had seen wondrous things he could not now fathom. Who is he to have such a remarkable vision? He is not of the race or the religion of this Jesus, so why had he been so affected?

He recalls the rabbi's words that night at the campfire— "Are we not all of the race of man?"—and how his skin had appeared as black as Simon's. That could have been a trick of the light, of course, for the shadows had been growing long in the Garden of Gethsemane.

"Simon," a voice intones, interrupting his musing as he walks alone down the deserted road.

He halts and looks around, half expecting to see his friend Dismas bar-Dismas come in search of him. "Yes?" he calls, but he sees nothing, so he shrugs and continues along the hard-packed roadway.

"Simon."

Simon spins around, and again he sees no one. But this time when he turns back, someone is blocking the way in front of him. For a moment he doesn't recognize the man. Then with a gasp Simon realizes he is looking at Jesus.

"No, it cannot be!" Simon falls to his knees, muttering the rabbi's name.

"Rise, Simon," Jesus says. "Did I not say we would walk together again?"

"My Lord, forgive me for my doubts," Simon whispers, afraid to look up at him.

"In my travail, you used your tunic to wipe blood from my eyes. Look now at that garment, Simon."

Simon had clutched the torn patch of cloth all during the crucifixion, later discovering it still gripped tightly in his fist. It was so drenched with blood that he had considered throwing it away. But something had compelled him to save it, as if unwilling to let go of Jesus. This morning he stuffed it in his traveling bag, and he reaches into the bag now and takes it out.

"Open it," Jesus declares, "and gaze upon the sign."

The cloth is approximately one foot square and stiff with dried blood as Simon unfolds it. He looks at the cloth, then glances up questioningly at Jesus, who merely smiles. When Simon looks back at the cloth, his eyes widen in wonder, for the brownish encrusted blood is reddening and becoming moist again. It begins to flow from the cloth onto the dirt at Simon's feet, leaving the material a lustrous white—a white more brilliant than the fabric had been the day it was woven.

Not all the blood drains away. Some of what had been a random pattern remains now in the form of a strange, unfamiliar symbol. The top looks like a crescent moon resting with the points facing upward and just touching at the peak. Centered in that circle of moon is a five-pointed star, with the bottom two points shooting downward like beams of light and forming a pyramid with the horizontal line of the ground. Connecting the ground to the crescent circle is a T-shaped cross, much like the one that bore Jesus upon Golgotha.

"What . . . what is this wondrous thing?"

"Trevia Dei—the three great roads to God that are one," Jesus says. "It is a symbol of the different paths men shall take in seeking their Father."

"I don't understand."

Reaching out, Jesus touches Simon upon the forehead and then the heart. Simon feels a tingling sensation, then finds himself surrounded by a bubble of light. All of his senses are intensified: Colors become more vibrant, smells sweeter, sounds more resonant, even the hard earth feels exquisite beneath his feet.

Still gazing at the image on the cloth, he sees the Trevia Dei transform into three separate symbols that slowly lift into the air and pull away from one another. The top turns and forms a crescent moon and star. The pyramid doubles and folds upon itself into a six-pointed star. Finally, the transept of the cross lowers, forming a cross with four arms.

Suddenly Simon is transported to a new time and place, and though the experience is unlike anything he could have conceived, he is neither frightened nor mystified. From some distant vantage point, he gazes back upon a bright blue ball suspended in a black void, and he knows without understanding how that this sphere is the home of man.

His vision expanding, he sees marvelous winged machines streaking like chariots through the sky, cities ablaze with lights that never flicker, buildings taller than the Tower of Babel. But he also sees men and women with skin as dark as his own being chained and crowded onto slave-trading boats, Jews being herded by the thousands to slaughter in death camps, millions of men and women of all races and nations being killed by terrible engines of war. . . .

Simon looks at the cloth in his hands. The Star and Crescent, the Star of David, and the Cross have once more come together into the blood-red symbol Jesus called Trevia Dei.

"You have seen?" Jesus asks.

"Yes, Lord," Simon answers. "I don't know why I was chosen to view such astonishing things, but I have seen and will never forget."

"In time you shall see and understand more, for the Trevia Dei shall teach you," Jesus tells him. "It is a sign for man's journey to God. I have chosen you, Simon, to be keeper of *this sign until you are no longer able. Then you must find one who is worthy, who in time will find another, who will pass it to yet another for fifty generations to come . . . until the time Trevia Dei is to be revealed."*

"Yes," Simon replies, looking again at the marvelous symbol upon the cloth. "I will do as you say, my Lord, always. . . ."

There is a faint rustle of wind, and then Simon looks up to discover he is again alone. For an instant he thinks it was all a dream, but then he sees in his hands the cloth bearing the Trevia Dei, and any remaining doubt vanishes. He falls forward on the ground, giving a prayer of thanks that he has been chosen and a prayer of entreaty that he be worthy of so great a trust.

TOBIAS WATCHED AS Simon of Cyrene prayed aloud, and he realized at that moment that he was no longer Simon but was again looking upon him. That awareness pulled him out of the vision, and the prison walls closed back around him.

"Now you know," Hermitimos said.

"Yes," Tobias replied. "Now I know."

"This is a great commission," the old man said.

"I am not worthy of such a thing."

"They say that you are worthy."

Hermitimos waved his hand, and again Tobias saw Simon of Cyrene standing before him, but this time with other men and women beside him. All of the Keepers looked at him with beatific smiles.

"Will you accept this honor and this obligation?"

"Yes," Tobias said. "I accept."

Hermitimos lifted from beneath his tattered robe a necklace bearing an exquisitely carved silver case. Tobias had never seen it before and wondered how he had kept it hidden from the guards. But with the thought came the instant understanding that the necklace could be seen only by those the Keeper permitted.

Opening the case, Hermitimos removed a folded piece of cloth, the very one that Simon had been carrying when he met Jesus on the road from Jerusalem.

"Accept this in service to the Lord, and in the knowledge that God loves His children regardless of the path they take to Him."

Those were the final words of Hermitimos, who handed Tobias the necklace and cloth and then fell lifeless to the prison floor.

NOW, FORTY-THREE YEARS later, Tobias sat on the edge of his hard bed, clutching the Trevia Dei cloth in his hand. He smiled as he recalled how he had escaped the prison. It had been the final gift of Hermitimos, a lesson given in death to the new Keeper. Tobias had been holding the necklace against his heart when the guards came to remove the old man's body, and he realized the necklace wasn't the only thing they were unable to see. Tobias himself was invisible, thanks to the power of the cloth bearing the Trevia Dei symbol, and he simply followed as they carried the corpse out of the prison and tossed it into an unmarked grave.

But it was only an old man's body that they buried, for as they covered it over with dirt, Tobias became aware of Hermitimos smiling at him from the distance. He was no longer an old man but the vibrant young monk who had first been given the Keeper's commission. As he and the other Keepers turned and headed toward the setting sun, Tobias followed, knowing that somewhere far to the west he would discover why he had been chosen and what he was destined to do.

"Thank you, Hermitimos," Tobias whispered as he tucked the cloth into the silver case and lay back on his bed.

It had been a long journey that ultimately led here to

Toledo, and now he wondered if the letter from Jean
Fournier was a sign he had yet another journey to undertake. At first he had doubted that a message from the likes
of Fournier would hold any key to his destiny, but something had shaken him upon reading the name Peter the
Hermit. He had known Peter many years ago and had even
thought the monk shared many of the qualities of Hermitimos. But something must have happened to him, if indeed
he had turned from the truth of Trevia Dei and now was
spreading the call for holy war.

"Give me a sign," Tobias whispered, clutching the necklace tight against his chest. "Show me what must be done,
where I must go."

He felt the bed shudder, then fall away from beneath him.
For an instant he was weightless, floating in air. But then
he alighted on hard ground and became aware of the acrid
smell of burning ruins. Blinking his eyes, he struggled to see
through the smoke, to figure out where he had landed and
what it might portend.

*TOBIAS STANDS ON top of a high parapet, a pall of smoke
hanging over the fortress, which he recognizes at once as
Masada. Below are enormous iron-plated towers from which
the Romans are using ballistae to hurl large stones high up
into the fortress. The constant pounding of the barrage as
missiles slam into the barricades has unnerved the defenders, and with the latest assault by fire, he knows their fate is
sealed.*

*Even as Tobias stands watching, a catapulted boulder
brings down a large section of charred wood and stone, and
he can hear the cries of fear and alarm from the defenders
inside the fortress.*

*The Zealot leader Eleazer is preparing to address his fol-
lowers in the fortress courtyard. And while Tobias, having*

translated the writings of the first-century historian Josephus, knows what is to come, he is helpless to do anything to
change their fate.

"Long ago, my generous friends, we resolved never to be
servants to the Romans or to any other but God himself,
who alone is the true and just Lord of mankind," Eleazer
calls out to the crowd. "The time is now come to make that
resolution true in practice. It is now clear that Masada will
be taken within a day's time. But though the Romans may
breach our walls, they need not breach or break our spirit."

Some of the assembly voice their approval; others call
for Eleazer to explain what they must do.

"First, let us destroy our belongings and our money and
put to the torch what remains of the fortress, so that the
Romans shall not claim what little earthly wealth we still
possess. But let us not destroy our provisions, for they will
serve as a testament that we were not subdued for want of
food but that we chose death over slavery."

He pauses as he looks around him, taking in each of the
nearly one thousand people present.

"And finally, my faithful friends, let us indeed choose
death, at our own hands, so that no Roman sword may stain
this sacred ground with Jewish blood."

"But suicide is a sin, is it not?" someone calls out.

"Yes, and the final sin," another says, "for there is no
asking God for forgiveness."

"It is a sin," Eleazer admits. "But I have contrived a way
in which the sin would rest on only one of us. Ten will be chosen to execute all the others. They will then draw lots among
them, and one of those ten will execute the nine, leaving the
sin of suicide on him alone."

"Yes, that is the way we must do it," a man shouts, and
others take up the cry, until the entire assembly is shouting
its assent.

"When do we do this thing?" someone asks.

"In a few minutes," Eleazer replies. "I have already sought volunteers from among our greatest warriors, and from them I have chosen ten who shall be the instruments of our glory. Let us use the time that remains to embrace our beloved and to offer up prayers in praise of our Lord."

Eleazer calls out the names of the ten executioners, and as they take up their swords and join their leader in the center of the courtyard, others go about setting fire to what remains of the fort. The rest of the assembly gather in small groups, sharing kisses and warm embraces, chanting and singing of the glory of God.

As the executioners begin their terrible work, Tobias sees two among them, a man and a woman, slip away. His vision allows him to follow, and he watches as they place a scroll in an earthen jug, then fill the cavity with straw and seal the lid with wax to protect the document for the day it might be found.

They carry the urn and a shovel to a room deep in the fortress. Even through the thick stone walls, they can hear the terrifying sounds from above, the moans and cries and prayers of the dying.

"Hurry," the woman says. "We must not let it be found."

The man drops to his knees to scoop up dirt with the short-handled shovel, the pungent odor of freshly turned earth filling the chamber.

"Hurry," she urges. "We don't have much time!"

"I'm almost deep enough." He gasps for breath as he increases his labor.

Another scream, this one so close as to make both of them jump. Then from outside comes a mournful dirge:

*"Yeetgadal v' yeetkadash sh'mey rabbah
B'almah dee v'rah kheer'utey."*

"Give it here," the man says, dropping the shovel and reaching up toward the vase.

"Is it deep enough? This must not fall into the wrong hands," the woman says, handing it to him.

"It has to be. We have no time left."

> *"Yeetgadal v' yeetkadash sh'mey rabbah*
> *B'almah dee v'rah kheer'utey."*

Above, the chanting of the Kaddish grows fainter as the voices trail off one by one.

The woman keeps vigil by the stairs as the man quickly fills the hole, tamps the dirt, and tosses the shovel to one side. "The shovel," she whispers excitedly, gesturing at where it lies.

"Of course," he says, realizing it is evidence of the burial site. He snatches it back up, then scrapes his foot over the ground, hiding any remaining marks of the dig.

The woman is again peering up the stairs at the doorway above as the man comes over and places a hand on her shoulder.

"It's time for us to go."

"Do you think it's safe?" she asks, fear evident in her eyes as she looks up at him.

"We have done all we can do. Whether the door opens upon Heaven or Hell is now up to God."

Outside, the cries and prayers have stilled, replaced now by the soft whisper of the wind.

In vision, Tobias follows the man and woman outside, where he can see that the killings are complete, the ten executioners also dead at the hands of the one they chose by lot. It is a gruesome sight, yet there is something peaceful, almost poetic, in the way these patriots of the Holy Land lie in one another's last embrace.

Arm in arm, the man and woman walk through the still and silent courtyard, past the bodies of parent and child, warrior and priest, then through the fortress gates and out to the edge of the Masada cliff. There they gaze down upon the Roman troops, who are already gathering for a final assault up their crude earthen ramp.

They pray aloud together, first to his God of the Jews, then to her Christian messiah. With a final embrace, they step forward and leap into the void.

Suddenly, Tobias senses the presence of another, not a participant in the events but someone who has also been witnessing it in a vision. It is a young woman, and with a start Tobias realizes he recognizes her. He starts to speak her name, but she seems unaware of his presence, perhaps even unaware that this is anything more than a dream.

And there is someone else on hand, the faint figure of a man standing at some distance, gazing toward them. He is tall, with dark, flashing eyes that seem neither cruel nor kind. Most surprising is that he is not a Jew or a Roman or even a Christian like Tobias. He is an infidel.

THE VISION PASSED, and Tobias found himself back in his own bed. He knew with certainty why he had been shown the vision and what he now must do. He would travel to Jerusalem and then to the fortress of Masada to unearth the urn and the scroll inside. He had no idea what the scroll contained, but he knew his God-given task was to find it. And the first step in carrying out that great commission would be to accompany Philippe Guischard to Constantinople.

"I WILL TRAVEL with you to Constantinople," Tobias told Philippe after they said matins in his library the next morning.

"The Grand Master will be very pleased," Philippe replied with genuine excitement.

"I am not making the journey to please the Grand Master," Tobias said, "but to serve the Lord."

"Yes, yes, of course, as are we all."

"I intend to ask Rachel Benyuli to accompany us."

"Brother Tobias, she was not at vespers last night, nor did she join us at matins," Philippe said.

"I would not expect that she would," Tobias replied.

"She is your assistant, yet she does not follow the daily offices?"

"She's Jewish," Tobias reminded him.

"Yes, I am aware of that. But I assumed that you took the poor woman in so that she might complete her conversion to the true faith."

"I hired Rachel as my assistant because she is very learned and a great help to me in my work. I have no intention of trying to convert her to Christianity."

Philippe's jaw dropped in surprise. "Then you would condemn her soul to eternal damnation?"

"I don't accept that," Tobias said. "It is not for me to choose the path by which she approaches God."

"If you will not save her, then I will," Philippe declared.

Tobias chuckled. "I think you'll find that Rachel is not only smart but a young woman of strong conviction in her own faith. You will not succeed."

At that moment Rachel joined Tobias and Philippe. She curtsied slightly and said, "Good morning to you, Tobias."

"And to you, Rachel."

She smiled at Philippe, but without warmth. "Good day, Monsieur Guischard. I trust you slept well in a strange bed."

"I was quite comfortable, yes," Philippe replied. "And long before you came to this house, I served as assistant to Tobias, so the bed is not unfamiliar."

"I am pleased." She turned to Tobias. "Will we be working on the Missal of Silos today?"

"No," Tobias answered. "Instead you will help me prepare for a journey. I am going to Constantinople."

The young woman looked surprised and concerned. "That is a very great distance."

Tobias grinned. "For someone my age, you mean. But I shan't be alone. Philippe is going, and I was hoping you'd consent to accompany us. To ease your journey, Philippe and I will gladly share a kosher diet, though I cannot promise that will always be possible."

Rachel looked visibly relieved. "I will begin preparations at once. And I will seek dispensation from my rabbi for those occasions when such a diet cannot be maintained."

CHAPTER 9

WEST OF CONSTANTINOPLE

Tobias and his companions neared the pilgrim encampment four days' march from the city of Adrianople, where they had spent several days resting and gathering supplies following the arduous land and sea voyage from Toledo. They had started by land to Barcelona in eastern Hispania, then by boat around Italia to Nicopolis in Greece. From there it was a long land journey through the Greek provinces of Epirus, Thessaly, Macedonia, and Thrace to the broad plains of the western approach to Constantinople, which lay twenty miles to the east.

For this leg of the journey they had joined one of the many caravans of pilgrims who used Adrianople as a final staging point en route to Constantinople from their homes scattered through Europe. But while Pope Urban had exhorted the masses to flock to Constantinople to buttress the forces being gathered by Peter the Hermit for the assault on Jerusalem, the pilgrims had found a less than warm reception in that city. Its ruler, the Byzantine Emperor Alexius Comnenus, had encouraged Urban to send mercenary forces to help him fend off the Seljuk Turks in Asia Minor, but he had not expected such a disorganized group of regular citizens with virtually no military training. After discovering they had pillaged their way through his Balkan provinces, he decided to keep them at some distance from the city while he arranged for their passage across the Bosporus, where they could take their chances with the Turks while Alexius awaited the trained soldiers that the pope promised would follow.

Most of the two dozen people in the caravan were on foot, with several horse-drawn wagons bearing kegs of water, wine, and other supplies. Whole families had made the pilgrimage, as if their march on Jerusalem were some sort of religious procession so blessed by God that the infidels would fall back without a fight as the glorious host approached. Few weapons beyond simple swords and pikes were in evidence, and the only shields were the crosses embroidered on the front of the long surcoats of the men. On a knight these surcoats protected metal armor and chain mail from the corrosive effects of weather and battle, but on these pilgrim soldiers they covered only the coarse-spun clothing of the farmers and tradesmen they had been back home.

About a mile outside the encampment, the caravan was stopped by several soldiers who rode among the pilgrims asking questions. When the lead horseman approached Tobias and his group, Philippe stepped forward, motioning to his companions that he would speak for them.

"Je suis Ducas, émissaire du Empereur Alexius," the horseman said, using the language common to most of the pilgrims. *"Qui êtes-vous?"*

Replying in the Greek of Constantinople rather than French, Philippe told Ducas, "I am Philippe Guischard, a Disciple of the Way. I am traveling with Tobias Garlande, a learned transcriber of ancient texts."

"Ah, you are men of education," the emperor's emissary said in Greek, intrigued by Philippe's command of the language. "That is most unusual among—" He swept his arm to take in the line of pilgrims. "—among their sort." He turned his attention to Rachel, who was standing beside Tobias. "Is she your wife?" he asked Philippe.

"She is in my employ," Tobias replied, also in Greek.

"Why have learned men such as yourselves come to Constantinople with the likes of these?"

"To join the glorious battle, of course," Philippe declared.

Ducas clucked his tongue and shook his head. "Then you are educated but not very smart. You bring an old man and a young woman on a military campaign? Do you even know what this struggle is about?"

"We are answering Pope Urban's call to all Christians to liberate the Holy Land," Philippe declared.

"No. You are here because Emperor Alexius asked the pope for help in beating back the Turks, who threaten to overrun our city. We expected warriors, bowmen, knights," he said, "but what do we get? Women and children, feeble old men. Even the young men are worthless. Untrained and unarmed, they do little more than descend like locusts on our fields and plunder our people. Thousands of pilgrims, all besotted with the wine of adventure and the dream of making manifest the will of our Lord."

"Sir, do you malign our service to the Lord?" Philippe asked somewhat petulantly.

Ducas chuckled again. "I do not malign your desire to serve the Lord. I just do not believe these misfits are the army capable of doing it."

"Surely, among all these people, there are some knights."

"Very few." Ducas snorted derisively. "If you want to know this army of pilgrims, you need go no further than the pitiful example provided by their leader and prophet."

"Peter the Hermit is here?" Tobias said hopefully.

"Yes, he is here," a different man said in French.

Ducas turned on his horse to see that another rider had come up. A tall man with graying black hair, he wore the same surcoat as the pilgrims but over chain mail too shiny ever to have seen action.

"Ah, Raymond," Ducas said in a tone of false deference. "You are here to escort these pilgrim recruits to your camp?"

"Where is Peter?" Tobias asked in French of the man named Raymond. "I'm an old friend and would like to see him."

"I'll bring you to him when we reach the encampment."

"Who are you?" Philippe asked.

"Raymond of Amiens."

"Amiens? Peter is from Amiens," Tobias said.

"Yes. I have known him since our youth." Raymond looked pensive. "But perhaps not as well as I thought." Seeing their questioning expressions, he gave a dismissive wave of the hand. "It is of no importance. Come, I will take you to Peter and his army."

"Army!" Ducas scoffed as he pulled on the reins to turn the horse. "I will leave you to your army of peasants." He rode away, signaling his guards to follow.

Philippe introduced himself and his companions to Raymond of Amiens, then said, "The emperor's emissary doesn't think much of Peter's cause or his army."

"No, and not without some cause."

"What do you think of the pilgrimage?" Philippe pressed. "Is it not a glorious adventure?"

"I will let you judge for yourself," Raymond replied. "Now we must be on our way." He spun his horse around and rode up and down the line of two dozen travelers, calling out in French, "Let us move along, now! The pilgrim city awaits just beyond that hill!" He galloped to the front of the line, then pulled to a halt and dropped down off the horse's back. Handing the reins to one of his aides, he led the caravan on foot toward a distant rise.

TOBIAS STOOD AT the crest of the ridge and took in the encampment below. He had expected to find the orderly rows of tents and disciplined processions of soldiers and support staff of a traveling military camp, but what he gazed upon was pure chaos. This rendezvous point for Peter the Hermit's army of peasants was more like a makeshift city thrown together with debris and detritus that had been stolen and carted off from the villages the caravans passed through along the way.

Tobias held Rachel's arm with one hand and his walking staff with the other as they started gingerly down the rocky path that led into the heart of the camp. As they passed the first crude and lopsided canvas-and-wood structures, they found themselves among a crowd of peasants who milled about the makeshift streets and alleys, trading goods and carrying out business as if this temporary camp were a bustling city.

As the new arrivals pushed their way through the crowd, Tobias was struck by the odd combination of heat and stench and sound, and thought that an artist's rendering of Hell could not have been more graphic. There were more than a thousand tents and temporary buildings, housing many thousands of people, yet nobody seemed to be inside. Countless fires were burning, over which turned spits of sheep, goats, and swine. There was a babble of laughter and music, but it sounded discordant, demonic, the voices loud and angry.

Tobias heard Rachel gasp and grip his arm more tightly. She quickly averted her gaze, and when he turned in the direction she had been looking, he saw what had upset her. Just inside the open flap of one of the tents, a naked man and woman lay coupled on the ground, making no effort to preserve their privacy. Seated nearby on a rock, another naked man was holding up a wineskin, squirting a stream of red liquid into his gaping mouth, with equal parts splattering against his chin and chest. Looking around in astonishment, Tobias saw several more acts of fornication, one involving several people at once.

"What is this debauchery?" he said in disgust.

"Have you not heard?" Raymond said sarcastically. "Pope Urban has granted absolute remission of all sins."

"But surely that is for sins already committed, not an invitation to go forth and commit sins anew."

"I agree," Raymond replied. "But neither Peter nor Walter share that view."

"Walter?"

"Walter the Penniless. He's Peter's second-in-command."

"I don't know this Walter the Penniless," Tobias said, "but I do know Peter—or at least I thought I did. He is fanatical in his devotion and would never associate with such . . . with such depravity."

"You speak of Peter the mendicant of Amiens," Raymond replied. "But we are far from France, and the hermit is leading an army of thousands. He is determined to use whatever means are required to keep his soldiers from abandoning the field before battle is engaged. If that includes a liberal interpretation of the pope's edicts, Peter is convinced it is God's will."

"Then he condones this behavior?" Tobias said, shaking his head. "Or worse, participates in it?"

Raymond laughed. "Peter? With a woman . . . or even a man? Never. But he is not above letting his flock rut at will—" He abruptly caught himself and said to Rachel, "I apologize for my coarse manners." He turned back to Tobias. "What I mean is that Peter has decided it will benefit the campaign to allow the pilgrims their liberties in advance of battle. And so he has told them that the pope has promised that their past and future sins shall be remitted if they reclaim Jerusalem or die in the endeavor."

They entered a large open area that served as a public square. Raymond halted and gestured toward a small hillock at the far end. A short man in a coarse brown robe stood atop the mound, surrounded by several hundred pilgrims who were looking up intently at him.

"And there is Peter the Hermit," Raymond declared as he led them toward the gathering.

Tobias recognized at once the long, lean face and sharp nose rather like an eagle's beak. As they grew closer, he saw how truly filthy the barefooted monk had become, his long hair a tangle and his robe shredded at the hem and sleeves. Peter had always been an ascetic, fond of spending time in caves and forests, but never had Tobias seen him so unkempt and wild as he looked now, repeatedly stabbing his finger toward heaven and haranguing the crowd.

Tobias and his companions slipped into the outer edge of the crowd until they were close enough to hear Peter's words.

"Go, brothers, go with hope and faith to the great battle against the enemies of God, who for so long have dominated Syria, Armenia, and the whole of Asia. Their outrages against our Lord are legion. They have defiled the sepulcher of Christ and the marvelous monuments of our faith. They have forbidden pilgrims to set foot in a city whose worth only Christians can truly appreciate. Are these facts not sufficient to unleash your swords? To unbind your tongues so that you may bear witness against these unholy blasphemers?"

He spat out the last word as a curse, and the crowd took up the chant, crying out, "Blasphemers! Blasphemers!"

"Go and show your worth! Go, you soldiers of God, and your fame shall spread across the entire world. Do not fear losing the Kingdom of God because of the tribulation brought by war. If you fall prisoner to the infidels and face their worst torments for your faith, you will save your heavenly soul at the same moment you lose your earthly body. Do not hesitate, most dear brethren, to offer your lives for the good of your neighbors. Do not hesitate to go because of love for your family, your kingdom, or your riches, since man owes his love principally to God. You shall have the greatest happiness one can have in this life, which is to see the places where our Lord walked and spoke the language of men."

"Deus vult!" the crowd shouted. "God wills it!"

"Remember the words of our Holy Father, Pope Urban,

when he declared: 'Such a cry would not be unanimous were it not inspired by the Holy Spirit. Let this be, then, your war cry to announce the power of the God of Hosts. And whosoever undertakes this journey shall carry upon him the form of the cross. Let you bear the cross on your sword, on your breast, on your weapons and standards. Let it be for you either the sign of victory or the palm of martyrdom, and also the symbol to unify the dispersed children of Israel. It will continuously remind you that Jesus Christ died for you and that for Him you should die.' "

Again the crowd cheered.

"And remember, my fellow warriors for Christ. By committing to this Holy War, all sins forever are forgiven!"

Peter literally shouted the last words, and they were met with enthusiastic cheers and applause.

Peter climbed down off the hillock, and the crowd began to disperse, returning to their tents and hovels. As they parted, Tobias saw that Peter was walking over to a donkey that, oddly, was practically denuded of hair.

"What happened to his beast?" he asked Raymond.

"His followers have plucked out tufts, believing it to be sacred."

Peter was speaking to another man, and the contrast between them was striking, one short and swarthy, the other tall and blond, with a regal air about him.

"Is that Walter the Penniless?" Tobias asked.

"Yes. He's one of the few knights among us, and his poverty is self-imposed, as he comes from a family of considerable wealth," Raymond said of the man known in French as Gautier Sans-Avoir.

"Then he is to be honored for his vow of poverty," Philippe put in.

"I suppose so," Raymond replied, "if you can overlook that, while on the march here, Walter and his followers plundered and burned entire villages if they did not convert to the Holy Roman faith. And these were not the infidels

Pope Urban has sent us to defeat. He killed hundreds of Byzantine Christians and Jews."

Tobias sensed Rachel stiffening beside him, and he heard her choke back a little gasp. He looked at her and shook his head, warning not to say that she was a Jew.

"I thought the war was to retake the Holy Lands from the Muslims."

Raymond sighed. "Muslims, Jews, even the Byzantines— to Walter and his kind, they are all the same."

"And Peter?" Tobias asked.

"For many years I've been his friend, or at least as close to a friend as a man such as Peter the Hermit can have. I've pleaded with him to stay true to the teachings of our faith, to win converts not through the sword but through acts of kindness."

"I know Peter, or did a long time ago," Tobias said. "I cannot believe that such an appeal, coming from a friend, would fall on deaf ears."

"It is not that his ears are deaf, but that his heart has grown cold. I fear it is the influence of Walter."

"I must speak with Peter—and with this Walter the Penniless," Tobias declared.

"Yes, Raymond, will you arrange it?" Philippe asked. "Tobias and I bring greetings from Lourdes and wish to offer him our services."

Tobias held up his hand. "First, I would speak with Peter alone."

Philippe seemed taken aback. "What business do you have that cannot be said in front of me?"

"Please," Tobias said softly. "I am but a simple transcriber of documents, while you have become an envoy to the Holy See. But grant me this indulgence, that I might greet an old friend in private."

Philippe's expression confirmed that Tobias had taken the right approach in appealing to the younger man's inflated sense of importance.

"Very well," Philippe said with the slightest of sighs. "But do not say anything that would betray the spirit of our glorious cause."

"Come," Raymond said, "I'll bring you to his tent."

CHAPTER 10

Why do we wait?" Walter the Penniless protested as he paced back and forth across the broad expanse of the tent that served as headquarters for the pilgrim force. "Emperor Alexius grows weary of our presence. And the merchants of Constantinople, rather than welcoming us as defenders of the faith, rob us with the prices they charge for the most basic goods. We should push on across the Bosporus."

Peter gave a dismissive wave. "Are not sheep, goats, and swine being cooked, even now, to feed us? It is not yet time to go."

"If we wait too long, the enemy will increase its forces, and I fear our time will never come," Walter said.

Peter was about to reply when he saw that his protégé, Raymond of Amiens, had entered the tent with an elderly pilgrim.

"Excuse me, Peter," Raymond said as they approached. "This man wishes to speak to you."

"A new pilgrim?" Peter looked the stranger up and down with a dubious frown.

"An old friend," Tobias replied with a nod.

Peter cocked his head slightly, as if searching his memory. His lips crooked into a smile, and he declared, "Tobias? Can it be?"

Tobias reached out and gripped Peter's forearm.

"It's been . . . how long?" Peter asked.

"Many years. Too many."

"You come from France?"

"No, Toledo."

"Ah, I'd heard you were there." Peter turned and gestured for Walter to approach. "This is Walter the Penniless, who leads our soldiers."

Walter eyed the older man suspiciously. "You must be Tobias Garlande. I have heard of your work in the libraries of Toledo."

The two men clasped hands in a cautious greeting.

"Is it true that you translate heathen texts?" Walter asked. "The works of Greeks and Muslims and other unbelievers?"

"There are far-more-learned scholars poring over the sacred texts of Christianity. If my meager skills can help uncover what knowledge our Lord has seen fit to bestow on these so-called unbelievers, so be it."

Peter, looking impatient at their exchange, interjected, "Do you bring an army of the faithful from Castile?"

"I'm afraid not. My assistant, Rachel, and I have made the journey at the behest of Philippe Guischard."

"Philippe? He is here?" Peter said, looking around.

"He waits outside. Do you know him?"

"Only by name, as a faithful servant to the Grand Master in Lourdes."

"Yes, and that is why I've come." Tobias leaned forward and said softly, "May we speak in private, Peter?"

"Of course." Peter turned to Raymond and Walter. "Please leave us for now."

"As you wish," Walter said, his tone betraying disapproval. "But consider, Peter, what I was saying. Our army grows weaker with each day we remain encamped."

"I will think on this," Peter replied. When Walter and Raymond were out of earshot, he turned to Tobias. "My 'penniless' friend grows impatient. He wants to march on the Holy Land now. I have tried to tell him we are not yet ready to do battle."

"That's what I wanted to discuss," Tobias said.

"Don't tell me you, too, are eager to do battle."

"Quite the opposite. I have come to ask you to call off this war."

"What?" Peter gasped. "Do you not realize we are doing this in response to a holy commission from Pope Urban himself?"

"Peter, we have known each other a long time, since our early days in the Sacred Order of Trevia Dei—"

"Via Dei, the one path to God," Peter cut in. "We are now Disciples of the Way."

Tobias pinched the bridge of his nose and sighed audibly. "Peter, Peter. I had hoped that you would have stayed true to the words of our Lord, when he said that Trevia Dei is the three great paths to God that are one. Can't you see that this entire war against Jews and Muslims is contrary to that great commission?"

"Your interpretation—the old interpretation—has been shown to be false," Peter said. "When Jesus spoke of the three roads to God, he meant the Holy Trinity: Father, Son, and Holy Spirit, exemplified by our own sacred trinity of Via Dei, Catholic Church, and Jesus Christ."

Tobias was struck by how closely Peter's words matched the letter from Grand Master Jean Fournier. "And so you are prepared to kill, in the name of Jesus?" Tobias asked.

"I am going to defend the faith in the name of Jesus. If Jews and Muslims get in the way, then their deaths are of little consequence."

"What has happened to you, Peter? I remember you as a pious man, a holy man, a member of the Sacred Order of Trevia Dei."

"It is not for me to gauge my own piety or holiness, but I

trust it has strengthened, for God has graced me with the power to see His light." Peter shook his finger in warning. "You are welcome to join our army, but do not obstruct our holy quest."

"Then you will not listen to reason?"

"Reason?" Peter sneered. "When faith is strong, reason can but follow."

"Then I will take my leave and think on what you have said," Tobias replied. "Perhaps we can continue our discussion at another time."

Tobias left the tent and found Raymond waiting outside.

"You have seen and heard?" Raymond asked. "Is he the Peter you knew?"

"He has changed," Tobias said.

"Yes. He was once a humble priest, a hermit sought out by a handful of the faithful who heard of his holiness. But now he has all this." Raymond took in the crowded encampment with a wave of his hand. "An army at his feet, he has become drunk with power."

"I fear you are right."

"I would ask about your servant girl . . ." Raymond started.

"Rachel is no servant. She is my assistant."

"Your assistant," Raymond corrected himself. "She is a Jewess, isn't she?"

Tobias's eyes narrowed. "Yes," he admitted. "Raymond, you won't tell—"

"Fear not." Raymond held up his hand. "But you must caution her to be very quiet about it. Without the Saracens to fight against, our soldiers slake their thirst on the blood of helpless Jews and even the local Christians."

"Then it's true that Walter and his men have put even fellow Christians to the sword?" Tobias said in dismay.

"The Byzantine Christians hold no allegiance to Rome, and if they refuse to swear allegiance to Urban, then yes, they are considered infidels and treated as such."

As they walked toward where Philippe and Rachel were waiting, Raymond put his hand on Tobias's shoulder, bidding him stop for a moment. "I would tell you something," he said. "But I must have your assurance that you will keep it secret."

"You have my word," Tobias promised.

Raymond looked around to make certain he could not be overheard. "I learned a few days ago that Walter, with Peter's consent, planned to raid a nearby village and kill all of its Jewish inhabitants."

"Did he?"

"He carried out the raid, but he was surprised to find there were no Jews there."

"So his information was wrong."

Raymond shook his head. "No, there were twenty-six Jewish residents. But the night before, I stole into the village and warned them to flee."

"You took a big chance," Tobias said.

"Do you think I was wrong?"

"Of course not. You were doing God's work. But I'm surprised the Jews believed you."

"They didn't at first," Raymond admitted. "I told them to leave before the soldiers came—that they didn't even have time to gather their belongings."

"They must have thought it a trick to leave their belongings for the army," Tobias said.

"Yes. But then it happened."

"What happened?"

"A child, carrying coals from one pit to another, accidentally set fire to a bush." Raymond shook his head, and his eyes grew large as he envisioned the scene.

"The bush burned, but was not consumed," Tobias said.

Raymond gasped. "Yes! How did you know?"

"It was the way God made himself known to Moses. It would be God's way of telling the Jews that you were speaking the truth."

"After that, they listened," Raymond said. "All twenty-six were saved from the sword."

"Surely, you have found favor in God's sight."

"But not in the eyes of Peter or Walter, should they ever discover what I've done."

CHAPTER 11

NEW YORK CITY

T im O'Leary stood at the bathroom mirror in his room
on the seventh floor of the Marcel Hotel. He almost
didn't recognize himself, with his hair dyed black
and a pair of woven extensions fashioned into *payos,* or
sidelocks, worn by Hassidic men. Contact lenses changed
his eyes from blue to brown, and a black suit completed the
effect.

O'Leary gathered up the clothes he had worn while carrying out the bombing the previous day and placed them in
a plastic shopping bag, which he set beside the door. A few
minutes later, he draped a *tallit katan* prayer shawl around
his neck and tucked it under his vest, then donned a Huckel
black hat. Retrieving a small brown suitcase from the bed,
he snatched up the plastic bag and headed out into the hall.
As he walked to the elevator, he passed a trash chute and
discarded the bag containing his Hawaiian shirt, cargo pants,
and sneakers.

"I am Joshua Kohane, an Israeli national," he said, prac-
ticing his new name as he patted his breast pocket to confirm he had his passport.

As the elevator doors opened, two uniformed policemen
stepped out into the hall. O'Leary caught his breath, then
forced himself to remain calm as he moved past the men
and into the elevator. When his suitcase bumped against one
of the officers, he said softly, *"Selach li."*

"What?" the man said, looking back at O'Leary.

"*Selach li* . . . ex-excuse me," O'Leary replied in broken English.

"Sure," the officer said, hardly taking any notice of the Hassidic Jew.

As O'Leary pressed the lobby button, he heard the officer say to his partner, "Room 705."

"I hope the son of a bitch is there. This will be a good collar."

The doors slid closed and O'Leary felt his heart beating rapidly. His room was number 705.

Two more policemen were stationed in the lobby, one watching the elevators, the other standing by the reservation desk, keeping an eye on the front door. O'Leary walked by them without making eye contact, then pushed through the door and stepped out onto Twenty-fourth Street. As he did so, a taxi glided to a stop and a young couple got out, the man carrying an oversized art folio.

"You can't really have an understanding of art until you appreciate the evolution of aesthetic sensibility," the man said with the intensity of youth.

"As if you do," the woman snapped back, looking quite miffed as she barreled past him and into the hotel lobby.

O'Leary ducked into the cab and placed his suitcase on the seat beside him. "Kennedy Airport, the international terminal," he said as he read the cabbie's ID, which gave his name as Hamzah Hasan.

"Yes, I take you," the driver replied. Seeing that O'Leary was looking at the ID, he added, "You are Jewish?"

"Yes."

"I am Muslim. But in this country, we all get along together."

"Yes," O'Leary replied, not wanting to get involved in a conversation.

"There is a big conference coming, of Jews, Muslims, and Christians. Big, important people," the driver continued. "They want us to look to God for help. We do not need politicians, who only make things trouble."

"Yes, I know," O'Leary muttered, trying not to encourage the man.

"It is called People of the Book. That is from my religion," he added proudly. "We are all children of the prophet Abraham and revere the same book, the old Bible. So we are all People of the Book."

"Maybe their meeting will help," O'Leary said.

"I pray it is so. Things have not been good for Muslims in New York since 9/11." The cabbie was pensive for a moment. "No, not good at all."

O'Leary didn't respond, and after a few more attempts at conversation, the driver gave up.

MID-ATLANTIC

One hour out of New York aboard an American Airlines flight bound for London, Tim O'Leary swiped a credit card on the seatback satellite phone and dialed a number in Italy. He fidgeted with the brim of his hat, which was cradled on his lap.

"Lupo grigio," the voice at the other end answered.

Gray wolf was the code name Fr. Antonio Sangremano used for himself, and O'Leary replied with his own prearranged code, in Hebrew: *"Ad me'ah ve'esrim shanah"*— May you live to be 120.

There was a long beat of silence, followed by a sigh. "I'm very disappointed with you, Joshua."

"I'm sorry."

"You have made us look bad in the eyes of our friends."

O'Leary knew this was a reference to the group Migdal Tzedek, which had succeeded in killing Professor Efraim Heber, whereas he had failed to dispatch Fr. Michael Flannery.

"It couldn't be helped, *Grande Padrone*," O'Leary said.

"Where are you now?"

"On a plane, en route to London."

"You should not have left New York until the job was completed," Sangremano scolded.

"The—uh—situation became untenable."

"Return and finish your work," Sangremano ordered.

"*Sì, Grande Padrone.*"

Hanging up the phone, O'Leary sighed deeply and closed his eyes, envisioning his next steps. Once inside Heathrow Airport, he would find a secluded restroom and change out of this costume and into the brown suit in his travel bag. Without the sidelocks and contact lenses, he'd match the German passport that was hidden in the lining of the suitcase. Switching to another credit card, he'd book himself on the next British Airways flight to New York under the name Horst Maas.

As for what he'd do once he arrived, he hadn't the slightest idea.

NEW YORK CITY

Fr. Michael Flannery, Preston Lewkis, and Sarah Arad were in a small interrogation room, away from the activity of the busy Midtown South Precinct station. As they scanned photographs in several large books of mug shots, a tall, lanky plainclothes officer appeared in the doorway, a mug of coffee in one hand, a small duffel bag in the other. His eyes were soft brown and his features rather bland, the one distinctive mark a white scar on his left cheek where a bullet had creased the skin. As he entered the room, he signaled the uniformed officer to leave.

"I'm Lieutenant Frank Santini; I'm taking over the investigation," he said as he placed his coffee mug on the table and sat across from them. "Have you turned up anyone promising?"

Sarah slapped closed one of the mug books and sighed. "I already told that other officer, this is getting us nowhere. The fellow I saw had blond hair and blue eyes. These men are all Middle Eastern."

"Yes," Santini said. "But he may have been wearing a disguise, possibly a blond wig."

"What makes you think that?"

Santini opened the duffel and pulled out three clear-plastic evidence bags containing a blue floral shirt, tan cargo pants, and a pair of sneakers. "Is this what he was wearing?" he asked.

Sarah examined the bags and nodded. "Yes, or clothing identical to these."

"Right after the bombing, we made a wide area sweep, and we found someone matching your guy's description at the Marcel Hotel, but he was gone. We found these in the trash bin in the cellar. He obviously ditched his disguise."

"Or he changed into a disguise," Sarah suggested.

Santini looked unconvinced. "Doesn't it make more sense to disguise yourself when you're about to commit a crime than afterward?"

"Usually. But I got a really good look at him, and I'd be willing to bet he wasn't wearing a wig when he brought that bomb into the deli."

"All right, look at it this way," Santini suggested, "Do you think a blond, blue-eyed—what did you call him? A California surfer? Does that fit the terrorist profile?"

"What about Timothy McVeigh?" Preston interjected.

"Yes, but this has the hallmarks of an Islamic terrorist attack," Santini countered.

"What makes you so certain?" Preston asked.

"Well, we had a little incident here a few years ago with some planes and the World Trade Center. It was in all the papers. Surely you heard of it."

"I didn't mean to make light of that, I was just—"

"Sorry," Santini said with a wave of his hand. "I shouldn't

have spouted off like that. It's just that—well, I lost two
brothers that day, both firefighters."

"I'm sorry for your loss," Flannery said, looking up from
the mug book.

"Thank you, Father. Like I said, I had no right to spout
off. But, to answer your question, Mr. Lewkis, we've received a communiqué from an Islamist group taking credit
for the bombing."

"Communiqué?" Sarah asked. "How did you receive it?"

"By e-mail this morning. Most of our tips, these days,
come by e-mail."

"Could I see it?"

"Sure. . . . I've got a printout." He reached into his coat
pocket and withdrew a piece of paper, which he unfolded
and handed to Sarah. She and her companions read the terse
message:

> To all Americans:
>   Know that you are not safe, no matter where you live or
> where you travel. After 9/11 you thought we could not
> strike again, but today we have shown you that the arm of
> Allah is long. This is but the first of many strikes to come.
> Prepare yourself for the judgment of Allah, the Merciful,
> the Compassionate.
>
>   Crusaders for Allah

"Most of your tips come by e-mail?" Sarah asked.

"At least eighty percent."

"And how many of those prove to be crackpot?"

"Almost all," Santini admitted.

"This is another one," she said dismissively as she pushed
the printout across the table to him. "It isn't even a good
hoax."

"How do you know?"

"They call themselves Crusaders for Allah. No Muslim
would ever refer to himself as a crusader."

"She's right," Flannery put in. "They save that term for us Christians."

"All right, you've told me who it wasn't," Santini said with an air of resignation. "Who do you think it was?"

"First, the bomber didn't attack a Jewish deli in order to scare the public. His target was much more specific." She turned to her companion. "I believe the bomber was after Father Flannery."

"What?" Santini laughed. "Why would someone be after a Catholic priest?" He looked at Flannery. "I mean, bombing a restaurant is a bit excessive, even for a victim of one of those sex scandals. You're not involved in anything—?"

"How can you ask him such a thing?" Preston demanded in a quick flash of anger.

"I'm Catholic myself," Santini said. "I take no joy in questioning a priest, but times have changed, I'm afraid."

Flannery put out his hand to calm Preston. "Lieutenant Santini has every right to ask such a thing, given the way some of my fellow priests have behaved. But to answer your question, Lieutenant, no, I have committed no such sin."

"Then why, in heaven's name, would someone want to kill you?"

"For the same reason they brought down those airliners last week," Sarah said. "They also tried to bring down the plane Father Flannery was on. And when our associate, Professor Heber, missed his doomed flight, they killed him at his home in Jerusalem."

"They? Who are they?" Santini asked. "And what's the connection between those airplanes, Father Flannery, and that professor?"

"The connection is the upcoming People of the Book symposium here in New York. Those planes each carried prominent organizers of the event, such as Professor Heber and Father Flannery. As for who's behind those attacks and yesterday's bombing, it's obviously a group that's determined to stop it from taking place."

"People of the Book, eh?" Santini said. "I've heard of that. Leaders of all religions are gathering to find some sort of common ground."

"Not all religions," Flannery said. "Just Jews, Muslims, and Christians."

Santini nodded. "Well, that's a good idea, all right, if you're able to pull it off. So, who do you think is so hell-bent—?" He turned to Flannery. "Excuse my language, Father. Who'd be trying to stop it?"

"Via Dei, for one," Flannery said. "It violates their steadfast belief that there's only one path to God."

"Via Dei?" Santini asked, squinting as he searched his memory. "Never heard of them."

"Not many have," Flannery said. "It's composed of extremely conservative Catholics and even a few fundamentalist Protestants. Their stated goal is to protect the Church, but they've been denounced by the pope."

"Via Dei," Santini repeated, taking a pad from his breast pocket and writing down the name. "All right, I'll look into it."

"Will you be needing us much longer, Lieutenant?" Flannery asked. "I'm to present a paper at the symposium, and I'd like some time to prepare for it."

"I'm finished for now." He gave each of them a card. "If you see anything, hear anything, or just think of anything that might be helpful, please give me a call."

CHAPTER 12

NEW YORK CITY

Preston Lewkis answered the light knock on his door at the Algonquin Hotel and discovered Sarah Arad in the hallway, a bottle of wine cradled in her arm. He just stood there in silence a long moment, taking in her beauty.

"Are you going to invite me in?" Sarah asked with a bemused smile. "Or are you going to leave me out here like a door-to-door wine salesman?"

"What? Oh, no, come in, come in," he stammered, stepping back.

Placing the bottle on a little table in the entryway, Sarah wrapped her arms around Preston's neck, leaned into him, and kissed him deeply. He returned the kiss with enthusiasm.

"You have no idea how long I've been wanting to do that," she said. She pulled a corkscrew from her pocket and set it next to the bottle of Recanati's Special Reserve.

"It's one of Israel's best wines," Sarah said. "Mostly cabernet sauvignon with a touch of merlot. I hope you've got some glasses; I'd hate to drink wine this fine from the bottle."

"Oh, I don't think we'll have to do that." Preston crossed the room and brought back a pair of water glasses from the bedside stand. Then, working the cork out, he poured a small amount into a glass, swirled and sniffed, then tasted it.

"Excellent," he said as he filled both glasses.

Tasting the wine, Sarah gave a languorous sigh and whispered, "Let's see, chocolate, sage, cloves . . . with a hint of eucalyptus and tobacco that blends well with the ripe berry flavors. And it has a smooth, long-lasting finish."

"I didn't know you're an oenophile."

"Me?" She chuckled. "Hardly. I got that off the ad copy. You have to wonder, though, where the tobacco comes in. I mean, is it a ground-up cigarette butt?"

Preston laughed. "It's delicious, cigarette butt and all." Seeing her enigmatic smile, he asked, "What are you thinking?"

"Just wondering what a nice Jewish girl like me is doing with a *goy* like you."

Preston drained his glass, then set it down and reached for her. "Why don't we find out?"

TIM O'LEARY WAS wide awake in his room at the Bedford Hotel when the telephone rang at six in the morning. He had flown to London, then taken the next available flight back to New York, and had slept very little during the past thirty-six hours. He was looking forward to a good night's rest once he successfully completed his mission.

"Guten tag?" he said, answering the call.

"Horst Maas?"

"Ja."

"This is the concierge. You ordered a limo?"

"Ja."

"It's here."

"Danke. I'll be right down."

The vehicle turned out to be a Lincoln Town Car, and O'Leary was a little disappointed it wasn't a stretch limo. But it would serve his needs, so he tossed his carry bag onto the backseat and slid in beside it as the door was held open for him.

"Where to, sir?" the driver asked, getting back behind the wheel.

"Stuyvesant Hall," O'Leary said. "Know where it is?"

"Yes, sir. Are you in town for the conference there?" the driver asked.

"*Ja,*" he replied curtly.

O'Leary leaned back in the seat as the car worked its way through the traffic and pulled up in front of the convention hall, named after Peter Stuyvesant, last governor of the original Dutch colony.

"Take me around back, would you, please?"

"There's no entrance back there."

"There's a loading dock," O'Leary said. "I'm meeting someone there."

The driver pulled back into traffic, then turned into the drive that had a sign reading DELIVERY AND EXHIBITOR SETUPS. The back of Stuyvesant Hall was empty, a large concrete area surrounded by a high fence.

"Over there, by the trash bins," O'Leary said.

"Why do you want to go there?"

"Just do it."

The driver complied and pulled the vehicle to a halt alongside the bins, then turned around to find his passenger holding a pistol with a long silencer.

"Get out," O'Leary ordered, waggling the barrel of the gun. Opening his own door, he stepped out with the driver and gestured the man over to the nearest trash bin.

The driver looked ashen, but he did as directed. He turned and started to speak, but O'Leary pulled the trigger, the bullet entering the man's chest and knocking him back against the trash bin.

O'Leary quickly opened the bin and lifted the body into it, then shut the top. Returning to the car, he snatched up his carry bag and removed a chauffeur's jacket and hat. Donning the disguise, he stuffed the empty bag under the front seat and slid into the driver's seat. A moment later he was pulling out onto the early-morning traffic and heading uptown.

*   *   *

Preston Lewkis jerked awake at the sound of the phone ringing, and as he reached for it, he knocked the receiver off the hook. He slapped his hand around on the nightstand until he found it.

"Hello?" he said groggily.

There was a chuckle on the other end. "I was going to ask if you were ready yet, but it sounds like you're just waking up."

"Michael—what time is it?" Preston looked at the digital clock on the stand. "Oh, it's seven forty-five. We were supposed to meet at seven thirty, weren't we?"

"Yes. But we can skip breakfast and just get a roll or something before going to Stuyvesant Hall. The opening session begins at nine thirty."

"No, no, you go on down to the restaurant and order breakfast for both of us," Preston said. "Any kind of eggs will do. I'll be down before you know it."

"I called Sarah's room to ask her to join us, but she didn't answer. She may have been in the shower."

"I'll get in touch with her," Preston said. "I'll see you soon." He hung up the phone.

"Am I the one you're going to get in touch with?" Sarah asked from her side of the bed.

"You want to have breakfast with Michael and me, then go to the convention hall?"

"Um, when?" she asked.

"About fifteen minutes ago."

"I've got to shower and get dressed. There's no way I can make it down in time for breakfast."

"We could save time by showering together," Preston suggested.

She gave a low, sexy laugh. "Now, I ask you, Preston, if we shower together, is that really going to *save* time?"

"You have a point there."

Sarah sat up and began dressing. "You go on down. Tell Michael I'll join you before you leave."

"Shall I get you something to go?"

"Just order me a coffee and some toast."

"Okay."

"Oh, and by the way, Michael is a priest. You aren't going to have a sudden urge to confess what we did last night, are you?"

"I'm a Protestant, remember?"

"I was just making sure." She leaned over and kissed his cheek.

TIM O'LEARY LEFT the limo parked in front of the Algonquin Hotel on Forty-fourth Street, telling the doorman he was picking up a guest. The doorman nodded as O'Leary straightened the chauffeur's hat and went inside.

As he started toward the registration counter, he hoped that the information Sangremano had provided was correct and that his target was registered at the hotel. He was about to ask the clerk when he noticed the restaurant across the lobby. On a hunch, he approached and peered inside. Sure enough, his target was on hand, seated at a table with the same man and woman who had been with him in the deli. The men were finished with their meals, while the woman was working on an order of toast.

The woman was undoubtedly the Interpol agent mentioned in news reports of the deli bombing. She had gotten a look at him, but he appeared quite different now in his suit and with his hair dyed black, and he was confident she would not recognize him.

Approaching the table, O'Leary asked in a thick brogue, "Would you be Father Flannery, now?"

Looking up, Flannery and his companions saw a young man in a chauffeur's coat and hat. A silver name tag over his jacket pocket read HENNESSY.

"Yes, I'm Father Flannery," the priest answered.

"Good," O'Leary said, grinning broadly. "'Tis always good when the dispatcher sends me to the right place, which is a darn sight less often than I'd wish it t'be. I'm your limo driver. I'll be taking you to Stuyvesant Hall."

"I didn't order a limo," Flannery said. "I'm not sure I can afford it."

"Sure'n not to worry, Father," O'Leary replied. "You'll be speaking at the conference, will y'not? The conference has picked up the tab. And I guess 'tis divine intervention that your driver is also a countryman. You're from the Erin isle, are y'not? Me, I'm from Connemara."

Flannery smiled. "Dublin, though I've lived in Rome for many years."

"Which explains why I could'na place your accent." He stepped back and gave a flourish of his hand. "Well, Father, we'd best be off, if your friends dinna mind."

"Well, thank you, Hennessy." He turned to his companions. "It seems we'll be traveling in style."

O'Leary shook his head. " 'Twas nothing said about other passengers."

"But we're going to the same place. Surely the car is big enough for three."

"Aye." O'Leary scratched his head as he debated what to say. Having others in the car would complicate things. "The company is very strict about unauthorized passengers."

"That's all right, then," Flannery said. "We'll take a taxi. Thank you anyway."

"No, no, no," O'Leary exclaimed, grinning broadly. "When it comes to following the rules of my boss or yours," he gestured upward, "then surely your boss carries the day every time." He motioned for the others to follow. "Come along with you, then. Just dinna tell anyone what I've done. It'd cost me my job, for sure."

CHAPTER 13

WEST OF CONSTANTINOPLE

Tobias Garlande and his companions were sitting outside the tent Raymond of Amiens had provided them. The air was thick with the aroma of cooking and the smoke of hundreds of campfires. Rachel Benyuli had managed to purchase enough ingredients for a goat stew, which she had prepared in as kosher a manner as possible and now simmered in a kettle over dancing flames. Tobias and Philippe Guischard were on a log near the fire, enduring the smoke in an effort to drive away the bugs.

"Peter the Hermit is not the man I once knew," Tobias said, shaking his head.

Philippe was paring an apple, and he tossed the peels into the fire. "How has he changed?"

"It is as if his soul had changed. He has been made sick with the bloodlust of the Holy War."

"The Holy War is pleasing to God," Philippe said.

"How does it please God to slaughter His children?"

"Only those who do not know Him are being killed," Philippe countered.

"Do you think the Jews don't know God?" Tobias challenged. "They have known Him for almost three thousand years. Do you think the Muslims do not know God? They have known him for more than four centuries."

"Perhaps they know God, but they do not serve Him. The Holy War serves God."

"I don't think so," Tobias said. "I think this war serves Pope Urban."

"But the pope speaks with the voice of God."

"Would you give to a mere mortal the power of God?" Tobias asked.

"Of course not."

"Then do not claim that the pope speaks God's words."

"I believe he is inspired by God."

"Or by Satan," Tobias replied.

"Our supper is ready," Rachel said, taking the pot away from the fire.

"Tobias," Philippe said, "it would be wise not to speak so boldly in front of others. Just as we must keep our own counsel about Rachel being a Jew, so too should you keep your ideas to yourself. If the wrong person were to hear you, we would all be in great danger."

"I believe Philippe is right," Rachel said as she spooned a serving of stew into a pan for Tobias. "I do not worry about myself, for I am of no consequence. But you are a learned man, doing important work transcribing ancient documents, so that generations yet unborn will be able to learn from the wisdom of the ages."

A LEAGUE FROM where Tobias and his companions were having supper, a husband and wife and their three children were trapped in a ravine, surrounded by several dozen armed soldiers. Walter the Penniless, wearing a cassock emblazoned with a red cross, stood at the top of the ravine, looking down at the pitiful family. He lowered the tip of his sword toward them.

"Seize the Jews," he ordered. "Bring the miserable wretches to Peter's tent."

Several of Walter's men leaped into the ravine and jerked the family roughly to their feet.

"Come, you heathen sinners!" one of the soldiers shouted

as he struck the man on his back with the flat of his sword. The others laughed.

With their hands tied behind their backs and ropes looped around their necks, the hapless procession was paraded through the camp. Men, women, and children of the Peasant Army shouted obscenities. Men and boys urinated as they passed, and several women bared their breasts. The family of Jews hung their heads in shame and fear.

"And now, you are to be mocked and scourged, as you mocked and scourged our Savior!" one in the crowd shouted.

"Kill them! Kill them all!" another yelled.

"Burn them at the stake!"

"Repent! Repent, sinners! It is your last chance!"

The family did not answer the taunts and challenges.

"Make way, make way here!" Walter shouted, opening a path for the procession by slashing his sword to and fro, forcing the crowd to part.

The noise and excitement grew to a fever pitch, spreading throughout the entire encampment until it reached the tent of Tobias, Rachel, and Philippe.

"What is it?" Tobias called out. "What's going on?"

"Jews!" someone shouted nearby. "We have captured Jews, and we are going to burn them alive!"

"Tobias!" Rachel gasped, grabbing his arm.

"Careful, child," Tobias whispered, patting her hand reassuringly. "Say nothing that will put you in danger."

"Come," Philippe said excitedly as he stood from the log where he was seated. "We must bear witness!"

As Tobias stared at Philippe, he felt the familiar sensation of entering a vision. The sounds of laughter and mocking voices began to recede as the smoke whirled about, blotting out the surrounding buildings and people.

TOBIAS IS STANDING upon a smooth stone surface alongside hundreds of pilgrims, many carrying curious-looking travel bags. He can sense a great uneasiness among them, great fear and suffering. There is smoke, but not the smoke of campfires. It rises from the chimneys of two enormous iron machines that are sitting on iron rails on either side of the stone platform. Behind each of the machines is a row of huge carriages, hooked together in a long line.

Red banners flutter from poles attached to the iron machines, and in the center of each banner is a white circle. Inside the circle is a broken cross, an aberration of a sacred symbol. The hooked cross is unfamiliar, but Tobias senses something evil about it.

He hears a loud disembodied voice that seems to come from everywhere. One might think it the voice of God, but it sounds more like the voice of Satan.

"Attention! When you are ordered to board, do so immediately. Those who fail to board immediately will be punished severely!"

In addition to the crowd of men, women, and children in obvious distress, there are soldiers who carry strange weapons. On their uniforms they wear armbands that mimic the red banners with the hooked cross. Somehow, the smaller versions look even more sinister.

"Attention! When you are ordered to board, do so immediately. Those who fail to board immediately will be punished severely!"

Tobias feels the crowd begin to move, herded along like sheep, prodded by the men in the red armbands. The people cling to one another in fear and confusion.

The soldiers punch and poke and beat people, seemingly at random. Occasionally some pilgrims fall to the ground, and the soldiers, like rats attacking a piece of bread, converge on them, pummeling and kicking them mercilessly.

"Jewish swine, onto the trains!" the men with the armbands yell.

Jews, Tobias thinks. These are Jews, being herded like animals. But for what purpose?

The vision shifts, and Tobias finds himself in a large room, filled with naked men. Small wisps of vapor begin wafting into the room from vents, and the men cry out, some cursing, many praying. They cough and gasp, and Tobias realizes that something in the air is killing them.

They claw at the doors and walls, struggling to escape, but the exits are locked. They begin slipping, falling, piling up on one another until there is a great mound of naked human flesh.

Tobias watches as the bodies are dragged out of the room and loaded onto carts. The carts are pushed to another building, where huge chimneys belch out smoke. Inside are ovens, unlike any Tobias has ever seen. There, the bodies are taken off the carts and thrown into the flames.

"Enough, enough!" he cries out, closing his eyes tightly against the vision. "I have seen enough. Please, God, show me no more!"

"TOBIAS?"

He opened his eyes and saw that, thankfully, the vision had ended.

"Yes?"

"You say show you no more, yet we have seen nothing," Philippe said. "I believe we should go and bear witness."

"Yes," Tobias said. "Yes. I know now, we must go."

"Hurry," Philippe urged. "Otherwise the spectacle will be over before we arrive."

Philippe started ahead, pushing his way through the crowd of people who also sought to witness the event.

Tobias and Rachel followed, but well behind Philippe, allowing them to speak in private.

"You had a vision," Rachel said. It wasn't a question. She had been with him long enough to know of his visions.

"It—it is too horrible to contemplate."

"But your visions come from God, do they not?"

"Yes."

"Then, if God gave you the vision, there is a purpose, and you must contemplate it."

Tobias was quiet for a long moment as he gathered his thoughts. "I saw soldiers herding men, women, and children, like sheep, into carriages without horses."

"Without horses? I don't understand."

"There were many, connected in a line. They rolled on iron bands, pulled behind a machine of great power."

"And horses were pulling the machine?"

"There were no horses," Tobias said with a dismissive wave. "I have seen such things before in visions. I have seen carriages going very fast, much faster than any horse could run. I have even seen carriages that fly."

"How marvelous it would be to have such visions," Rachel said.

"Sometimes there is a price to pay, and I paid it today when I looked into the bowels of hell itself."

Rachel put her hand to her mouth. "Hell?" she said in a short, frightened voice.

"Yes, for Satan himself could not formulate a greater evil than I beheld. The people who were driven onto the carriages were taken to a great building where they were forced into a room that removed the breath of life from their bodies."

"They were killed?"

"Yes, by having the breath of life taken from their bodies. Their chests heaved and their nostrils flared as they took in air, but the air did not nourish them."

"I don't understand. Why were they killed?"

"Because they were Jews," Tobias said simply.

"Then the Holy War will continue far into the future?" Rachel asked in a resigned voice.

"I don't believe these were holy warriors," Tobias told her. "I don't believe these soldiers were even making a pretense of serving God. They were serving Satan, and they knew it."

"How many Jews were killed?"

"You mean how many *are* to be killed. I believe my vision was far into the future. None of those whom I saw being killed have even been born yet."

"Then, how many are to be killed."

Tobias paused for a long moment before he answered. "Millions," he said with quiet resignation. "Millions will be killed."

"Is there nothing we can do to prevent it?" Rachel asked, her lips quivering.

"I fear nothing can be done until all three religions learn to love, honor, and respect one another, not only as human beings, but as God's own children."

"I pray such a thing will come about someday," Rachel said.

By now they had reached the center of the camp, where hundreds had gathered to witness what would happen next.

"Oh, Tobias, God in heaven, look!" Rachel said, pointing to five posts that had been driven into the ground.

The father alone stood taller than the post to which he was tied, his arms wrapped around it in front of him, his robe pulled off his shoulders to bare his back. The other posts rose above their prisoners, especially over the youngest child, who looked in fear at his sisters on either side of him.

There were piles of wood at the base of each post, and beside each one stood a soldier holding a whip. Peter and Walter were pacing back and forth in front of the family.

"Do you now repent of your sins?" Peter asked, pointing at the man. "Do you beg Jesus Christ, He who is the Son of God, to forgive you of your sin of heresy?"

"We have committed no heresy," the man exclaimed in terror.

Peter nodded, and the first soldier swung his whip with all his might. The lash popped loudly as it struck flesh, and the man cried out in agony.

"You are a debaucher!" Peter said, and again he signaled the man holding the whip.

Peter accused his prisoner of the sins of pride, greed, lust, envy, gluttony, wrath, and laziness, and after each accusation, the lash fell upon his back.

"Now," Peter said. "Tell us who betrayed us and warned you we were coming."

"I will tell you nothing," the man said, barely able to speak against his pain.

Peter walked over to a nearby fire, picked up a burning brand, and tossed it onto the pile of wood that lay stacked around the man. The flames caught hold, and the wood began to burn.

"Peter, no! What are you doing?" Tobias shouted. He started forward, but Philippe pulled him back.

"Do you want to be the next one to burn?" Philippe asked.

"Yes!" Tobias replied. "If it will stop any others from dying, I will be next!"

"Keep him back," Peter said, indicating Tobias. Two soldiers stepped forward and blocked his way.

"Jew, tell us what we want to know, and we will pull the flame away," Peter promised.

"Tell them, Jacob! Please!" his wife pleaded.

"No!" Jacob replied, his voice racked with the pain of the fire. "Miriam, say nothing! We are going to die anyway, but if we tell him nothing, no one else will die!"

"Jacob! Jacob!" the woman screamed in grief and agony as the flames leaped so high that they covered her husband.

Tobias looked into the faces of the witnesses and was shocked by how little pity he saw. Most were curious, as if watching an entertaining spectacle. Some looked joyous, as if they were deriving sensual pleasure from seeing another man's agony. As Jacob screamed, a few laughed out loud.

Finally the screaming stopped, and all that could be heard were the sobbing of Jacob's wife and children and the snapping and popping of the fire as it consumed his mortal remains. The air hung heavy with the cloying smell of burned flesh.

Peter turned to the woman. "If you tell me what I want to know, I will let you and your children go. If you do not, I will burn your children before you, one at a time."

"No!" Raymond of Amiens suddenly shouted, appearing from the middle of the crowd. He walked out into the clearing to face Peter. "Do not do this, I implore you."

"Raymond, my old friend, have you lost your will?" Peter asked, his tone almost mocking. "If you do not have the strength to see God's work carried out, then leave it to those of us who have girded our loins with righteousness and resolve."

"This is not God's work. This is the work of the Devil," Raymond declared.

Peter's eyes flashed angrily, and he said in an undertone, "Careful, Raymond, that you do not presume too greatly upon the security of friendship."

"Let them go, and I will tell you what you want to know," Raymond said, loud enough for the crowd to hear.

"You will tell me what?"

"I will tell you who among us warned the Jews to flee."

"Who was it?"

Raymond pointed to the woman and her three children. "Let them go," he said.

Peter stared at Raymond for a long moment; then he nodded to one of his soldiers, who used his knife to cut loose Miriam and her three children.

"They are free," Peter said.

"You must take an oath, with God as your witness, that you will not bring them back after I have spoken. They must be free from further harm and given safe passage home."

Peter waited a long moment, then finally declared, "In the name of our Lord, I give you my word that all shall be done as you have asked."

Raymond turned to Miriam. "Woman, take your children and flee now."

Nodding, the woman led her children away. A path opened up through the crowd, which seemed no longer interested in the Jews but intent instead on learning who Raymond would denounce and what Peter would do to the one he named.

"They are gone," Peter said. "Tell me now, who among our brethren has betrayed us?"

"It was I," Raymond declared.

If Tobias expected to see a look of shock on Peter's face, he was disappointed. The monk merely stared at the younger man. Finally, he nodded.

"Yes. I thought as much. Seize him," Peter ordered. "Tie him to one of the remaining stakes."

"No!" Raymond called out as Peter started to walk away. "You won't do this. You can't do this. We were children together. We have been friends our entire lives."

Peter halted and looked back at Raymond. "Yes, we have been friends for many years, yet that friendship meant nothing to you when you betrayed me."

"I didn't betray you," Raymond replied. "I was trying to save you from yourself. For surely, when you commit such a sin, it places your immortal soul in jeopardy."

"You, who by your actions have betrayed this holy mission, this war for Christ, you worry about my soul?"

"Yes, for I am your friend."

"I have no friend but God," Peter replied.

"Then for the love of God, you cannot burn me at the stake!" Raymond pleaded.

"You speak of the love of God, when it is you who are in need of redemption." Peter stroked his chin. "Very well, I will not burn you."

"Thank you, Peter. In God's name, I thank you for your mercy and—"

"I will kill you myself," Peter declared. "Out of recognition of a lifetime of friendship, I personally will send you to the next life, there to stand before the throne of God in the presence of Jesus, to expiate your sin."

As Raymond was dragged to one of the posts and his arms tied back around it, Peter began exhorting the crowd.

"Let this be seen by all, and know by my action that all who turn away from the one true path to God, the path of Jesus Christ, will face death in this life and lose all hope of redemption in the life to come. I weep tears of sorrow and bitterness that I must kill he who has been a friend my entire life, he who is like a brother to me, yet who has betrayed me."

As Peter spoke, he walked behind Raymond and wrapped a rope around his neck and the post. Looping a stout stick through the rope, he began twisting it, drawing the rope tighter and tighter around Raymond's neck.

Raymond's face turned red, and he struggled for breath.

"Come," Philippe said to Tobias and Rachel. "Let us go, before this is over."

"Yes," Tobias said, tears flooding his eyes. "It is better that we go."

"Oh, that poor—" Rachel started to say, but Philippe jerked her arm sharply.

"Say nothing," he hissed, "lest unfriendly ears hear."

He led Tobias and Rachel back through the crowd, who were more intent on the spectacle than on their departure. They kept moving until they reached their own tent.

When they were safely inside, Tobias said to Philippe, "Surely you see now the danger of what Peter has been preaching."

"No, Tobias, I believe Peter is right," Philippe said. Before Tobias could respond, Philippe held up his hand. "I do not approve of all his methods, but he is right in preserving the one true faith, the only path to God."

"Even if that doctrine were true, it is befouled now with such evil as we have witnessed in this place," Tobias countered.

"Tobias, let's return home," Rachel said.

"No. God brought me here for a reason. I do not yet know what it is, but I feel I must obey His will. It is you that I worry about."

"Me?"

"You saw what Peter did to those Jews. If he finds out about you . . ."

"If you stay, I stay," Rachel said. "I owe my allegience to you. I couldn't leave you to face danger, while I flee back home."

"There won't be any danger for me. No, I should never have brought you here. After all, I am a Christian. You are a Jew."

Rachel smiled and tenderly touched the older man's hand. "You are a Christian who speaks what he believes. That is almost as dangerous as being a Jew."

Tobias nodded. "True. But still, I must stay."

"I have an idea," Philippe said, his voice soft but exceedingly firm. "A way to keep Rachel safe."

"Then speak quickly, for her safety is of the utmost importance."

Philippe turned to Rachel. "You're a Jew, but I am an envoy to the Holy See," he declared with a hint of arrogance. "If you were to marry me, I could provide for your safety, for who would harm the wife of a Via Dei official?"

CHAPTER 14

NEW YORK CITY

As participants of the People of the Book symposium arrived at Stuyvesant Hall for the opening session, they were confronted by several dozen protesters.

"Don't sell out Christianity!" one of them exclaimed as she hurried from taxi to taxi, thrusting flyers at the people who emerged.

"Jesus is Lord! Jesus is Lord!" others chanted as they waved their placards:

I am the way, the truth, and the life. No man cometh unto the father but by me. John 14:6

And many false prophets shall rise, and shall deceive many. Matthew 24:11

He that believeth and is baptized shall be saved. He that believeth not shall be damned. Mark 16:16

Sarah Arad sat beside Preston Lewkis in the far backseat of the Lincoln Town Car. As the limo pulled to the curb in front of the hall, she peered through the tinted window, taking in the scene. She spied a couple of men in suits, one standing near the entryway, the other walking among the protesters, and guessed they were from the security detail.

Her musings were interrupted by the driver, who said to Michael Flannery, "Father, your two guests will get out here. There's an entrance around back for the presenters. A reception, I believe."

Flannery turned to his companions. "You should come with me. I'm sure they'll let you—"

"Go ahead, Michael," Preston said. "We'll meet up with you inside."

"Yes," Sarah agreed. "I'd like to see how they're handling security."

The driver started to get out, but Preston had already exited the limo and reached back to assist Sarah. She felt perfectly safe but was pleased at how tenderly he wrapped his arm around her as he escorted her through the gauntlet of protesters. Reaching the front door, they showed their credentials and were ushered inside.

"There's Dr. Geer," Preston said, nodding toward a tall bespectacled man who stood off to the side of the lobby with a knot of other distinguished-looking people.

"Dr. Geer?" Sarah asked.

"Thomas Geer of Yale. He's to theology what Stephen Hawking is to physics. Come, I'll introduce you."

"Okay." Sarah smiled. "I'm always intrigued by brilliant men."

"Damn. And I'd hoped there was a chance for me."

Sarah playfully jabbed his arm.

"Dr. Geer," Preston said as they approached.

Geer looked up from the paper he was reading and smiled broadly as he offered his hand. "Dr. Lewkis. So good to see you again."

"This is my friend and fellow archaeologist, Sarah Arad."

"It's very nice to meet you, Miss Arad," Geer said.

"Aren't you presenting a paper?" Preston asked.

"Yes."

"Then, shouldn't you be at the reception?"

Geer looked confused. "Reception?"

"Isn't there a reception for all the presenters?"

Geer shook his head. "No, not as such." With a sweep of his arm, he took in the group of men and women around him. "We've been asked to gather here while they make some adjustments to the order of presentation."

"All the presenters are here?" Sarah asked

"Why, yes," Geer replied, looking around. "Except Dr. Houghtaling and Father Flannery, who have yet to arrive."

"Oh, God!" Sarah exclaimed. She looked around the lobby and saw a corridor that headed toward the back of the convention hall. Halfway down the corridor was a lighted EXIT sign.

"Hurry!" she shouted, pulling away from Preston and breaking into a run toward the corridor.

"What is it?" Geer called out in confusion. "What's going on?"

Sarah had to slow down to press through a throng of people who were clustered around the doorways that led into the main lecture hall. She heard Preston yell, "Make way! Make way!" And then he was at her side, pushing people out of the way as he made a path toward the corridor.

There were some angry remarks as people were jostled, but Preston continued to yell until they began to move aside, clearing a path toward the corridor.

Sarah noticed a uniformed security guard moving to cut off their path. He did not appear to be armed but was speaking into a walkie-talkie. Clearly he had no idea what was going on and was calling for assistance.

"Preston, can you take care of him?" Sarah shouted.

Preston nodded and immediately sprinted to his right, racing to intercept the guard. He looked like a linebacker going in for the tackle, and sure enough, he launched into a crackback, rolling block at the guard's knees. While it was illegal on the playing field, it was effective, and the guard went sprawling onto his back, his walkie-talkie skidding across the floor in the opposite direction.

"A gun! She has a gun!" someone shouted as Sarah drew her Beretta and raced down the corridor. She hardly slowed as she barreled into the push bar on the exit door and shouldered it open, setting off a piercing alarm.

Sarah found herself on a concrete dock. Several steps led down to the loading area, and across the way she saw that the limo was parked by a set of trash bins. Michael Flannery was backed up against one of the bins, with the driver aiming a handgun at him.

The alarm caused the man to spin around, and Sarah shouted, "Drop the gun!" She stood with her feet shoulder width apart, her arms extended and locked at the elbow, her pistol in a two-hand grip, pointed at the driver.

"Michael, run!" Preston called out as he emerged onto the loading dock.

The driver suddenly jerked back around and fired, his bullet ricocheting off the trash bin where Flannery had been standing. The priest was already in a run, and as the driver swung his gun toward him, Sarah pulled the trigger.

The Beretta bucked in her hand, the bullet striking the driver in the shoulder. As he dropped to one knee, he brought up his gun and got off a single round at Sarah, but it missed and hit the brick wall just behind Preston. Sarah fired a second time, the slug slamming into his midsection and knocking him onto his back.

Both Sarah and Preston jumped down from the loading dock and ran toward the downed shooter. Sarah kept her gun extended as she approached and kicked his pistol away.

The shooter was obviously dying as he clutched at the fatal wound just below his rib cage. He gasped for breath, his eyes wide with shock as he stared at Michael Flannery, who had hurried back and was kneeling at his side.

"What is your name, my son?" Flannery asked. "Your real name."

"O-O'Leary, Father. Timothy P-Patrick O'Leary."

"Why did you want to kill me?"

" 'Twas a holy mission."

"A holy mission to kill?" Preston said incredulously.

"Aye, an oath I took—to obey the G-Grand Master." He managed to reach up and grip Flannery's lapel in his bloody fist. " 'T-wasn't personal, F-Father."

"You are Via Dei," Flannery said with a nod.

"Aye." O'Leary groaned, his jaw tightening in agony. "Father . . . p-please . . . Extreme Unction . . ." He released Flannery's jacket, his hand dropping to his chest.

"Do you confess your sins?"

"I do c-confess," O'Leary said, his voice weaker. "And I beg for . . . for remission of my sins."

Flannery made the Sign of the Cross.

"May the Lord in His love and mercy help you with the grace of the Holy Spirit. May the Lord who frees you from sin save you and raise you up."

"Latin, Father," O'Leary gasped. "P-Please . . ."

"Misereatur vestri omnipotens Deus et, dimissis peccatis vestris, perducat vos ad vitam aeternam."

O'Leary grabbed Flannery's hand and squeezed it hard. Then, with a final rasping rattle, he quit breathing, his sightless eyes staring upward at the sky.

As Flannery closed O'Leary's eyelids, a pair of police cruisers roared into the back lot, their lights flashing and sirens wailing. Four officers jumped from the vehicles and took positions behind their open doors, their guns trained on Sarah, Preston, and Flannery.

"Freeze!" one of them yelled.

"Officer, I can explain," Preston began, starting toward the policemen.

"I said freeze!" the officer shouted again. "Put your hands up!"

"Do what they say," Sarah ordered quietly. She laid her own pistol on the ground, then raised her hands.

* * *

LT. FRANK SANTINI placed Sarah's Beretta Model 71 on the table in front of her in the squad room at the Midtown South station. "Lieutenant Arad," he said, "you've been in New York less than a week, and you've already fired your gun more than I have in the last three years."

"And saved lives each time," Preston noted.

"Don't get me wrong, Dr. Lewkis, I'm not condemning her. Just an observation, that's all."

Sarah dropped the magazine out of the grip and opened the pistol to make sure there was no round in the chamber. Then she replaced the magazine and put the pistol back in her purse.

"You were right, by the way," Santini said.

"I beg your pardon?"

"The bomber was a blue-eyed blond. We found O'Leary's prints on the handle of the attaché the bomb was in."

"But O'Leary's hair was dark," Flannery said.

Santini shook his head. "Dye job."

"I should have made him when he came into the café at the Algonquin," Sarah said, frowning.

"And you were right that Father Flannery was the target all along," Santini continued. "You say it was to break up this ecumenical conference?"

"Yes, I'm sure of it," Sarah said.

"I don't understand why anyone would want to do that."

"Have you been over to Stuyvesant Hall yet, Lieutenant?" Preston asked, and the officer shook his head. "Well, you should. There are more protesters down there than at a Halliburton stockholders' meeting."

"Who's doing the protesting?" Santini asked.

"Right now it's evangelical Christians. But if truth be told, there are elements in each religion that don't want to see this symposium succeed," Preston said.

"Yes, well, I just wish they were holding it in London or Rome—better yet, Amsterdam," Santini offered.

"Amsterdam?" Preston asked.

"Yeah, Amsterdam. Nobody there would care one whit about a religious conference."

"I'm afraid the U.S. was the only suitable place," Flannery said. "No other country has such a diverse population or as much religious freedom as your Bill of Rights offers."

Santini nodded. "I suppose you're right. But combine the First Amendment with the right to bear arms, and you can get quite a potent brew." He turned to Sarah. "Now, Lieutenant Arad, we'd best find some new digs for the good Father and you folks."

"Digs?" she said.

"A place to stay."

"What's wrong with the Algonquin?" Flannery asked.

"No, he's right, not the Algonquin," Sarah said. "There have already been two attempts on your life. We need to move you."

"I'm not leaving New York until after the symposium. It's too important and has already cost too many lives. I won't let them run us out of—"

"You don't have to leave the city," Santini assured him. "I just want you in a safe house somewhere."

"I agree," Sarah said.

"All right," Flannery said. "If you think it is best."

Picking up the phone on the table, the lieutenant dialed a number. "This is Santini. I need a hole for three. And I'm not talking one of our usual holes. These are VIP." He nodded a couple of times. "Yeah, sounds perfect. Get me a car; I'll take them myself."

SANTINI GAVE A quick walk-through of the safe-house apartment on Central Park West. "This is plenty big for all three of you. Three bedrooms—one a bit small, mind you, but—"

"That's mine," Flannery said quickly.

"He fancies himself an ascetic," Preston teased.

"It's small, but it's no monk's cell," Santini said as he reached through a doorway and flipped the light switch, revealing a bedroom that was modest in size but tastefully decorated.

Santini continued down the hall to the kitchen.

"There's a well-stocked refrigerator and pantry, so you don't have to risk another restaurant or delivery." He stopped and turned to Sarah. "Are you kosher?"

"No."

"Good."

He brought them back into the living room, where they had first entered.

"There are plenty of books, a stereo but only classical CDs, I'm afraid, and a TV."

"What a beautiful view of the park," Sarah said as she looked through the window.

"Yeah, I suppose," Santini muttered with the indifference of someone who had lived all his life near the park. "As you saw on the way up, the elevator opens right in the apartment, and it won't come this high without the special code I gave you. Also, the stairway doors can't be opened from the outside. Once you're here, nobody can get in unless you allow them."

"It does seems quite secure," Sarah agreed.

Preston walked over to a small desk and began examining it. He ran his hands over it, then opened one of the drawers. "Who does this apartment belong to?" he asked.

"It has three years remaining on a five-year lease. Right now, the City of New York holds the lease."

"And the furniture?"

"It came with the apartment."

Preston pulled the desk out from the wall and looked on the back, then whistled. "This is an old piece."

"Yeah," Santini said apologetically. "It was here when we seized the place, and the city didn't want to spend any funds to refurnish it."

"You're joking," Preston said.

"No. We tried to get some new furniture up here but were turned down."

Preston chuckled. "No, Lieutenant, when I said this piece was old, I meant antique. This is a John Dunlap, probably around 1780 or so."

"John Dunlap? Is that something important?"

"A similar piece, probably not as nice as this one, recently sold for twenty thousand dollars."

"Damn! Who would've thought?"

"How is it that the city maintains an apartment like this?" Flannery asked. "Are there that many people who need hiding?"

Santini nodded. "More than you might think. This place belonged to a high-level drug dealer. When we busted him, we confiscated everything he had, including a paid-up five-year lease."

"The fellow was living well," Preston said.

"Yes, they usually do."

"Well, we thank you for the use of the place," Flannery said.

"I wish I could convince you to stay put here for as long as you're in our city."

"It's tempting," Flannery said. "But I must deliver my report at the People of the Book symposium."

"When?"

"It was going to be today. But after what happened, they rescheduled me for tomorrow."

"All right," Santini said. "You've got my card. So before you go to the conference hall tomorrow, give me a call and I'll see to it you get there safely."

"Thanks." Flannery shook the lieutenant's hand.

Santini said good-bye to the others, then pressed for the elevator and headed back to the street.

"Are you ready to present your paper?" Preston asked when they were alone.

"Yes," Flannery answered. "Thankfully, the scroll was fully photographed before Via Dei stole it."

Sarah came over from the window. "And the translation has been completed?"

"Yes, which is what I'll present to the symposium."

They were talking about the ancient scroll that had been discovered a year earlier in the ruins of Masada, where in 73 AD a thousand Jewish Zealots committed suicide rather than surrender to the Romans. While it was similar to others found in caves near Qumran, the Masada scroll was surprising because it contained a hitherto unknown Gospel of Jesus that predated the four Gospels of the New Testament. Of equal mystery was how the scroll ended up at a sacred Jewish site with no connection to first-century Christians.

Flannery, Preston, and Sarah had worked to unravel the mystery of this scroll written by Dismas bar-Dismas, son of the Good Thief crucified beside Jesus. One of the more surprising aspects of the scroll was that it contained a strange symbol, similar to one representing the secretive and reactionary organization Via Dei.

"What I don't understand," Preston said, "is why Via Dei is still after you. They have the scroll now. What else do they want?"

"It's pretty obvious, isn't it?" Sarah said. "It's not only the scroll they consider their sacred property. It's the message the scroll contains."

"Yes," Flannery agreed. "And that's why they're desperate to keep it from being revealed."

CHAPTER 15

NABLUS

When Israeli army trucks rolled through the West Bank town of Nablus in a show of force, scores of young Palestinians came out to throw rocks. The soldiers didn't react until three masked men wielding AK-47s appeared from the crowd and began spraying the trucks with automatic fire. As often happens, the response was far greater than the attack, and the soldiers killed not only the gunmen but two of the young rock throwers as well.

Sixteen-year-old Da'ud al-Tawil was in the crowd, and he cradled his dying friend, Omran Radan, in his arms. Two weeks later, he went to see local Hamas leader Ahmad Faruk.

"What do you want?" Faruk asked.

"I want to be a *shahid*."

"A martyr? You are too young."

"How old must I be to die for my faith?" Da'ud asked.

"How old are you?"

"I am the same age as Omran Radan, who was killed by the Israelis. I want to kill Israelis."

Faruk stroked his beard for a moment. "It is a great honor to commit the ultimate act of devotion. Do you think you can do this?"

"Yes," Da'ud insisted.

"What is your name?"

"I am Da'ud al-Tawil."

"In order to be a *shahid,* you must act with a pure heart, Da'ud. You do this for Allah, not for personal revenge. Do you understand?"

"Yes."

"If you do this for Allah and for your people, paradise is just on the other side of your thumb. With your thumb, you push the detonator, and you are instantly transported to paradise." He stared a long moment into the teen's dark eyes. "But if you do it for selfish reasons, you will not be rewarded."

"I do this for Allah and Palestine," Da'ud said.

"Go back home, Da'ud al-Tawil. Go back home and think hard about this thing. Come see me again tomorrow. If you still want to do it, I will find a way."

"Tomorrow," Da'ud said as he nodded respectfully.

WHEN DA'UD RETURNED the next day, he saw a red, black, white, and green Palestinian flag attached to the wall. Faruk handed him a black-and-white checkered *kaffiyeh* and told him to put it on. As he wrapped it around his head, Faruk handed him an AK-47.

"Stand in front of the flag," he ordered.

Da'ud held the weapon up and looked at it. "Is it loaded?" he asked.

"No."

"Why have you given it to me?"

"You will hold it as the video is being made."

Da'ud nodded, then moved in front of the flag and watched as another man put a video camera on a tripod, then set up a microphone.

"Say something," the cameraman said.

"What am I to say?"

"That's good enough. I needed to adjust the sound."

"Will this be shown on television?" Da'ud asked.

"Yes," Faruk replied. "It will be shown all over the world. You will be famous and honored as a martyr for Allah."

"Will my parents see it?"

"Yes."

Da'ud smiled broadly. "They will be proud of me."

"Do your parents know you are here?"

"No."

"That is good." Faruk handed Da'ud a piece of paper. "This is what you will read."

Da'ud scanned the paper, then nodded.

"Begin," the cameraman said as Faruk backed away, leaving the boy in front of the flag.

"I cannot live in peace," Da'ud recited, "when our holy and sacred places are being violated by infidels who humiliate our religion. I cannot live while my brothers and sisters are prisoners of the Americans and the Jews."

Da'ud shifted the AK-47 on his shoulder, pointing the barrel heavenward.

"Even now, there is a gathering in the great city of sin, New York, where Christians, Jews, and traitors to Islam are meeting to form one religion, a religion of heresy. By my martyrdom, I send a message to my Islamic brothers and sisters that we reject such blasphemy."

His eyes welled with tears, but his expression was joyous as he read the final words:

"I am happy that I will soon be in paradise, while the gates of hell will open to receive the infidels I shall kill with my martyrdom. All praise be to Allah."

"That's good," the cameraman said.

"Do you want to see the video?" Faruk asked.

"Yes, very much," Da'ud said eagerly.

The cameraman put the video in a VCR, rewound it, then hit the PLAY button.

Da'ud watched his death message in silence. When it was finished, he looked up at Faruk and said somberly, "That's the last thing anyone will ever see of me, isn't it? My mother, my father, this is what they will see."

Faruk, sensing perhaps that Da'ud was having second thoughts, embraced him and declared, "How brave you looked. What an inspiration you will be. Children will see the video and praise your name. Infidels will see the video and be inspired by your courage to become Muslims. You will be honored, forever, in our hallowed hall of martyrs."

"Yes," Da'ud said, his smile returning. "They will remember me, won't they?"

"And, when you are remembered, you are never really dead," Faruk said. "You will live in paradise forever and in the hearts and minds of our people for as long as there is a Palestine."

"I am ready," Da'ud declared.

JERUSALEM

Wearing a yarmulke and carrying a backpack onto which had been sewn an Israeli flag, Da'ud looked like a Jewish schoolboy as he boarded the bus. No one would suspect that the pack contained twenty pounds of C-4 explosive and another twenty pounds of nails.

"Pretty day today, isn't it?" the bus driver asked, smiling at Da'ud as he got on. "A strong young man like you should be walking on a day like today."

Da'ud smiled back but didn't answer. Ahmad Faruk had told him to find a spot close to the greatest number of people, so he took a seat near the center of the bus. A girl about his age smiled at him from across the aisle, and he felt a twinge of attraction. He chastised himself for allowing even the hint of such a thought. She was no better than a whore, he told himself, with her head uncovered and wearing a tight school dress that left little to the imagination.

"See my airplane?" a little boy asked, holding up a plastic toy that Da'ud recognized as an F-16 in Israeli colors. The boy ran down the aisle, holding it over his head and making the sound of a jet.

"Judah, come back here!" the boy's mother called from her seat a few rows ahead of Da'ud. "You are disturbing the other passengers."

"Let the boy play," a middle-aged woman said, smiling at the mother. "They are young for such a short time."

Judah continued to run up and down the aisle, eliciting smiles from everyone but Da'ud.

As the bus moved slowly through the traffic, Da'ud knew enough Hebrew to make out snippets of the conversations of the other passengers. Judah's mother and the middle-aged lady were talking about children. A pair of men were arguing about a soccer match they had seen on television. A young couple were discussing a novel they had read. The conversations were both mundane and disconcerting. Da'ud had wanted them to be monsters, but they seemed quite ordinary, no different from people he had known his entire life.

Da'ud stuck his hand in his pocket and found the detonator switch. He gingerly touched it with his thumb.

"Remember," Faruk had told him. "Paradise is just on the other side of your thumb."

"Are you ill?" a girl's voice asked.

Da'ud turned to see that the girl across the aisle was leaning toward him. The material of her dress pulled slightly, revealing a glimpse of the top of her breasts.

"Wh-what?" Da'ud stammered, trying not to look at her indecency.

"You're sweating and shivering," she said. "Are you ill?"

Da'ud's eyes opened wide, his jaw tightening as he stared at her. She was there to tempt him, he suddenly realized, to entice him away from the promised paradise.

She seemed to read his mind, her look of concern transforming to abject fear. She threw her arms in front of her, drawing back away from him as she shouted, "No! No, please don't—"

Shutting his eyes, Da'ud recited the *Shahadah* as he pushed the button.

A huge fireball blew out both sides of the bus, sending body parts and twisted metal across the street. Nearly a block from the explosion, a diner at a sidewalk café was splashed with some hot liquid, and he looked down to discover a small plastic airplane had crashed into his soup.

CHAPTER 16

NEW YORK CITY

Fr. Antonio Sangremano opened the door of the apartment Via Dei kept at the Helfand House on Central Park West and greeted Benjamin Bishara, head of the militant Jewish group Migdal Tzedek, or Tower of Justice.

"Is he here?" Bishara said curtly, pushing past the Catholic cleric.

"Mehdi?" Sangremano said, referring to Mehdi Jahmshidi of the Islamist organization Arkaan, or the Fundamentals. He followed Bishara into the living room. "His plane arrives tomorrow."

Bishara spun around and glowered at Sangremano. "I thought you had brokered a truce—at least until after the People of the Book symposium."

"You're talking about the bus bombing in Jerusalem."

"Twenty-two dead! If that's his idea of a truce—"

"I've already asked him about that, and he insists Arkaan wasn't involved."

"If that's true—which I sincerely doubt—then perhaps we're dealing with the wrong person. If the head of Arkaan can't keep the Palestinians from strapping on bombs and blowing up our people, then what good is he?"

"Let's not lose our focus," Sangremano urged, taking a seat and gesturing for Bishara to sit across from him. "So far Mehdi has upheld his end of the plan. His people brought down those planes, as promised."

Bishara started to sit, then stood again and paced across the room, looking quite agitated. "I'm not comfortable with this . . . this pact in hell you've sold me. Yes, Arkaan brought down those planes. And my people took care of Professor Heber and a few other loose ends." He stopped in front of Sangremano's chair and stared down at him. "But what of Via Dei? You've had no trouble pulling our strings, but when it comes to your own, what have you to show?"

"If you're referring to—"

"One priest," Bishara blurted, holding up his forefinger. "You assured us he'd be out of the picture, but now you don't even know where he is. I'm beginning to wonder if you have the nerve to kill one of your own."

"Michael Flannery is not one of my own. Far from it."

"He's a fellow priest."

"An illegitimate one," Sangremano said. "He opposes everything Via Dei stands for."

"So do we," Bishara said with a rueful smile.

"Not everything," Sangremano reminded him. "We share quite a bit in common, more than either of us will ever share with Mehdi Jahmshidi and his Arkaan fanatics."

"Then why are we dealing with them?"

"Because in this single matter, we share the common goal of ending this People of the Book heresy before it takes root. And because it offers the chance to see how Arkaan operates. One day that may prove quite beneficial for both of us."

"Divide and conquer, eh?" Bishara said.

"Keep your friends close, and your enemies closer," Sangremano replied. "For 'misery acquaints a man with strange bedfellows,'" he added, betraying his habit of sprinkling his speech with literary allusions.

"And when this is all over, what do we do? Turn on Arkaan, then on each other?"

"We both know that the world—our worlds—will never be safe with the likes of Arkaan on the loose. As for you and me, yes, we have very different interests, but they are interests that can coexist, don't you think?"

Bishara dropped into the chair across from Sangremano. "Yes, I suppose so. But only until your Messiah returns and sweeps my people into the abyss." He chuckled. "That is, unless our Messiah comes first."

"I sincerely pray that when the Messiah comes, you will see that yours and ours is the same."

Bishara sighed. "So what do we do now? What's to be done about Father Flannery? He mustn't be allowed to address the symposium."

"I admit that the Flannery—solution—has been uncommonly difficult to achieve. But not to worry, we shall take care of him," Sangremano proclaimed.

"I should hope so. After all, he's just one priest, and you've had experience with final solutions that have involved millions."

"Oh, no," Sangremano said, shaking his head and stabbing a thumb toward Bishara. "You won't hang the Holocaust on me."

"Tell me, Father, exactly what did Pope Pius, or your Via Dei, for that matter, do to prevent the Holocaust?"

"What could the pope, or any of us, have done? The Vatican was in the middle of occupied Rome."

"Oh, I understand the situation perfectly," Bishara countered. "In August 1942, after more than two hundred thousand Ukrainian Jews had been murdered, Ukrainian Metropolitan Andrej Septyckyj wrote to the pope, advising him that the Nazis were a regime of terror more dangerous than the godless Bolsheviks. What was the pope's reply? He advised Septyckyj to 'bear adversity with serene patience' and quoted the Psalms."

"That is but one incident," Sangremano replied.

"Would you like another? A month later, Monsignor Giovanni Battista Montini, whom the world would know as

Pope Paul VI, wrote to Pius that the massacres of Jews had reached frightening proportions. Yet that same month, when the American representative to the Vatican warned Pius his silence was undermining his moral prestige, the pope dismissed those concerns, saying he couldn't verify rumors about crimes against the Jews. *Verify rumors*," he repeated, emphasizing the words.

"We each have our cross to bear," Sangremano said.

Bishara started to protest, then saw Sangremano's mischievous expression and found himself smiling.

"All right," Bishara said. "I'll give you a pass on the Holocaust—just this once. But that still leaves the problem of Father Flannery."

"Since dead men tell no tales, our problem will be resolved soon enough, with finality," Sangremano assured him.

"And what of the symposium itself?"

"I propose we take a closer look. You got my text message yesterday?"

"Yes," Bishara said. "And I've made the arrangements."

"Good. Then as soon as Mehdi arrives, we'll plan our visit to Stuyvesant Hall. You have our passes?"

Bishara nodded. "Three floor passes. We'll be attending as guests of the House of Abraham."

"Very fitting for three of his oldest children."

FR. MICHAEL FLANNERY sat down at the eighteenth-century John Dunlap desk and booted up his laptop. Glancing over at Preston Lewkis and Sarah Arad, who were on the couch having their morning coffee, he said, "I'll check my e-mail, then if either of you wants to use it . . ."

As he turned back to the computer, an instant message popped up on his screen:

> Mongo: *Father Flannery, this is David. Remember me from the plane?*

"David," Flannery exclaimed, then glanced back at his friends. "It's an IM from David Meyers, that fellow who saved our flight." As he started tapping out his reply, Preston and Sarah came up and stood looking over his shoulder.

> Micflan: *Of course I remember you. But, how did you find me on the Internet?*
>
> Mongo: *The Web is my world, remember? Sometimes I think of this as my reality, and the real world as virtual.*
>
> Micflan: *LOL. How are you doing, David? I've thought about you since our grand adventure.*
>
> Mongo: *I'm doing fine, thanks. But I've been doing a little investigating into what that was all about.*
>
> Micflan: *What have you found out?*
>
> Mongo: *Have you ever heard of Antonio Sangremano or Via Dei?*

Sarah placed a hand on Flannery's shoulder. "You'd better take this offline. Someone could be intercepting." Flannery nodded and again started typing.

> Micflan: *We shouldn't discuss this online. There must be others out there with your skills. Well, maybe not at your level, but good enough to be reading our IMs right now.*
>
> Mongo: *I'm using encryption, but you're right. Someone could be using other methods, such as tracking keystrokes. That's why I've sent a friend to see you.*
>
> Micflan: *That's not a good idea. There have been a couple of attempts on my life, so the police have me in a safe house. I'm sure you can understand that I can't tell you where I am.*
>
> Mongo: *Your elevator door will open in thirty seconds.*
>
> Micflan: *That's not possible. It won't come to this floor unless I summon it.*

> Mongo: *Her name is Ann Coopersmith. Keep your head down, Padre. I've decided you're one of the good guys.*

The instant message window closed, leaving the words: MONGO IS OFFLINE.

Even as Flannery was staring at his computer screen, the elevator door opened, revealing an attractive black woman who appeared to be in her late twenties. She was dressed in a gray business suit and walked into the living room with total calm and an air of authority.

"Father Flannery?" she said, looking at the stunned trio.

"Who are you? How did you get here?" Preston demanded.

"You must be Ann Coopersmith," Flannery said, standing from the desk and approaching.

Ann smiled and offered her hand. "Since you're wearing the collar, I take it you're Father Flannery. David told me you might have guests. Professor Lewkis, I presume?" She grinned. "And you must be Sarah Arad, with Israel's counterterrorism unit."

"I won't ask how you got up here," Flannery said. "Practically nothing David can do surprises me. I'd like to know, however, how you managed such impeccable timing."

Ann reached into the leather portfolio she was carrying and produced an iPhone. As she turned the screen toward them, Flannery saw the full text of the instant message exchange.

"I was listening in," Ann explained. "Or rather, looking in. It was David's idea. He loves melodrama."

Sarah Arad moved closer to the woman and folded her arms in front of her, as if sending a message that she had no intention of shaking hands. "Well, Ann Coopersmith, you seem to know who we are, but other than your name and connection to David Meyers, we know nothing about you."

"I'm a freelance journalist. About two years ago I was doing an investigative piece on computer hackers, which led me to David."

"Would you like some coffee?" Flannery asked, seeking to defuse the tension in the room.

Ann smiled. "That would be lovely. Black, please."

Flannery showed her to the couch and poured a cup from the Bodum coffee press.

As Ann sat down, she opened her portfolio and pulled out some photos and papers, which she spread out on the coffee table.

"That's Father Antonio Sangremano," Flannery said, recognizing the prelate in one of the pictures.

"You know him?" Ann asked.

"Yes. He was one of the most powerful men in the Prefettura dei Sacri Palazzi Apostolici."

Ann looked confused.

"The Prefecture of the Sacred Apostolic Palaces," Flannery explained. "They administer the Vatican buildings and serve as our State Department."

"You said he *was* in the Prefecture. What about now?"

"He went into hiding about a year ago after—" He glanced at his companions as he debated how to describe Sangremano's role in the theft of the Masada scroll, which had resulted in multiple deaths ordered or carried out by Sangremano himself. "After something of a scandal."

"One that involved Via Dei, no doubt," Ann said.

"You know of Via Dei?" Flannery asked.

"I'm learning. They've been around a long time, and this Antonio Sangremano is the current grand master." Ann looked through the papers and pulled out another photo. "What about this fellow?"

Flannery shrugged. "No, I'm sorry, I don't know him."

"That's Mehdi Jahmshidi, head of the Islamist group Arkaan," Sarah said. She leaned forward from her chair on the opposite side of the coffee table and tapped another photo that was half-covered by the other papers. "And that's Benjamin Bishara, head of our own little band of Jewish terrorists, Migdal Tzedek."

"What do you know of these two men, Jahmshidi and Bishara?" Ann asked.

"I know a great deal about both of them," Sarah said, leaning back in her chair. As she eyed the young journalist closely, she seemed to be weighing how much to reveal. Finally she said, "We're off the record?"

"Everything's off the record for now. I'm just getting background and trying to help David, as he's helped me many times in the past."

"All right, here's what we know," Sarah replied. "Benjamin Bishara was only twelve when he joined the Ha'Irgun Ha'Tsvai Ha'Leumi B'Eretz Yisrael, or National Military Organization in the Land of Israel, which for obvious reasons was known simply as the Irgun."

"The militant Zionists who helped create the state of Israel," Ann put in.

"Yes. In July 1946, Bishara took part in the Irgun bombing of the King David Hotel in Jerusalem. Ninety-one people were killed: twenty-eight Brits, forty-one Arabs, seventeen Jews, and five others."

"Weren't future prime ministers David Ben-Gurion and Menachem Begin in the Irgun?" Preston asked.

Sarah nodded. "They warned the British to evacuate the hotel, but the Brits didn't take the warning seriously, saying they wouldn't take orders from Jews and insisting nobody leave the building."

"What about Bishara?" Ann asked, betraying a hint of impatience.

"After Israel got her independence, some of the more radical elements in the Irgun broke away and formed Migdal Tzedek, the Tower of Justice. Bishara rose through the ranks, primarily by being more ruthless than anyone else. Over the years he has been involved in at least a dozen attacks against Palestinians, for the express purpose of preventing any rapprochement between Israel and Palestine. We believe, but have not been able to prove, that he also has committed terrorist acts against Israelis, making it appear they were Palestinian attacks. In this way he has helped fan the flames."

Sarah picked up the photo of Mehdi Jahmshidi.

"And here, my friends, is the pick of the litter. Mehdi Jahmshidi is personally responsible for over fifteen hundred deaths, by his own hand and by recruiting gullible young men for martyrdom." She dropped the photo onto the table in disgust. "Of course, he is not eager to make that sacrifice himself."

"That's quite an unholy trio you have there, Ann," Preston commented.

"Yes," she replied. "Now, what would you say if I told you that they have joined together in a common cause?"

"These three?" Sarah shook her head. "I would say it's impossible."

"I wouldn't reject the idea out of hand," Flannery put in. "I've learned from history that fanaticism of any stripe makes for odd alliances. Given the right circumstances, such an alliance, while unlikely, is possible."

"Not only possible, it is fact," Ann declared.

"Is that what David wanted to tell us?"

"Yes. And that the three of them are planning to attend the People of the Book symposium."

"They're coming here?" Sarah said incredulously.

"They may have arrived already."

"How do you know?"

"David has been tracking them on the Internet and discovered that Bishara was making the arrangements for the others. But they're using assumed identities, obviously, and for the moment the Web trail has gone cold."

"You and David Meyers must be pretty close for him to trust you with all this," Sarah said, eyeing the other woman suspiciously.

Ann laughed lightly. "I'm a journalist, and I know a good

story when it presents itself." She waved a hand over the papers on the coffee table. "All he needed to win me over was all this, though he is quite charming."

"And quite a talker, it seems," Sarah added.

"He's more than just talk," Ann said. "He's really quite impressive."

Flannery chuckled.

"You don't think so, Father?" Ann asked.

"Oh, quite the contrary. I wholeheartedly agree. I'm just remembering something David said about not having much luck with women because he's such a computer geek."

Ann smiled. "There are some of us who find that very attractive. But I wouldn't call him a geek. Brilliant and charming is far more apt a description."

"We've established that you and David share a trust," Sarah said, looking eager to change the topic. "And now we are expected to trust you?"

"That's your call entirely. I promise you this: Anything we do or say will remain off the record until you give the okay, with one proviso."

"Which is?"

"When this thing breaks, I get an exclusive. If you're able to go on the record with anyone, it's me, not Larry King or Jon Stewart."

"That seems fair," Flannery said, looking back and forth at his companions.

"Fine," Sarah agreed. "Now, it looks as if we've got some work ahead of us. What else have you got there?" she asked Ann, indicating the pile of papers.

"I was hoping you could tell me," the journalist replied as she picked up one of the documents.

CHAPTER 17

I n the pilgrim camp twenty miles from the city, Rachel Benyuli sat at a small table, transcribing a document her master had recently translated. Philippe Guischard stood just outside the tent, gazing in at her as she worked. He had grown increasingly consumed with lust for this servant girl, for that's all he considered her despite Tobias Garlande's insistence that she was an assistant and their equal. The old man could call her what he wanted, Philippe mused, but that didn't change her status or fate. Philippe would have her, either by marriage or by force, if need be.

Philippe knew that whether she agreed to his advances or not, the very act of lust was a sin and that he was in mortal danger, doubly so having pledged himself to the Order of Sanctity of Via Dei:

> *It is a dangerous thing to gaze too long upon the face of a woman. Avoid the kiss or embrace of a woman lest you be contaminated by the sin of lust. Remain eternally before the face of God with a pure conscience and a sure life.*

Marriage was permitted only for the elite among Via Dei, but Philippe did not worry that the Grand Master might disavow this one. He was emboldened by the proclamation of Pope Urban, granting prior absolution of all sins to anyone who took part in the Holy War. Not only would a violation of the Order of Sanctity be forgiven, but also the sin of lust. An unsanctioned marriage could be annulled upon return to France without risk of mortal sin. And if Rachel refused marriage and he were forced to take her by force, that would be forgiven as well.

However, Philippe considered himself a man of principle, a decent man at heart. He did not wish to violate Rachel but to obtain her willing consent. And he had every confidence that he could win her over.

"My dear," he said, entering the tent and approaching where she was seated.

As Rachel looked up from the document, Philippe was too self-absorbed to see the fear so evident in her eyes.

"Yes, m'lord?" she replied.

"Have you considered my offer?"

"Your offer, m'lord?"

"To marry you," Philippe said.

Rachel hesitated a long moment before finally replying, "M'lord, as you can see, Tobias depends on me for so many things." She gestured at the documents spread before her. "I don't know what he would do if I were to abandon him."

"Tobias is a foolish old man," Philippe said with a patronizing smile. "He wastes his life translating ancient texts that have no meaning today."

"Tobias says that true knowledge always holds meaning," she replied.

"Knowledge . . . yes, I see." Philippe circled the desk until he was standing next to Rachel. "Remember what your own Bible says of knowledge and its dangers. In Genesis it is the woman who tempts the man and thus falls from grace. I fear that in this instance, it is the old man who is the tempter."

"This work is very important to Tobias, and he depends on me."

"Child, you have seen how the soldiers of Christ deal with Jews. Would you see yourself burned at the stake?"

"God forbid," Rachel said with a shudder. .

"God does forbid it, if you will only accept Him as your Savior." Philippe placed a gentle hand upon her shoulder, then withdrew it when she tensed with fear. "As I see it, you are twice in jeopardy, once for your mortal life here in this world, and more importantly for your immortal soul in the next. The only way to save yourself is to accept the divinity of Jesus Christ and the one path to salvation that he offers."

"But Tobias says that three paths lead equally to God. Surely my faith, as one branch of Trevia Dei, offers the same salvation, provided I am a true and reverent servant of God."

Philippe frowned. "It matters not how reverent you are, if you do not accept the kingship of our Savior, who died for your sins. Tobias, having rejected that most basic of tenets of the one true faith, has forfeited his own soul. And he condemns the souls of all whom he corrupts, yourself included."

"But through the symbol of Trevia Dei, the great Rabbi Jesus—"

"Enough!" Philippe cut her off. "You speak of Jesus as if he were a . . . a mere mortal. The mystery of Trevia Dei was not given to the Jews or the infidels. It was revealed to us alone as the embodiment of the blessed Trinity. I ask you, how could it refer to three religions, since the false religion of Islam did not even exist at the time of Jesus?"

"I have often wondered the same," Rachel admitted, "though to the Lord nothing is impossible. And I am not a Muslim but a Jew."

"Yes, you are one of His chosen people, and so there is hope for you yet. Remember, Jesus himself was a Jew, as were His disciples. But on the rock of Peter, Jesus built a new religion and declared it the only path to salvation."

"I cannot abandon the religion of my birth, of my father."

Philippe shook his head slowly. "Then I am sorry for you, my dear. I will do what I can to save you, but unless you convert to the true faith or consent to be my bride, I see little hope for you."

* * *

"SOLDIERS ARE ARRIVING! New soldiers!" someone shouted, running through the encampment. "Turn out! Turn out all, and greet the soldiers of Christ!"

A few moments later, Tobias returned to his tent in search of Philippe and Rachel. "Did you hear the news?" he asked. "Soldiers have arrived from Castile." He held out a hand to Rachel. "Come, let us meet them. Perhaps they bring news from Toledo."

"The document?" Rachel asked, indicating her work.

"Place it in the satchel and put it under the blankets. It will be safe."

"Perhaps Rachel shouldn't go." Philippe raised his voice as he continued, "She is a Jew, and we have seen how dangerous it is to be a Jew in this encampment."

Tobias's eyes flashed in anger. "And the danger is increased by your making so vocal a pronouncement."

"Tobias, it is not a secret that can be guarded for long. I've told her that she has but two options: convert and make a public confession of her acceptance of the divinity of Christ, or accept my proposal of marriage."

"And how long would you accept a wife who was Jewish before insisting she proceed with the first option?"

"One must come to the Lord of one's own accord, not through force."

"Tell that to the Jew burned at the stake," Tobias said, and when Philippe started to protest, he held up a restraining hand. "Enough. As I understand it, you have approached Rachel on this matter many times, and each time she has refused both options." He turned to Rachel. "Is that not so?" he asked, and she nodded.

"You refuse at your own peril," Philippe told Rachel haughtily.

"It is her decision to make," Tobias reminded him. "And if we are honorable men, we will accept that decision and do what we can to save her from harm. And one way we can do that," he said, lifting his finger in admonition, "is to keep silent about who she is."

"Yes, yes, of course," Philippe said. "I meant no harm. I am only trying to do what is best for both her temporal body and her immortal soul."

"Then please, make no further pronouncements, lest someone hear."

"I will be guarded," Philippe promised. "Shall we go now and see these new soldiers for Christ?"

"Why don't you go ahead?" Tobias suggested. "Age is slowing these legs. Rachel will accompany me."

"I don't mind waiting for—"

"Please, go on and we'll follow. See if there's any news from Toledo."

Philippe looked back and forth between them, then nodded and departed from the tent.

Tobias turned and saw that Rachel had finished stowing away the documents and other supplies. "Shall we go?" he asked as she came over and took his arm. "I hope you don't mind that I sent Philippe on ahead of us."

Rachel grinned. "No, Tobias. I don't mind at all."

THE ARRIVAL OF a mounted force of about one hundred soldiers created quite a stir in the camp. Unlike the majority of the peasant army, these were all young, strong, well-armed men who appeared to have some discipline about them as they rode through the makeshift streets to the large central court.

"I am Ferdinand of Castile," their leader announced as they pulled to a halt. "Who is in charge here?"

Peter the Hermit stepped forward from the crowd. "I am in command."

"You must be the one they call the Hermit," Ferdinand said, seeing the contrast between Peter's ragged robe and his own shining armor and crisp white chasuble emblazoned with a large red cross.

"I am Peter," he replied by way of acknowledgment.

Turning in his saddle, Ferdinand signaled his men to dismount. He, too, dismounted and dropped to one knee, his soldiers following suit.

Sir Ferdinand extended his sword in his hands, palms upraised. "In service of the Lord, I submit myself, my men, and my sword to your command."

"Rise, Sir Ferdinand," Peter replied. "Retain your sword and give your men leave to enjoy the welcome of our people."

"Thank you, sir." Ferdinand stood and slid his sword back into its sheath.

"Who are they?" Peter asked, gesturing toward the rear of the column, where four men stood chained together.

"Infidels we captured in Castile and brought with us so that you might mete out justice."

"Sir Ferdinand!" a voice called from the edge of the crowd. "What news have you from Castile?"

Ferdinand turned, looking irritated that someone from the crowd had spoken when he was in audience with the leader. Then he saw who had addressed him, and said in surprise, "I know you, do I not?"

"I am Tobias Garlande of Toledo."

"Yes, Tobias el Transcriptor. We have met before. What news would you have?"

"What is the latest from Castile?" Tobias asked. "Although I am not Castilian by birth, I have developed a great affection for the country. Tell me how it fares."

Ferdinand pursed his lips. "It is not good. As we continue to free regions from Moorish control, they are pushing back, wreaking havoc throughout the countryside. They know their days are numbered in the Holy Land, and they intend to take back control of all Hispania. No one is safe. They are destroying crops, poisoning wells and streams, burning houses, robbing our people, raping our women, and killing Christian and Jew alike."

"What of Toledo?" Tobias asked. "When we left, the truce was holding."

"And so it remains for the time being. But with al-Aarif gone, there is no one to keep his people in check, and Toledo could soon face the same depredations at Moorish hands."

"Al-Aarif gone?" Tobias asked. "Where?"

"He is missing, perhaps dead."

"Or off raiding the countryside," Philippe put in, stepping forward a few feet away from Tobias.

"Sir Ferdinand," Peter called, regaining the knight's attention. "Enough news of Castile. We have other lands to concern ourselves with."

"When do we proceed to the Holy Land?" Ferdinand asked.

"Soon," Peter replied. "Soon."

Tobias watched the proceedings for a few more minutes, then turned to Rachel. "I am tired. I am going back to our tent to take a nap."

"I will accompany you," she said.

"Philippe, are you coming?" Tobias asked.

"Not just now," he replied. "I would talk with some of these men."

"Very well." Tobias turned to Rachel. "Come, my dear."

"Tobias," Rachel asked as they walked away through the crowd. "Do you believe what Ferdinand said? Do you really think the Moors are attacking Christians?"

"I have no reason to doubt him," Tobias replied.

"But why? Christians, Muslims, and Jews have lived together for centuries throughout Hispania."

"Yes, but that was under Moorish rule. The same has been true in Jerusalem, where Jews have lived alongside Muslims, and where Christians were allowed to make pilgrimages to the holy sites. But all that is changing."

"Why?"

Tobias shrugged. "In Hispania, it has to do with power. The Moors had it, and now the Christians are taking control. I'm sorry to say that we Christians are proving to be a lot less tolerant, and it seems the Moors would rather fight than be forced into exile."

"Do you think that will happen?"

"It will if there aren't more men like al-Aarif on both sides of the struggle. And now, with this ill-advised war, I fear hearts will only harden."

"Then there's no hope?" Rachel asked as they approached their tent.

"There's always hope. Someday, perhaps wise men of all three religions will realize what must be done, and they will come together in love of God and mutual respect."

"That will be a wonderful thing."

"Yes," Tobias agreed. "But that day is not yet at hand, and until it is, I fear there will be more trouble."

"Like your vision of Jews being put into a room where they are killed by the air they breathe?"

"Yes. And worse," he added ominously.

BACK INSIDE THE tent, Rachel resumed work on the document she was copying. Tobias retired to a curtained-off area and lay down on the blanket-covered straw that served as his mattress. He started to drift off to sleep, then realized the images that danced around him were not those of a dream but of a vision.

TOBIAS STANDS ON a crowded street at the heart of a great city, larger than any he has ever seen or imagined. The houses and buildings loom overhead like mountains, recalling the biblical tower of Babel.

Hearing a noise like the rushing of wind, Tobias looks

over at the tallest of the buildings and sees one of the great silver birds of earlier visions as it flies toward it. He wonders if the flying carriage will slow and land on the building, like a bird upon on a tree.

But the silver bird does not even slow down as it hurtles through the air and strikes the building at full speed, halfway between the ground and the heavens. There is a thunderous explosion, followed by smoke and flames that pour from the windows of the building.

For an instant, Tobias wonders if this is a normal occurrence in this city of the future. But then he hears the terrible screaming and shouting as people appear at the windows, trapped by the growing conflagration.

As Tobias tries to make sense of what is happening, he hears another great roar, and a second silver bird comes flying at unimaginable speed toward a twin tower just beyond the first. The impact causes an enormous explosion as the second building erupts in smoke and flames.

More people gather to watch, many weeping openly. He hears the piercing sound of horns, louder than those that felled the walls of Jericho. And large wheeled carriages, moving by their own power, rush through the streets toward the buildings.

"Oh, dear God!" a woman shouts. "They're jumping!"

Tobias sees it as well, so many people leaping from so great a height that often there are two or three in the air at the same time. Even though he knows this is a vision of an event that won't happen until far in the future, he cannot help but feel horror and sympathy for the victims.

Suddenly, one of the towers shudders and comes crashing down, collapsing upon itself and sending out huge billowing clouds of smoke. The other tower follows, leaving an almost deafening silence as the city fills with ash.

Suddenly Tobias is no longer enveloped in a cloud of smoke, nor is he in the middle of the street surrounded by weeping people. Instead he's in a room, watching the same scene shrunken in size in the window of a black box. Seated in a chair, staring at the moving image on the box, is the man Tobias first saw in vision inside one of the silver flying carriages. There are tears in the man's eyes, his face fixed in an expression of unimaginable sadness.

Sensing he is not alone, the man turns from the box and stares directly at Tobias, who recognizes him at once as a fellow Keeper. The man curls his thumb and two fingers into a circle and places his hand upon his chest, and Tobias returns the Keeper's sign.

"You can see me," Tobias says without speaking.

"Yes."

"You can hear me?" Tobias asks excitedly. "I have never spoken with a Keeper before."

"Perhaps it is important that we speak now," the man in the chair says.

"You know Castilian," Tobias said.

"No, I am speaking English," the man replies.

"Yet I hear you in my own language. This must be what it means when it is written, 'And they were all filled with the Holy Ghost, and began to speak with other tongues, as the Spirit gave them utterance.'"

"Yes," the other Keeper replied. "All things are possible when we speak through God."

"I was there," Tobias says, pointing to the moving picture in the black box. "How is it that you are seeing it in that window?"

"It is called a video. For you, it has not yet happened. For me, it is a recording of something that has already happened. Just as you can record your thoughts on paper, so can we record an image of events."

"Were men directing the silver birds?" Tobias asks.

"Yes."

"And they directed the birds to fly into the buildings—to kill others?"

The Keeper nods sadly.

"But why?"

"It is what happens when those who claim to follow God's will instead follow their own."

Tobias nods. "This is true in my time, as well. We have begun a war to claim the Holy Land for Christendom. I fear it is but an excuse to kill in God's name."

"I know of your wars, your Crusades." The Keeper points to the images on the box. "Some say this is the result of the hatred first spawned by the Crusades."

"Can you not stop it?" Tobias asks.

"There is a gathering here of Christians, Jews, and Muslims. There will be many brilliant men and women, good people from all three faiths."

"Trevia Dei," Tobias intones.

"Yes, Trevia Dei."

"You must not fail," Tobias says as the vision begins to fade. "You must not fail."

"WHAT DID YOU say?" Rachel asked as she pushed aside the curtain and stood over Tobias.

"You must not fail . . . must not fail," the old man repeated, his eyelids fluttering as he stared blankly toward the ceiling.

"Tobias, are you all right?" She knelt down and touched his shoulder.

He blinked a couple of times, then looked toward Rachel, who was backlit by the bright sun pouring through the open flap of the tent beyond. The burning buildings were gone, the Keeper and the moving images in the box were gone. Tobias was back in his own time and place.

"You were having a vision," Rachel said.

"Yes." He pinched the bridge of his nose. "Child, I fear no one realizes the seeds of destruction that are being sown here."

NEW YORK CITY

Fr. Michael Flannery jerked upright in his chair. He had been watching a documentary about 9/11 in order to prepare for his presentation at the symposium, but he had fallen asleep with the remote in his hand.

What a strange dream, he mused, but with that thought came the sudden awareness that it had been no dream. The vision came flooding back, and he recalled every word the old Keeper had said, ending with the words, "You must not fail."

Flannery remembered the other time he had seen the old Keeper—on the plane right after it had almost crashed. Why had he reappeared now?

Flannery knew the answer. The vision, like the ability to communicate in each other's tongue, was a message from God, one that spoke with the sureness of the old Keeper's voice when he declared, "You must not fail."

"We must not fail," Flannery repeated aloud.

"You sure have that right," a voice said, and Flannery spun around to see Preston Lewkis stretched out on the sofa. He had likely been there the entire time, yet he had not seen or heard anything out of the ordinary.

Preston's presence did not cause Flannery to question if the vision had merely been a dream. Instead he was strengthened in the sure and certain knowledge that it had been real. But the vision did not belong to the present or the past, nor had it taken place here in New York City or on the fields of the Crusades. No, what the two Keepers experienced had existed in God's time and place.

"So be it," Flannery whispered as he rose from the chair, refreshed and ready to face whatever awaited him.

CHAPTER 18

WEST OF CONSTANTINOPLE

The four men were stripped naked and staked out on the ground, their bodies forming a cross with their feet together at the transept. Their legs were smeared with animal fat; then a fire was lit. As the fire grew hotter, their feet began to bake, and they screamed in agony.

More than a thousand of Peter's pilgrims were gathered around, laughing and jeering. Philippe Guischard stood among them, his eyes gleaming in excitement. At first, he believed that to enjoy such pain in others would be sinful. Then he remembered that he had been absolved of all sins—and that the victims were Muslim infidels brought in chains from Castile—and therefore he could enjoy the spectacle without guilt as they underwent trial by ordeal.

Peter the Hermit circled the victims, looking down at each man's face as he exhorted them, "Confess your sins. We know that you have raped our women, burned our villages, murdered our people. Confess now, and your agony will not be prolonged."

"We are . . . innocent!" one of them screeched, his words so distorted by pain as to be almost unintelligible.

"Make the fire hotter," Peter demanded, and more wood was added. Their feet turned black, and the flesh began peeling away from the bones.

"Confess and repent!" Peter shouted. "Denounce your

false prophet and accept Jesus, and a merciful God will accept you into His bosom!"

As the roar of the fire grew louder, the cries of the victims diminished into weak whimpers, and finally silence.

"Do you repent?" Peter shouted.

"Peter," Walter the Penniless said, and Peter turned toward him. "They are dead."

Peter had worked himself into a frenzy, and he struggled to calm his breathing as he continued to circle the blackened remains of the four prisoners. Finally he stopped walking, closed his eyes, and exclaimed in a booming voice, "On your knees! Everyone, on your knees!"

The crowd instantly dropped to the ground, Philippe among them. Peter remained standing, his hands clasped together in prayer.

"Lord, we ask that you look with favor upon what we have done here. We tried, diligently, to save the souls of these deluded heathens, but they would not heed your word. Send them now to hell to dwell with the others who know you not. Amen."

"Amen," the crowd responded as one.

As PHILIPPE HEADED back to the tent, he felt a strange stirring in his loins, an unexpected excitement. He wished Rachel had not left with Tobias but had stayed to see what happened to the four infidels. Surely if she had heard them cry out in their agony and had smelled their burning flesh, she would be more receptive to Philippe's entreaties to become his wife.

He moved quickly through the crowd, eager to recount all he had seen.

"Ah, Philippe, you're back," Tobias said as the younger man entered the tent, out of breath from running. "Are you all right?"

"Tobias," Philippe exclaimed, "I have just witnessed a

wondrous spectacle. I only wish that you and Rachel had been there."

"What was it?"

"I saw the Lord's justice meted out on those four infidels captured by Ferdinand," Philippe said, his voice rising with exhilaration. "They were laid out so." He found four sticks and placed them on the ground in a cross. "And here, where their feet met, was a fire."

"Fire?" Rachel said with a gasp.

"Yes, my dear," Philippe said, not noticing how she cringed at his words. "And not just an ordinary fire. Their legs had been coated with animal fat so that, as the fire intensified, their flesh blackened like an overbaked haunch of meat."

"How horrible!" Rachel said, shaking with anger and disgust.

"You should have been there," Philippe told her. "It would have done you good to have witnessed a trial by fire. You wouldn't so quickly reject my offer of marriage—or the chance to acknowledge Jesus as your Lord. For the suffering experienced by those four sinners is only just beginning. The gates of hell have been opened to them now, and they will burn for all eternity."

"How awful." Rachel shuddered in revulsion, then turned away and hurried from the tent.

"It is not something you can run from!" Philippe called after her.

"Enough!" Tobias said sharply.

"I am only trying to save her immortal soul."

"Rachel is a moral, God-fearing woman. Her immortal soul is in less danger than yours or Peter's or anyone else who takes pleasure in killing in the name of God."

"Careful what you say, old man," Philippe said angrily, pointing at Tobias. "Word could get back to Peter."

"I hope it does. In fact, I intend to make certain that word gets back to him." He strode from the tent.

"What do you mean?" Philippe asked, following outside.

Tobias halted and looked back at Philippe. "I intend to see Peter now, to tell him that I don't approve of this."

"You don't approve of what?"

"Of *this*." Tobias took in the entire encampment with a sweep of his arm. "The trials by fire, the entire pilgrim march, I reject all of it."

"You're going to say that to Peter?"

"I am."

"Then you go to see him at your peril," Philippe said, following a few steps as Tobias turned and headed deeper into the encampment. "Watch your tongue or you're a dead man," he called after him. "A dead man."

WHEN TOBIAS WAS shown into Peter's tent, he found the pilgrim leader seated at a small dining table, holding a large joint of meat that had been blackened over an open fire. Remembering Philippe's description of the feet of the Muslims, Tobias closed his eyes for a moment to force that image from his mind.

Peter tore off a large strip of meat with his teeth, then put down the joint and poked a dangling piece into his mouth. "Tobias," he said by way of greeting. He pointed to a platter that held a couple more joints. "Come, dine with me."

Again, Tobias envisioned the victims' burnt feet. "I've already eaten," he lied, fighting a twinge of nausea.

"Perhaps you would share a glass of wine, then?"

Tobias wanted to say no but decided that drinking the wine would put them on a more intimate basis so they could talk more freely.

"Yes, thank you," he said.

Peter picked up a copper goblet, wiped it out with the sleeve of his garment, and filled it from a wine amphora. As he handed it to Tobias, he leaned to one side and passed wind. With a small sigh of relief, he said, "Drink it in good health."

Tobias held the goblet toward Peter in a silent toast, then took a sip. "Peter, I would have a word with you."

"Never let it be said that I wouldn't speak with an old friend," Peter replied. "What of those soldiers who arrived? Aren't they magnificent?"

"Quite impressive."

"I didn't see you when we sent to the Lord those four Muslim prisoners. They had been raping and looting throughout your beloved Castile, so I'm sure you would have approved of their fate."

"No, Peter, I do not approve of what happened to them," Tobias said, setting down the goblet.

Peter looked genuinely surprised by Tobias's response. "Surely, if you love God, you cannot object to what we did today. They were unbelievers. Even worse, they were believers in the false teachings of Muhammad."

"And so you killed them?"

"Yes, for the glory of God, I killed them."

Tobias shook his head. "You did not kill them for God. You killed them for reasons of your own, so do not put their blood on God's hands."

Peter glared at Tobias for a long moment. "You had best be careful what you say, Tobias. Friend or not, I will not hesitate to condemn you for the crime of heresy."

"Yes, I saw how you treat old friends when you murdered Raymond of Amiens, who by all reckoning was a good and God-fearing man."

"Guards!" Peter shouted. "Come at once!" He jabbed his forefinger at Tobias. "I have tried to show you the way, but you will not listen. Instead you continue to pervert the meaning of Trevia Dei. We will see how strong your faith is when you burn at the stake."

Two guards came running in, brandishing their swords.

"Seize him," Peter demanded, pointing at Tobias. "Take him outside and tie him to the stake, then call everyone to come watch him burn."

The guards stared at Peter as if they didn't understand, then looked at each other.

"Is your faith strong enough to withstand the flames?" Peter asked.

Tobias's expression remained unchanged.

"Take him now," Peter demanded angrily. "I grow weary of looking at him."

"Sir, take who?" one of the guards said gingerly.

"Who? This heretic and sinner who calls himself Tobias of Toledo."

"You want us to find this person Tobias?" the other guard asked.

Peter looked at the two men as if they were crazy. "Find him? What do you mean 'find him'? He is right here! Seize him, I say."

Again, the guards looked at each other in confusion.

"Sir," one of them said ever so cautiously. "There is no one here."

"Are you blind?" Peter shouted. He leaned toward Tobias and pointed, the tip of his finger no more than half an arm's length from the old man's face. "He is right here! Now seize him!"

"Sir, there is no one there!" This time the guard's voice was filled with frustration and concern for their leader's sanity.

"Peter, they cannot see me," Tobias said calmly.

"What do you mean? Of course they can see you. You are right there."

"They can neither see nor hear me," Tobias said.

"Then I will take care of you myself. Guard, give me your sword," Peter commanded, holding out his hand.

The guard looked over at his comrade, who nodded for him to do as ordered. He turned the sword around and handed it hilt-first to Peter.

"Now, let us test your faith!" Peter said with a malevolent smile.

He drew the sword back, but when he tried to thrust, it would not move. He pushed as hard as he could, but he could not make the sword move forward.

"What is this?" Peter demanded, his anger replaced by fear. "How can this be?"

Tobias pulled a locket from under his tunic. Opening it, he removed a piece of white cloth that bore the symbol of Trevia Dei in blood as moist and bright as the day it had been formed.

Peter jerked his hand away from the sword, dropping it as if it were a hot poker. He put his hand to his throat as he looked at the cloth bearing the familiar symbol. "What is that?" he asked.

"Sir, shall we call a physician?" one of the guards asked in concern over Peter's strange behavior.

"No, no, get out, both of you!" Peter said with a wave of his hand.

The guard picked up his sword; then the two left the tent as quickly as they had entered.

"Who are you?" Peter asked.

"I am the same Tobias you have always known," he replied. "I am also the Keeper."

"Keeper? The keeper of what?"

"I am the Keeper of the symbol of Trevia Dei. It was entrusted to me by the Keeper who came before, and I shall pass it on to the one who follows. The symbol you see here is formed by the blood of Christ."

"Sanguis Christi?" Peter said, shaking his head. "That cannot be. This blood is fresh."

"Yes, for it is the blood of the living Christ. And it will remain fresh until the end of days."

"What do you want with me?" Peter asked, backing away from the table.

"I want you to end this spectacle of torturing and killing Jews and Muslims."

"They are our enemies."

"No, they are not. They are our brothers and sisters, for we are all children of Abraham. We are all People of the Book."

"I will kill no more as spectacle," Peter promised, looking genuinely afraid. He held up his finger. "But I am going to the Holy Land to set them free."

"They are already free," Tobias said. "At least they were, before you started this unholy war. Were Christians not allowed full access to the holy sites?"

"Access?" Peter said. "Why should anyone grant us access to what is rightfully ours?"

"Peter, believe me when I say that I have seen the future. I know what fruit these seeds shall bear, and it is bitter fruit indeed."

"Why are you here?" Peter challenged. "If you don't believe in our Holy War, why have you come?"

"I'm not sure."

"Perhaps God told you to come. After all, Pope Urban himself issued the call, and he speaks for God."

"I do not believe God has chosen me—or any true Christian—to kill His children."

"Then perhaps you have come for the scroll," Peter suggested with a conspiratorial smile.

"Scroll? What scroll?"

"I knew that would interest a translator of ancient documents. And this scroll will be the most important document you have ever translated."

"What scroll?" Tobias asked again.

"A gospel account of Jesus by one who walked with him. I speak of the scroll written by our founder, Dismas bar-Dismas, the son of the Good Thief who died on the cross beside our Lord."

You know where to find the scroll of Dismas?" Tobias asked, barely able to contain his excitement.

"I know that it is in the Holy Land."

"How do you know this?"

"Why are you here?" Peter countered.

"I am here because I believe my Lord wants me to be here."

"And do you not think there is a reason for that?"

Tobias didn't answer.

"Perhaps the Lord wants you to help me find the scroll and to see for yourself the true meaning of Trevia Dei."

"What if the scroll confirms the three paths that are one?" Tobias asked.

Peter laid a hand on his old friend's forearm. "Come with me, and together we shall uncover the true meaning of our Lord's greatest secret."

Tobias was silent a long moment, then tilted his head slightly and asked, "When do we leave for Jerusalem?"

"Ah," Peter replied. "So now you have joined the Holy War."

CHAPTER 19

NEW YORK CITY

Following the near-shooting of Fr. Michael Flannery, security around Stuyvesant Hall was tightened for the second day of the People of the Book symposium. Demonstrators, to their chagrin, were moved across the street, where they were restricted to marching in a long oval behind yellow-and-black sawhorses. There were almost as many uniformed police officers, standing with their backs to the convention hall as they kept a close watch on the marchers.

Because the main demonstration area was limited, the police had worked out a schedule, rotating the marchers every two hours, with the spillover restricted to an area farther down the street from the main entrance. Christians who opposed the symposium used the primary area the first two hours, followed in turn by atheists, Muslims, Jews, and finally by supporters of the ecumenical gathering.

When the police car bearing Flannery, Preston Lewkis, and Sarah Arad arrived at the conference hall, the atheists were taking their turn marching around the oval, shouting slogans and waving signs that read:

God didn't make man
Man made God

What is the way, the truth, the light?
Secular Humanism!

People of the Book
need a better reading list

As Flannery stepped from the patrol car, he scanned the protesters across the street and saw one young man who was shouting more vociferously than most as he jumped up and down to be seen over the phalanx of police. When Flannery read the fellow's sign, he grinned and motioned for Preston and Sarah to take a look.

"He's godless but not humorless," Flannery said as he gestured toward the man, whose sign bore five handwritten lines of text:

Jesus Saves
Moses Invests
Muhammad Profits
Atheists don't need to:
They're already well-endowed

The police escort ushered Flannery and his colleagues into Stuyvesant Hall and over to the security desk, which was outfitted with walk-through metal detectors and X-ray machines for inspecting the bags of everyone entering the building. As the two men were emptying their pockets and placing their briefcases on the machine, Sarah withdrew a letter from her purse and gave it to the security officer, who opened and read it:

Office of the Commissioner, NYPD
To Whom It May Concern:
    The bearer of this letter is Lt. Sarah Arad, accredited
by the Israeli National Police, Interpol, and the New York
City Police Department.

In her capacity as a law officer, providing security for the People of the Book symposium, she is authorized to carry a firearm in and around Stuyvesant Hall.

> *For the commissioner,*
> *Martin Kelly, Police Adj.*

"Go on in, Lieutenant Arad," the officer on duty said as he handed back the letter. "We were told you'd be coming."

"Thanks." Sarah placed her purse on the X-ray machine, stepped through the metal detector, and retrieved her purse on the other side.

"Well, Michael, it looks as if they managed yesterday's opening session without us and the symposium can get down to serious business today," Preston said as they walked through the lobby toward the meeting area. "What do you think?"

"I think we have to succeed," Flannery said.

They headed into the main hall where the symposium was being held. The large square room was about four times the size of a basketball court, with rows of seats facing a raised stage against the far wall. Along the left and right walls were booths and tables hosted by the various organizations that had been invited to attend. In the far right corner, beside the stage, was a food court with several vendors and about a dozen tables.

"Father Flannery," someone called as they entered the hall.

"Rabbi Persky," Flannery said, walking toward a tall, dignified-looking man with a gold-trimmed yarmulke that covered his bald pate. "How nice to see you again. These are my friends, Sarah Arad and Preston Lewkis."

After they shook hands and exchanged greetings, Persky said to Flannery, "I hope you don't mind, when we were putting together discussion groups, I asked for you to be on my panel."

"Not at all," Flannery assured him.

"Come. I'll introduce you to the third member of our group. We go on in about fifteen minutes."

"Don't worry about us," Preston said when Flannery looked over at him. "We'll wander around the floor a bit."

Persky led Flannery over to the food court, where a Muslim cleric was seated at one of the tables.

"This is Imam Salim Madari of Detroit," Persky introduced. "Imam, I'd like you to meet Father Michael Flannery of the Vatican."

The two men shook hands, then the rabbi brought over three cups of coffee, and they began talking about their upcoming panel discussion on interfaith projects.

"It pains me to admit it," Madari said, "but a national poll of American Muslims indicates only about ten percent have ever participated in an interfaith project."

"We're all guilty of that," Flannery replied. "When we Christians say interfaith, we generally mean Protestant and Catholics coming together."

"At least your Catholic churches aren't being bombed by the Baptists," Persky put in.

"It's a two-way street, Rabbi," Madari said. "Let's not forget that there are more bombs going off in mosques than in your temples and churches."

"You're not blaming the Jews?" Persky asked.

"Gentlemen, please." Flannery held up his hand. "Isn't this symposium to put an end to such things?"

"You're right," Persky said. "Imam, I'm sorry if I came off a bit too self-righteous."

"I'm sorry, as well," Madari said. "Let us resolve to set an example for others."

"*Assalamu alaikum,*" the rabbi intoned in Arabic.

"*Shalom aleichem,*" the imam echoed in perfectly pronounced Hebrew.

"*Pax vobiscum,*" Flannery repeated.

* * *

"DOCTOR LEWKIS, LIEUTENANT Arad," a woman called, and Preston and Sarah turned to see Ann Coopersmith, accompanied by a tall, rather gangly young man with wire-rimmed glasses.

"This is David Meyers," Ann said. "David, this is—"

"Dr. Preston Lewkis," David cut in, "professor of archaeology at Brandeis, graduate of Washington U. in St. Louis, cross-country runner in college, came in seven hundred thirty-fourth in the Boston Marathon two years ago, author with Daniel Mazar of *Liturgical Archaeology: Lessons Learned at Qumran*."

"What about my favorite color?" Preston asked.

"I don't believe that's ever been documented," David replied.

"Well, to complete your dossier, it's orange, but burnt orange, not the flashy type," Preston said.

"And you are Sarah Arad," David said.

Sarah held up her hand. "I'll pass on the personal history, if you don't mind."

David smiled self-consciously. "It goes without saying that I lack social skills."

"Well, social skills or not, we're both very grateful for what you did for Father Flannery," Sarah told him. "He's a good friend, and we wouldn't have liked to see him wind up in the drink."

"Yes, well, I was on that airplane, too, so I was highly motivated."

"When did you arrive in New York?" Sarah asked. "I thought you were in Rome."

"This morning. I hoped to catch you at your apartment, but you'd already left. By the way, you left the coffeepot on, so I shut it off."

"You were in our apartment today?" Preston asked. "How did you get in?"

"It was easy."

"For that matter, how did you get here, on the floor?" Sarah asked, tapping the floor pass on David's jacket lapel. "The symposium is by invitation only."

"By arranging an invite," he replied.

Sarah took out her cell phone and dialed a number. "This is Lieutenant Sarah Arad of Interpol. Could you verify badge number P178 please?" She listened a moment, then repeated, "David Meyers of Sikeston, Missouri, reporting for *Tikkun* . . . all right, thank you very much."

"That's a Jewish interfaith magazine," David explained. "Do you want the phone number?"

Sarah smiled as she put her cell phone back in her purse. "I'm sure you have that covered, as well," she said. "I just wanted to see if you were reckless enough to counterfeit a floor badge. I'm glad you weren't."

David glanced around. "Where's the padre?"

"Well, he's—" Preston started, then smiled and pointed. "—right up there."

At that very moment, Flannery was taking a seat on the stage alongside the rabbi and a Muslim cleric. Dr. Thomas Geer stepped up to the podium and tapped on the microphone. As the sound reverberated through the room, people settled in their seats or turned toward the stage from the exhibition booths at the sides.

"Ladies and gentlemen, welcome to day two of the People of the Book symposium. The three members of our first panel need no introduction, other than their names. Two have already made individual presentations, and their colleague will be featured at the closing session—an event we all eagerly await. Today they join us for a panel discussion titled 'Interfaith Cooperation, Three Paths to a Single Goal.' May I present Rabbi Yev Persky, Imam Salim Madari, and Father Michael Flannery."

Following enthusiastic applause from the four hundred or so people in the audience, the three men began their discussion. After several minutes and the first question from the audience, David Meyers turned to Sarah and the others and asked if there was someplace they could talk.

"How about the food court?" Preston suggested.

"Too crowded," David said, shaking his head. "I need to show you something in private."

"What do you have?" Sarah asked.

"Dynamite."

"I'll have security find us a private room," she said, then headed toward the lobby.

Just then someone in the audience called out, "Father Flannery, you've been quoting the Gospels, but I don't recall that last verse. It's from Dismas, isn't it?" he asked, referring to the gospel Flannery was going to present during the final session.

"Why, yes," the priest admitted. "I'm afraid I got a bit ahead of myself—I should've saved that for the final presentation, but sometimes I find myself mixing Dismas with Matthew, Mark, Luke, and John."

"Then you expect Rome to add Dismas to its canon?" another person asked.

"I can't predict if it will be incorporated into the New Testament," Flannery replied. "It will take several years of detailed study and validation before any decision is made."

"How many years?"

"Could be as many as a hundred."

"Is it authentic or a hoax?" someone called out.

"Well, of course, that's the question that everyone will be asking during the long validation process," Flannery replied. "And it's going to be very difficult to prove, since the document was stolen."

"Difficult? Try impossible," another questioner said.

"We heard you carbon-dated the papyrus to the first century, but not the ink," a man in the first row said.

Flannery looked a bit uncomfortable. "I'd really like to

hold any discussion of the Dismas scroll until my presentation."

"How old was the ink?" the man pressed.

"What I'll say now is that tests on the ink were inconclusive."

"So it could be real?" one person said, with another adding, "Or a hoax."

"Which is it, Father Flannery?"

The priest raised his hands to settle the crowd. "What I believe is this: Dismas bar-Dismas walked with Jesus and wrote a gospel. Now, as to whether or not the Masada Scroll will be validated as that gospel and included in the New Testament, well, you'll have to attend the final session for my findings."

Sarah returned then and led the others from the hall and back through the lobby to a side room that was used for smaller gatherings. It held a half-dozen tables with four chairs at each.

David placed his laptop on one of the tables and booted it up. Tapping a few keys, he opened an e-mail. "Here's what I wanted you to see. It was sent to Mehdi Jahmshidi from MWDS."

"What's MWDS?" Preston asked.

"Medical Waste Disposal Solutions," Ann answered for David. "They're headquartered in Newport News, Virginia, but they service hospitals as far south as Florida and west to the Mississippi."

"Service how?"

"They dispose of bloody bandages, used hypodermic needles, expired medicines, and the like."

"I still don't make the connection," Preston said. "Why would a medical waste company be in touch with the head of Arkaan?"

"It's simple," David replied. "Hospitals use cobalt-60 for radiation therapy, and cesium-137 in medical gauges and radiotherapy machines. And they also use a lot of medical-grade plutonium."

"Yes, I see," Sarah said, nodding. "We're talking radioactive material here."

"But it's medical grade," Preston noted. "It's not like they're dealing with enriched uranium."

"No, we're not talking about a nuclear bomb," David agreed. "But a dirty bomb, perhaps. And even in smaller amounts, less than a thimble, for instance, of medical-grade plutonium . . . well, if it were dissolved, made into an aerosol, and introduced into the ventilation system of an office building, it would kill every living thing on an entire floor."

"You think a bunch of terrorists have the skills to do something like that?" Preston said dubiously.

"They had the skills to bring down two airplanes," David reminded him.

Preston nodded. "I guess you're right, which leads to the next question. Have they gotten their hands on radioactive material?"

"Read the e-mail," David said, angling the laptop so the others could see the screen.

From: gchambers@mwdsolutions.com
To: mj@gulfexportsltd.com
Subj: Disposition of Waste Material
   We have the following material available for final disposition:
   1. 2,000 used hypodermic needles
   2. 50 pounds of soiled gauze and bandage material
   3. 500 grams of source decay material
   4. 100 pounds of bed linen
   5. 30 sets of soiled scrubs
   It is understood that in dealing with items 1,2,4, and 5, you will follow the regulations as covered by the Resource Conservation and Recovery Act. With regard to item 3, you will adhere to the Code of Federal Regula-

tions, Title 10, Chapter 1, Part 62, and additional sec-
tions.

Compensation is as previously agreed.
Glen Chambers, CEO, MWD Solutions

"So, David, let's see if I've got this correct," Sarah said. "MJ is Mehdi Jahmshidi, and Gulf Exports Limited is some sham company he's set up. Five hundred grams of source decay material means it's low-level radioactive waste, the disposal of which comes under the Code of Federal Regulations."

"Exactly," David confirmed with a nod.

"And the other stuff?" Preston said. "The needles, soiled bandages, and bed linen is just for cover, right?"

"It's probably been disposed of already. This e-mail is just to cover Chambers's ass," David said. He looked up at Ann and Sarah. "Pardon the language."

"I think 'cover his ass' puts it quite well," Sarah replied.

"So, where's the radioactive material now?" Preston asked.

"I wish I knew." David shut down and closed his laptop.

"Do you think our government knows about this?" Ann asked.

"Quite possibly," David said. "They monitor these waste companies pretty closely, especially the ones that use injection wells."

"Injection wells?" Sarah asked.

"Wildcatters who drill dry wells are often able to recover their losses by allowing their wells to be used for waste disposal," he explained. "They're called injection wells and are monitored closely because of the possibility of contaminating the water table."

"Won't they pick up on this, then?" Preston asked.

"I doubt it."

"Why not? I mean, once you pointed it out, it was pretty obvious, even to me. I'd think the intelligence community would pick up on it quite easily."

"Except a company like MWDS probably sends out a hundred or more of these e-mails a month. And I doubt, seriously, that there is anything about this one that's any different from any of the others."

"The addressee?" Sarah suggested.

"Jahmshidi and Arkaan have gone through scores, if not hundreds, of e-mail and Internet name changes," David said. "As far as I can tell, this particular e-mail address was never used before or after this message. To be honest, I was lucky to pick up on it."

"So, here's where we stand," Sarah said. "We don't know where the stuff is and we don't know how Jahmshidi plans to use it. But I think we can safely say we know the target."

"This symposium," Preston declared.

"Precisely."

"All right, David, you're the smart one here," Preston said. "How will he do it?"

"The easiest way would be through the ventilation."

"What do we do now?" Preston asked. "Go to the police?"

"You think they'll believe us?" Ann asked. "They can be pretty cynical about unconfirmed threats. On the other hand, since 9/11 they take things a lot more seriously. What we need is a police officer we can trust."

"I know just the man," Sarah said.

"Santini?" Preston asked.

"Yes," she replied as she took out her cell phone.

CHAPTER 20

NEW YORK CITY

And the purpose of your visit to the United States, Dr. al-Halid?" the customs officer asked.

"I'm to deliver a paper at the People of the Book symposium," Mehdi Jahmshidi replied, nodding toward the passport that identified him as Hassan al-Halid. The fake passport was necessary, because he knew he was on the watch list of Homeland Security, Interpol, and almost every other intelligence agency.

"Oh, yes, I've heard about the symposium," the officer said. "Bringing together peoples of all religions, it's a wonderful thing. I hope you are able to bring it off. Anything to declare?"

"I have brought nothing but my clothes, the Qur'an, and some of my work," Jahmshidi said.

"What are these?" a second officer asked as he rummaged through Jahmshidi's carry-on bag. He held up a sealed six-pack of Binaca peppermint spray.

"Breath freshener." Jahmshidi took a matching one from his breast pocket and squirted an atomized cloud into his mouth, then smiled.

"I know what it is. Why so many?"

"I find I need it when I eat your—how do you call it?—your fast foods. I don't like to run out. Would you care to try?" He held forth the spray.

"Thanks, but no." The officer dropped the packet into the

bag and zippered it, then nodded to his colleague, who stamped the passport and returned it to Jahmshidi.

"Enjoy your stay in America, and good luck with the symposium."

"Thank you," Jahmshidi replied.

The head of Arkaan headed out of the terminal and found a cab, directing the driver to the Dunn Hotel near Columbus Circle in Midtown Manhattan. After checking in, he followed the bellman up to his room. As the bellman was preparing to leave, he asked the man, "Which way is east?"

"East? That way," the bellman said, pointing toward the window.

"Thank you."

The bellman waited a moment longer.

"Thank you," Jahmshidi said again, motioning for the man to leave.

The bellman gave a slight sigh and started to leave, then hesitated at the door. "I made a mistake," he said. "That's west. East is the opposite direction."

Jahmshidi waited until the door closed behind the bellman, then he took out a small compass and turned it slowly in his hand. As he suspected, the bellman had been right the first time but changed his answer when he realized he wasn't getting a tip.

Jahmshidi looked at the clock and consulted a pocket schedule to get a time adjustment. Opening his suitcase, he laid out his prayer rug for the *Dhuhr Salat*, or midday prayer. Then, because he had a few minutes before prayer, he read his Qur'an:

> *When your Lord inspired the angels: Verily, I am with you; make ye firm then those who believe; I will cast dread into the hearts of those who misbelieve—strike off their necks then, and strike off from them every fingertip.*

If Jahmshidi did not already know in his heart that what he was doing was the right thing, Surah VIII of the Qur'an reinforced his resolve.

> O ye who believe! when ye meet those who misbelieve in swarms, turn not to them your hinder parts; for he who turns to them that day his hinder parts, save turning to fight or rallying to a troop, brings down upon himself wrath from God, and his resort is hell, and an ill journey shall it be!

As the time for *salat* approached, Jahmshidi put down the Qur'an and began his *wuduu*, or cleansing for prayer.

Starting with his right hand, he washed both hands up to the wrists, three times. Then he rinsed his mouth three times and cleaned his nostrils by sniffing water and blowing out three times. Next he washed his face three times, then his right and left arm, up to the elbows, three times each. With his thumbs and fingers, he rubbed both ears once, then washed both feet up to and including his ankles three times, beginning with his right foot.

That done, he stood at the end of the prayer rug and, raising his hands beside his face and lowering them to his sides, he recited, *"Allahu Akbar"*—God is great. With his hands placed over his stomach, he continued by reciting the "Key" that opened the prayer:

"Bismil laahir rahmaanir raheem. Al hamdu lillahi rabbil 'aalameen. Ar rahmaanir raheem. Maaliki yawmid deen. Eyyaaka na'budu, wa eyyaaka nasta'een. Eh'denas siraatal mustaqeem. Siraatal lazina an'amta 'alayhim; ghayril maghdoobi 'alayhim waladdaaleen."—In the name of God, most gracious, most merciful. Praise be to God, Lord of the universe. Most gracious, most merciful. Master of the day of judgment. You alone we worship; You alone we ask for help. Guide us in the right path, the path of those whom

You blessed; not of those who have deserved wrath, nor of the strayers.

Bowing, he continued the prayer, dropping to his knees and falling prostrate on the rug.

FR. ANTONIO SANGREMANO was at his apartment window, looking down at Central Park, when the phone rang. Walking over to the desk, he answered and heard a familiar voice.

"Any word from our friend?" Benjamin Bishara asked.

"All's quiet on the eastern front," Sangremano replied, amused by his slight play on words.

"He should be here by now. I checked with the airline; his plane arrived on time."

"Let's hope the Americans haven't picked him up on their watch list."

Bishara chuckled. "We could make a lot of money by letting the Americans know the name he's traveling under."

"He'll contact us in due time," Sangremano said.

"I suppose so," Bishara agreed. "But I don't like it. Making us wait for him gives the impression he's in charge, and I don't intend to let him suffer that delusion."

Sangremano laughed. "I didn't think you would."

"I know that you and I have been on opposite sides," Bishara said cautiously, "but in this unholy alliance, I'd like to suggest—"

"An alliance within the alliance?" Sangremano interrupted.

"Precisely. After all, we've much more in common with each other than with our Muslim partner. What do you say?"

"Great minds think alike," Sangremano replied by way of agreement, leaving out the potentially contradictory second half of the famous quote: *and fools seldom differ.*

"Good. Let's find a time to meet alone, so we can develop our strategy."

"Agreed," Sangremano said.

After the phone call concluded, Sangremano removed a small piece of paper from his billfold, then called the number that was written on the paper. When the call was answered, he said, "There is one path, one way."

"Via," said the person on the other end of the line.

"Dei," Sangremano replied. "I am in New York and was given your number."

"How may I serve you, Grand Master?"

"We should meet," Sangremano said.

LT. FRANK SANTINI leaned across the table in one of the interrogation rooms at the Midtown South Precinct station and shook his head in amusement as he looked back and forth between David Meyers and Sarah Arad. "Now, let me get this straight. You're saying that someone is going to make an atomic bomb out of . . . what? A few glow-in-the-dark watch faces or something?"

"Not a bomb like Hiroshima," David said with a frustrated frown. "I said a dirty bomb. That's when—"

"I know, I know," Santini said dismissively. "I've heard of dirty bombs. We've had some lectures on it."

"So you must know that a dirty bomb set off in Times Square, using ten pounds of TNT and a pencil-size piece of cobalt, would create enough radiation to give anyone exposed a one-in-a-hundred chance of dying from cancer."

"Isn't that something to worry about?" Sarah asked.

"I'm not so sure," Santini replied. "Your probability of dying of cancer in your lifetime is already about twenty percent. This would increase it to, what, about twenty-one percent?"

"What if the bomb went off in a concentrated area, like the floor of Stuyvesant Hall?" David asked.

"In the first place, how are they going to get a bomb in there? We've got that place sealed tight—even tighter than normal, given all the kooks outside protesting. And even if they did get in and set it off, those who weren't killed or wounded by the explosion itself could easily evacuate before being exposed to any more radiation."

"So, you aren't going to do anything?" Sarah said incredulously.

Santini sighed. "I didn't say that. But you can't expect a full-court press, hazmat suits and all, based on a hunch." He paused and rubbed his forehead. "I'll tell you what—I'll see if we can get Geiger counters down there. That will lessen the likelihood of anyone getting onto the floor with anything radioactive."

"That's a start," Sarah said.

"I know you think I'm turning my back on this, but believe me, without more specific evidence, there's nothing more I can do."

"How about investigating that Medical Waste Disposal Solutions outfit?" David asked.

"Because you hacked an e-mail off the Internet? As far as I'm concerned, it's just a routine letter they write every day, dealing with getting rid of medical waste. You yourself said they send out hundreds of e-mails just like that one. And even if it did make me suspicious, it's way out of my jurisdiction. Take it to the feds, if you're so convinced. Just be careful; you as much as admitted you got hold of it illegally, so the target of any investigation could end up being you."

David started to object, but Sarah placed a restraining hand on his forearm and said to the police lieutenant, "Thanks for your help." She turned to David. "We should get back to the symposium."

Leaving the interrogation room, David and Sarah met up with Preston Lewkis and Ann Coopersmith, who had waited for them downstairs. As they headed outside, Sarah and David recounted their meeting, after which David announced, "I'll join you at the symposium later. I'd like to do a little more snooping around."

"Nothing too dangerous, I hope," Sarah said.

"Don't worry about me. My credo is: 'If all else fails, try running the other way.' "

The others laughed.

"I'll go with David," Ann announced. "I can feel that Pulitzer in my hands already."

"Pulitzer my hind leg. It's my body she wants to get her hands on."

"Oh, David, I thought we were keeping that a secret," she teased, wrapping her arms around his neck and blowing in his ear.

David blushed. "There's a cab," he said as he quickly flagged it down.

Preston and Sarah watched as they got into the taxi and drove off. Then Sarah started toward the curb, saying, "I'll get us a cab."

Preston caught her arm. "Let's walk a bit first."

"You want to walk?"

"New York is the greatest town in the world for walking, especially with you."

CHAPTER 21

NEW YORK CITY

Piccolo Ristorante at Third Avenue and Nineteenth Street was long and narrow, with table seating for twenty-four and a row of bench tables along one wall that sat another twelve. An intimate bistro popular with young couples, it featured an exposed beam ceiling, painted wood floor, pictures of the Mediterranean coast, and wall sconces bearing sprays of colorful flowers.

Antonio Sangremano and Benjamin Bishara were at a table for two in the far-right corner. When the waiter brought the lunch menus, Sangremano said, *"Questo è un luogo molto bello. Mi fa pensare all'Italia."*

"Grazie. Ci piace pensare che."

The waiter left, and Sangremano, said to Bishara, "That wasn't polite of me. I said to him—"

" 'This is a beautiful place. It makes me think of Italy,' " Bishara translated. "And he replied, 'Thank you. We like to think that.' "

Sangremano clapped softly. "I didn't know you spoke my language."

"Sometimes it is good to keep such things to oneself. I also speak Arabic, but please do not tell Mehdi."

"Then you are a good man to have on my side." Sangremano hesitated, then added, "You *are* on my side, aren't you?"

"That's the purpose of this meeting, isn't it?"

"Yes, I suppose it is."

The waiter left a basket of rolls, and Bishara broke one open and slathered a generous amount of butter on it.

"That's dairy—not kosher at dinner," Sangremano pointed out.

Bishara chuckled. "If you've done your homework on me, and I'm sure you have, you know I don't care about that. I may even order the spaghetti carbonara with bacon."

"With you Jews, it has always been more about culture and politics than religion, hasn't it?"

"It's a matter of survival," Bishara replied. "Do you know what the population of Israel is? About five million. That's a touch less than the Jewish population in the United States. Or put another way, it's about one million fewer than the number killed by the Nazis. So you see, with us it is first, last, and always about survival."

"Believe me, Benjamin, speaking for Christians world-wide, both Catholic and Protestant, I can assure you we have no wish to eliminate the Jews—though I regret to admit that wasn't always the case. We have nothing but compassion for what you've been through."

"I don't think our friend Jahmshidi shares your compassion."

Just then Bishara's cell phone vibrated, and holding up his finger by way of saying "time out," he took the call, saying, "Hello? Who is this?"

"Hassan al-Halid," the caller replied.

"Al-Halid," Bishara repeated, nodding to Sangremano that it was their comrade, Mehdi Jahmshidi, using his alias. "So you made it to America, I see. I hadn't heard from you and was beginning to worry."

"I'm at my hotel now. Have you heard from our friend?"

"Yes, he and I spoke this morning," Bishara said.

"Is he in New York?"

"Yes. You can reach him on his cell."

"Good. Perhaps we can set up a meeting for eight tonight."

"Eight o'clock is good. Do you have a place in mind?"

"Al Bustan on Third, between Fiftieth and Fifty-first. I am told this is a good place to eat, and that we will not be bothered there."

"That sounds fine. I'll meet you there at eight."

A moment after Bishara closed his phone, Sangremano's rang and he answered it. He nodded to Bishara as he said, "Hello, Dr. al-Halid."

"I've just spoken with Bishara. We are hoping the three of us can get together this evening."

"All right. Tell me where and when, and I'll be there."

"Al Bustan on Third between Fiftieth and Fifty-first at seven thirty," Jahmshidi said.

Sangremano almost questioned the time but held his tongue. He didn't want Jahmshidi to realize he had overheard the call with Bishara, and he suspected the earlier time was no mistake. Evidently Jahmshidi also wanted to make an alliance within this unholy alliance.

MEHDI JAHMSHIDI PUT down his cell phone and turned to Ahmad Faruk, who was seated on the couch in his room at the Dunn Hotel. "The martyrdom operation in Jerusalem was well done," Jahmshidi said. "You were very careful not to connect it to Arkaan, and yet it has let everyone know that our struggle goes on. Where did you find the martyr?"

"In Nablus. Da'ud al-Tawil came to me after the Israelis killed his friend, and he asked to become a *shahid*. I was able to use him for that operation, thus allowing Nidal to come to America with me."

"How many do you have?" Jahmshidi asked.

"Five. Six, counting myself."

"Nidal is with you?"

"Yes. We are delegates to the People of the Book symposium."

"And the others were already here, as we planned?"

"Yes. They are students at universities," Faruk said.

"Are you certain all five can be trusted?"

"They have all dedicated themselves to Allah and our sacred cause," Faruk assured him. "They are ready for martyrdom. Yes, they can be trusted."

"And you?"

"If I can serve Allah better in death than in life, I will gladly sacrifice myself," Faruk declared. "What about the bombs? Will we be assembling them here?"

"The plan has changed. You won't be using bombs."

"Guns?" Faruk asked, and Jahmshidi shook his head. "Then what? We cannot kill many with knives or our hands."

Jahmshidi picked up a small breath freshener, no larger than a cigarette lighter. Pointing it toward his mouth, he pushed it twice, releasing a tiny spray.

"You will be using something like this," he said.

Faruk shook his head. "I don't understand."

"Not this one," Jahmshidi said with a smile, "but one of these." He opened his suitcase and took out one of six matching Binaca fresheners, which he handed to Faruk.

"You just squirt them?" Faruk asked, lifting it toward his mouth.

"No!" Jahmshidi said. "Push that button and we'll both be dead within seconds."

Faruk jerked his thumb away. "Are you sure it will work?"

Jahmshidi held up his finger, then lifted the phone and dialed the front desk. "Would you send the bellman named Nicholas to room 911 please? I forgot to tip him when I arrived and would like to correct that."

Within minutes there was a knock on the door, and Jahmshidi let him in. The bellman looked quite cheerful, as it was not often that a guest summoned him back for a tip.

"You wanted me, sir?" the bellman asked, looking as if he was making a supreme effort not to thrust out his hand for the money.

"The air conditioner doesn't work," Jahmshidi said. "I wonder if you would take a look at it?"

"Why, certainly," Nicholas said, momentarily confused. "But it's quite cool in here already."

"Yes, it's too cold, but I can't seem to turn it off."

"Right away, sir."

The bellman turned toward the wall thermostat but had gone only a step when Jahmshidi jumped up from his seat and pricked him on the neck with a straight pin.

"What the hell?" Nicholas slapped his neck as he spun around to see what had happened. Suddenly he fell to the floor, foaming at the mouth and convulsing. Within a few seconds he was dead.

"As you can see, it works," Jahmshidi said, looking down at the dead man.

"You didn't spray him."

"Praise Allah. If I had, we'd be lying beside him. It's just as deadly inhaled or through the skin. Now, help me get him out of here."

Checking to make certain the hall was clear, Jahmshidi and Faruk carried the bellman's body into the service room directly across the hall. There, they pushed him down the trash chute, dropping him into the bin in the basement.

Returning to the room, Jahmshidi called the front desk. "I sent for the bellman, but he never came."

"We sent Nicholas up, sir."

"Perhaps someone else needed him," Jahmshidi said.

"Shall I send up another bellman?"

"No, thank you. I'm going out shortly; I'll leave that tip for Nicholas at the front desk."

"He'll be very pleased, sir."

Hanging up the telephone, Jahmshidi looked over at Faruk. "Stay in touch. I'll let you know when it is time."

"A THIRD PERSON will be joining us," Mchdi Jahmshidi told the waiter at Al Bustan. "We'll order your grilled *kafta* special then. For now, we'll just have coffee."

"Very good, sir," the waiter said as he withdrew.

"What is *kafta*?" Sangremano asked.

"Minced, skewered lamb with chopped onions and spices."

"Maybe we should order now; I'm sure Benjamin will be here any moment," Sangremano said. He knew better, but he was letting Jahmshidi take the lead.

"Bishara won't be here until eight. I asked you to come a half hour early so we could speak alone."

"Oh?" Sangremano raised his eyebrows.

"In any organization that has three members, it is inevitable that alliances will be formed, two against the one. I see this arrangement as being no different."

"That's the mathematics of such an organization," Sangremano replied. "Unless everything is unanimous, it will always come down to a ratio of two to one."

"That is why we should be allies," Jahmshidi declared. "After all, we share ancient grievances with the Jews. And in recent times they have invaded our land, laying claim to it based upon their presence two thousand years ago. Let's face it, you and I both know that the Jews are pushy people."

"You may have a point there," Sangremano said. "So tell me, just how is this alliance between us to work?"

"First, we both agree that we will not make a separate alliance with Bishara."

"I have no problem with that," Sangremano said.

"Second, we will share information with each other."

"What sort of information?"

"Nothing specific at the moment, but if either of us learns something, we must agree to share with the other."

"All right," Sangremano agreed.

For the next few minutes, they discussed over steaming cups of coffee how they might help each other. And then Jahmshidi looked up and said, "Ah, here is Benjamin now. We can order."

"Am I late?" Bishara asked, looking puzzled that Sangremano and Jahmshidi were already seated at the table.

"Not at all," Jahmshidi replied. "In fact, you are early. We are all early." He smiled as he raised a hand to summon the waiter. "We must be hungry."

CHAPTER 22

Rabbi Yev Persky stood before the audience in Stuyvesant Hall and gave the prayer, first in Hebrew, then in English: *"Sh'ma Yisrael, Adonai Eloheinu, Adonai echad. Baruch shem kevod malchuto, l'olam va'ed.* Hear, O Israel, the Lord our God, the Lord is One. Praised be His name whose glorious kingdom is forever and ever."

He continued his prayer, adding verses from the New Testament and Qur'an, and ending it with, *"V'ahavta le're'e'cha kamocha.* And love your neighbor as yourself."

The number of attendees had increased steadily during the day, and now more than a thousand voices responded with an amen, bringing day two of the symposium to a close.

"A wonderful prayer, Rabbi," Imam Salim Madari said as he, Persky, and Fr. Michael Flannery stood talking while the delegates filed out of the hall. "I feel as if we made some real progress today."

"Thank you," Persky said. "I feel the same sense of hope. What do you think, Father Flannery?"

"I particularly appreciated what Imam Madari said at the opening of the session," Flannery replied. "In fact, I liked it so much that I wrote it down."

Flannery unfolded a piece of paper from his pocket and began to read.

" 'I am profoundly Muslim, but I recognize the importance of having a dialogue with Christians and Jews, emphasizing our common belief in the one and only God. In a sense, we are all ecumenical no matter our faith, as long as we remain brothers under God's keeping.'"

Flannery folded the paper and put it away.

"Gentlemen, as far as I'm concerned, if we come out of this meeting with a universal agreement upon that one theme, we will have achieved success."

"Yes," Persky agreed. "It also addresses the fears of so many of the protesters, that our individual faiths will lose their identity. I think this proves they will not."

"Ah, I see my friends," Flannery said. "Gentlemen, I look forward to tomorrow's session."

After exchanging good-byes with the clerics, Flannery walked over to where Preston and Sarah were standing.

"I haven't seen you around today," he noted.

"We ran across your friend, David Meyers," Sarah said.

"He's in New York? I thought he was still in Rome."

"He's with Ann Coopersmith," Preston said.

"Still playing the sleuth?"

"Yes. And he may have uncovered something very disturbing."

"In what way?"

"A dirty bomb," Sarah said, then explained how David had intercepted e-mail that appeared to connect Mehdi Jahmshidi with a medical waste disposal company. "There's not that much radioactive material involved, but within close confines, not much is needed."

"Did you tell the police?"

"I talked to Lieutenant Santini, but he wouldn't promise anything more than to try to equip the security guards with Geiger counters."

"Well, forewarned is forearmed," Flannery said. "With the police alerted, I'd think it would be difficult to bring something like that into the hall."

"I don't know," Sarah said. "One thing I've learned is to never underestimate the ingenuity of someone determined to do you harm—especially if he's willing to sacrifice his own life."

"By the way, you didn't happen to see your old friend Sangremano today, did you?" Preston asked. "If he's involved in all this, he may try to sneak in as a delegate."

"No, I didn't. But I find it hard to believe he'd be a party to something that could kill hundreds, maybe thousands of people."

"What about the planes that went down?" Preston asked.

"That has the trappings of Arkaan. We have no proof Sangremano or anyone else was involved in that. Via Dei is not above murder, that's for sure, but mass murder?" Flannery shook his head doubtfully.

"I know you don't want to think that about a fellow priest," Preston said. "But you remember what happened in the Jerusalem catacombs, don't you?"

"Of course," Flannery replied. "I'll never forget the catacombs."

"Sangremano killed two of his accomplices, and he would have killed you, too."

"Indeed, he tried," Sarah put in. "But for now the only person linked to a possible dirty bomb is Mehdi Jahmshidi, and it wouldn't be unlike him to do something like this on his own. But Sangremano has allied himself with Jahmshidi, which makes him an accomplice, whether or not he takes part or even knows about it."

FLANNERY LAY IN bed that night thinking about what his friends had said. Could Antonio Sangremano, formerly a top official in the Vatican's Prefecture of the Sacred Apostolic Palaces, be involved in a plot to down airliners merely to stop an ecumenical symposium? Was he really so evil? Or was he so desperate to keep secret the message of the Dismas scroll that he believed he was doing the Lord's work, regardless of the number of innocent victims?

As he drifted off to sleep, he found himself reliving that day a year earlier when he confronted Antonio Sangremano in the catacombs at the Mount of Olives.

FR. MICHAEL FLANNERY was led down a long flight of stone steps. As he descended, the air became cool and dank, and there was a musty, familiar scent that he recognized at once, because he had been here several times before. Even without being able to see through the hood, he knew he was in the catacombs of Jerusalem.

At the bottom, his captors led him through a doorway and into a room, where at last they removed his hood and cut free the plastic tie binding his arms. As he stood rubbing his wrists, he looked around the long stone chamber lit by a few flickering candles. The ancient Christian graffiti revealed his precise location: the catacombs on the Mount of Olives.

Flannery was led through a passageway to a second, smaller room. Lit by torches, this chamber was considerably brighter, revealing three ossuaries in the same positions they had occupied for the last two thousand years. One, he knew, was the stone coffin of Shimon bar Yonah—the original name of the Apostle Peter. Another, bearing cross marks, read: "Shlom-zion, daughter of Simon the Priest." Flannery had been in this very spot before.

In the center of the room was a table covered with white linen. Seated behind the table were three men in white ecclesiastical robes. They wore masks, but not the hooded ones used by his kidnappers. These were the type worn by revelers at masked balls. Somehow, the masks with their paganlike satiric connotations, paired with priestly vestments, seemed a sacrilege against the holy orders.

But what really caught his eye was the bright red symbol embroidered on the front of the linen. It was the sign of Via Dei, similar to but not precisely the same as the one on the scroll of Dismas bar-Dismas.

"Sit down, please, Father Flannery," the man in the middle of the triumvirate said, indicating the facing chair. His voice held no anger, only a cajoling warmth.

"You know my name," Flannery said without surprise as he sat down across the table from the three men.

"Of course we do." He motioned for Flannery's kidnappers to depart, and as they filed out of the room, he turned back to the priest. "In fact, Father Flannery, we know everything there is to know about you."

"Do you, now?"

"When you were seventeen, you won the Irish National fifteen-hundred-meter race. Your trainer, the famous Irish runner Ron Delaney, wanted you to work toward the Olympics, but even then, you wanted to enter the priesthood."

"That was in the newspapers," Flannery said. "It couldn't have been that hard for you to look up."

"What about Mary Kathleen O'Shaughnessy? Will I find her name in the newspapers? She thought you were going to marry her, didn't she?"

Flannery didn't reply. That episode had been one of the most difficult periods of his life, and it wasn't something he wanted to talk about, especially with someone who had brought him here against his will.

"You broke her heart when you became a priest. Not a parish priest, mind you, but a Jesuit, an honored scholar, with a major in archaeology. You are now regarded as the leading religious archaeologist in the Catholic Church, and indeed, one of the leading archaeologists in the world." The man paused, his lips curling into a smile. "But there came a time when you realized you had a problem . . . a drinking problem."

"I have not had a drink—"

"In twelve years, nine months, two weeks, and three days," his inquisitor interjected.

"All right," Flannery acquiesced. "You do know quite a bit about me. Now I want to know who you are."

"I think you already know, Father Flannery." The man gestured toward the symbol on the linen covering. "After all, we did try to recruit you once. You do recall that, don't you?"

"Yes, I remember."

"Father Flannery, we are offering you a second chance now to join us . . . to become a member of Via Dei."

"Why would I want to do that?"

"Who exactly do you think we are?"

"A secretive organization, like the Knights Templar."

"We are not a modern-day Knights Templar, though indeed, one of our most illustrious members, Peter the Hermit, first preached the Crusades and was a mentor to those who founded the Knights Templar. Our members also served with the Legions of Constantine and the armies of Charlemagne. We advised Jeanne d'Arc; we were at the Battle of Constantinople, and with the founders of the New World. Ah, yes, Father Flannery, our movement is a noble and holy order, begun and ordained by Jesus Christ himself to protect the Church and his blessed name."

"You believe Via Dei was personally founded by Jesus?"

"I do."

"I have done some of my own research," Flannery said. "I know that the Via Dei have been excommunicated from the Church. Why would the Church do that if, as you say, it was founded by Jesus?"

"We have our enemies, even within the Vatican."

"Is it any wonder you have enemies? The Church is blamed for the Spanish Inquisition, the murder of hundreds of thousands of Jews and Muslims during the Middle Ages, the slaughter of innocents in the New World. Upon closer examination, it appears that these acts were encouraged by a secret cabal within the Church. Might that be Via Dei?"

"If Via Dei appears sinister, Father Flannery, it is only a mask—like the ones we are wearing. We don such a mask in order to keep out prying eyes. Our members are not

Church outcasts who have created their own society within the greater whole. Indeed, we count among our membership many of the popes who have sat on the throne of St. Peter."

"What do you want with me?" Flannery said impatiently.

"We have brought you before this tribunal to offer you a great honor. We will admit you, this very day, into our ranks, conferring not only full membership but also knowledge of the deepest mysteries of our Mother Church. Father Flannery, these are secrets you have spent a lifetime trying to uncover. They are known to a precious few—to an elite even among Via Dei. All this we offer you."

"That's why I was kidnapped?"

"I would prefer to say, that is why we had you brought to us."

"Do Islamist terrorists recruit all your initiates?" Flannery said pointedly. "Or just me?"

"We have an unusual situation and a unique opportunity now," the leader of the tribunal replied. "As you know, 'misery acquaints a man with strange bedfellows.' And in our current situation, let's just say that it serves our interests to ally ourselves with some of those bedfellows against a mutual enemy."

There was something about the man's vocal pattern and the way he quoted Shakespeare's *The Tempest* that struck Flannery as familiar, but he couldn't quite place it.

"What's the catch?" Flannery asked. "You can't want me because I'm such a prize. There has to be some catch."

"Ah, yes, the catch. Well, it is simple—something that, as a member of Via Dei, you will want to do, for once the full mysteries are revealed, you will understand that what we ask is merely the fulfillment of God's plan."

With that, he turned and nodded to the man on his right, who reached under the table and lifted a heavy object. Even as he was placing it atop the table, Flannery recognized it as the urn unearthed at Masada.

"Yes, the scroll of Dismas bar-Dismas," the leader continued.

His smile hardened into a scowl as he turned the urn onto its side to reveal that it was empty.

"We had made arrangements to obtain the scroll, but unfortunately, even the best-laid schemes of Via Dei 'gang aft a-gley,' and leave us naught but grief and pain for promised joy," he said, paraphrasing the famous poem by Robert Burns about plans going astray. He seemed amused by his own verbal play, and his smile returned. "And so, the catch, as you so eloquently put it, is that you shall bring us the Dismas scroll."

"Why do you need the scroll?" Flannery asked. "Once our research is finished, its contents will be evaluated by the Church and a determination made as to whether or not it is to be included in the Holy Word. But even if it isn't, the full text will be published—the Israelis will insist on that. So either way, within or without the Church, you will have access to everything the scroll contains."

"That is not enough," the man shot back, the first hint of annoyance in his tone. "It is very meet, right, and our bounden duty that we should at all times, and in all places, have control of the scroll."

Flannery looked curiously at the masked man, who had used such an archaic expression. Even more peculiar was that it was not Catholic but from the Anglican Book of Common Prayer: *It is very meet, right, and our bounden duty, that we should at all times, and in all places, give thanks unto thee, O Lord, holy Father, almighty, everlasting God.* Either he was subtly pointing out that the influence of Via Dei extended beyond the Catholic Church, or this was but another example of the man's penchant for literary allusion.

Again Flannery was reminded of someone he knew but could not quite place. Filing away the observation for the time being, he leaned closer to the table and asked, "Does

Via Dei wish to possess the scroll, or merely keep the world from learning its secrets?"

The spokesman sighed. "All right, Father Flannery, I am going to tell you something that has never been revealed to anyone outside Via Dei during the two thousand years of our existence. We know that the symbol—our symbol—is found on the Dismas document. Suppose I tell you that the symbol of Via Dei was given directly to Dismas bar-Dismas by Jesus Christ himself, who appeared to Dismas on the road from Jerusalem the day after his resurrection."

"It was given to Dismas?" Flannery asked.

"Yes."

"That is what your legend tells you?"

"It is not legend, sir; it is truth!" the leader declared, his tone sharpening noticeably.

"It is sometimes hard to separate legend from fact," Flannery countered.

"Fact, yes, but not truth. And surely, Father Flannery, you are intelligent enough to know the difference between the two."

"Yes, I know the difference. But in this case truth is not good enough. You are asking me to help you obtain one of the most important documents ever discovered in the history of Christianity, knowing full well that you will deny the world and the wider body of Christians access to that document. To even consider such an action, I will need fact. What facts have you?"

"We have the fact that Dismas wrote his gospel long before those of Matthew, Mark, Luke, John, or even any of Paul's epistles. We have the fact that Dismas gave his scroll to his successor, Gaius of Ephesus, who then founded Via Dei. Therefore the Gospel of Dismas, by rights, belongs to us. But somehow, at the very beginnings of Via Dei, the scroll was lost, and we alone, for two thousand years, have known of its existence and have searched the earth for it."

As Flannery listened, he suddenly remembered where he had heard that voice before.

"What proof do we have?" the man continued. "Why, the Via Dei symbol itself. Do you think it mere coincidence that a first-century document bears the very symbol long held sacred to our organization? Isn't that proof enough that Dismas bar-Dismas is the father of Via Dei, through his successor and our founder, Gaius of Ephesus, and that his gospel must by all rights be returned to us?"

"And you want me to return it," Flannery stated.

"In so doing, you will be fulfilling an act of God."

"What about the murder of Daniel Mazar? Was that an act of God?"

The man hesitated, apparently having been unaware that Flannery knew of what happened at the lab. His tone grew strained, defensive, as he declared, "The professor was killed by Palestinian terrorists."

"But you are in possession of the urn."

"Yes."

"If terrorists killed Professor Mazar, how is it that you have the urn?" Flannery pressed. "Was it the work of those strange bedfellows you spoke of?"

"It . . . it wasn't supposed to happen that way," the man replied, sounding increasingly uncomfortable. "We sought only the scroll, not anyone's death."

"Those bedfellows of yours killed not only Daniel Mazar but three Israeli guards. When you unleashed them, did you really expect anything less would happen, or did you merely wash your hands of it?" When the man hesitated, Flannery added, "As you wash your hands of so many things at the Prefettura dei Sacri Palazzi Apostolici, Father Sangremano?"

The man seemed to reel back at being identified as Fr. Antonio Sangremano, one of the most powerful men in the Prefecture of the Sacred Apostolic Palaces, which administered the papal palaces and served as the State Department of the Vatican. Regaining his composure, he began to speak but was interrupted by one of his comrades.

"Michael, m'lad . . ."

Flannery turned in surprise to the man on the right. "My God," he gasped, for he knew this priest, as well. "Father Wester, you?"

Sean Wester, the archivist who had been Flannery's friend for so many years, sighed as he removed his mask and laid it on the table in front of him. "Michael," he repeated. "Like a son, I have loved you all these years. Like a son." He ran his hand through his hair, then shook his head, almost sadly. "The time has come, Michael, m'lad. Where do your loyalties lie? Do they lie with the Holy Roman Catholic Church and Via Dei, an instrument of its protection, created and ordained by Jesus Christ himself? Or do you ally yourself with the enemies of the Church?"

Flannery shook his head. "I do not consider myself an enemy of the Church."

"Then you will lead us to that which is rightly ours? The sacred scroll of Dismas bar-Dismas?"

"I don't know where it is."

"You are lying, Father Flannery," the tribunal leader said from behind his mask. "You have been a part of their team from the very beginning. You have seen the scroll; you have touched it, smelled it, read it. Don't you see? . . . You have already achieved something that generations of members of our organization have not been able to accomplish. That is why we consider you worthy of entry into the deepest level of Via Dei."

"Yes, I have done all those things," Flannery admitted. "But the scroll is still the property of the Israelis. After our initial inspection, we've had access only to photocopies. The scroll itself has been kept in a vault with the urn, and if it wasn't there when your agents raided the lab, then I have no idea where it is today. Or perhaps those bedfellows of yours found it but are holding out on you."

"Tell me this, Michael," Wester said. He placed his palms on the table and leaned toward Flannery. "And it's the truth I'll be wanting and expecting from an old friend. If you knew where the scroll was—and I understand you do not—but if you did, would you be willing to tell us?"

"Not for a minute," Flannery replied resolutely.

Wester leaned back in his chair, his eyes registering intense sorrow and regret. "I was afraid of that." He looked over at the other two. "We've done all we can do. We'll get nothing more from Father Flannery."

The man in the middle removed his mask then, confirming that he was Fr. Antonio Sangremano, first secretary to the subprefect of the Prefettura dei Sacri Palazzi Apostolici, a powerful Vatican insider known for sprinkling his speech with quotations.

The third inquisitor also removed his mask, and Flannery recognized him as Boyd Kern, an American lawyer who served as counsel to the Inquisitor of the Tribunal of the Prefecture. Like Sangremano, Kern held a position quite high within the hierarchy of the Church.

As Flannery looked from one man to the other, he came to the sudden realization that he was undoubtedly the only nonmember of Via Dei who could identify these three men as key members of an organization that for two thousand years had gone to great lengths to guard its secrecy.

"I'm not going to get out of here alive, am I?" Flannery said with no trace of fear or pleading in his voice. Rather he evinced a calm acceptance of his fate.

"I'm sorry, Michael," Father Wester replied.

"Tell me one thing first. How high does this go . . . in the Vatican, I mean?"

"The Vatican?" Wester asked, looking momentarily confused. "You think all this is at the bidding of the Vatican? You don't understand Via Dei . . . not really. The Vatican is no more than a sideshow. A means. Via Dei is the end. The alpha and the omega."

"Tell me, Sean, are you the one who's going to kill me?"

"Father Wester is under enough strain," Sangremano interjected. "Do not increase that strain by pleading for your life."

"I have no intention of doing so," Flannery declared.

"That is to your credit, and it confirms why you would make a valuable addition to Via Dei. This is your last chance. Are you going to help us?"

" 'What you are going to do, do quickly,' " Flannery stated, using the words Jesus had uttered in commanding Judas to deliver him to his death.

Raising his hand, Sangremano extended his thumb and two fingers and drew a cross in the air. *"In Nomine Patris, et Filii, et Spiritus Sancti. Amen,"* he intoned. "May God have mercy on your soul."

He turned toward the doorway that led to the entry hall and clapped three times. There was a single clap, sharper and louder, in return.

Sangremano clapped again and shouted, "Come in here!"

He was answered by a flurry of reports, and this time Flannery realized it wasn't hands clapping but gunshots echoing through the catacombs.

"Father Flannery! Get down!" a woman's voice echoed from beyond the chamber.

With the athleticism that had made him a good runner in his youth, Flannery dived from the chair and rolled behind the ossuary of Shlom-zion. A bullet ricocheted off the wall behind him, and he spun around to see that Sangremano had pulled a revolver from beneath his robe and was waving it about wildly. Flannery ducked to avoid another shot, then saw that Father Wester had leaped in front of Sangremano and was struggling for the gun. There was a muffled report, and Wester's body jerked backwards. He slumped to the floor, his lifeless hands releasing their grip on the other man's arm.

Someone appeared in the doorway, and Sangremano got

off a round, forcing the person back. His next bullet centered on Boyd Kern's chest, and as a crimson pool spread across the front of his snow-white vestments, Kern dropped to his knees, his lips silently mouthing the word *Why?* as he sprawled facedown on the stone floor, one arm reaching out toward his killer. But Sangremano was already gone, having snatched a torch off the wall and disappeared into a small passageway at the back of the chamber.

CHAPTER 23

NEW YORK CITY

Even as Michael Flannery lay in bed grappling with his memories, fifteen miles away in Flushing, in the borough of Queens, several men were arriving at Saint Bonavita Catholic Church for a special meeting. They walked through the darkened parking lot toward a side entrance, carrying canvas bags that held their ceremonial robes.

Saint Bonavita was named after an obscure saint of the fourteenth century, known for his charitable works and deep prayer life. The church guide listed its outreach programs and the various groups that used the church for a meeting place. One group identified itself as a "men's group providing information aimed at helping people develop their spiritual life and apostolate." Very few parishioners realized that the men's group was a chapter of Via Dei.

Although Via Dei had been disavowed by the Vatican in 1890, it had merely gone underground and was now so secret that few bishops or even cardinals were aware it still existed. The entry in the *Catholic Encyclopedia* regarded Via Dei as an oddity of history.

Via Dei (Latin for "The Way to God") was a very secretive international prelature of the Roman Catholic Church, comprising ordinary lay people and secular priests headed by a prelate known as the Grand Master. The organization

made the claim that it was founded by Jesus after His res-
urrection. Active during the Crusades; some attribute the
origin of the Knights Templar to Via Dei. In 1890, Via Dei
was disavowed by Pope Leo XIII, who said in his Papal
Bull: "Those who belong to Via Dei, though making claims
to serve the Lord, are heretics who, in their secret initia-
tions and meetings, use the holy name of Jesus to secure
power within the Church. From this day and for all time,
Via Dei is outside the protection of the Church."

Despite the papal bull, Via Dei continued to recruit members, called Disciples of the Way and assigned to secret cells
throughout the world. Saint Bonavita housed the largest cell
in America and the largest outside Rome.

The dress code for regular meetings was extremely casual,
with members attending in everything from work clothes to
golf outfits. On special occasions, such as initiations and tonight's visit by the Grand Master, the disciples wore their
official garb of brown cassocks and hoods. Emblazoned in
bloodred over the heart of the cassocks was the Via Dei
symbol containing elements of the Cross, the Star of David,
and the Star and Crescent.

When the dozen members had formed a circle in the
church sanctuary, the beadle opened the meeting by asking,
"Grand Master, would you do us the honor of reciting The
Order of Sanctity?"

"I would be honored," Antonio Sangremano replied.

Each disciple sank to his knees, bowed his head, and
clasped his hands together, gripping a small whip that sym-
bolized both the scourging of the Lord and the one each had
endured upon being initiated into Via Dei.

"Renounce your own will for the salvation of your soul.
Strive everywhere with pure desire to serve the Holy Trinity
of Via Dei, the Catholic Church, and Jesus Christ. Feel now
the pain of the scourging received by our Lord."

In unison the disciples lashed their backs with their whips and exclaimed, "This I will do, so help me God."

"It is a dangerous thing to gaze too long upon the face of a woman. Avoid the kiss or embrace of a woman lest you be contaminated by the sin of lust. Remain eternally before the face of God with a pure conscience and a sure life."

"This I will do, so help me God," they responded as they again lashed themselves.

"Avoid idle words and laughter. There is much sin in any conversation that is not for the glory of the Lord."

"This I will do, so help me God," came the response, punctuated by the snap of the whips.

"In order to fulfill your holy duties so that you may gain the glory of the Lord's mercy and escape the torments of hellfire, you must obey the Grand Master of our Sacred Order of Via Dei. Do you swear now, so to do?"

They lashed themselves yet again. "I swear to always obey our Grand Master."

"The Sacred Order of Via Dei, the Catholic Church, and our blessed Lord are the trinity that guides our lives, symbolic of the Holy Trinity of Father, Son, and Holy Spirit. You will protect the sanctity of Via Dei by whatever means necessary. There is only one path to salvation, and it is the mission of Via Dei to protect that path. Destroying an enemy of Via Dei is doing the work of the Lord. Do you accept our doctrine?"

Once more the whips flailed, and the disciples cried out, "I accept the doctrine."

"Rise now, Disciples of the Way, and greet one another in brotherhood."

After each man had acknowledged the person on either side, Sangremano made a speech that focused on the ecumenical symposium that was taking place in Manhattan. After giving some background on how it had been organized and the major players behind the People of the Book movement, he said, "We must not let this symposium succeed, for it seeks nothing less than to merge all religions into one false doctrine. Would you see our Lord, Jesus Christ, declared nothing more than a prophet, on the order of Moses and Muhammad? Our Holy Catholic Church, which has civilized and Christianized the world for the last two millennia, will exist no more."

"No!" someone shouted.

"Never!" another added.

"Then what are you prepared to do?" Sangremano challenged. "How great is your love and how far are you willing to go in order to prevent such a blasphemy?"

"All the way!" a disciple shouted.

"Whatever it takes!"

IT WAS NEARLY midnight before the meeting began to break up, primarily because so many of the disciples wanted to speak to the head of Via Dei, to kiss his ring and receive a personal blessing. One disciple hung back, watching the others crowd around the Grand Master while making no effort to get closer himself. He was a tall, gangly fellow with nondescript features. Sangremano took particular notice of him and waited for him to come over, but the man kept to himself, even as the crowd thinned.

Finally, it was Sangremano who approached and broke the ice. "Is there something I can do for you, brother?" he asked, extending his hand.

The man kissed the Grand Master's ring. "We have spoken by e-mail and phone. I am the Hermit."

Sangremano smiled. "At last we meet. Come, let's go outside."

When they were alone in the darkened parking lot, the man who called himself the Hermit said, "I ran a check on Benjamin Bishara and Mehdi Jahmshidi, as you requested."

"What have you found?" Sangremano asked.

"Nothing on Bishara. But your friend Jahmshidi has been very busy."

"Busy doing what?"

"For one thing, getting his hands on some nuclear material."

Sangremano's eyes widened in shock. "A bomb? Are you telling me that Jahmshidi has an atomic bomb?"

"No. But he does have radioactive material, enough to make a dirty bomb."

"Do you know what he plans to do with it?"

"Based on some of his communiqués with associates, my best guess is that he plans to use it at the symposium."

"How big a blast will it produce?"

Hermit shook his head. "It's not the blast that is important. It's the radioactivity that will be released."

"I see."

"There's one thing I don't understand," the Hermit said.

"What's that?"

"When the head of Arkaan does something, he likes to generate as much publicity as possible. If he releases some radioactivity, it will cause cancer, yes, and probably a lot of the people who are exposed will ultimately die from it. But it's not instantaneous. Most will die quite a few years after exposure."

"I see what you mean," Sangremano said, breathing in deeply as he weighed the information. "Any political statement made by such a bomb would be greatly diluted by the time factor."

"Exactly."

"Well, I suppose we'll have to wait and see what happens, won't we?" Sangremano said.

"I suppose so. In the meantime, I am to be your bodyguard."

"I beg your pardon?"

"I am your bodyguard," the Hermit repeated. "New York can be a rough town, especially for a stranger. I was selected by our beadle to ensure that you get safely to your apartment tonight."

"I see. While I assume you have experience in this area, I confess you do not appear the bodyguard type."

The disciple grinned. "Many have mistaken my physique for weakness, when in fact it contributes to speed and surprise. After military service, I spent years studying martial arts. It has proved valuable in my day job."

"What is your profession?" Sangremano asked. "And if we're going to be working together, I'd rather call you by your name than Hermit."

"I'm one of New York's Finest." He held out his hand. "Frank Santini, proud to be at your service."

"And I'm pleased you'll be at my side, Officer Santini."

"Lieutenant," he corrected.

"Ah, Lieutenant Santini." Sangremano shook his hand. "I'm grateful that you and your fellow disciples are going to such efforts to assure my safety."

ANN COOPERSMITH SAT reading the *Daily News* on the couch in David Meyers's East Ninety-third Street apartment while he sat nearby at the dining room table, tapping away on his laptop. She turned the page and began a short metro story:

POLICE STILL BAFFLED
BY MYSTERY OF MISSING MAN
by Adriana Wilcox
Daily News Staff Writer

Devoted husband Nicholas Joiner, who was working as a bellman at the Dunn Hotel on Columbus Circle, was weeks away from getting a degree at night school when he mysteriously disappeared.

"It was his birthday," mourned Diane Parker, Joiner's

anguished bride of two months, who reported him missing Thursday when he did not show up for a cele-bratory dinner party she had planned. "He was going to start teaching school next year. He already had a job lined up and was so looking forward to it. It just isn't like him to take off without telling me or his mom. I fear that something terrible has happened to him."

The Dunn Hotel concierge told police that Joiner had been summoned to a guest's room, but the guest reported that he never showed up. The police are ask-ing anyone who might have seen Joiner or know his whereabouts to contact them.

Fellow hotel employees said that Joiner was univer-sally admired for his tenacity in pursuing his dream of becoming a high school social studies teacher. He had spent six years attending classes at . . .

Ann was interrupted by David's calico cat, which jumped onto the couch and into her lap. Tossing the newspaper onto the coffee table, she kicked off her shoes and curled her legs beneath her as she gently stroked the cat.

"Where did you leave T while you were traveling around the world?" she asked David.

He nodded toward the ceiling. "My upstairs neighbors kept him."

"That was nice of them."

"Well, they felt they owed me."

"For what?"

"John Kersey is a Korean War vet who draws a pension for a wound he got in the army. There was some mix-up somewhere, and he didn't get his check for three months. I tapped into the system, found what was wrong, straightened it out, and got him his money, plus interest."

Ann smiled. "You're a good man to know, David."

T purred and rubbed his head against her arm.

"I think your cat likes me," she said with a little laugh.

"T, you're a dog. You'd go home with her in a minute, wouldn't you?"

"Don't listen to him, T. He's just jealous, that's all." She turned back to David. "Why do you call him T, anyway?"

"*T* for 'trouble.' He was nothing but trouble when I found him. He used to pick through the garbage cans out back, and people would throw things at him. I sort of adopted him—or he adopted me."

"Good for both of you." She gave the cat a vigorous rub, which he seemed to relish. "And you are one lucky cat, Mr. T."

"No!" David exclaimed. "Just T. Never Mr."

She snuggled her face against the cat's and whispered, "I can call you whatever I want, can't I?"

"Aha! I found him!" David suddenly exclaimed.

"Who? Jahmshidi?"

"Yes. He's using the name Hassan al-Halid, and he's staying at the Dunn Hotel on Columbus Circle."

"That's odd," Ann said, reaching over and picking up the newspaper again. "I was just reading about a bellman at that hotel who disappeared."

"What bellman?" David said almost distractedly as he continued to type on the laptop.

"At the Dunn Hotel," Ann repeated. She tapped the paper. "It's in the *Daily News*."

Coming over from the table, David took the tabloid from her and quickly read the article.

"It says he was on his way to see a guest when he went missing. I wonder what the room number was."

"Why?" Ann asked.

"Maybe this isn't as big a coincidence as it seems."

"You think Jahmshidi may have had something to do with it?"

"It's possible," David said.

"That's a bit of a stretch, isn't it? Just because they're in the same hotel doesn't mean Jahmshidi is involved. I mean, what's the motive?"

"I don't know, but I can try to find out if this goes any deeper."

"How?"

"Most hotels keep their room calls in their computer. All I have to do is tap in and see what room called."

"How will you do that?" she asked.

"They take credit cards, so they must be online. And if they're online, I can get in."

David spent the next few minutes tapping away on the laptop, following what proved to be a blind alley. He started over, and a short time later exclaimed, "I'm in!" He started typing hurriedly. "Here it is. Nicholas Joiner's last call was to—son of a bitch." He said the words with awe, almost reverence.

"What is it?" Ann asked, pushing the cat off her lap and going over to the dining room table.

"He was summoned to room 911."

"The date of the World Trade Center attack," she said as the reality sank in.

"And that's no coincidence," David continued. "According to hotel records, the guest in room 911 is—"

"Hassan al-Halid?" she said.

"Precisely. Our very own Mehdi Jahmshidi."

"He must be involved or at least know what happened to that poor bellman."

"And what do you propose we do?" David asked. "March over there and demand the truth?"

"Why not?" Ann replied. "We reporters do that all the time. It's called aggressive journalism."

"It's also called dangerous," David countered. "Don't forget, this guy already murdered nearly four hundred people on those planes. There would have been more—me included—if he had succeeded in downing our flight."

"Which you managed to stop. Which is why I want you to go with me."

"To do what?"

"To interview Mehdi Jahmshidi. Safety in numbers, you know."

"Ann, maybe you didn't notice," David said as he bent his arm to make a muscle, "but there's not much here. Nada. Zilch."

Ann laughed. "I'm not talking about you protecting me physically. My lord, I'm stronger than you are."

"Then what sort of protection can I offer?"

"Your mind, David. You're the smartest person I've ever met."

"So, I'm supposed to protect you with my mind? How do you figure that?"

"How am I supposed to know? You're the smart one," she replied.

David stared at her for a long moment; then he started chuckling. "I'll prove how wrong you are about how smart I am," he declared. "I'm so dumb that I'm gonna go with you."

"Good!" She leaned over and kissed his cheek.

"Wow, that was easy," David said, grinning self-consciously. "All I had to do was agree to risk my life."

"Other men have done far more for a kiss from me," Ann teased. "Now, bring along that laptop, and let's see if you can earn yourself another."

CHAPTER 24

WEST OF CONSTANTINOPLE

Philippe Guischard stood outside the blacksmith's tent, which was little more than a high canvas roof suspended on poles with a circular opening in the middle to vent whatever smoke did not disperse through the open sides. The taut canvas shook like a drum with each blow of the blacksmith's hammer, punctuated by a flash of white sparks that burst from the hellish red glow of the forge.

Entering the tent, Philippe laid a cautious hand on the hilt of his short sword and approached the open forge. He felt a twinge of fear as he wondered why Walter the Penniless had summoned him to such a place. The blacksmith was silhouetted in the light of the burning coals, and as Philippe's eyes adjusted to the light, he realized with a start that the man was in fact Walter himself. The soldier leader was working on a piece of glowing, red-hot steel, holding it with tongs as he hammered it against the anvil. Bright white sparks flew with the fall of each hammer blow.

"You are with Tobias Garlande, are you not?" Walter asked, hardly glancing at Philippe as he continued to hammer. The steel was taking the shape of a long dagger, and he submerged it in water, causing a gush of steam.

"Yes, I am with Tobias," Philippe replied.

Walter held the piece of steel up, looked at it, then laid it back on the anvil and started hammering again. "Do you believe as he does?" he asked over the sound of ringing steel on steel.

"What do you mean?"

"I am told the old man believes the ancient myth that there are three or even myriad paths to God, rather than the one true road."

"Yes, that is what Tobias believes."

"And you?" Walter raised the hammer a moment as he examined the younger man's face, waiting for an answer. "What do you believe, Philippe Guischard?"

"I believe in the one true path to God through His son, Jesus Christ. As for three paths, the only three that are one lie within the Holy Trinity."

Walter nodded, then began striking the steel again. Between the ringing hammer blows, he said, "I could have someone forge this blade for me. But I may have to depend on it, and if so, I like the assurance of knowing it has been properly fashioned."

"Yes. I have always believed that a wise policy."

"It is the same with an army of men. When I lead them into battle, I must know they have been properly trained and their ranks properly filled." He gave the blade a final mighty strike, then leaned away from the anvil and sighed. "I grow weary of waiting."

"Waiting?" Philippe asked.

"I joined this expedition to carry my sword for the Lord so that we might rid the Holy Land of infidels. And I brought with me many who are driven by the same noble purpose."

He dipped the steel in the water again. This time he left it there as he wiped the back of his hand across his face. His forearms were pocked with tiny scars from the glowing embers.

"But my soldiers grow fat and lazy, and they defile themselves with the whores of the camp because their sins have been forgiven. We grow weaker by the day, yet still we remain here, waiting."

"Yes . . ." Philippe didn't know what else to say or what was expected of him. He both hoped and feared that Walter would get to the point of why he had been summoned.

"Do you know what I think, Philippe?"

"No, m'lord, I do not."

"I believe Peter's resolve to march on the Holy Land has weakened. And I believe it has weakened because of the influence of Tobias."

"Why do you say that? I didn't think Peter held Tobias in such regard."

"Tobias visited Peter recently, after the purification of the Muslim prisoners. Tobias was upset that the infidels were killed, and he spoke to Peter about it."

"Yes, that is my understanding."

"It has had its effect on Peter," Walter said.

"In what way?"

"Something Tobias said or did is causing Peter to lose his will." Walter pulled the knife blade from the water and felt its point. Satisfied, he laid it down to cool more slowly in the air.

"Peter the Hermit is a courageous and reverent man," Philippe said. "I do not believe he can be influenced by another. Especially one who espouses heresy."

"And yet, something strange happened during their last meeting," Walter insisted. "Since that meeting, Peter has not been the same. That is why I summoned you."

"But what has that to do with me?"

"You are Tobias's companion. Because you follow him, whatever sin Tobias commits you commit as well."

"That isn't true. I believe in the one, true path to God," Philippe declared. "And I do not follow Tobias but travel with him only out of duty, bound to an oath I made to our Grand Master, who believes Peter and this pilgrimage to be the agents that will bring Tobias back into our fold."

"Ah, but I fear quite the opposite is happening, and the pilgrimage itself may be in danger from Tobias preaching his heresy." Walter came closer and gripped Philippe's shoulder. "The Grand Master is not here to advise us. But we both know that he would have us undertake whatever action is needed to protect Peter and our glorious cause. Would he not?"

"Of course. But how? What must we do?"

"We must stop Tobias from infecting Peter and others with his heresy. To do so, he must be eliminated."

"You mean killed, don't you?"

"Yes, and his servant girl, as well."

"No," Philippe declared, surprised at his boldness.

Walter's eyes narrowed in anger. "No?"

"Let me convince Tobias that he is wrong. A contrite and repentant Tobias will not only strengthen Peter's resolve, it will strengthen the resolve of all."

"You don't really believe you can turn a man like Tobias back to the true path, do you?"

"Let me try."

Walter tightened his grip on Philippe's shoulder. "And if you fail?"

"We both may still be able to get what we want."

Walter looked at him curiously. "What I want is to break camp and lead my men to Jerusalem, with or without Peter's peasant rabble. But what of you, Philippe Guischard? What, precisely, do you desire?"

WHEN PHILIPPE RETURNED to his own tent, he found Rachel Benyuli seated at the table with Tobias standing behind her, pointing at something on a scroll spread before them. Philippe felt a sudden surge of jealousy. Why was it that she allowed an old man to take such casual intimacy with her, while steadfastly rejecting any of his overtures? Didn't she realize that he held her life—and Tobias's, as well—in his hands? Without his intervention, Walter the Penniless and his men would be here now, making an end to them both.

"Ah, Philippe," Tobias said, looking up and smiling. "Did you have a pleasant walk?"

"Yes," Philippe responded almost sullenly. "What are you working on?"

"A transcription of the *Apologia*, written by Tatian in the third century. It's really quite fascinating."

"I've just been speaking with Walter the Penniless," Philippe announced as he moved past them, nervously gripping the hilt of his sword.

"Productive, was it?" Tobias said sarcastically.

"It was, and you should be thankful, as I convinced him to give me another chance to speak to the two of you."

"Oh?"

"Tobias, you are in danger, great danger." Philippe returned to the table and stood in front of them. "And Rachel, my dear, you are in the greatest danger of all. Tobias may survive, despite his heresy, because he is a Christian. But you don't even have that protection. You are a Jew, a non-believer."

"Why are you bringing this up now?" Tobias asked.

"Because I am concerned for you—for both of you. Walter fears your influence on Peter, and he warns of the most dire punishment for you both. But I begged him to let me speak to you one more time. Tobias, you must abandon this heresy of three paths to God. And Rachel, you must renounce your religion, convert to Christianity, and become my wife. That is your only salvation."

"I cannot and will not abandon my religion," Rachel declared. "And while I'm grateful for your concern, I won't marry someone I don't love. And I do not love you."

"Likewise, I will never turn my back on the truth of Trevia Dei," Tobias said.

Philippe pinched the bridge of his nose and shook his head. "In that case, your only hope is to run away."

"Run?" Rachel asked. "Run where? How?"

"I feared you'd be obdurate about this," he said, "so I

took the precaution of acquiring some horses. They're being held near the western edge of the encampment. Gather your things quickly, and I'll take you to them."

"And what of you, Philippe?" Tobias asked. "Will you be coming with us?"

"No."

"Won't you be in danger for helping us?"

"Great danger, I'm afraid," Philippe replied. "But I won't stand by and see the two of you killed, which is what will happen if you remain here."

Tobias stared at Philippe a long while, weighing the younger man's words and what they should do.

"I speak the truth, Tobias," Philippe insisted. "If you will not change your course, and if she will not convert, both of you will die."

"I believe you," Tobias proclaimed. "Which is why you must come with us."

"Don't fear for me. Walter wants you gone, one way or another, and you will be. He may be tempted to punish me, but I can convince him that I'll be more useful to him on the battlefield, where the Lord can take whatever vengeance He sees fit."

Tobias turned to Rachel. "Go and gather our things. I would have a word with Philippe before we leave."

Nodding, Rachel headed to the back of the tent, leaving the two men alone.

"Is there nothing I can say to convince you to join us?" Tobias asked.

Philippe shook his head. "My place is with the pilgrims. We are doing the Lord's work in reclaiming the Holy Land for His people."

"Very well, if that's your decision," Tobias said. "If there's nothing more I can do or say, then—"

"There is one thing, Tobias."

"Yes?"

Philippe looked over at Rachel, who was stowing their belongings and preparing for the journey. "I would speak with you alone," he said softly to Tobias, motioning for them to go outside.

When they had passed through the open flap of the tent, Tobias grasped the younger man's forearm. "What is troubling you, my friend?"

Philippe glanced around to confirm no one was nearby. Then he drew in a deep breath and declared, "I know that you bear a great secret."

"I have no secrets," the old man said dismissively.

"What of the necklace you wear and the treasure it contains?"

"This?" Tobias patted the front of his robe over the locket. "It is not a secret. It was a gift from a friend a long, long time ago."

"I know something of this gift," Philippe said. "I've known of it since my years under your tutelage in Toledo, yet I've told no one, not even the Grand Master. Is it not a gift that, one day, you must pass to another? Perhaps that time is now."

Tobias looked puzzled. "What are you saying?"

"Now is the time for you to pass the necklace and its knowledge to me."

Tobias drew in a deep breath. "Why should I do this?"

"You are in your final years, and your life is in danger. What if something should happen to you before you pass along the gift . . . what if its power were to fall into the wrong hands?"

"Power?"

"Yes."

"Power?" Tobias repeated. "Do you think that is what this is all about?"

"I know that you have been graced with immense power," Philippe said, "power that was bestowed upon you with the gift of that necklace. Many years ago, when you were deep in vision, I heard you speak of a Keeper—of many Keepers of this great secret. You are one of them, are you not?"

"And if I am?"

"Then now is the time for you to bestow that power on someone who understands its value and will wield it for good and for God."

Tobias pulled back from the younger man. Looking disheartened, he said, "I was wrong about you, Philippe. Even though you fell sway to those who have perverted the intent of Trevia Dei, I believed it was due to your religious fervor and that in time you'd rediscover the truth we have borne witness to since the days of Jesus Christ and his disciple, Dismas bar-Dismas. Now I see that your fervor is little more than a thirst for power." Tobias lifted the locket from beneath his robe. "This is what you want," he said. "But this you shall never have."

Philippe's expression hardened, his mouth twisting into a malevolent scowl. He was about to speak, when five knights on horseback came galloping through the encampment and pulled to a halt in front of the tent.

"Seize him!" the lead knight shouted, pointing his sword at Tobias. Just then Rachel appeared in the doorway, and the knight waggled his sword at her and said, "Seize both of them!"

"No!" Philippe cried out as he leaped between the horsemen and his companions.

"Stand aside!" the leader ordered.

"I will not!" Philippe exclaimed, drawing his own sword to do battle. "If you would seize them, you must first come through me!"

Two of the knights dropped down from their horses and approached, engaging him in battle. As their swords clashed, the blades rang loudly, reverberating through the encampment. Several pilgrims came out of their tents to see what the commotion was about. Seeing the armed knights, they quickly ducked back inside to avoid getting caught up in the conflict.

Philippe and his adversaries moved back and forth as they fought for advantage. The clanging continued as their shuffling feet kicked up sand and dust. Philippe weaved and bobbed, parrying a slashing attack here, returning with a long thrust, dancing about to keep the two men always in front of him.

Suddenly Philippe's sword was knocked from his hand, leaving him defenseless as one of the knights thrust his sword forward. With a groan, Philippe clutched his belly and fell facedown on the ground.

"Philippe!" Tobias called, rushing toward him.

"Get back!" the knight shouted, pulling him away from Philippe's prostrate form.

Dismounting, the leader strode over to Tobias. He drew his knife from its scabbard and made a wide slashing arc across the old man's throat.

"My lord!" Rachel gasped in alarm.

The knight stepped back, chuckling in amusement at the woman's scream and the fear in Tobias's eyes. His knife had drawn no blood. Instead, it had sliced the chain of Tobias's necklace, sending the locket spinning through the air. Tobias tried to go after it, but one of the knights jerked him back, while the leader pressed the tip of his knife against his throat, pushing in just enough to get his attention, then pulling the knife away.

Raising a hand to his throat, Tobias felt dampness, then saw some blood on his fingers.

"Next time it will be more," the leader said. Turning his back on Tobias, he remounted and called back to the other knights, "Take them away."

Two knights took hold of Tobias, the other two grabbed Rachel, and they dragged them over to where the horses were standing. When Tobias tried to look over his shoulder at Philippe, he was struck in the face.

"Keep your eyes straight ahead! Don't turn around. Don't try to run away."

"Please see to Philippe," Tobias begged. "I fear he's gravely hurt."

"Enough! Say nothing more unless you are spoken to!"

The knights looped a rope around Tobias and another around Rachel, then mounted back up. They started through the encampment, forcing their prisoners into an uncomfortable trot to keep up with them.

CHAPTER 25

WEST OF CONSTANTINOPLE

Y ou can get up now; they are gone," a voice said, and
Philippe Guischard turned his head and looked up to
see Walter the Penniless seated atop his horse, holding the reins of a second horse in tow.

Philippe raised himself onto his hands and knees and
looked around to confirm that Tobias and Rachel were no
longer in sight. Then he stood and brushed the dirt from his
tunic. There were no wounds on his body. He was totally uninjured as he stood scanning the ground around him.

"Let's go."

"Just a minute," Philippe said as he continued to search
the ground.

"What are you looking for?"

"It's nothing."

"Obviously it's something."

"Just a necklace. It belongs to Tobias."

Walter chuckled. "Well, he won't be needing it any longer.
Come, let's go."

"I'd like to have it," Philippe explained as he searched the
area.

Walter looked at him suspiciously. "This necklace, is it
worth a great deal?"

"No, not at all," Philippe lied, not wanting to reveal what
he suspected the locket contained. He halted and turned to
the knight. "It has sentimental value only."

"Then forget it," Walter declared. "We are here to serve the Lord. There is no place for sentimentality."

Philippe was about to protest but thought better of it. He took a last glance around, making sure the locket would not be found until he came back for it. Walking over to Walter, he looked up at the knight and said, "You will keep your promise?"

"The one we made at the blacksmith's tent when you told me what you really desire?" Walter said, grinning as he teased the younger man.

"You know what I'm talking about," Philippe said a bit petulantly.

"Yes, I will execute Tobias but let his young servant live."

"When I ransom her life," Philippe reminded him.

Walter hooked one leg over the saddlebow and laughed. "I must admit, this is pretty clever of you. The girl will think you defended her bravely, then paid to ransom her life. Out of gratitude, she will marry you."

Philippe allowed himself the hint of a smile.

"Unfortunately for you, she will not do it."

Philippe's smile vanished. "Of course she will."

Walter shook his head. "I know people like her, women of honor and integrity. She will not compromise herself to marry you, not out of gratitude, not out of admiration for your heroics, not even to save her own life."

"I don't believe you."

"Of course you don't. You possess neither honor nor integrity; therefore, you have no understanding of those who do."

"You'll see," Philippe insisted. "She'll marry me."

"Come, let's go," Walter said, tossing him the reins of the second horse.

For a moment Philippe forgot all about the locket and the treasure it contained, his thoughts filled instead with images of Rachel and how he would soon possess her as his wife. But as he mounted the horse and followed Walter, he suddenly felt something pull at him, and he turned back toward the tent. He thought he saw a flash of light, perhaps something silver that was reflecting the sun. He fixed the position in his mind, determined to return in a few hours and possess not only a woman but also a power only a few had ever witnessed.

THE FIVE KNIGHTS slowed their horses to a walk as they led Tobias and Rachel from the encampment and across an open field toward a prearranged meeting place in a small copse of trees. Hearing hoofbeats, one of them turned in his saddle and saw a knight closing on them at a gallop from the encampment.

"Is that Walter?" he called to his comrades.

"I'm not sure," the leader said as he strained to see through the cloud of dust from the approaching horse's hooves. The rider was dressed like them, but instead of wearing a light riding cap, he had on his iron casque battle helmet, which had a fitted nose protector that obscured his face.

Suddenly the rider was upon them, and they realized too late he was brandishing his sword. The curved, unusually thin blade flashed once, and the leader of the knights went tumbling from his saddle, his head nearly severed from his body. Another slashing motion and a second knight went down. The third was dispatched with a mighty thrust of the mysterious warrior's sword.

One of the two remaining knights shouted a curse as he dropped the rope that was secured to Rachel and spurred his horse forward. The other knight realized he was alone, and he released the rope that was tied around Tobias and galloped after his comrade.

The helmeted knight sheathed his sword and pointed at the riderless horses. "Get mounted, quickly!" he ordered. "Come with me."

"Where are you taking us?" Tobias asked.

"To safety," the man replied.

Freeing themselves from the ropes, Tobias and Rachel mounted two of the horses, then followed at a gallop as the knight led them away from the copse and the pilgrims' encampment beyond. After a ride of several minutes, they passed through a gathering of large boulders, and the stranger held up his hand, signaling them to halt.

"We need to let the horses rest," he said. "We should be safe here."

The knight dropped from his horse and walked over to Rachel, holding out his hand to help her dismount. After assisting Tobias, as well, he finally lifted the helmet from his head.

"It's you!" Rachel gasped.

Tobias also was staring at the tall olive-skinned man. "Don't I know you, sir?" he said cautiously.

The man gave a flourish with his hand, declaring, "I am al-Aarif of Toledo." He turned to Rachel and added, "Again, my lady, I have placed my sword in your service."

"A knight?" Rachel said in disbelief. "A Christian warrior?"

Al-Aarif's dark eyes flashed with humor. "They would hardly admit an infidel among their ranks. But I thought it best to wear this outfit while passing through the Christian lands." He reached into the folds of his tunic. "I believe this is yours," he said to Tobias, holding forth the Keeper's locket and broken chain.

"Yes!" Tobias said excitedly as he wrapped his hands lovingly around it. "How did you come by it?"

"I was in hiding in the encampment when they took you prisoner. I heard the commotion, but when I reached your tent, you were already gone. I found the necklace lying in the dirt and guessed it was yours."

"Philippe . . . do you know what happened to him?" Tobias asked.

"Philippe Guischard?"

"Yes. He was gravely wounded protecting us."

Al-Aarif shook his head. "I saw no sign of him. They must have taken him away."

"Why aren't you in Toledo?" Rachel asked.

"When Ferdinand of Castile and his men pillaged Toledo and took some Moors as prisoners, I followed in disguise. I have been hiding in the encampment ever since."

"Then you must have witnessed the murder of your fellow Muslims," Tobias said.

Al-Aarif nodded solemnly. "I saw it. I knew them well, but I was alone in a sea of hostility. I could do nothing."

"I'm so sorry," Rachel whispered. She reached out as if to touch his arm, then held back.

"Come," al-Aarif said. "Our horses are rested, and we must begin our journey."

"Are you taking us back to Toledo?" Tobias asked.

Al-Aarif shook his head. "No. We travel to Jerusalem."

"Jerusalem? Isn't that too dangerous?" Rachel asked.

"The journey, perhaps, but we will be treated as guests among the Saracens. We'll be safe there, at least until the pilgrim army arrives."

"But why Jerusalem?" she asked.

Al-Aarif looked at Tobias. "Ask him why we go. He knows. He was there, in my vision."

"It was you!" Tobias blurted. "Before we left Toledo, I had a vision of a man and woman burying a scroll in an urn at a place in the desert called Masada. Someone else was sharing my vision—a man, a Muslim. . . . You were the one I saw."

Al-Aarif nodded. "Yes, I was there. I watched, as you watched. And now we must find and rescue the scroll."

"What scroll?" Rachel asked. "And why is it so important that Tobias find it?"

"I can't answer that yet," al-Aarif replied. "I only know that Allah wants me to bring you to Masada."

Tobias reached out and gripped al-Aarif's arm. "Truly, you have been sent by God."

CHAPTER 26

NEW YORK CITY

The elevator doors opened, and Ann Coopersmith stepped out into the ninth-floor hallway of the Dunn Hotel. David Meyers extended his arm to keep the doors from closing and to hold the elevator in place.

"Ann, wait," he said.

"What for?"

"It's after ten."

"So?"

"He's probably in bed already."

"Nonsense, nobody goes to bed at ten o'clock. The news doesn't even come on until eleven."

"Still, I'm beginning to think this isn't such a good idea."

"Beginning? You've been whining ever since we left your apartment. Come on, don't be a wuss," she taunted.

David shook his head. "I thought you're counting on me being smart enough to protect you. Well, my mind tells me this isn't a good idea."

"Nothing's going to happen," Ann insisted.

"How do you know?"

"Because I've done this before. It's called ambush journalism. When you surprise someone, they don't have time to react. When their guard is down, they'll say things they had no intention of revealing."

"I'm sorry, but I just don't feel good about this."

Ann smiled. "Okay. Go back to the apartment. I'll talk to him, then meet you there and tell you what he said."

David felt the blood draining from his face, and his stomach rose to his throat. "You—you're going through with this, aren't you? No matter what I say?"

"Yes, but you don't have to. I'll be fine."

Summoning every ounce of courage, David stepped out into the hall and let the elevator doors close behind him. "If you're going, so am I."

Leaning into him, she kissed his cheek and whispered, "It'll be all right, David. Trust me."

As they walked slowly down the hall, they were startled when a door opened directly in front of them. A maid came out of the room, carrying a tray.

"Oh, por favor, perdóname, señor," the woman said.

"No es nada," David replied.

"It's nothing my foot," Ann teased as the maid left. "You nearly jumped out of your skin."

"Like you didn't?"

"Shh. We have to be serious."

They continued down the hall until they reached room 911. Looking at each other for a moment, they nodded in unison. Then Ann took a deep breath and knocked.

"Who is it?" The voice from inside was muffled.

"Mr. Mehdi Jahmshidi, I'm a reporter for *The New York Times.*"

"The *Times*?" David whispered.

"Well, I will be if I get this story," she replied.

The door was jerked open, and the man inside snapped, "What did you call me?"

"You're Mehdi Jahmshidi, are you not?" Ann asked.

"My name is al-Halid. Hassan al-Halid. You have the wrong person."

"Our mistake," David said. "Come on, let's go." He reached for Ann's arm, but she remained put.

"Mr. Jahmshidi, we aren't with the police or the FBI or any government agency. I'm a reporter, and I just want to get your side of the story before it breaks in the media. Wouldn't you like to have your story told, in your own words?"

"You have the wrong person," he repeated, scowling.

"It will just take a few minutes of your time and—"

Jahmshidi closed the door on them.

Ann started to knock again, but David grabbed her arm and held it fast. "Let's go, Ann. I mean it."

"He's lying. You saw his picture, and that's Mehdi Jahmshidi."

"Let's go," he said through clenched teeth.

Ann stood her ground a second longer, then sighed and followed David back down the hall.

EVEN AS ANN and David were heading for the elevator, Jahmshidi was making a room-to-room telephone call, which was answered by Ahmad Faruk on the third floor.

"Two unwelcome visitors just left. One is a very thin white man, the other a black woman—very pleasing to look upon."

"Are they still in the hotel?" Faruk asked.

"They should be getting on the elevator about now."

"Do not worry," Faruk said.

"SHALL I GET you a taxi?" the doorman asked as David and Ann left the hotel.

"No, thanks. It's such a beautiful night, we'll walk," David said.

"Very good, sir. Have a nice evening."

"Thank you."

The air was soft, almost sensual as they started down the street.

"There's something about the city on a summer night," David said. "It makes you feel so alive."

Ann leaned against him. "I know what will make you feel even more alive."

Smiling, he wrapped his arm around her. "You have something special in mind?"

"I'm sure we can come up with something," she said, her voice low and alluring.

David took in a short audible breath. "Are you sure, Ann? Didn't you call me a wuss?"

"That was before."

"Before what?"

"Before you proved yourself my hero."

"Hero? Hardly," he scoffed. "You did all the talking. I just stood beside you, shaking."

She laughed. "Didn't you hear me shaking, too?" She stopped walking and turned to him. "David, you really are a hero in my eyes. And in my heart." With that she pulled him to her, meeting his lips with a slow, tender kiss.

They were interrupted by the sound of a car stopping and someone calling to them, "Do you need a taxi?"

Smiling, Ann pulled away from David and glanced over at the taxi. "Yes, let's take a cab," she told David. "I can't wait to get to your apartment." She started toward the curb.

David halted abruptly. In all the years he had lived in the city, no cabbie had ever solicited him like this. "Ann, wait!" he called.

Ann must have also realized something was wrong, for she had already stopped in her tracks. She looked over her shoulder at David, her eyes wide with fear. Just beyond her, the driver was leaning through the open window, a long-barreled pistol in his hand.

"Run!" David shouted, reaching out to grab her.

The muzzle of the pistol flashed, the gunshot a muffled clap because of the silencer on the barrel.

Ann staggered slightly, then clutched at her chest as she spun around toward David, blood oozing through her fingers. "D-David," she gasped, her voice weakened by shock and pain.

David grabbed her just as the taxi driver fired a second time. He felt a hammer blow to his shoulder, and he went down, pulling Ann with him to the ground.

The taxi took off, its tires spinning wildly as it sped away from the curb.

"Ann?" David said. He felt her weight on top of him, heavy and still. "Ann!" he shouted in fear.

Rolling her off him, David leaned over and shook her gently, then with increasing urgency. Her eyes were open but vacant. Her lips were parted, but there was no breath, no sign of life.

"Oh, my God, Ann!" He leaned back, unaware of the blood seeping through the shoulder of his jacket. Looking around helplessly, he started to cry out, "Help me! Somebody, please help me!"

LT. FRANK SANTINI had just arrived at Midtown South to work the night shift and was standing at the locker in his office, changing shirts. Because of the juxtaposition of two mirrors, he had an unobstructed view of his back. The skin was laced with white ridges, old scars from his initiation into Via Dei as a Disciple of the Way. He wore a more noticeable mark of that initiation in the scar on his left cheek, which he claimed was from a bullet but was really acquired when he turned his head at the wrong moment during the initiation and caught the tip of the flagellum.

Since joining the police department, Santini had provided security for many visiting dignitaries, from heads of state to three U.S. presidents. After 9/11, he headed the honor guard at the funerals of three officers from his precinct who were killed in the collapse of the towers. But as a devout Roman

Catholic and member of Via Dei, the greatest honor ever bestowed on him was to provide personal security to the Grand Master during his return trip to Manhattan earlier that evening.

As he finished dressing, he recalled how surprised he had been when Father Flannery first mentioned Via Dei a few days ago. Santini had claimed to know nothing of the group, which was what he had been trained to do. Revealing the secrets of Via Dei, even its mere existence, violated their rules and would result in the severest punishment. He could only guess what that punishment might be, because as far as he knew, no one had ever betrayed the order.

Santini had just sat down at his desk to do some paperwork when the watch sergeant knocked on the door, then leaned into the room. "Lieutenant?"

"Yes, Booker?"

Sgt. Raymond Booker was several years older than Santini and quite a bit heavier, his thinning hair cut close to the scalp. He looked even more solemn than usual as he announced, "There's been a shooting over near Columbus Circle."

Santini shrugged. "That's Midtown North."

"One of the victims asked to see you. Says he's been working with you on a case."

"An officer?"

"No, civvie."

Santini shook his head. "That's ridiculous. I'm not working with any civilians on anything."

"He said it has to do with the People of the Book symposium, and he—"

"What's his name?"

Booker looked at a slip of paper he was holding. "David Meyers. He was struck in the shoulder, and a woman with him was killed." He again consulted the note. "Name of Ann Coopersmith."

"Damn." Santini leaned back in his chair and sighed. "Okay, where is he?"

"St. Vincent's."

"How bad is he hurt?"

"Don't know." Booker turned to leave, then looked back. "Answer me something, would you, Lieutenant?"

"If I can."

"Somebody blew up a restaurant, somebody tried to off a priest, and now a woman's been killed, all to stop that People of the Book gathering. What makes these lunatics so hell-bent on stopping people of different faiths from coming together?"

"Fear, I suppose . . . that all the religions will get mixed into one, and we'll wind up with none at all."

"Given the way God-fearing folk are killing one another, that might not be such a bad idea," Booker said.

Santini stood from his desk. "I'd better get over to the hospital and see what this is all about."

"Want me to come along?"

Santini shook his head. "That won't be necessary."

DAVID MEYERS WAS in a private room at the far end of the trauma wing. Because it was late, the lights had been dimmed, with the end of the hall even darker because several bulbs had burned out.

As Frank Santini approached the room, he halted and peered into the darkness ahead. No one was on duty outside the room, though he had confirmed with Midtown North that a police guard had been authorized.

This is too damn easy, he thought as he slipped his hand into his coat pocket and gripped the handgun. This wasn't the police-issued weapon he wore at the small of his back but an unregistered pistol with all markings filed off and a silencer on the snub-nose barrel.

Santini stood outside the hospital room for a moment, then quietly pushed open the door and peered inside.

David Meyers was in the bed, with his head elevated as high as the bed could go. *What an easy shot,* he thought as he started to ease the pistol from his pocket.

"Michael, is that you?" someone called from inside the room.

Sticking his head through the doorway, Santini saw that Preston Lewkis and Sarah Arad were also there. For an instant he considered killing all three, for the Grand Master had made it clear during the drive back to the city that they were all to be considered targets of opportunity. Flannery, on the other hand, was the primary target, and Santini knew a triple murder might result in almost impenetrable security around the priest.

Dropping the pistol back into his pocket, he stepped into the room. "Where's the guard?" he asked.

"Guard?" Preston said.

"There's supposed to be a police guard out in the hall. No one's there."

"Father Flannery went to the morgue to see Ann's body, and the guard went with him," Sarah explained.

"He shouldn't have done that. He's not from my precinct, but I can submit a delinquency report."

"No, please," Sarah said. "I told him to go."

"*You* told him to go?" Santini asked, his voice betraying his irritation. "You've no authority to give orders to a New York police officer."

"Sorry—poor choice of words. What I meant to say was I asked if he'd go with Father Flannery, who's in as much danger as David. I showed him my Interpol credentials and told him I'd cover while he was gone."

"You may have been right to ask, but he shouldn't have agreed. He should've stayed here and called for backup to accompany the priest. But don't worry, I won't come down on him." He turned to David. "How bad are you hurt?"

"He's in a lot of pain," Preston said, approaching the bed.

"I'm fine," David insisted. "The doctor says it isn't serious." His eyes welled with moisture. "Maybe not for me, but . . . but for Ann—" He choked back his tears.

"Ann Coopersmith—she was a freelance reporter, right?" Santini asked, and David nodded. "How well did you know her?"

"She was my fr—" The words caught in David's throat as tears streamed down his face. For a long moment he couldn't speak, and then at last he managed to say proudly, "She was my girlfriend." As he wiped away the tears with his good hand, he noticed that Michael Flannery had just returned to the room. "You saw her, Father?" he asked.

"Yes."

"You prayed for her?"

Flannery nodded.

"Good. I'm not Christian, but she was. I know it would've meant a lot to her."

"Mr. Meyers, did you see who shot you and Miss Coopersmith?"

"Not exactly. It was dark, and he was in the cab."

"A cab?"

David described how the cabbie stopped to offer them a ride, then opened fire when they approached.

"That makes no sense," Santini said. "Why would a cabbie start shooting? Unless he wasn't a cabbie."

"Didn't you hear?" Sarah asked.

The lieutenant looked at her questioningly.

"He wasn't a cabbie. A detective came by about a half hour ago and said they found the taxi dumped in Central Park with the real driver in the backseat, shot dead."

Santini shook his head in frustration. "I was on the phone with Midtown North not ten minutes ago. They should've briefed me on that." He took out his pad and jotted a few notes. "Hopefully the taxi will yield some forensics. All we have to do next is figure out who stole the cab and shot Miss Coopersmith and you."

"David has a theory," Preston put in. He gestured to David. "Go on, tell him."

"Just before it . . . it happened, we confronted Mehdi Jahmshidi, the head of the Islamist terror group Arkaan."

"Jahmshidi? Are you certain?" Santini said as he scribbled furiously on his pad. "Where is he?"

"At the Dunn Hotel, though I'll bet he's long gone by now. He's using the name Hassan al-Halid, and he's the one who reported a bellman had gone missing at the hotel. It was in today's paper."

"Yes, I know of that case." Santini looked up from the notepad. "Are you saying Jahmshidi is the killer?"

"He probably killed the bellman, but he wasn't driving the cab."

"It had to be one of his men," Sarah interjected. "The driver was Middle Eastern; David gave the detective a full description."

"I'll bet his friends were also involved," Preston offered.

"What friends?"

"Benjamin Bishara and Antonio Sangremano."

"Father Antonio Sangremano of the Vatican?" Santini asked, looking more than a bit surprised.

"Formerly of the Vatican," Flannery corrected. "I'm impressed. You know your Church hierarchy."

"I'm a good Catholic, Father."

"Yes, that very Sangremano," Preston continued. "He's with a fringe group called Via Dei, and Bishara heads the militant Jewish group Migdal Tzedek."

"First, I find it hard to believe that a high Vatican official would let himself get caught up in this mess."

"He's not with the Vatican any longer," Flannery reminded the lieutenant. He didn't want to say more, since Sangremano had gone into hiding following the shooting in the catacombs, and Israeli authorities were keeping the incident under wraps while trying to take him into custody.

"Once in the Vatican, always in the Vatican," Santini

replied. "And what would he have in common with those Muslim and Jewish terrorists?"

"All we know is that there have been communications between the three," Preston said, "and they share a mutual hatred for everything the People of the Book movement stands for."

"And they're here," Sarah added. "All three have come to New York during the symposium, which can hardly be a co-incidence."

"I'll look into all this," Santini promised, closing the notepad and tucking it back into his jacket pocket. "Really, I will. But they may have their own agendas in coming to New York, and right now I'd say Mehdi Jahmshidi and his lot are the most likely candidates for employing violence." He turned to David. "Do you know how long they'll keep you here?"

"The doc thinks I can go home tomorrow, as soon as they're sure there's no infection."

"Good. If I have any more questions, where can I reach you?"

"I'll be at my apartment until after Ann's funeral."

"That's probably not a good idea."

"The lieutenant's right," Sarah agreed. "If they realize you aren't dead, they may try again, and your address would be pretty easy to find."

"He can stay with us," Flannery offered.

"Perfect." Santini said. "The safe house is the best place until we track down and arrest this Jahmshidi fellow." He started toward the door, then looked back at David. "Oh, and one other thing. When they schedule the funeral, let me know and I'll arrange for a Uni—a uniformed officer—to take you, just to be on the safe side. Maybe I'll take you myself."

Santini gave a slight wave and headed down the hall.

CHAPTER 27

NEW YORK CITY

While Ann Coopersmith had many friends and colleagues, that only partly accounted for the large crowd that turned out for her funeral. The suggestion that her murder was somehow connected to the People of the Book symposium brought out hundreds of the curious.

Following a service at the family church in Long Island City, a large contingent traveled to nearby Calvary Cemetery. As the young priest gave something of a New Age homily, Preston Lewkis and Sarah Arad stood nearby with David Meyers and a tall distinguished-looking man with a trim gray beard, a vested pinstripe suit and blue tie, and the quiet demeanor of a banker.

"Stop touching it," Sarah whispered to the man.

"I'm sorry," Fr. Michael Flannery replied, quickly dropping his hand. He moved his mouth awkwardly, as if uncomfortable in his skin.

"Enough. Do you want it to come off?"

"Sorry," he repeated. "This beard is killing me. I should never have agreed—"

"Better to get killed by a fake beard than a real bullet," Sarah said bluntly.

"I still don't see why I had to dress up like this."

"Because you're a target. There have already been two attempts on your life; there's no sense tempting fate."

"I know you're right. But still, I feel . . . silly."

The casket bearing Ann's remains was moved to the catafalque beside the grave. Then the family priest walked up beside the coffin and intoned, "My brothers and sisters, we are gathered here to help deliver the soul of our dearly departed Ann Coopersmith into the company of God. Our sister has made a clean oblation and acceptable sacrifice of love toward God, man, and the universe, and there she shall dwell forever. Amen."

The assembly responded with their own amen.

The priest stepped away from the coffin to allow Ann's mother and father to approach. The elderly couple stood by the coffin for a long moment, remembering moments from the past, lamenting her stolen future.

There was a commotion off to the side, and Flannery turned to see a young Middle Eastern–looking man in an oversized coat jostling his way through the edge of the crowd. Someone screamed, and one of the other mourners leaped at the intruder and knocked him to the ground. As the man tried to struggle to his feet, those closest to him began scattering in all directions.

"Down!" Sarah Arad shouted, throwing herself at Flannery and tackling him.

As Flannery went sprawling to the ground, he caught sight of the intruder, who was on his feet again. He was staring directly at Flannery, grinning malevolently, when suddenly he disappeared in a flash of light. The ground shook as the air shattered with an explosive boom, leaving a cloud of smoke and dust. As it slowly dispersed, Flannery uncovered his eyes and saw several bodies lying a few feet from the center of the explosion, with other people down on their knees or staggering away from the carnage, choking and screaming. Many were covered with blood and had severe wounds, but Flannery saw that Ann's parents and the priest were far enough away to be uninjured.

Sarah was helping Flannery to his feet when David

Meyers ran up and pulled at her arm, calling out, "There! Look over there!" He was pointing to a black car parked on the nearest of the small roadways that crisscrossed the cemetery. A man had just run up to the vehicle and was jerking open the door.

"It's Jahmshidi! I'm sure of it!" David exclaimed.

"I see him," Sarah said.

Drawing her pistol, she started running toward the car, but Mehdi Jahmshidi was already in the driver's seat and saw her coming. Throwing the vehicle into gear, he backed onto the road and drove off in reverse, racing the wrong direction down the one-way street.

Gaining the roadway, Sarah halted and raised her Beretta, steadying it in both hands as she fired three rounds. The vehicle swerved, and for a moment she thought she had struck the driver, but he was merely avoiding an oncoming car. She couldn't risk another shot and watched in frustration as he expertly spun the vehicle around and sped off in forward gear through one of the exit gates. She knew that in a few seconds he would make a clean escape on the Brooklyn-Queens Expressway.

By the time Sarah returned to the others, the sirens of emergency vehicles were blaring. She found Flannery with his disguise removed as he knelt beside one of the bodies and performed Extreme Unction.

When the last rites were administered, Flannery looked up at Sarah, his eyes flooded with tears. "God help us," he whispered. "We are dealing with madmen."

THE NEXT DAY, David Meyers was at a desk in the safe house, his calico cat perched in his lap. *The New York Times* lay on the table, folded to a story bearing the headline: BOMB BLAST AT FUNERAL KILLS 4, INJURES 12.

The story quoted police officials offering several theories as to why a bomb had been set off, but there was no mention of a possible link to the People of the Book symposium. Nor did they name Mehdi Jahmshidi or his terror group Arkaan, though Sarah had provided a full report, including her attempt to apprehend a man who looked like Jahmshidi.

The most startling revelation in the story was that the severed forearm of the bomber, its fingers still clutching the detonator, had been found at the bottom of the grave, where it had landed after the blast. It was undergoing forensics analysis in an attempt to determine the identity of the suicide bomber.

David stared morosely at the photo of Ann Coopersmith that accompanied the article and choked back tears as he recalled the budding relationship that now would never be realized.

"I miss her, T," he whispered as he stroked the cat. T seemed to sense that David needed comforting and leaned into his chest and purred appreciatively.

"Enough," he declared, not to the cat but to his overwhelming sorrow and self-pity.

Pulling his laptop in front of him, he began tapping on the keyboard. He called up the log file of a code-breaking utility that he had been running for several days to analyze a copy of the code stream he had intercepted on the airliner when it was under attack.

As he scanned the log to see if the utility had highlighted any sections of code, he muttered, "Hello, what's this?"

A code string several screens long had been highlighted and overlaid with new code. David quickly copied and pasted the new string into one of his hacking programs and ran the code.

"You son of a bitch, I've found you!" David shouted at the screen.

The code had connected him to a hacker's computer in real time, displaying stroke by stroke as the hacker entered new code. The stream suddenly collapsed to a small icon at the bottom of the screen, and David saw an address being typed into a narrow text window above. It was the section of www.nyc.gov for the New York City Department of Transportation. As David watched, the hacker logged into the restricted portion of the site and began examining traffic choke points, computer-controlled traffic lights, and police traffic communications.

"You're good," David said to the screen as he realized the hacker was manipulating traffic signals to create a citywide gridlock. "Damn good—but not as good as Mongo."

David started typing.

TEHRAN

Taped to Kamal al-Khazar's computer monitor were small photographs of the two Boeing 767 airplanes he had managed to bring down by hacking into the satellite control system. He joked to his comrades that he needed only three more to become an ace. If he could count trains, he was already an ace, having wrecked four of them by sending incorrect switching signals, causing collisions.

Today he hoped to dramatically increase his count of destroyed vehicles—this time automobiles—by disrupting traffic in New York City.

"What?" he exclaimed in Arabic, his smile vanishing. "What is this? What is going on?"

The code that Kamal had painstakingly typed was flashing on and off, then suddenly disappeared from his screen, leaving behind an animated cartoon of an American cowboy in a ten-gallon hat. The cowboy was holding a lasso, which he flung offscreen. The rope became taut, and the cowboy pulled in what he had lassoed: a bearded man in a turban and robe.

Kamal began typing in a desperate attempt to disconnect from the server he had hacked, but he was unable to regain control of his own computer. He was about to reach for the power button, when the cartoon abruptly disappeared and was replaced by a message in English:

> YOUR ENTIRE SYSTEM HAS BEEN FRIED. YOUR SLOPPY SECURITY HAS ALSO LET US DESTROY THE SYSTEMS OF EVERYONE ON YOUR DIRECT ACCESS LIST. THIS HAS BEEN A CLOSE EN-COUNTER OF THE WORST KIND.
> HAVE A NICE DAY. ☺ MONGO.

Kamal gasped. His computer could connect remotely to virtually every PC throughout the Arkaan organization. He also had frequent contacts with al-Qaeda, Hamas, Hezbollah, and several other radical organizations. If this hacker Mongo was telling the truth, he had exploited the pathway from Kamal's PC to severely cripple or even wipe out the wider Islamist network.

Kamal stared in fear at the Blue Screen of Death, the far-from-affectionate nickname for the blank screen of a dead Windows PC. He frantically tried to restart the computer, but it would not boot up.

Grabbing his cell phone, he called an Arkaan associate and discovered that the man's computer had flashed a message in Arabic from Kamal al-Khazar confessing that he secretly worked for the American CIA and had trashed the PC at their behest. Rebooting resulted in the dreaded blue screen. Phone calls to contacts at Hamas and Hezbollah confirmed that their systems had also been fried, with Kamal purportedly confessing to be the culprit.

Kamal covered his eyes with his hands, trying to erase the flood of images of beheadings of infidels that he had uploaded to the Web. He had taken great pleasure in broadcasting their pain and humiliation, and now, if he didn't act quickly, he would likely suffer the same fate.

"Allahu Akbar," he intoned as he removed a revolver

from his desk drawer and raised it to his temple. Cocking it, he repeated the phrase "God is great" and pulled the trigger, spraying the Blue Screen of Death with his blood and brain matter.

CHAPTER 28

NEW YORK CITY

David Meyers stood watching the entrance of the Hotel Musée from across the street. It had taken some effort to track down where Mehdi Jahmshidi had gone after abruptly checking out of the Dunn Hotel in the wake of the disappearance of the bellman. But in a stroke of luck, he had intercepted one of Jahmshidi's cell phone calls related to the crippling of the Arkaan computer network. He was then able to track the terrorist leader to this small Upper East Side hotel, several blocks from the Metropolitan Museum of Art.

David waited until he saw Jahmshidi leave the hotel and get into a taxi; then he crossed the street and entered the lobby. Shifting his shoulder bag, he gave a nonchalant smile to the woman behind the front desk as he headed to the elevators, looking like any other guest.

Getting out on the sixth floor, he headed down the hall and nodded at an elderly man who shuffled past and disappeared around the bend to the elevator corridor. David walked slowly, listening as the elevator door opened and closed. When he was satisfied he was alone on the floor, he opened the shoulder bag and removed an electronic device about the size of a cigarette pack. Wired to it was what looked like a credit card, which he inserted into the key-card lock of room 632. He pressed some buttons on the device, and several LED lights began flashing.

David looked around nervously, making sure no one came out into the hall. After almost two minutes, the LEDs turned solid green, and he slid the card from the lock and turned the doorknob. There was a click, and he pushed open the door.

David saw Jahmshidi's prayer rug on the floor, facing east. He stepped gingerly around it, careful not to disturb how it was lying. Taking a toolkit from his bag, he installed a listening device in the telephone and a pair of small, powerful video cameras in the overhead return-air register and behind the smoke alarm. Then he opened his laptop, confirmed the devices were working properly, and programmed a hidden controller to transmit the signals through the hotel's wireless network.

Smiling at his handiwork, David made his way back down to the lobby, where he gave the desk clerk a pleasant good-bye and headed down the street toward Central Park. A half hour later he was back in the safe house, eating a can of chili and watching Jahmshidi's hotel room on the monitor of his computer.

T jumped up on his lap, and David stroked the cat, saying, "I know, it's boring right now, T. But I promise, it's gonna get interesting. And we're gonna nail him. You and me, T, we're gonna nail his hide to the barn door." He chuckled. "I've always wanted to say that to somebody."

But as quickly as the laughter came, so did the tears as he remembered the terrible price Ann Coopersmith had paid in helping him take on Jahmshidi and his comrades.

"I'm gonna nail your hide, you bastard!" he hissed, blinking against the tears as he focused on the monitor.

FR. MICHAEL FLANNERY, Preston Lewkis, and Sarah Arad were in one of the interrogation rooms at Midtown South Precinct. Sarah was on the phone with Natan Schuler, her superior at the Israeli counterterrorism unit YAMAM.

"We've issued a warrant for Benjamin Bishara and are asking the Americans to arrest him so we can begin extradition," Schuler said. "We're pretty sure, now, that he's responsible for the murder of Professor Heber."

"What about that fellow Moshe Goldman and his dispute with Heber over *The Sacrifice of Abraham*?" Sarah said.

"We think Goldman's lying about that," Schuler replied. "We've found evidence linking him and the murder to Migdal Tzedek."

"How about Arkaan and Via Dei?"

"I've read your reports, but we've found nothing solid to link the three groups," Schuler replied.

"They're definitely working together," she insisted.

"I don't doubt it, but I'm having no luck convincing anyone else. We've confirmed a mutual interest in the People of the Book gathering. According to Moshe Goldman, Bishara is in the U.S. to break up the symposium. It's not such a leap to believe all three groups are working toward that common goal."

Sarah heard the door open, and she turned to see Lt. Frank Santini come into the room. "I have to go now," she said into the phone. "I'll talk to you later."

Santini sat down, then slid a piece of paper across the table.

"We got a good set of prints from the hand of that bomber." Santini smiled ruefully. "I have to tell you, it pretty well sickened our fingerprinter, Miss Marwell. I think it was the first time she printed just a hand."

"Did you find a match?" Sarah asked.

Santini shook his head. "Not in the U.S. database. But you were right, Miss Arad, the Israelis had a match. The bomber was a terrorist named Ishaq Nidal. What I don't understand is why he bombed a funeral. I mean if he wanted to make a statement, why not a police station or military recruiting office? If he just wanted to kill a lot of people, there are a lot more in the crowd outside Shea Stadium, right near the cemetery."

"It wasn't just a terrorist act," Sarah replied. "It was another attempt on Father Flannery."

Santini held up his hand. "I'm not denying someone wants the good father dead. But this was a Muslim terrorist from that group run by Jahmshidi. What's it called?" Santini reached for the paper.

"Arkaan," Sarah said.

"Yes, Arkaan. Why would Arkaan want Father Flannery dead?"

"Same reason the Jewish group Migdal Tzedek and the Christian group Via Dei want him dead," she replied.

"You shouldn't call Via Dei Christian," Flannery put in. "They're anything but."

"Look," Santini said, rubbing a hand through his hair, "I appreciate that these three groups have no love for that symposium of yours. And you were right that this Jahmshidi fellow was behind the murder of Ann Coopersmith and the bombing at her funeral. But you yourselves proved the fellow who tried to kill Father Flannery wasn't a Middle Eastern terrorist. And there's nothing to connect those Jewish and Christian groups to anything or anyone."

"My government has issued a warrant for the leader of Migdal Tzedek," Sarah told him.

"Yes, I heard. But while we know Arkaan is a terror group, and the Israelis say the same about Migdal Tzedek, there's no proof that Via Dei, if it exists at all, is a terror group. And even if it is, what's the likelihood that Christians, Jews, and Muslims would come together for anything?"

"Isn't that what they're doing at the symposium? Albeit for good."

Santini sighed. "I get your point. But it's all pretty much conjecture here."

Sarah leaned across the table and looked the lieutenant in the eye. "What isn't conjecture is that the leaders of these three groups, Mehdi Jahmshidi, Benjamin Bishara, and Antonio Sangremano, arrived under assumed names in

New York within twenty-four hours of each other, and each has a connection to the recent murders."

"Father Sangremano?" Santini said incredulously. "A former Vatican official? How is he connected? Even if he belongs to Via Dei, there's no evidence it's anything like Arkaan or Migdal Tzedek."

"Sangremano is the head of Via Dei. He told me so himself," Flannery said without elaborating. "And I'll bet that Tim O'Leary fellow who tried to kill me was a member."

"Isn't Via Dei something of a fraternal organization, like the Masons?" Santini said.

"I'm well aware of the good work done by the Masons," Flannery replied. "But, trust me . . . Via Dei is nothing like that. And right now, Via Dei is intent on disrupting the People of the Book symposium."

"Arkaan and Migdal Tzedek have that same goal," Preston put in. "So, isn't it reasonable to believe they've decided to work together, if only this once?"

"Ironic, isn't it?" Flannery said.

"How?" Santini asked.

"Here we have three leaders of the most radical and violent elements of their respective religions doing the very thing they're trying to prevent. They are uniting their efforts."

"I hope you're wrong," Santini said. "God help us, I hope you're wrong. I simply cannot imagine any Vatican official joining forces with someone like Mehdi Jahmshidi."

CHAPTER 29

JERUSALEM

The sun hung high in the sky when the travelers first saw Jerusalem spread before them. The journey from Constantinople had been long and arduous, but al-Aarif had led them safely through all dangers. Now he stood with Tobias Garlande and Rachel Benyuli as they looked upon the holiest city in the world.

Jerusalem was surrounded by hills laced with low-growing scrub brush and rocks. A massive wall encircled the city, affording protection to the flat-roofed houses and domed buildings crowded within its streets. Inside the wall, also, was a monument to Islamic faith, the Dome of the Rock, a spectacular octagonal mosque built around the rock from which Muhammad ascended to heaven. The rock was equally sacred to Christians and Jews, for the Ark of the Covenant was placed upon it inside the Holy of Holies of the First Temple. And it was here that Jesus drove away the moneychangers.

As the travelers approached Jerusalem from the northeast, they stopped at the pool of Bethesda, where Jesus had performed a miracle and which now was a part of the system of reservoirs and cisterns that supplied the city. Al-Aarif ground-tied their horses, then followed his companions to the upper bath. He had long since disposed of the Christian uniform he had worn in Constantinople, and he was dressed now in the flowing black robe of a desert prince, with a black *kaffiyeh* headdress held in place by a red *agal*, or circlet of rope. Tobias and Rachel had also abandoned their pilgrim clothing and wore simple white hooded robes.

"Come," al-Aarif said after a few minutes. "I have a friend in the city who will feed and shelter us."

"Wait, please, just for a moment," Tobias said.

"Yes, please," Rachel added.

Al-Aarif smiled at his two friends. He had been here before, but it was their first time. "I understand," he said. "I have seen this holy place many times, and still I am touched by the spirit of God when I am here."

Tobias walked past the ruins of the colonnades that surrounded the remains of the large spring-fed upper bath. As he stood beside Rachel, gazing upon the rippling, shallow waters, he recited from chapter five of the Gospel of John:

" 'There was a feast of the Jews, and Jesus went up to Jerusalem. Now, there is by the Sheep Gate a pool, which is called Bethesda, having five porticoes. In these lay a multitude of the sick, blind, lame, and withered, waiting for the moving of the waters; for at certain seasons an angel of the Lord went into the pool and stirred up the water. Whoever then first stepped in was cured of whatever disease afflicted him. A man was there who had been ill for thirty-eight years. When Jesus saw him lying there, He said to him, "Do you wish to get well?" The sick man answered Him, "Sir, I have no man to put me into the pool when the water is stirred up, and another steps down before me." Jesus said to him, "Get up, pick up your pallet and walk." Immediately the man became well and picked up his pallet and began to walk.' "

After a few more minutes, al-Aarif came up beside them and said softly, "Come, it would be best to find my friend's house before dusk."

"Yes, I understand," Tobias replied.

Returning to where their horses were tied, al-Aarif walked the animals down toward the city, with Rachel at his side. Following close behind, Tobias used his staff to help negotiate the uneven, rock-strewn ground.

Bypassing the small Sheep Gate, they entered the city through the larger Middle Gate along Jerusalem's east wall and headed down one of the main thoroughfares, busy with merchants and their customers, from butchers and vegetable mongers to street performers dancing for coins. As they led their horses deeper into the city, they passed Christian churches, Jewish synagogues, and Muslim mosques. Members of all three faiths were worshiping in their own quarters of the city with no apparent animosity.

"If only the people back home could see this," Tobias said. "I wish they could experience the brotherhood among all who worship the same God."

A few minutes later, al-Aarif halted and declared, "We are here."

"Where?" Rachel looked around in confusion, for all she saw in front of them was an opulent building.

"Here," al-Aarif said, indicating what appeared to be a royal palace. "The house of Sultan Barkiyaruq." He approached one of the guards at the entrance and called out in Arabic with a tone of authority, "I am al-Aarif of al-Andalus, nephew of al-Mamun of Toledo, and I and my companions are here to visit the Sultan Abu al-Muzaffar Rukn ud-Din Barkiyaruq bin Malik Shah, son of the great Jalal al-Dawlah Malik Shah. Announce us, and have your man see to our horses."

"Yes, at once," the soldier replied obsequiously.

"Al-Aarif, I am most impressed that you know the sultan," said Tobias, who was fluent in Arabic.

"There is some question as to whether Barkiyaruq is truly the sultan," al-Aarif confessed, reverting to Castilian, the language shared by Tobias and Rachel. "While he's of the Seljuk Sultanate and the oldest son of the Sultan Malik Shah, who died five years ago, the succession has come under dispute because his three brothers are making the same claim. There seems to be a temporary truce, however, and for now Barkiyaruq rules Jerusalem."

Once inside the palace, al-Aarif and his companions were led by one of the servants into a room and asked to wait. The room was enormous and almost devoid of furniture, with intricately carved white walls and a high, vaulted ceiling. The floor tiles were a deep blue inlaid with geometric designs in gold.

After a short wait, a side door opened and a rather short, corpulent man swept into the room, wearing a flowing white robe and a headdress held in place by an emerald-encrusted *agal*. Because the hem of the robe touched the tiled floor, he appeared to glide toward them, his dark eyes glistening with delight, his broad smile nearly obscured by his heavy mustache and beard.

"Al-Aarif, my old friend," the sultan exclaimed in Arabic as he approached with his left arm extended.

Al-Aarif kissed Barkiyaruq's hand. "Allah has granted me the pleasure of seeing you again, Your Highness."

Barkiyaruq looked over at Tobias and Rachel. Fixing an admiring gaze on the young woman, he said to al-Aarif, "How delightful of you to grace the palace with the beauty of this woman." He extended his left hand toward her.

Following al-Aarif's lead, she gave a slight curtsey and kissed his hand. "I am Rachel Benyuli, Your Highness," she said in Arabic. While not as proficient in the language as Tobias, she could carry on a simple conversation.

Barkiyaruq eyes widened. "Ah, you speak our language. I am most honored." He then turned to Tobias but did not extend his hand, as he had to the others.

"Your Highness, may I present Tobias Garlande, known far and wide as Tobias el Transcriptor of Toledo," al-Aarif said by way of introduction. "He is a scholar with a knowledge of many languages, including our own. And he is a man of faith, morality, and exemplary courage."

"Tobias," Barkiyaruq said, finally extending his hand and accepting the older man's kiss. "I am honored to be in the presence of a personage of such qualities."

"I fear that al-Aarif exaggerates my worth. But the honor, Your Highness, is mine," Tobias replied in Arabic.

"You have traveled far?" Barkiyaruq asked.

"All the way from Hispania," al-Aarif said.

"Then please, you must join me for some food and drink. And you will make my house your home during your stay in Jerusalem."

AN HOUR LATER, their stomachs stuffed with a dozen elaborately prepared delicacies, al-Aarif warned the sultan of the danger that lay ahead should Peter the Hermit, Walter the Penniless, and their pilgrim army follow through on their promise to cross the Bosporus and march on Jerusalem. To his surprise, Barkiyaruq burst into laughter.

"I have heard of this band of ruffians who camp in the fields outside Constantinople and get drunk and grow fat and lazy as they boast of great victories to come. I think that Emperor Alexius will soon tire of their presence and send them home. I do not believe we need worry."

Al-Aarif shook his head. "I wish I could agree with you, Your Highness, but I think this pilgrimage could prove to be troublesome."

"I shall take your warning under advisement. In the meantime, make yourselves at home in our Holy City."

"Al-Aarif?" Tobias whispered.

His companion held up a finger and nodded. Al-Aarif knew what Tobias wanted, having discussed it in great detail during the long weeks of their journey.

"Your Highness, as I mentioned, Tobias Garlande is a scholar. It is his desire, while in Jerusalem, to examine and transcribe some of the city's historical documents."

"And so it shall be," Barkiyaruq declared. "I shall tell the keepers of our ancient writings that you are to have unfettered access."

"My most sincere thanks, Your Highness," Tobias replied.

* * *

For the next few weeks, Tobias haunted the libraries, government buildings, churches, synagogues, and mosques of Jerusalem, pulling out dusty and sometimes deteriorating scrolls and manuscripts for study and possible transcription. Most were no older than the eighth century, when writing became more prominent and scholars increasingly recorded the core traditions of their societies, including religious texts and legal codices.

While Tobias was undertaking his initial research, he had no immediate need for the services of Rachel, so he asked al-Aarif to look after her. Al-Aarif eagerly undertook the task and took great delight in showing Rachel the wonders of the city, giving equal attention to the religious sites of Christianity, Judaism, and Islam.

As Rachel waited for al-Aarif on the morning of their third week in Jerusalem, she examined her reflection in a hand mirror, paying particular attention to the golden chain and pendant he had given her the day before. The first time she had met al-Aarif, when he came to her rescue in Toledo, she had felt an immediate attraction, which intensified in Constantinople when he fought off the soldiers who would have killed her and Tobias. Her feelings were nurtured during the long journey across the desert, and they blossomed fully in this magical city.

For a long time, al-Aarif had said nothing to indicate he felt the same, which had made her fear her feelings were unrequited. But yesterday he had given her the golden chain and pendant and told her it was a pledge of his deep affection. When Rachel had gently chastised him, saying he should not spend his money on such extravagances, he had assured her that he would gladly spend ten times as much as an expression of his feelings.

She was particularly looking forward to his visit today, because last night he had sent word he had something he must tell her. Rachel smiled, recalling how secretive he had been, sending the message with one of the palace servants. There was no need for such mystery, since she already knew that he was going to ask her to marry him.

"Yes, I will," Rachel said to her reflection in the mirror. "I will marry you."

As she practiced her response, she tried various facial expressions, from joyful to serious, and everything from a simple yes to a more formal and solemn reply, testing the words in both Castilian and Arabic.

"Al-Aarif, are you sure this is what you want?" she asked the mirror. "I am Jewish and you are Muslim. Can our love bridge the gap between our cultures and religions?"

She looked very sober for a long moment, closely studying her expression in the mirror. Then she laughed.

"Yes!" she exclaimed. "Our love can bridge any divide. Yes, al-Aarif, I will marry you."

"Mistress Rachel," a servant girl said in Arabic as she entered the room. "Prince al-Aarif is here."

"Thank you, Kalila," Rachel answered as she hurried to greet al-Aarif. She found him standing with his back to her just outside the doorway. "Al-Aarif, God's love be with you today," she greeted him, adding shyly, "and mine."

Rachel's smile faded when he turned and she saw his troubled expression.

"What is it?" she asked. "What troubles you?"

"Yesterday I sent word I had something to tell you."

Rachel felt her heart fall, certain from the look on his face that he did not intend to propose.

"I am afraid I must leave you," al-Aarif said, his voice almost a whisper.

Rachel gasped. Her knees weakened, and she struggled to look calm.

"The pilgrim army has pushed south across the Bosporus. Barkiyaruq has asked me to accompany his soldiers to engage and repel them."

"No!" Rachel exclaimed. She gently touched his cheek. "You could be killed. Please, stay with me."

Al-Aarif shook his head. "As much as I love you, and as much as I want to stay with you, I cannot refuse the sultan. Were I to do so, I would be a man without honor."

"Honor? What is honor if it gets you killed?"

"I must go," al-Aarif said. "Do I have your prayers?"

Rachel was sobbing now and did not reply.

"We worship the same God, and I sincerely hope you will pray for me in my trial by fire."

"Yes," Rachel said, wiping away her tears. "Yes, I will pray every day for your safe return."

"And when I return, we shall be together . . . forever." He took her into his arms and held her close.

"I FEARED AS much," Tobias said when Rachel told him that al-Aarif would be accompanying Barkiyaruq's Saracen army to do battle with the advancing French force.

"Please, do something," Rachel begged as she knelt in front of the old man. "He will listen to you."

"What would you have me do?"

"Ask him not to go."

"I take it you've already tried. What was his reply?"

"He called it a matter of honor—as if I care anything about that."

"Oh, but you must," Tobias told her. "A man without honor has no self-respect. And if he has no respect for himself, he has no respect for anyone or anything else." He gently lifted Rachel's face so that she was looking up at him. "You say you are in love with al-Aarif, whom we both know is a man of great honor. If you take that away, he will no longer be the man with whom you fell in love."

Rachel was silent a long moment before answering, "I know you're right. I just wish there was something I could do. I feel so helpless, doing nothing."

"You said he asked you to pray for him?"

"He did."

"Then you must do so, with all your heart. I shall do the same."

Rachel's voice was hesitant but a bit more assured as she replied, "Surely, with our prayers, God will keep him from harm."

"I am certain of it."

Rachel breathed deeply, calming her thoughts and emotions. She looked over at the table beside them and ran her hand across some of the manuscripts Tobias had gathered during the past few weeks.

"Have you found what you were looking for?"

"The Dismas scroll?" Tobias shook his head. "I've searched everywhere, but it's nowhere to be found."

"Perhaps such a gospel doesn't exist," she suggested.

"Oh, I'm certain it exists," Tobias replied. "I watched in a vision as it was being placed in an urn and buried at a fortress called Masada. It was my hope that it had been unearthed and is now somewhere in Jerusalem, but that doesn't appear to be the case. I've searched every library, every archive, all in vain."

"If God brought you here to find it, you shall do so," Rachel insisted.

"Yes, but to do that, we must travel to Masada," Tobias said. "And we cannot attempt such a journey without al-Aarif, so we must double our prayers for his safety."

Rachel's eyes brightened. "My prayers have already been answered."

"How so?"

"I know that you're destined to find the Dismas scroll, and if al-Aarif must accompany you, then surely God will deliver him safely to us."

CHAPTER 30

XERIGORDON

Al-Aarif sat astride his horse and looked toward the fortress at Xerigordon, where a large force of pilgrim soldiers had taken refuge. Reports had come back to the Saracen army from spies within the infidel ranks, describing internal rifts that had all but split the invading army into two camps. Following al-Aarif's departure from Constantinople with Tobias and Rachel, a large contingent of Germans and Italians had swollen the ranks of Peter the Hermit's army to almost twenty thousand, encouraging Peter to give the order to cross the Bosporus and march on the Holy Land. While Walter the Penniless continued to lead the majority of the forces with the assistance of the French knight Geoffrey Burel, about six thousand Germans and Italians, with a smattering of French, had set off on their own under the command of the Italian knight Rainald of Breis.

Rainald's force ran into trouble almost at once. Jealous of the booty the French had carried off on several raids of local villages, Rainald marched on Nicaea, which had already suffered a humiliating defeat at the hands of the French. With no siege equipment, they had no chance of breaching the six-mile-long city wall with its 240 turrets. And so they rode off into the countryside, pillaging as they went and eventually taking control of the lightly garrisoned fortress at Xerigordon, which they planned to use as a staging area for further raids.

But they soon found themselves trapped by an overwhelming Muslim force, headed by Yaghi-Siyan, the Turkish emir of Antioch, and reinforced by the Saracens of Jerusalem. Rather than attack the fortress directly, Yaghi-Siyan decided to lay siege, knowing that the fortress had no internal water supply.

Off to al-Aarif's right, someone shouted, "Loose!" He turned in his saddle to see a Saracen ballista hurl a fifty-pound stone, black against the sky, into the outer wall of the fortress. The heavy projectile struck with terrible effect, shattering sections of the palisade and sending jagged wooden shards flying in every direction.

Al-Aarif saw Yaghi-Siyan riding toward him. The emir was an imposing figure, tall and muscular, and did not look like the slave he once had been. His master, Barkiyaruq's father, Malik Shah, had given him the governorship of Antioch several years after capturing the city in 1085.

"Tell me, al-Aarif, do you still think we should have attacked on the first day?" Yaghi-Siyan asked as he pulled up alongside the Moorish prince.

"I see now that your way is better," al-Aarif replied.

Yaghi-Siyan chuckled. "But yours is the more honorable way, yes? Better to kill them by the sword than to have them die of thirst."

"Many of our men would have died as well," al-Aarif admitted.

"You are a man of honor and courage," Yaghi-Siyan said. "I am pleased the sultan sent me such a commander. But alas, I must protect the lives of thousands—and extract retribution for thousands more killed by these infidels. Remember, al-Aarif, we did not start this war. We did not invite them to our land. And now, it is only fitting that we end it here, in a manner that will send their comrades running back to their homes." He pulled back on the reins, turning the horse. "Do not worry, friend. It has been almost a week; they cannot hold out much longer." He kneed the animal and galloped back toward his troops.

The ballista let fly another stone, joined by several more, each striking the crumbling walls of Xerigordon.

INSIDE THE FORTRESS, the defenders were in agony. They had learned too late that the only supply of water was from outside the walls, with only a few barrels on hand for the half-dozen men who had been stationed there when the pilgrims attacked. When Rainald's army of six thousand found itself surrounded by a Muslim force almost six times as large, they had been forced to retreat inside the fortress with little food and not enough water for a day. Now, five days later, they were baking in the sun, their lips and tongues swollen with thirst.

"We must surrender before we all die," Philippe Guischard told Rainald of Breis as they walked through the courtyard, inspecting the sorry state of the troops. Philippe had been eager for personal glory and wealth, and Peter had convinced him to accompany Rainald as Peter's eyes and ears when the Italians and Germans broke from the main force.

"Surrender?" Rainald said mockingly. "And be put to the sword?"

"Better to die by the sword than by thirst."

"Slaughter some of the horses," Rainald told him.

"Is this some sort of ritual sacrifice, a prayer for rain?" Philippe asked.

"No. It is a matter of survival. Slaughter the horses so that we may drink the blood."

"I . . . I don't think we should do that. It seems an unholy act."

"Would you rather drink your own urine, as others are doing?"

"I . . . I don't know." Philippe put his hand to his forehead. "I can no longer think."

"Surrender!" someone yelled, and Philippe and Rainald looked to see where the voice was coming from. "We're all going to die! We must surrender!"

Most of the soldiers were lying in the shadow of the west wall, moving as little as possible in the afternoon heat. But then they spied one of their soldiers scurrying up a ladder to the south parapet. He climbed atop the wall and began waving his arms at the Muslim army beyond.

"We surrender!" he shouted. "We surrender!"

"Get that man down from there!" Rainald ordered.

When no one immediately complied, he cursed and snatched up a bow from the ground beside a soldier who was either asleep or dead. Nocking an arrow, he took careful aim at the man on the wall, who continued to wave his arms and shout at the enemy beyond.

Rainald released the arrow, which whistled through the air and buried itself in the soldier's neck. The man clawed at his throat, gurgling and sputtering as he grabbed hold of the protruding tip of the arrow. His knees buckled, and he fell forward off the parapet.

"A pity," Rainald muttered as he tossed aside the bow.

"Yes. The poor man was delusional with thirst."

"No, not him. Pity that he fell outside the wall. We could have drunk his blood, as well."

JERUSALEM

Tobias Garlande was having a troubled sleep. After tossing about for several minutes, he sat up in bed and stared into the darkness. The room began to lighten, and he saw someone standing there. For just a moment he thought a servant had come into his room; then he realized he had seen this man before.

"I am Tobias," he said. "Can you hear me?"

"I am called Michael," the vision replied.

"Are you St. Michael, the angel of the Lord?" Tobias asked in wonder.

"No, I am a man. And like you, I am a Keeper."

Tobias nodded in understanding. "Yes. We have visited before, once in the metal bird that flies."

"It is called an airplane."

"A wondrous thing. There must be many wonders in your time."

"All wonders fall short of the glory of God."

"And there is no better commission than to be in service to the Lord," Tobias replied. "But I fear I have failed Him."

"Because you have not yet gone to Masada?"

"Masada . . . the place of my vision. The scroll is there, is it not?"

The dark figure nodded.

"Tell me, Michael, as you are from a time yet to come, will I succeed? Will I find the scroll?"

"I don't know," came the reply. "But I can show you where it lies hidden."

With that, Tobias felt himself being swept away, not in the metal bird called an airplane, but through a brightly lit tunnel that opened upon the ruins of a mountaintop fortress.

"Masada," he whispered.

The walls of the ancient fortress grew transparent, as if fashioned of the finest crystal. As the Keeper Michael pointed, Tobias saw through the crystal walls a light that glowed deep in one of the lower chambers. As he stared at the light, he realized it was a glowing urn, buried in the chamber floor. And the light within the urn was a scroll, the Gospel of Dismas bar-Dismas.

Tobias gasped with wonder and whispered, "Then I *will* succeed in uncovering the scroll."

"That I do not know," Michael told him. "For the scroll shall remain buried at Masada until this future time, a thousand years distant, and it is my destiny to play a part in its discovery. Your destiny is to make the journey to Masada. Beyond that, I cannot see. If it is God's will that you uncover it, then God's will be done."

"But how do I know what is God's will?" Tobias asked.

Before his question could be answered, the vision faded and was gone, and Tobias found himself sitting alone on his bed.

"Masada," he said, then repeated it over and over, a bit louder each time. "Masada . . . Masada . . . Masada."

"Tobias!" Rachel called. "Tobias, are you all right?"

Tobias blinked and looked around. There was no sign of the man named Michael, and he was again alone in his room. He was still sitting on the bed, but the darkness had been pushed away by the first light of dawn.

"Tobias!" Rachael called again, knocking on the door between their rooms.

Tobias got up from the bed and walked over to the door. Opening it, he saw Rachel standing with a lamp in hand, an anxious expression on her face.

"What is it, child?" he asked. "What is wrong?"

Seeing that Tobias was well, Rachel gave à relieved sigh. "Nothing is wrong," she said. "Nothing at all."

"My dear, you really shouldn't worry about me so much," Tobias said. "It makes me worry about you."

Rachel grinned. "I will try not to give you any cause for worry."

XERIGORDON

On September 29, 1096, eight days after the siege of Xerigordon had begun, a lone knight walked out of the fortress, carrying a white flag. Yaghi-Siyan signaled that he was to be given safe passage.

"Water, please, water," the man said in Arabic as he

staggered to a halt in front of the Turkish emir. His throat was so swollen that he could scarcely be understood.

"Have you come just to ask for water?" Yaghi-Siyan asked angrily.

"My lord, Rainald of Breis, wishes to discuss terms."

Yaghi-Siyan smiled and rubbed hands together. "Give him water," he ordered, then turned to al-Aarif. "Bring your men back to Jerusalem. Tell Sultan Barkiyaruq that Allah has granted us a great victory."

Al-Aarif gave a slight bow, then mounted his horse and rode to where the force sent by Barkiyaruq was gathered. He signaled them to follow, then began the long ride back to Jerusalem, carrying word of the defeat of the Christian force.

INSIDE THE FORTRESS, Rainald wept tears of bitter defeat. "I arrived with six thousand and have less than two thousand still alive," he said. "I have failed my Lord."

"We should feel no shame, sir," Philippe Guischard told him. "We fought bravely and well. Now we have no choice but to ask for terms. The Christian world will long remember the courage we showed here."

Rainald looked up at Philippe with ill-concealed disgust. "You were begging me to surrender at the first sign of thirst. What do you know of courage?"

"I know that we accomplished nothing by prolonging the siege," Philippe replied. "Perhaps if you had listened to me, four thousand more would still be alive, and Yaghi-Siyan would have been generous with his terms to avoid battle. Now, we know not what his terms will be."

"There will be no terms," Rainald replied.

"Sir, they are at the gates!" one of his officers called.

Rainald nodded. "Let them in."

The gates swung open and trumpets blared from beyond. Drums beat a pulsing rhythm as Yaghi-Siyan entered on horseback, followed by several hundred foot soldiers, all dressed in billowing green trousers, white shirts, and gold waistcoats. They marched in step to the drums, carrying pikes from which colorful streamers fluttered in the breeze. All were armed with gleaming scimitars held at the waist by bright red sashes.

A long double-column of bowmen marched through the gates and split into two columns that turned left and right and headed up two sets of stone stairs to the parapet. They quickly fanned out around the perimeter of the wall, standing at attention with arrows nocked on their bows.

"We are all going to be killed," Philippe said to Rainald, his voice weak with fear.

"For the glory of God," Rainald replied, resigned to their fate.

Yaghi-Siyan held up his hand, and the drums and trumpets were stilled, the only sound the fluttering of the pennants.

"Which one of you is Rainald of Breis?" Yaghi-Siyan called in Arabic, and one of his soldiers stepped forward and translated into the French common among Europeans.

"I am Rainald, commander of this fortress," Rainald declared, stepping forward. His words were translated for the Turk.

Yaghi-Siyan made motion with his hand, and a dozen two-wheeled carts were rolled into the fortress and placed at different spots around the courtyard.

"Those casks contain water," Yaghi-Siyan said. "As your men lay down their arms, they may approach and drink."

When the translation was given, one of the defenders shouted, "Water!" With an almost animal-like roar, his comrades threw down their weapons and ran to the carts. They crowded around the casks, drinking from long-handled dippers, then waiting their turn to drink again. One cart had been brought near Rainald, and Philippe and the other officers drank eagerly, but Rainald stood his ground.

"Are you not thirsty?" Yaghi-Siyan asked.

"I am," Rainald admitted. "But I will let my men drink their fill first."

"And if no water remains after they have slaked their thirst?"

"I will remain thirsty," Rainald declared.

"Are you prepared to accept my terms?"

Rainald looked at his soldiers, weaponless as they crowded around the water carts, each group surrounded by Yaghi-Siyan's armed soldiers. It was, Rainald realized, a clever way of taking control of them. He glanced up at the bowmen on the walls, then back at Yaghi-Siyan.

"I have no choice but to accept," he said.

"The terms are harsh."

"I knew they would be."

"Each of your men will be allowed to decide his own fate," Yaghi-Siyan explained. "He can choose to convert to Islam and live, but as a slave. Or he can remain true to the Christian faith and die."

"I have made my decision," Rainald said. "I will not renounce my faith."

Yaghi-Siyan listened to the translation and nodded. "I expected no less. You shall be the last to die."

"Let me be the first," Rainald said.

"You are in no position to dictate when you will die."

"Then I ask it as a favor from one who worships the same God, though in a different faith. Grant me this wish."

"Why do you wish to die first?"

"I want my men to see that their leader was true to his faith until the last breath."

Yaghi-Siyan smiled. "I grant your request. I will also accord you the honor of dying by my own hand." He removed his personal water-skin from around his neck and handed it to Rainald, saying, "You will not die a thirsty man."

Rainald lifted the skin to his mouth and drank eagerly. His throat was so swollen and dry that the water burned going down. He knew drinking so fast after such a long thirst would make him ill—if he wasn't about to die anyway. He laughed aloud.

"How can you laugh in the face of death?" Yaghi-Siyan asked.

"I laugh, because I have found joy in the Lord."

PHILIPPE GUISCHARD TOOK a final drink of water, dropped the dipper into the cask, and turned away from the cart. He looked over and saw Rainald handing a water-skin to the Muslim leader, who hung it around his neck and then slid from his horse's back. As Philippe watched in stunned silence, Rainald faced his soldiers, who were spread throughout the courtyard, and called out, "Men, I go to face the judgment of my Maker. I leave it to you to examine your hearts and choose to follow me into the arms of our Lord or enter into a new life as servants of Allah."

Turning back to Yaghi-Siyan, he bowed to the Turk and remained bent forward, his gaze fixed on the ground. As Yaghi-Siyan drew and raised his scimitar, Philippe heard Rainald say softly, "Into Your hands I commend my spirit."

The blade of the scimitar flashed in the sun, and Rainald's head fell forward, while his body crumpled backwards.

A number of Christians cried out in fear and anger. Some started toward their leader but were stopped by the pikes and scimitars of the Muslims surrounding them.

"Hear me!" Yaghi-Siyan called out to the captives, pausing to allow the translator to repeat the command. "Each of you may choose whether you shall live as a slave or die. Those of you who will convert to Islam and accept Muhammad as the true prophet, move to this side." He pointed the scimitar to his right. "You shall live, by the grace of Allah. Those of you who refuse to renounce your faith, move to the other side. You will receive the same justice as your leader."

"No!" one of the Christians shouted. "We are warriors for Christ! I will not turn my back on our Lord!"

"The choice is yours," Yaghi-Siyan said. "Renounce Christianity, convert to Islam, and live as a slave until you are able to purchase your freedom. Or remain true to your faith and die."

"I shall die!" someone cried out, and others joined in shouting their defiance. But nearly as many chose to renounce Christianity, and they walked away from their comrades to the area designated by the victors as the Place of Conversion.

CHAPTER 31

NEW YORK CITY

The phone rang, awakening David Meyers in the bedroom he was using at the safe-house apartment. Groggily, he leaned over to the nightstand and answered it, muttering, "Hello?"

He heard a dial tone and thought that whoever called must have hung up. Then a voice came from the speaker of his laptop, which sat glowing on the mattress beside him.

"Hassan al-Halid."

Sitting up and pulling the computer onto his lap, he stared at the monitor and saw Mehdi Jahmshidi, who had answered the phone in his hotel room, giving the alias he was using in New York. The image from the webcam David had secretly installed was a bit fuzzy but easy to make out.

"We shall meet on the train," the caller said, his words picked up by the bug in Jahmshidi's telephone. He spoke English with no trace of an accent.

"At the scheduled time?" Jahmshidi asked.

"Yes."

"Do not fail as Ishaq Nidal failed," Jahmshidi said.

Ishaq Nidal, David knew, was the suicide bomber who had killed four people at Ann Coopersmith's funeral.

"I will not fail."

"Allahu Akbar," Jahmshidi said.

"Allahu Akbar," the caller replied.

Jahmshidi hung up the phone then walked out of the range of the smoke-alarm camera. David tapped the touchpad and switched to the feed from the webcam in the return-air register. He saw Jahmshidi sitting on the couch, but otherwise doing or saying nothing.

David stared at the screen, wondering what Jahmshidi's caller meant when he mentioned a train. Was he meeting Jahmshidi or someone else? Or was he planning another terrorist attack?

Again the phone rang, and Jahmshidi walked over to answer it, saying, "Al-Halid."

"Allahu Akbar," the caller replied.

They spoke in Arabic, and while David didn't understand the language, he was capturing the stream to a voice-activated translator. He opened the program and looked in the dialogue window.

The translator was far more accurate when programmed to a known voice. In this case, it had trouble with many of the words and offered a best-guess translation. Sometimes it was so far off that the words in the dialogue window were almost nonsensical:

> VOICE 1: *The eternal.*
> VOICE 2: *Great God.*
> VOICE 1: *When commencement surgery?*
> VOICE 2: *Daytime.*
> VOICE 1: *Martyrs in profusion?*
> VOICE 2: *Abundant seek to nurture Allah*
> VOICE 1: *Great God.*
> VOICE 2: *Great God.*

When the phone call ended, David copied the short dialogue into his word processor and studied it, correcting what he could and putting his notes in parentheses. At first he wondered why Jahmshidi's alias was translated as "the eternal," but then he did a Google search on "Arabic Halid," and the first Web site that popped up said, "In Arabic, *halid* is an adjective meaning 'eternal.'"

David completed his translation of the translator and read it over:

> Jahmshidi: *This is Al-Halid.*
> Caller: *God is great. (Allahu Akbar)*
> Jahmshidi: *When does the operation begin?*
> Caller: *During the day. (Today? Tomorrow?)*
> Jahmshidi: *Do you have enough martyrs?*
> Caller: *Many want to serve Allah.*
> Jahmshidi: *God is great.*
> Caller: *God is great.*

With the reference to martyrs, David was certain the call had something to do with suicide bombers. Obviously an attack was being planned, but when and where? He knew he should warn someone, but whom? Lt. Frank Santini? And what would he say? That an attack was being planned for some unknown place at some unknown time?

He drummed his fingers on the mattress as he contemplated what to do. He doubted Santini or anyone else would believe him. And how would he explain where he got the information, sketchy as it was?

"It was a cinch, Lieutenant," David said aloud. "I have his room bugged three ways from Sunday." He shook his head. "Yeah. Santini is going to buy that."

David considered awakening Father Flannery, Preston Lewkis, and Sarah Arad, but he decided to let them sleep for the time being.

"C'mon," he whispered as he turned back to the computer screen. "Give me something more. Something solid."

CHICAGO

Rhoda Peters stood on the platform of the Metra station in the Chicago suburb of Glenview, waiting for the commuter train that would take her to her job downtown.

"Seven fifty-two southbound. Stay clear of the tracks," a robotic-sounding voice said over the PA system.

With its bell clanging, the train came to a stop and the doors slid open. A half-dozen morning commuters hurried aboard.

"My God!" Rhoda gasped as she stepped onto the nearest car.

There were twenty passengers already on board. Some had their heads back, their eyes and mouths wide open. A few were leaning forward with their heads between their legs. Others were lying in the aisle. All were dead.

As the reality sank in, Rhoda began to scream. She turned to get off the train before the doors closed, but her knees buckled. Her scream became a choking gurgle as she pitched forward through the open door and fell lifeless onto the platform.

CHAPTER 32

NEW YORK CITY

F r. Michael Flannery stood in the kitchen of the safe-
house apartment and poured several generous dollops
of half-and-half into his morning cup of coffee. Setting down the carton, he added three teaspoons of sugar and
stirred it with the spoon.

Taking the mug into the living room, he sat on the couch
and contemplated the dream—or more accurately, the
vision—he had experienced during the night. He had witnessed the frustration of a fellow Keeper at not being able
to fulfill his destiny of finding the Dismas scroll. In the vision, he and the man named Tobias had been able to communicate, and Flannery took Tobias to Masada and revealed
the site where the scroll lay buried.

But how could that be? If Tobias unearthed the scroll a
thousand years ago, why was it still there last year? Was
Tobias fated to fail in his mission? Had Flannery unwittingly
shown the old man the path to his own death?

His musings were interrupted by Sarah Arad, who came
into the living room and said, "My, you look deep in thought
this morning."

Sarah was standing just inside the doorway, holding a cup
of coffee in both hands. Automatically, Flannery stood.

"Heavens, Father Michael, you don't have to stand every
time I enter a room." She gave a slight wave of her hand.
"You flatter me."

"A reflex, I'm afraid," Flannery replied. "Won't you join me?" He waited for her to sit in a plush chair across from the couch, then sat back down.

"So, what were you thinking about so intently?" Sarah asked. "The symposium?"

"Well, my thoughts never drift too far from the symposium. But just now I was thinking about the scroll."

"Yes, it's in my mind often," she said. "Sometimes I almost wish we hadn't found it, only to lose it again."

"Well, I give thanks to God that we had it long enough to make copies so it can be studied and authenticated."

"How can we authenticate it, without the original?"

"We had it long enough for carbon dating, and the papyrus was first century."

"True."

"Still . . ." Flannery said mysteriously.

"Still what?"

"If it was found during the Crusades, why was it still there a thousand years later?"

"Crusades? What are you talking about?"

Realizing he had said more than he intended, Flannery forced a smile. "It's nothing; just some foolish musings. My research turned up an eleventh-century scribe named Tobias who spent his life locating and transcribing early-Christian documents."

"And you think this scribe may have found the Dismas scroll?"

"I'm not sure, but there's some evidence he knew of the Dismas gospel and may have seen it. Much of what we know about early Christian history is the result of Tobias's diligence. In many cases, his transcriptions are all we have of first- and second-century documents."

"If he found the Dismas scroll and hid it again, don't you think he'd have made a copy?"

"A copy?" Flannery asked, his voice rising in interest.

"Surely, if such a diligent scribe had found a document as important as the Dismas scroll, he would have made a copy."

"A copy, yes!" Flannery exclaimed. "I should've known that. Next time I'll ask him, but I'm sure that's it."

"Ask him?" Sarah said, looking confused. "What do you mean, next time you'll ask him?"

"What?" Flannery replied, now so deep in his own thoughts that he could barely follow the conversation.

Sarah laughed. "You're just like my father. Sometimes he'd say something that only he and God could understand. Only I'm not sure God always understood."

"Turn on the TV!" Preston shouted as he rushed into the room.

"Good morning, sleepyhead, did you have a good night?" Sarah asked.

"The TV!" Preston said again, snatching up the remote and aiming it toward the set. He switched channels until he found a news show.

"—and so now Vienna joins the list," a reporter was saying off camera. "That brings the number of attacks to fifteen. Back to you, Claire."

"Fifteen what?" Sarah asked.

"Suicide bomb attacks during the night," Preston replied. "They're happening all over the world."

"For those of you who are just tuning in, here is a recap," the blond anchorwoman said. Her name, Claire McKenzie, was displayed at the bottom of the screen. "In the last eight hours there have been a series of terrorist attacks all around the world."

She consulted a piece of paper on her desk.

"So far attacks have occurred in London, Paris, Brussels, Madrid, Berlin, Copenhagen, Rome, Tel Aviv, Lisbon, Warsaw, Moscow, Manila, Rio de Janeiro, Berne, and now Vienna. Yes, even traditionally neutral Switzerland seems to have been drawn into this world upheaval. Exact figures as to the number of casualties are not yet in, but early estimates suggest the total may be in the hundreds. So far we—"

She stopped midsentence and put a finger to her earpiece. Nodding, she looked back at the camera.

"This just in, we have videotape from an organization that calls itself Defenders of the Faith. We are going to play that for you now."

"Defenders of the Faith?" Preston said. "Have you ever heard of them?"

"No," Sarah and Flannery said in unison.

The studio shot was replaced by a grainy home video. There was a grisly familiarity to the video, which featured a bearded turbaned man staring at the camera with an AK-47 leaning against the wall behind him.

"That's Mehdi Jahmshidi!" Sarah said. "This isn't Defenders of the Faith; it's Arkaan."

Jahmshidi began speaking in English.

"This morning I, Mehdi Jahmshidi, Servant of Allah the Most High, and the Defenders of the Faith began our work. We have joined hands with like-minded Muslims, Christians, and Jews to protect our faiths from those godless souls who would create one world faith, one world order. We have conducted martyrdom operations all over the world, carried out by the courageous and faithful who are now in paradise, enjoying the rewards of their good work on Earth.

"The Defenders of the Faith call attention to the satanic gathering that is taking place in New York City. We will not allow the so-called People of the Book symposium to continue, for its goal is to create a false doctrine that is not true to any faith.

"That is the work of al-Shaitaan—Satan—and we call on all Muslims, Christians, and Jews around the world to rise up in protest and in defense of our unique faiths."

Jahmshidi pointed his finger at the camera. "To all who

attend the symposium, what happens to you will not be on our conscience."

The picture went black for a moment; then once more Claire McKenzie's image filled the screen.

"That was a tape of Mehdi Jahmshidi, leader of the Islamist terrorist group Arkaan, but now declaring himself to be in partnership with—"

The sound was abruptly cut off, and the screen displayed a network logo and the words: World Satellite News Alert. The notice cross-faded to a black woman seated at a news desk.

"This is Althea Gale in Chicago," the woman said. "World Satellite News has just confirmed that there has been a possible terrorist attack on a commuter train on its way downtown. More than twenty people are believed to be dead. We have some footage from the Glenview Metra station."

A live shot showed a sitting train with police cars and ambulances lined up about a hundred yards away. Rescue workers in full biohazard suits were going in and out of the train, some carrying equipment, others transporting covered bodies on stretchers.

Althea Gale continued in voiceover, "The train passengers are believed to have suffered some sort of chemical or biological attack, but the agent has not been determined. It is also not known whether this attack is connected to the rash of suicide bombings around the world. In those incidents, explosive devices were employed, while there is no evidence of an explosion in this latest incident. We'll bring you more information as soon as it becomes available."

Preston clicked the remote, turning off the TV.

"It has to be related," Sarah said.

"But why attack a train in Chicago to protest a symposium in New York?" Flannery asked.

"Or blow up sidewalk vendors in Manila?" Sarah added.

"So, in light of all this, do we go to the symposium today?" Preston asked.

Sarah turned to the priest. "What do you think?"

"Of course I'm going," he replied. "If I don't, the forces of evil will have won."

IN HIS APARTMENT on Central Park West, Fr. Antonio Sangremano answered the telephone.

"Have you seen the news?" a man asked.

"Yes," Sangremano answered, recognizing the caller as Benjamin Bishara.

"Did you know what he was up to?"

"No."

"We need to talk."

"Where?

"Let's visit our so-called friend," Bishara said. "He's moved to the Hotel Musée."

"Yes, he told me. In a half hour, shall we say?"

"Fine." The phone clicked off.

DAVID MEYERS WAS in his bedroom in the safe-house apartment. He had woken up after the others, who were in their own rooms dressing for their outing to Stuyvesant Hall. He planned to remain behind, keeping track of the news via his laptop browser and also following events on the TV in Mehdi Jahmshidi's hotel room, which he could see via one of the hidden webcams. He now understood the reference to a train he had overheard during the night, and he felt guilty for not having reported it, despite having had virtually no details or corroborating evidence.

He had just taken a bite of a bagel when he heard, through the computer speaker, someone knocking on the door of Jahmshidi's room. Switching from the Web browser to the webcam image, he watched as Jahmshidi crossed the room and opened the door. He recognized the visitors at once:

Benjamin Bishara and Fr. Antonio Sangremano. The three men sat down on the couch and a nearby chair.

"Are you responsible for those suicide attacks?" Sangremano asked as soon as the door was closed.

"Not I," Jahmshidi replied. "We."

"We?" Bishara and Sangremano replied in unison.

"We have mutual interest in interrupting the symposium, don't we?"

"Not this way," Bishara said. "I never would have authorized suicide bombers."

"Nor I," Sangremano put in.

"Nonsense. You approved bringing down those airliners. There were many more killed in that operation than today."

"There were specific targets on those planes, some of the key people behind the symposium," Bishara pointed out.

"Someone had to take the next step," Jahmshidi countered. "It was obvious neither of you were going to."

"You should have discussed it with us," Sangremano said.

"That would have done no good. Christian and Jew," he said derisively. "Neither of you truly understand what it is to be a martyr."

"Our own Lord, Jesus Christ, was a martyr," Sangremano said. "And countless of His followers through the centuries— many at the hands of your people, I might add."

"And what were the six million Jews killed by Hitler, if not martyrs?" Bishara added.

"That is not martyrdom," Jahmshidi said with a backhanded wave. "They did not go willingly, gladly, to their deaths. Our martyrs do, and as each of them steps into paradise, he leaves behind a glorious testament to the faith of Islam."

"But you bombed cafés, shopping centers, bus stations, a school, a hospital," Sangremano said. "How do you expect something like that to rally others to our cause?"

"Our cause?" Jahmshidi asked. "We each, for our own

reasons, want the symposium to fail, but beyond that, we share no cause."

The three men stared at one another for a long moment; then Sangremano held up his hand and said with a sigh, "We are this close. We mustn't stop until we put an end to the People of the Book movement once and for all. Until that's accomplished, we should continue to work together."

He waited to see if Bishara would object, but the other man remained silent.

Turning back to Jahmshidi, Sangremano asked, "How many more suicide bombings do you have planned?"

"They are martyrdom operations," Jahmshidi corrected.

"All right, martyrdom operations. How many more?"

"The bombings are finished . . . for the time being."

"What about that Chicago train?" Bishara asked. "Was that part of this, as well?"

"That was an operational test."

"What do you mean?"

"We have isolated and strengthened a special agent. I needed to know how it would work in a confined area, and you saw just how effective it was. If it worked on a train car, it will also work in a conference hall."

Back at the safe-house apartment, David Meyers nearly dropped the bagel he was holding. Leaping up from the bed, he ran out into the hallway.

"Father Flannery!" he called down the hall. "Preston! Sarah! You've got to see this!"

CHAPTER 33

MASADA

S oon after al-Aarif returned to Jerusalem with word of
the defeat of the pilgrims at Xerigordon, he agreed to
take Tobias Garlande to the ancient Jewish fortress of
Masada. He wanted Rachel Benyuli to remain in the safety
of the palace, but she insisted on accompanying them, and
Tobias agreed, explaining that in his visions, she was always
on hand.

It was a tiring but not overly arduous journey by horseback south to the steep-sided rocky mount that rose high
above the nearby Dead Sea, with cliffs that plunged deep
into desert gorges. The trail to the top was too narrow for
horses, so they left them in the shade of some towering
boulders and made the ascent on foot along the ancient
Serpent Path. Rachel feared it would be too strenuous for
Tobias, but he seemed to grow younger and more vigorous
as he started up the trail, fairly leaping over rocks as he
climbed ahead of them. Periodically he would stop and recite portions of Flavius Josephus's *The Wars of the Jews*,
one of many works by the first-century Jewish historian that
Tobias had translated from the original Greek:

*There was a rock, not small in circumference and very
high. It was encompassed with valleys of such vast
depth downward that the eye could not reach their bot-
toms; they were abrupt, and such as no animal could*

walk upon, excepting at two places of the rock, where it subsides, in order to afford a passage for ascent, though not without difficulty.

Now, of the ways that lead to it, one . . . is called the Serpent, as resembling that animal in its narrowness and its perpetual windings; for it is broken off at the prominent precipices of the rock, and returns frequently into itself, and lengthening again by little and little, hath much ado to proceed forward; and he that would walk along it must first go on one leg and then on the other; there is also nothing but destruction, in case your feet slip; for on each side there is a vastly deep chasm and precipice, sufficient to quell the courage of everybody by the terror it infuses into the mind. . . .

Upon this top of the hill, Jonathan the high priest first of all built a fortress, and called it Masada.

As they neared the plateau bearing the ruins of the fortress, Tobias described how a band of less than a thousand Jewish Zealots held off a force of fifteen thousand Roman soldiers, who laid siege to the fortress from 72 to 73 AD. The Romans eventually built an earthen ramp to carry their ballista and other engines of war to the summit, but the Zealots decided to die at their own hands rather than surrender.

Since suicide was one of the greatest of sins, they devised a plan that would put that burden on but a single person. Josephus learned of their heroic sacrifice because several of the defenders hid out in the fortress and were found alive when the Romans entered. He recounted the Zealots' final hours in *The Wars of the Jews*:

They then chose ten men by lot to slay all the rest; every one of whom laid himself down by his wife and children on the ground, and threw his arms about them, and they offered their necks to the stroke of those who by lot executed that melancholy office.

And when these ten had, without fear, slain them all,
they made the same rule for casting lots for themselves,
that he whose lot it was should first kill the other nine,
and after all should kill himself. . . .

So, the nine offered their necks to the executioner,
and he who was the last of all took a view of all the
other bodies . . . and when he perceived that they were
all slain, he set fire to the palace, and with the great
force of his hand ran his sword entirely through him-
self, and fell down dead near to his own relations.

As Tobias walked among the stone ruins, he occasionally
closed his eyes and stood in silence, trying to perceive the
precise spot where the sacred gospel lay buried. But the
area looked a bit different from what he had seen in his
vision, and soon one section of ruins began to look like
every other. Finally he dropped onto a large stone and sat
shaking his head in frustration.

"Don't fear," Rachel said as she sat beside him and gently stroked his hand. "If the scroll is here, you will find it."

"Will I?" He looked up at her, his eyes betraying an un-
characteristic lack of conviction.

"Of course you will," she soothed. "God would not lead us
all this way, just to leave us empty-handed." She waited for
his response, but when he remained silent, she asked, "What
is it, Tobias? What do you fear?"

With a slight sigh, he took both her hands in his own.
"There's something I haven't told you. About my visions."

"What is it?" she said in concern.

"I . . . I'm not sure that I'm supposed to recover the
Dismas scroll. There's a man, someone I have seen here at
Masada."

"Al-Aarif?" she asked.

"While I've seen both you and al-Aarif here with me, this
is a different man from a different place and time. As long
ago as the scroll was written and buried, that many years in

the future is where this man named Michael is from. And through him I have learned that the scroll is to remain buried for another millennium, until he unearths it and reveals it to the world."

"I don't understand," she said. "Isn't it your own destiny to discover the scroll?"

"Yes, that's what I've seen, what I've believed."

"Then that's what you must do."

"But how can these two contrary destinies coexist?" Tobias mused aloud.

Rachel gave an ineffable smile. "Isn't destiny and mystery the province of the Lord? Let Him worry about resolving such enigmas. Surely you have been led here, and just as surely you must finish what you have begun."

He shared her smile and patted her hands. "You're right, my child. Let us find this great treasure of Dismas bar-Dismas." Standing, he looked around. "Where's al-Aarif?"

She shrugged. "I'll find him."

Rachel started forward, but just then a voice called out, "It's here! Over here!"

They both spun around and saw al-Aarif standing in the distance, frantically waving for them to join him.

"I've found it!" he cried out again and again as they hurried toward him through the ruins.

"Where?" Tobias asked, looking around but seeing nothing but crumbling walls.

"Down there," al-Aarif declared, pointing to the ground about twenty feet away.

Rachel scanned the ground and a nearby wall. "I don't see anything."

"Is it buried?" Tobias asked, walking forward and then kneeling to scrape at the ground.

"No, no," al-Aarif declared, coming over and lifting Tobias to his feet. "It's buried, but not here. Look down there . . . deeper." He pointed several feet away at nothing more than undisturbed ground. Tobias was about to protest, when al-Aarif repeated, "Deeper. Look deeper."

As Tobias stared at the ground, he felt something stir within his chest—a vibration, a lightness, that rose up his spine and filled his head. The ground began to shimmer, growing less solid, until it began to part and fade away, revealing a brilliant lantern of light deep below. Tobias was staring into an underground chamber, and at the heart of the chamber, a foot or two below the earthen floor, rested an urn that glowed with an ethereal light.

Rachel came up beside Tobias and whispered, "I feel something, but I . . . I cannot see."

"It's there," he assured her. "The Gospel of Dismas is at hand."

"Come," al-Aarif said, taking them by the arms. "There is a stairway."

He led them along the ruins to a hidden opening in one of the walls. They had to squeeze through, into a stone stairway that led to one of the lower rooms of the fortress. It took a few moments for their eyes to adjust to the light, but enough of the roof was missing to allow them to see without the use of a torch.

Al-Aarif led the way into a room directly below where they had been standing. The chamber was about ten feet wide by twenty feet long, with a hard-packed earthen floor and walls made of closely fitted stones. The low ceiling was a marvel of construction, fashioned of long stone slabs that traversed the entire width of the room.

Al-Aarif halted in the middle of the room. "What a strange feeling I'm having," he said as he looked around. "I've never been here, yet I know this place." He pointed toward the far end of the room. "That's where you'll find the manuscript you seek. It's in an urn buried by a man and a woman."

"Yes," Tobias replied.

"How is it that I know this?"

"Because you were here," Tobias said. "In my vision, you were with me when they buried the scroll."

"Yes," al-Aarif said. "I thought it was a dream, but now that you say the words, I know it was a vision. And I remember seeing you there as well."

Al-Aarif had brought along a small spade, and he started to dig. Within a few minutes, he found the urn. So as not to break it, he finished digging it out with his hands. Then, lifting the urn from the hole, he gingerly handed it to Tobias.

Tobias used the edge of the spade to cut through the wax that sealed the cover to the urn, then lifted it off and removed the scroll.

"Look how wonderfully preserved it is," he said in amazement.

"It's so much better preserved than most of the manuscripts we've worked on," Rachael said. "It looks no more than a few years old."

"When was it written?" al-Aarif asked.

"Just over a thousand years ago," Tobias said.

"How can it look so new?"

"The dry weather has helped. But I believe it has been preserved by the hand of God, for this document is at the very heart and soul of Christianity," Tobias declared.

"Without this document, the Christian faith wouldn't exist?" Rachel asked.

"That's not what I mean. Christianity has existed for one thousand years without this document, and I daresay it could continue without it until the end of time."

Tobias held the document to his nose and breathed in deeply.

"This gospel was penned by someone who actually walked with Jesus," he continued. "It was written by Dismas bar-Dismas, son of Dismas the Good Thief, who on the cross sought and was granted salvation by Jesus."

"It seems your long journey from Toledo has been worth-while," al-Aarif declared.

"Indeed," Tobias agreed. "What I am holding is a treasure beyond measure. Let the pilgrim knights battle for land and property. All the wealth in the world could not purchase this single manuscript."

CHAPTER 34

JERUSALEM

It wasn't until Tobias returned to Jerusalem with his companions and examined the scroll that he discovered the Trevia Dei symbol written in what appeared to be blood. It was, in fact, the very same symbol that was on the cloth he kept in the locket around his neck. He knew at once that this was the real and true Gospel of Dismas bar-Dismas.

Tobias and Rachel rolled the scroll out onto a long table, then weighted it down at each end, preparatory to transcribing it.

"Oh, this is rather unusual," he said as he scanned the characters. "It's written in both Greek and Hebrew. I don't believe I've ever seen a first-century document so constructed."

"Can you read it?" al-Aarif asked.

"Certainly. I'm proficient in the ancient forms of both languages."

For an exceedingly long time, he read in silence, experiencing an ineffable joy over the task at hand:

ΔΙΗΓΗΣΙΣ ΔΙΣΜΑΣ ΒΑΡΔΙΣΜΑΣ ΑΝΑΓΕΓΡΑΦΑΜΕΝΗ ΕΝ
ΧΕΙΡΙ ΑΥΤΟΥ ΕΝ ΕΤΕΙ ΤΡΙΑΚΟΣΤΩΙ ΑΠΟ ΤΟΝ ΘΑΝΑΤΟΝ
ΚΑΙ ΑΝΑΣΤΑΣΙΝ ΤΟΥ ΧΡΙΣΤΟΥ ΜΝΗΜΟΝΕΥΘΗΣΟΜΕΝΗ ΕΝ
ΤΗΙ ΠΟΛΕΙ ΡΟΜΑΙ ΥΠΟ ΤΗΣ ΕΝΤΟΛΗΣ ΠΑΥΛΟΥ ΤΟΥ
ΑΠΟΣΤΟΛΟΥ ΔΙΑ ΔΟΥΛΟΥ ΚΑΙ ΜΑΡΤΥΡΟΥ

ΕΓΟ ΔΙΣΜΑΣ ΥΙΟΣ ΤΟΥ ΔΙΣΜΑΣ ΓΑΛΙΛΗΟΥ ΚΑΙ ΑΓΓΕΛΟΣ
ΙΗΣΟΥ ΧΡΙΣΤΟΥ ΥΠΟ ΤΗΣ ΒΟΥΛΗΣ ΘΕΟΥ ΠΑΤΡΟΣ ΔΙΑ ΘΕΛΗ-
ΜΑΤΟΣ ΑΓΙΟΥ ΠΝΕΥΜΑΤΟΣ ΕΝΤΑΥΘΑ ΠΡΟΤΙΘΗΜΙ ΔΙΑΘΗΚΗ
ΠΙΣΤΕΥΟΝΤΟΥΣΙ ΚΑΙ ΠΙΣΤΕΥΣΟΝΤΕΣΙ ΚΑΤΑ ΒΟΥΛΗΝ ΑΥΤΟΥ

ΜΑΡΤΥΡΙΟΝ Ο ΕΓΟ ΔΕΔΩΚΑ ΠΑΝΤΩΝ Α ΙΗΣΟΥΣ ΤΕΤΕΛΕ
ΥΤΗΚΕ ΚΑΙ ΕΠΑΙΔΕΥΣΕ ΠΡΟ ΣΤΑΥΡΩΣΙΝ ΑΥΤΟΥ ΥΠΟ ΠΟΝ-
ΤΙΟ Υ ΠΙΛΑΤΟΥ ΗΓΗΜΟΝΤΙΣ ΡΟΜΑΝΟΥ ΙΟΥΔΑΙΑΣ ΥΠΕΡ
ΔΕΔΟΤΑΙ ΕΚ ΤΗΝ ΣΤΩΜΑΤΩΝ ΑΓΙΩΝ ΑΠΟΣΤΟΛΩΝ ΑΥΤΩΝ
ΠΡΟΣ ΕΜΕ ΑΛΛΑ ΠΕΡΙ ΣΤΑΥΡΟΣΕΩΣ ΑΥΤΟΥ ΦΕΡΩ ΜΑΡΤΥΡ-
ΠΟΝ ΙΔΙΟΝ ΚΑΙ ΠΕΡΙ ΤΩΝ ΑΚΟΛΟΥΘΗΣΕΩΝ ΜΕΧΡΙ ΑΝ-
ΑΒΕΒΗΚΕ ΕΙΣ ΤΟΝ ΟΥΡΑΝΙΟΝ ΠΡΟΣ ΔΕΞΙΑΙ ΤΟΥ ΠΑΤΡΟΣ
ΠΑΓΚΡΑΤΟΥ

ΤΑΥΤΑ ΕΣΤΙΝ Α ΟΙ ΠΙΣΤΕΥΟΝΤΕΣ ΑΠΟΜΑΡΤΥΡΟΝΤΑΙ
ΑΛΗΘΗ ΟΤΙ ΠΑΙΣ ΕΤΕΧΘΗ ΜΑΡΙΑΜ ΝΑΖΑΡΕΘ ΕΝ ΗΣ ΥΣΤΕΡΑ
ΚΥΡΙΟΣ ΑΥΤΟΣ ΥΠΟ ΔΥΝΑΜΕΩΣ ΠΝΕΥΜΑΤΟΣ ΑΓΙΟΥ ΠΑΡΑΔ-
ΕΔΗΚΕ ΥΙΟΝ ΕΙΝΑΙ ΒΑΣΙΛΕΑ ΤΗΣ ΒΑΣΙΛΕΙΑΣ ΥΠΕΣΧΗΜΕΝΗΣ
ΟΥΡΑΝΙΗΣ ΟΤΙ ΠΑΙΣ ΜΑΡΙΑΜ ΓΑΜΕΤΙΔΟΣ ΙΩΣΗΦ ΕΞ ΟΙΚΟΥ
ΔΑΥΙΔ ΤΗΣ ΑΝΕΥ ΜΙΑΣΜΑΤΟΣ ΚΑΙ ΜΗΤΡΟΣ ΤΟΥ ΚΥΡΙΟΥ ΜΕ-
ΜΑΝΤΕΥΕΤΑΙ ΥΠΟ ΤΩΝ ΠΡΩΦΗΤΩΝ ΙΣΡΑΕΛ ΣΩΤΗΡ ΚΑΙ
ΣΗΜΕΙΟΝ ΤΟΥ ΘΕΟΥ ΜΕΤΑ ΗΜΩΝ ΠΑΙΔΩΝ ΑΥΤΟΥ ΤΗΣ
ΔΙΑΘΗΚΗΣ ΟΤΙ ΟΝΟΜΑ ΑΥΤΟΥ ΙΗΣΟΥΣ

ΚΑΙ ΟΤΕ ΙΗΣΟΥΣ ΠΑΡΑΓΙΝΕΤΑΙ ΑΠΟ ΤΗΣ ΓΑΛΙΛΑΙΑΣ ΕΠΙ
ΤΟΝ ΙΟΡΔΑΝΗΝ ΠΡΟΣ ΙΩΑΝΝΗΝ ΒΑΠΤΙΣΘΗΝΑΙ ΘΟΡΥΒΗΤΟ
ΙΩΑΝΝΗΣ ΛΕΓΩΝ ΔΙΔΑΣΚΑΛΕ ΔΙΟΤΙ ΕΡΩΤΑΣ ΕΜΕ ΒΑΠΤΙΖΕΙΝ
ΟΤΕ ΕΓΩ ΧΡΕΙΑΝ ΕΧΩ ΥΠΟ ΤΟΥ ΥΙΟΥ ΑΝΘΡΩΠΟΥ ΒΑΠΤΙΣΘΗ-
ΝΑΙ

ΚΑΙ ΑΠΟΚΡΙΘΕΙΣ Ο ΙΗΣΟΥΣ ΕΙΠΕΝ ΑΥΤΩΙ ΑΦΕΣ ΑΡΤΙ
ΟΥΤΩΣ ΔΙΑΘΗΚΗ ΠΙΣΤΕΩΣ ΗΜΩΝ ΚΑΙ ΟΤΕ ΙΗΣΟΥΣ ΑΝΕΒΗ
ΕΚ ΤΟΥ ΥΔΑΤΟΣ ΚΑΙ ΙΔΟΥ ΗΝΕΩΙΧΘΗΣΑΝ ΟΙ ΟΥΡΑΝΟΙ ΚΑΙ Ο
ΘΕΟΣ ΕΥΔΟΚΗΣΕ

ΚΑΙ ΠΕΡΙΗΓΕΝ Ο ΙΗΣΟΥΣ ΠΑΝΤΑΣ ΤΑΣ ΚΩΜΑΣ ΚΑΙ ΠΟΛΕΑ
ΔΙΔΑΣΚΩΝ ΕΝ ΤΑΙΣ ΣΥΝΑΓΩΓ ΑΙΣ ΚΑΙ ΚΗΡΥΣΣΩΝ ΤΟ
ΕΥΑΓΓΗΛΙΟΝ ΤΗΣ ΒΑΣΙΛΕΙΑΣ ΣΥΝ ΜΑΘΗΤΑΙΣ ΟΙ ΕΙΣΙ ΣΙΜΩΝ
Ο ΛΕΓΟΜΕΝΟΣ ΠΕΤΡΟΣ ΚΑΙ ΑΝΔΡΕΑΣ Ο ΑΔΕΛΦΟΣ ΑΥΤΟΥ
ΙΑΚΩΒΟΣ Ο ΤΟΥ ΖΕΒΕΔΑΙΟΥ ΚΑΙ ΙΩΑΝΝΗΣ Ο ΑΔΕΛΦΟΣ
ΑΥΤΟΥ ΦΙΛΙΠΠΟΣ ΚΑΙ ΒΑΡΘΟΛΟΜΑΙΟΣ ΘΩΜΑΣ ΚΑΙ

ΜΑΤΘΑΙΟΣ Ο ΤΕΛΩΝΗΣ ΙΑΚΩΒΟΣ Ο ΤΟΥ ΑΛΦΑΙΟΥ ΚΑΙ
ΘΑΔΔΑΙΟΣ ΣΙΜΩΝ Ο ΚΑΝΑΝΑΙΟΣ ΚΑΙ ΙΟΥΔΑΣ Ο ΙΣΚΑΡΙΩΤΗΣ
Ο ΚΑΙ ΠΑΡΑΔΟΥΣ ΤΟΝ ΚΥΡΙΟΝ

ויבא אל נצרת אשר גדל שם וילד אל בית הכנסת ביום השבת כמשפטו
ויקם לקרא: והיתה רוח יהוה עליו לבשר לבשרה: ואיש היה בבת הכנסת
ובו רוח שמן ויצעק לאמר הניחה לנו ישוע הנצרי: ויצו ישוע את השמן
לצת ממנו וראו כלם את אלה ותפל אימה על כלם כי כלם בשלמן ובגבורה
מצוה לשמן לצאת: וידברו בו בבית ובבתי הכנסת ויצא שם ישוע בכל
הארץ ויומר ישוע שהוא מבשר מלכות השמים גם בעירים אחרות כי על כן
אותו: הוא שלח: ויהי קורא את בשרתו בבתי הכנסת ולעם עד שיחזרה הסגיר

ΜΕΤΑ Ο ΚΥΡΙΟΣ ΠΡΟΔΕΔΕΤΕΤΑΙ ΠΑΝΤΕΣ ΟΙ ΑΡΧΙΕΡΕΙΣ
ΚΑΙ ΟΙ ΠΡΕΣΒΥΤΕΡΟΙ ΕΖΕΤΟΥΝ ΚΑΤΑ ΤΟΥ ΙΗΣΟΥ ΜΑΡΤΥΡ-
ΙΑΝ ΕΙΣ ΤΟ ΘΑΝΑΤΩΣΑΙ ΕΝ ΤΗΙ ΑΥΤΗΙ ΩΡΑΙ ΒΑΡΑΒΒΑΣ Ο
ΖΕΛΩΤΗΣ ΚΑΤΑΛΙΚΑΣΩΘΗΣΕΤΑΙ ΠΡΟΣ ΤΟΝ ΘΑΝΑΤΟΝ ΚΑΙ
ΑΥΤΩΣ ΚΗΣΤΟΣ ΚΑΙ ΔΙΣΜΑΣ Ο ΠΑΤΗΡ ΕΜΟΥ

ΚΑΤΑ ΕΟΡΤΗΝ ΕΙΩΘΕΙ Ο ΗΓΕΜΩΝ ΑΠΟΛΥΕΙΝ ΕΝΑ
ΔΕΣΜΙΟΝ ΚΑΙ ΠΙΛΑΤΟΣ ΠΡΟΣΕΚΑΛΕΣΕ ΤΟΝ ΟΧΛΟΝ ΕΡΩΤΑΝ
ΟΝ ΗΘΕΛΟΝ ΠΑΡΕΔΟΘΗ ΠΡΟΣ ΣΕΑΥΤΟΙΣ Ο ΟΧΛΟΣ
ΠΡΟΣΕΚΑΛΕΣΕ ΒΑΡΡΑΒΑΣ ΚΑΤΑ ΝΟΟΝ ΑΥΤΩΝ ΒΑΡΡΑΒΑΣ
ΑΦΕΙΤΑΙ ΟΙ ΑΛΛΟΙ ΔΕΣΜΙΟΙ ΚΗΣΤΑΣ ΔΙΣΜΑΣ ΚΑΙ ΙΗΣΟΥΣ
ΣΤΑΥΡΟΥΝΤΑΙ

ΠΑΡΑ ΤΗΝ ΣΤΑΥΡΩΣΙΝ ΤΟΥ ΧΡΙΣΤΟΥ ΔΙΣΜΑΣ ΠΑΤΗΡ ΕΜΟΥ
ΠΡΟΣΕΚΑΛΕΣΕ ΙΗΣΟΥΝ ΜΝΗΜΟΝΕΥΕΙΝ ΣΕΑΥΤΟΝ ΟΤΑΝ
ΕΛΘΗΙ ΕΝ ΤΩΙ ΠΑΡΑΔΕΙΣΩΙ ΚΑΙ ΘΝΗΣΚΩΝ ΕΝ ΤΩΙ ΣΤΑΥΡΩΙ
ΨΥΧΗ ΤΟΥ ΠΑΤΡΟΥ ΕΜΟΥ ΕΣΩΘΗ

ΟΤΕ ΙΗΣΟΥΣ ΣΤΟΥΡΟΥΤΑΙ ΚΑΙ ΕΤΕΘΗ ΕΝ ΤΩΙ ΜΝΗΜΕΙΩΙ
ΑΥΤΟΥ ΗΓΕΡΘΗ ΕΚ ΤΟΥ ΘΑΝΑΤΟΥ ΑΠΟ ΤΟΥ ΑΝΑΣΤΑΣΕΩΣ
ΑΥΤΟΥ ΕΦΑΝΗ ΠΡΩΤΟΝ ΣΙΜΩΝΙ ΕΝ ΤΩΙ ΟΔΩΙ ΚΥΡΑΝΑΙΩΙ
ΚΑΙ ΩΙ ΤΟΝ ΣΥΜΒΟΛΟΝ ΔΕΔΩΚΕ ΤΟΤΕ ΚΕΦΩΙ ΤΟΤΕ ΤΩΙ
ΔΩΔΕΚΑ ΚΑΙ ΑΠΟ ΤΟΥΤΩΝ ΤΟΙΣ ΑΔΕΛΦΟΙΣ ΠΕΝΤΑΚΟΣΙΟΙΣ
ΑΥΤΟΘΕ

ΔΙΑ ΚΗΡΥΞΕΩΣ ΕΜΟΥ ΑΠΟΔΕΔΕΓΜΑΙ ΥΠΟ ΤΩΝ ΒΑΣΑΝΙ-
ΖΩΝΤΩΝ ΕΜΕ ΤΕΣΣΑΡΑΚΟΝΤΑ ΠΑΡΑ ΜΙΑΝ ΤΩΝ ΙΜΑΣΘΛΙΩΝ
ΕΛΙΘΑΣΘΗΝ ΣΧΕΔΟΝ ΠΡΟΣ ΘΑΝΑΤΟΝ ΚΑΙ ΕΝ ΦΥΛΑΚΑΙΣ

ΑΠΕΙΛΟΜΕΝΟΣ ΠΡΟΣ ΤΗΝ ΣΤΑΥΡΩΣΙΝ ΕΝΕΠΟΡΕΥΘΗΝ ΕΝ
ΤΩΙ ΠΕΛΑΓΩΙ ΕΚΙΝΔΥΝΕΥΣΕ ΤΑ ΡΕΥΜΑΤΑ ΚΑΙ ΤΟΥΣ ΟΔΟΥ-
ΡΟΥΣ ΚΑΘΑΠΕΡ ΤΟΝ ΛΑΟΝ ΕΜΟΝ ΟΙ ΜΗ ΕΛΑΒΟΝ ΤΟΝ ΚΥΡ-
ΙΟΝ ΑΥΤΩΝ

ΚΑΙ ΤΟΙ ΔΙΑ ΠΑΝΤΩΝ Ο ΚΥΡΙΟΣ ΘΕΟΣ ΕΜΟΥ ΠΕΦΥΛΑΚΕ
ΕΜΕ ΚΑΙ ΕΠΕΜΠΣΕ ΤΟΝ ΑΓΓΕΛΟΝ ΕΠΙΣΚΟΠΕΙΝ ΕΜΕ ΚΑΙ
ΑΠΟΔΕΔΕΙΓΤΑΙ ΤΗΝ ΟΔΟΝ

As Tobias absorbed the meaning, he felt a tingling
through his entire body, similar to what he experienced at
Masada and sometimes when having a vision. Looking up
from the document, he gazed at no point in particular and
saw an old man staring back at him. Without being told,
Tobias knew that he was Dismas bar-Dismas, the man who
had written the words upon this scroll.

There was a look of rapture on the face of Dismas, which
Tobias realized must match his own. Here, for the very first
time, Dismas was seeing his secret labor at last bear fruit.
After a thousand years beneath the ground, his words were
being read and understood.

"Who are you?" al-Aarif asked. "Have you come to hear
Tobias read the scroll?"

"Who are you talking to?" Rachel asked in confusion.

"To the old man in the corner," al-Aarif said, pointing.

"Have you been too long in the sun?" she asked. "There's
no one there."

"She cannot see or hear me," Dismas said. "Only you and
Tobias can see."

Tobias was stunned. This was the second time that al-
Aarif was sharing a vision, something no one on this side of
the veil had ever done.

"How is it," Tobias asked, "that my friend al-Aarif is
sharing my vision?"

"He is not sharing your vision, Tobias. This is his own
vision."

Rachel gasped at hearing Tobias and realizing that the

two men were experiencing something she was not. She started to speak, then held back, not wanting to interrupt and perhaps cause the vision to end prematurely. Instead she whispered in awe, "Surely al-Aarif has been blessed by the Lord."

"I don't understand," al-Aarif said. "Who are you?"

"I am Dismas bar-Dismas. My father, Dismas, died upon the cross beside Jesus. Before you is the story of the teachings of Jesus, as I heard them when He still walked upon this land."

"Praise be to Allah for allowing me to see such a wonder," al-Aarif intoned.

"Tobias," Dismas said, gesturing toward the scroll. "Please, read aloud in your own tongue, for where I am, all tongues speak the same praise of the Lord."

Tobias cleared his throat and began to read, his voice loud, clear, and impassioned:

The account of Dismas bar-Dismas recorded in his own hand in the thirtieth year from the Death and Resurrection of the Christ, set down in the City of Rome at the command of Paul the Apostle by a Servant and Witness

I, Dismas, son of Dismas of Galilee and messenger of Jesus Christ by the will of God the Father and commissioned by the Holy Spirit, do hereby set down a testament for believers and those who may come to believe, according to His will.

The witness I have made of all that Jesus did and taught before His Crucifixion by sentence of Pontius Pilate, the Roman prefect of Judea, was by the word passed from the mouths of the holy Apostles themselves to me, but of His crucifixion I bear direct testimony and of the aftermath until He ascended to Heaven at the right hand of the Almighty Father.

These are the things which the believers hold to be

true: that a child was born unto Mary of Nazareth, in whose womb the Lord Himself by the power of the Holy Spirit entrusted the Son to be King of the promised Kingdom of Heaven; that the child of Mary, wife of Joseph of the House of David, she without stain of sin and Mother of the Lord, was foretold by the prophets of Israel as the Savior and sign of God among us, His covenant people; that His name was called Jesus.

And when Jesus came from Galilee to Jordan unto John to be baptized, John was troubled, saying, "Teacher, why ask me to baptize thee, when it is I who should be baptized by the Son of man?"

And Jesus answered him saying, "Let it be so now, for such is a testament to our faith." And when Jesus arose from the water, the heavens opened up and God was pleased.

And Jesus went about all the cities and villages, teaching in the synagogues, and preaching the gospel of the kingdom with His disciples; Simon, who is called Peter, and Andrew his brother; and James the son of Zebedee, John his brother; Philip and Bartholomew; Thomas and Matthew the tax-gatherer; James the son of Alphaeus, and Thaddaeus; Simon the Cananaean, and Judas Iscariot, the one who betrayed our Lord.

Tobias stopped reading for a moment and looked up at the others. "Here," he said, "the words are written in Hebrew." Then to Dismas, who was still present in vision, he asked, "Why write this part in Hebrew?"

"I was guided by His hand, so to do," Dismas replied with no further explanation.

Tobias nodded, understanding so perfectly that he asked no further questions.

Clearing his throat, Tobias began to translate the Hebrew text:

And He came to Nazareth, where He had been brought up; and as was His custom went into the synagogue on the Sabbath day, and stood to read. And the Spirit of the Lord was on Him as He preached the gospel. And in the synagogue there was one who was by the devil possessed, and he cried out, saying, "Let us alone, Jesus of Nazareth." But Jesus commanded the devil to come from him, and when all saw this they were amazed that with power and authority Jesus did command the devil to depart. And they spoke of Him in the houses and synagogues, and the fame of Jesus went into every place of the country. And Jesus said that He would preach the kingdom of God to other cities also: for it was for this reason He was sent. And He went about, preaching in the synagogues and to the people, until His betrayal by Judas.

Once more, Tobias looked up. "And here the text returns to Greek." Clearing his throat again, he continued to read:

After He was betrayed, all the chief priests and the elders held trial against Jesus and sentenced Him to be put to death. At the same time Barabbas, the Zealot, was sentenced to death, and so were Gestas and Dismas, who was my father.

During the feast, the governor was accustomed to release one prisoner, and Pilate called upon the multitude, asking who they would want delivered to them. The crowd called for Barabbas, and in accordance with their wishes, Barabbas was released. The other prisoners, Gestas, Dismas, and Jesus, went to the cross.

During the passion of the Christ, Dismas, my father, called upon Jesus to remember him when He entered into Paradise, and even as he was dying on the cross, was the soul of my father saved.

After Jesus was crucified and laid in His tomb, He rose from the dead. He appeared after His resurrection, first to

Simon, who was on the road to Cyrene, and to whom He gave the symbol, then to Cephas, then to the twelve, and after these to five hundred brethren at once.

For my preaching, I have received at the hand of my tormenters forty-minus-one lashes of the rod. I have been stoned near to dead, and I have been thrown into prison under penalty of crucifixion. I have traveled by sea, I have been in danger from floods, robbers, and even from my own people who have not yet received our Lord.

And yet, through it all, the Lord my God has watched over me, has sent an angel to protect me, and has shown me the way.

When Tobias had finished reciting the opening section of the gospel, Dismas said, "Guard well the scroll, for it shall be sought by evil men, now and in the time to come. You must not let the true scroll fall into their hands."

"I will protect it," Tobias promised.

"Is he still here?" al-Aarif asked.

Tobias turned to al-Aarif. "Don't you see him? Don't you hear his words?"

"No," Al-Aarif replied, shaking his head.

Tobias looked questioningly at Dismas.

"He sees me not," Dismas said, "for these words are for you alone. But the time will come when al-Aarif will see far more."

Tobias started to speak, but Dismas interrupted with a raised hand.

"Say nothing. His time is not yet at hand."

As Tobias nodded, the vision faded, and once more the palace room held only Tobias, al-Aarif, and Rachel.

"Is he gone?" al-Aarif asked.

"Yes."

"What a wondrous thing," al-Aarif muttered.

"I must get started immediately," Tobias announced. "I have much work to do."

"But surely, Tobias, you can wait a few days before you start," Rachael told him. "The journey and the climb to Masada was long and hard. You should rest."

"I cannot, for my days grow short," Tobias replied.

CHAPTER 35

JERUSALEM

For the next several days, Tobias looked for papyrus worthy to use as a medium for the transcription of the Dismas scroll. Al-Aarif arranged with their host, Sultan Barkiyaruq, for rolls of unused papyrus to be brought to the palace room that Tobias was using as a scriptorium, and Rachel assisted in comparing them to the original scroll.

The challenge was far from easy, as papyrus had long since gone out of fashion, replaced first by parchment, manufactured from sheep or goat hide, and more recently by paper, invented in China in the second century but only recently imported to the West. Papyrus was made from the *Cyperus papyrus* plant, which grew in the fresh waters of the Nile, and was far less stable than either parchment or paper, as it was subject to mold in any but the driest of climates. Yet Tobias was insistent that his copy be produced on the same medium as the original.

On the third afternoon following their return from Masada, Tobias was at work in the scriptorium, rejecting yet another roll of papyrus, when Rachel appeared in the doorway.

"Here, look at this one," Tobias said, gesturing for her to approach. "It's the closest match yet. We must tell al-Aarif to bring more from the same library." Glancing up, he saw Rachel's worried expression. "What is it, child? Is something wrong?"

"It is Philippe," she said almost in a whisper. "He was at Xerigordon."

Tobias dropped the roll of papyrus and shook his head. "The poor man. I assumed he was with Peter the Hermit and the others. How do they know? Did they find his body?"

"No, he's here, in Jerusalem."

"Why bring him here? Weren't they all buried en masse at Xerigordon?"

"You don't understand," she replied, trying to calm her voice. "Not all of them were killed. Some have been brought to the city . . . as slaves."

"Philippe? A slave?"

Rachel nodded. "He's been sold to the household of a cloth merchant named Bin Haji."

"How did you find this out?"

"From al-Aarif. He saw a list of those spared from the sword at Xerigordon, and while he has no love for Philippe, he knew we'd want to do what we can for him, since he saved our lives at Constantinople."

"We must find this Bin Haji and send for—"

"It's already done," Rachel said. "Al-Aarif is with the merchant now, arranging for Philippe to visit us."

AN HOUR LATER, Philippe Guischard arrived at the palace of Barkiyaruq and was ushered into the scriptorium. He wore not only the tunic and short white skirt of a slave, but also the demeanor. Gone was his usual arrogance, replaced by a spirit-draining acquiescence that caused him to stand in the doorway with his eyes downcast.

Tobias hurried over and grasped the younger man's forearms. "Philippe, my friend. You are alive."

"Yes, sir," Philippe mumbled, still looking down.

"There's no need to call me that. We're equals."

Philippe shook his head. "No longer. I'm a slave."

"Not here," Rachel said, coming over to them.

"How did such a thing happen?" Tobias asked. "We heard all the pilgrims were put to the sword."

Philippe's eyes welled with tears. "Some of us were spared for a crueler fate."

"Don't worry about that," Tobias said, drawing Philippe through the doorway and into the room. "We'll find a way to free you from your master."

"My master?" Philippe said, looking up at Tobias in great distress. "I will never be free again."

"Surely there's a price he'll accept for—"

"I've already paid that price."

"Then we'll pay him more," Tobias assured him.

Philippe pulled away and backed toward the doorway. "You don't understand. . . ." He looked back and forth between Tobias and Rachel. "I've already paid the ultimate price . . . my soul."

Rachel held out a hand and took a step closer. "It's not your fault," she assured him. "You didn't choose to be made a slave."

"This?" Philippe said, looking down and gesturing at his outfit. "I care nothing about the state of my body. It's my soul that's been enslaved, and not by the infidels but by al-Shaitaan—by Satan himself."

"But we Christians have a greater power—"

"*You* Christians," Philippe said, cutting Tobias off. "You Christians, not we, for no longer may I number myself among the saved."

"What are you talking about?" Rachel asked. She again reached out to him, but he shrank from her.

Philippe closed his eyes, and as he spoke, his voice was calm with resignation. "At Xerigordon, I watched in awe as my fellow soldiers knelt before the infidels and bared their necks to the scimitar blades. But then it was my turn, and I tried. Truly, I tried." He opened his eyes, revealing a quiet desperation. "I thought my faith was strong, for it had been put to the lash in the sanctuary of Via Dei. Yet faced with the ultimate test, I failed."

"How?" Tobias asked. "There is no shame in accepting slavery in order to preserve life."

"Slavery I can stand. It's what I did to secure that slavery."

"What did you do, my son?"

Philippe dropped to his knees and covered his face with his hands. He did not cry but instead began to chant the *Shahadah* in a soft, wavering voice, *"La ilaha illa Allah wa-Muhammad rasul Allah"*—There is no god but Allah, and Muhammad is his messenger.

When Philippe started to repeat the Islamic profession of faith, Tobias pulled the younger man's hands away from his face. "Enough. You are not bound to any oath given at the point of a sword. That is, unless you truly believe what you were forced to say."

Philippe's shoulders slumped. "I . . . I don't know what to believe anymore." He looked up, not at them but into the distance. "I saw so much death out there. I confess, I no longer understand why God brought us to this land and what he would have me do."

"Come," Tobias said, helping Philippe to his feet. "The first thing He would have you do is regain your freedom. We must find out what price Bin Haji will accept for you, and once it is paid, we will grant you your freedom. Then you can freely profess the faith of your heart, be it Christian, Muslim, or Jew."

"I wish it were so simple," Philippe said. "Bin Haji won't sell me to you—" He glanced over at Rachel. "—to either of you. For it is unlawful for either Christian or Jew to own a slave in Jerusalem."

"But not for a Muslim," a voice declared, and they all turned to see al-Aarif standing in the doorway, a rolled-up piece of paper in his hand. "And so it has been done. I met Bin Haji's price, and now I am Philippe's legal master."

"And can grant him his freedom," Rachel said eagerly as she hurried over to al-Aarif.

"In time," he replied. "It is forbidden to purchase a slave merely to free him. For now Philippe must remain a part of my household. But that is a formality only."

With the hint of a smile, he approached the Frenchman who had treated him so disrespectfully in Toledo.

"Philippe Guischard, I, al-Aarif of al-Andalus, do hereby grant you leave to remain in the company of Tobias Garlande and Rachel Benyuli and to serve them as equals or however they see fit."

Turning, he handed Tobias the purchase agreement from Bin Haji.

AT FIRST, PHILIPPE exhibited a remarkable transformation. Gone was the arrogant self-righteousness that had previously dominated his character. And while he also lost the obsequiousness of a slave, he did seem to take pleasure in performing the most menial duties, and he quickly ingratiated himself to Tobias, whom he had once served as an assistant.

Rachel, however, did not share Tobias's conviction that such a transformation had taken place or was even possible. As a woman, she saw signs that Philippe was not entirely ingenuous, or at the least was not able to maintain a true change of character. It was nothing he said or did but more the way he looked at her, as if suppressing a desire to possess what he had been unable to win freely. She also didn't trust his flattering tone with Tobias. The real Philippe, she suspected, lurked below the surface, awaiting the right circumstances to be revealed.

In the meantime, Tobias finally found what he needed. It was Philippe, in fact, who suggested he give up searching for unused papyrus, since most of it would be far too new to match the unique nature of the Dismas scroll. Instead

Philippe organized a search of ancient papyrus manuscripts, and at the end of a first-century document titled *Periplus Maris Erythraei*, he found a long, unused section that was an almost perfect match, having been manufactured in the same century and locale.

Rachel was given the task of cutting the papyrus into a scroll matching the dimensions of the one found at Masada. When she was finished, it would have been hard to distinguish the original from the copy if not for the presence of the text.

At last Tobias was able to begin the painstaking transcription. In Toledo, he had either created a translation of an ancient manuscript or had merely copied the text so that others could read it in the original. Never before had he tried to reproduce the precise hand of the original author. When Rachel asked why it must be so exact, he confessed he didn't know, but that he felt compelled to produce a duplicate version in both content and appearance.

Tobias worked as quickly as possible, given the deliberate nature of the task. Rachel grew increasingly worried about his health and checked on him often, bringing his meals to the scriptorium and urging him to take periods of rest. Still, he could be found late into the night at his work table, huddled over the papyrus scroll and writing out Greek and Hebrew characters by the flickering light of a half-dozen guttering candles.

"HOW ARE YOUR guests, the old Christian man and his Jewess?" Sultan Barkiyaruq asked after summoning al-Aarif to his council room.

"They're doing well, Your Highness, and most appreciative of your beneficence," al-Aarif replied.

"The man is busy, transcribing ancient manuscripts?"

"Yes."

"Some have advised me not to allow that."

"But why, Your Highness?"

"They fear he is stealing the wisdom of the ages."

Al-Aarif shook his head. "I believe he is preserving that wisdom. And, Your Highness, for supporting that effort, your name shall be revered for a thousand years."

"My name?" Barkiyaruq said, stroking his beard.

"Each manuscript that Tobias transcribes bears an inscription with your name and seal."

The sultan's expression brightened. "We shall continue to offer our encouragement and support."

"Thank you, Your Highness."

"Now, al-Aarif, I am told you have purchased one of the pilgrim slaves of Xerigordon."

"Yes."

"Why would you buy such a creature?"

"I was asked to do so by Rachel."

"The Jewess?" Barkiyaruq asked, and al-Aarif nodded. "Why would she care about the fate of this one pilgrim?"

"She believes this slave, Philippe, saved her life."

"And you, al-Aarif, do you believe this as well?"

"No," he replied. "I think Philippe Guischard was in league with those who wanted to kill Rachel and Tobias."

"You are right in suspecting such a man," Barkiyaruq said. "I have little use for the cowards at Xerigordon who were so easily persuaded to deny their own prophet and be converted to ours. Keep a close eye on him."

"I will."

"After you return."

"Return, Your Highness? From where?"

"A new Christian army has crossed into our lands," Barkiyaruq said. "I have received word they are unlike the previous army that was driven back across the Bosporus. This time they have well-trained soldiers under the command of disciplined knights. They've laid siege to Antioch under the command of a man named Godfrey of Bouillon."

"Do you wish me to lead a force against them?" al-Aarif asked.

"I'm gathering an army to reinforce the beleaguered city. But I want you to go ahead with just a few men. Find out if Antioch will fall—and how much of a danger such a defeat would pose for Jerusalem."

"I will do as you direct, Your Highness," al-Aarif said with a slight bow of his head.

After his audience with Barkiyaruq, al-Aarif headed to the scriptorium and told Tobias, Rachel, and Philippe what he had learned.

"You must be very careful while I'm gone," al-Aarif said. "These Christians are not like Peter the Hermit's pilgrim band or the soldiers at Xerigordon. This army is very large and well organized."

"Will they reach Jerusalem?" Philippe asked.

"Yes, I believe they will." Seeing Philippe's barely restrained smile, he added, "Were I you, I wouldn't be so happy at the prospect. They may not look so kindly on those who renounced your savior and converted to Islam—even if only to save your life."

"Yes, but I am a Chris—"

"A true Muslim," al-Aarif cut him off with a raised hand. "You have made the *Shahadah*, and if you were now to recant, I would be forced to have you killed."

"No, I've done nothing like that," Philippe said, realizing the precariousness of his situation as long as he was in the land of the infidels. "My conversion is complete. I am Muslim."

Al-Aarif glared at Philippe so unwaveringly that Philippe could no longer meet his gaze and looked down.

"Tobias," al-Aarif said. "Might I have a word with you in private?"

"Yes, of course." Tobias turned to Philippe and Rachel, who left the room.

When they were alone, al-Aarif said, "You and Rachel must be prepared to leave as soon as I return."

"But my work is not yet done."

"You must finish within a fortnight. It will take that long for my journey, and I fear the Christian army may be at my heels when I return. If they storm Jerusalem, we're all in danger, regardless of our religion."

"Very well," Tobias said. "We will be ready."

"And, beware of Philippe. I don't trust him."

"He has given me no cause . . ." Tobias began, then nodded. "I'll be wary of him," he promised. "May God go with you."

"And may the blessings of Allah be upon you," al-Aarif replied as the two men grasped each other's forearms.

When al-Aarif emerged from the room, he found Rachel waiting for him in the neighboring foyer.

"Were you planning to leave without saying good-bye?" she asked as he walked up to her.

Taking hold of her hands, Al-Aarif gazed into her eyes. "No, I was planning to say something else." He pulled her closer. "I love you, Rachel Benyuli, and I want you to be my wife."

She started to reply, but her words melted into a long, passionate kiss.

CHAPTER 36

NEW YORK CITY

I don't know what to do with you people," Lt. Frank Santini said as he entered the interrogation room at Midtown South Precinct and found David Meyers and Sarah Arad seated at the table with a laptop opened in front of them. "You've been here so often, I should either give you badges or instruct my men to toss you out."

"David has something you need to see," Sarah said.

Santini sighed as he dropped into one of the chairs. "All right. What is it this time?"

David angled the laptop toward the lieutenant and tapped the mouse button, bringing a video program to the front. "I recorded this a little while ago," he said.

On the monitor, Antonio Sangremano could be seen seated on a sofa. The camera zoomed back slightly, revealing Benjamin Bishara beside him. Another change of zoom brought a third man into the frame, seated in a nearby chair.

Santini gasped and pointed at the monitor. "That's him!"

"Mehdi Jahmshidi," Sarah said. "He's on the most-wanted list of half the countries in the world."

"But what's he doing with Father Sangremano?"

"We told you," Sarah replied. "The three of them are working together to disrupt the symposium."

David dragged the mouse. "I'll turn up the sound."

Sangremano: *. . . We mustn't stop until we put an end to the People of the Book movement once and for all. Until that's accomplished, we should continue to work together. How many more suicide bombings do you have planned?*

Jahmshidi: *They are martyrdom operations.*

Sangremano: *All right, martyrdom operations. How many more?*

Jahmshidi: *The bombings are finished . . . for the time being.*

Bishara: *What about that Chicago train? Was that part of this, as well?*

Jahmshidi: *That was an operational test.*

Bishara: *What do you mean?*

Jahmshidi: *We have isolated and strengthened a special agent. I needed to know how it would work in a confined area, and you saw just how effective it was. If it worked on a train car, it will also work in a conference hall.*

Sangremano: *What did you use?*

Jahmshidi: *Sarin gas. We have enough to kill everyone in the convention hall. That is, unless you are too squeamish.*

Bishara: *Some things have to be done.*

Sangremano: *It is for the greater glory of God.*

The small video display on the monitor went black, and David shut down the program, then closed the laptop lid. "It was never going to be a dirty bomb," he said. "That e-mail about radioactive material was intended to throw anyone off the track. It was going to be sarin, all along."

Santini sat in total silence, shaking his head slowly. "We have been betrayed," he said, so quietly he could scarcely be heard.

"What?" Sarah asked.

"Just thinking aloud," Santini said, looking back up at David. "I should have listened to you earlier. Do you have any more?"

"What more do you need, Lieutenant?" Sarah asked. "Doesn't this prove they're working together?"

"Yes, which brings up another point. How did you get this recording?"

Looking a bit uncomfortable, David said, "I'll show you. I just need to connect via your wireless network."

Opening the laptop, he pressed a key to wake it from sleep, then launched a browser and entered an URL. An image of a bedroom appeared on the screen. David switched between camera angles, ending on an empty couch and chair—the same ones where Sangremano and his comrades had held their meeting earlier that morning.

"Where's that?" Santini asked.

"That's a live feed from Jahmshidi's room at the Hotel Musée," David explained.

"How are you getting that?"

"After I tracked Jahmshidi to the hotel, I sneaked in when he was gone and placed a couple of small cameras, which are connected to the hotel's wireless network. I can switch between cameras and control the zoom."

"Are you crazy?" Santini blurted. "Do you have any idea how serious that is? It's a felony that could put you away for five to ten years. Why would you do such a thing?"

"He killed Ann," David said bitterly. "I don't care if I go to prison, so long as we get Jahmshidi."

"This won't do it, you know," Santini told him. "We can't use any of this in court."

"No, but it can help us be ready," Sarah said. "And when they try something, we'll be there to stop them."

"Yeah, there's that," Santini admitted. He turned to David. "Can I get a copy of that video? Maybe I can find some hint of what they're planning and when."

"What's your e-mail address?" David asked, and as

Santini spelled it out, he entered it into a new message window. Then he attached the file and clicked the SEND button. He waited as the bar graph moved across the screen, then said, "You've got mail."

WHEN THE BUZZER sounded, Fr. Antonio Sangremano wiped his hands on a kitchen towel and headed through the apartment to the front door. He looked through the peephole, then unlocked and opened the door.

"Welcome, Lieutenant." He extended his hand bearing the Grand Master's ring.

Santini ignored the ring and brushed past him into the apartment.

"Is something wrong, Brother?" Sangremano asked, surprised by the treatment.

"Shut the door," Santini told him.

"Brother Santini, as Grand Master of Via Dei, I must tell you that I am uncomfortable with this behavior. I don't know what's wrong but—"

"I said shut the goddamn door!" Santini growled.

Sangremano's anger turned to fear. "All you had to do is ask," he said as he complied. "It wasn't necessary to take the Lord's name in vain."

"You hypocritical son of a bitch," Santini spurted, pressing his thumb against the Grand Master's chest. "You and two of the world's biggest terrorists hatch a plot to kill everybody in Stuyvesant Hall, and you take issue with my language?"

"Frank," Sangremano said. "Your first name is Frank, isn't it?"

"My first name is Lieutenant, which for a while I almost forgot. I only pray I haven't come to my senses too late."

Sangremano walked past the officer to a small cabinet against the wall. Kneeling down, he started to open the double doors on the front.

"Hold it right there!" Santini said, drawing his service revolver.

Sangremano held both his hands out to show they were empty. "I just want you to see something, that's all." Very slowly, he reached into the cabinet and removed an aluminum tube. Uncapping the end, he extracted a rolled manuscript.

"What's that?" Santini asked as he followed the older man into the dining room.

"I'm going to show you the greatest treasure of Via Dei . . . something less than a dozen people have beheld in the last two thousand years." He unrolled the papyrus scroll. "This is the actual gospel written in the hand of the founder of the Sacred Order of Via Dei."

"The Gospel of Dismas bar-Dismas?" Santini said, holstering his pistol as he looked down at the papyrus scroll. Upon joining Via Dei, he had heard the story of the founding of the order by the son of the Good Thief. "Where did you find it?" he asked, his voice quivering with awe.

"It is meet and right that Via Dei, and only Via Dei, have this document," Sangremano said. "And as Grand Master of Via Dei, it is my duty to protect it with my life. With the lives of hundreds, if not thousands, if need be."

"May I touch it?" Santini asked.

"Yes," Sangremano replied. "Feel its power, and you will no longer question what has to be done."

Leaning forward, Santini gingerly touched the scroll as he closed his eyes and breathed in its aroma.

"You feel it, don't you?" Sangremano asked.

"I do." Opening his eyes, he stared at the unfamiliar calligraphy. "What language is this?"

"Greek with some Hebrew."

"What does it say?" he asked eagerly.

Sangremano smiled. "In time, son. What we must concern ourselves with now is that renegade priest, Michael Flannery. He once had access to this, our most sacred document, and he intends to present a translation to the People of the Book—to the entire world—at the final session of that heretical symposium tonight." Sangremano waited until the lieutenant looked up at him, then said, "He must not be allowed to do that. He must be stopped."

Sangremano's words brought Santini back to reality. "No, I—I can't let you do that."

"It must be done, don't you understand?" Sangremano replied. "The contents of this scroll are for the sacred use of Via Dei only. No other eyes should ever behold it, no ears should ever hear the words spoken, except Via Dei. By revealing it at the symposium, that heretic will be offering our secrets to the pagan Muslims and to the Jew killers of Christ." He shook his head in defiance. "No, we cannot let such a thing happen, for whoever controls this scroll shall have the power to transform the world. It is vitally important that that power remain with Via Dei."

"But to kill . . ." Santini said a bit uncertainly.

"My brother, you have taken a sacred oath to Via Dei. You promised, when we met the other day, that you would uphold that oath and dispatch our enemies by your own hand, if necessary. Have you forgotten your oath?"

"I'll defend Via Dei against our enemies. But innocents? Hundreds of innocent people?"

"What are you talking about?" Sangremano said.

"I know what you're planning. And I won't let hundreds of people end up like those poor innocents on that train in Chicago."

"The lives of a few hundred people mean nothing when compared to the fate of the Dismas gospel."

"No," Santini said as he again drew his revolver and aimed it at Sangremano. "I won't let you murder all those people."

"The only way you will stop me is to kill me."

"I don't have to. I am placing you under arrest for conspiring with Benjamin Bishara and Mehdi Jahmshidi in the suicide attacks on—"

There was a dull clap, and Santini gasped and staggered forward, as if struck in the back by a baseball bat. He looked around in surprise and saw Mehdi Jahmshidi in the kitchen doorway, holding a pistol fitted with a silencer, from which curled a small wisp of smoke. The air smelled of cordite.

"You," Santini said, struggling to lift his gun arm.

Jahmshidi fired a second time, the bullet striking Santini in the chest. The lieutenant dropped to his knees, then pitched forward to the floor.

Jahmshidi hurried over and felt Santini's neck for a pulse, then looked up at Sangremano. "He's dead."

"You were right to stay in the kitchen, but you could've shown yourself a bit sooner."

"I wanted to hear what you were talking about," Jahmshidi said.

"What did that matter? He could've shot me."

"It is important to understand the thinking of one's enemy." He picked up the police officer's pistol.

"He's dead; who cares what he was thinking?" Sangremano said testily.

"He isn't the enemy I was talking about." Jahmshidi trained the police revolver on Sangremano.

"I see," Sangremano replied through lips drawn tight.

"What did you call Jews? Christ killers? And what did you call us? Pagans, wasn't it?"

"I was trying to draw him in, to put him at ease," Sangremano said. "You can understand that."

"Oh, I understand perfectly," Jahmshidi said. "Just as I understand that you are no longer of use to me."

Jahmshidi calmly pulled the trigger. This gun had no silencer, and the sound shook the room. The force of the blast knocked Sangremano backwards a few steps. He slapped his hand over the bullet wound in his upper abdomen and saw blood seeping through his fingers. He took a few staggering steps, reaching toward the dining room table as he fell forward. He managed to grab hold of the scroll and dragged it off the table as he went sprawling to the floor. He tried to pull it close, but his fingers went numb and the scroll slipped from his hand.

Jahmshidi watched in surprise and admiration as Sangremano's pained expression turned to rapture.

"*Introibo ad altare Dei*," the priest intoned. "I go to the altar of God."

Jahmshidi watched him die, then reached down to retrieve the scroll. Not bothering to wipe away Sangremano's blood, he rolled it up and slid it back into the aluminum tube. Then he wiped his prints from the two guns and put the police revolver in Santini's hand and the pistol with silencer in Sangremano's.

Jahmshidi punched a number into his cell phone and said to the person who answered, "I'm in Sangremano's apartment. He's dead."

"What happened?" Benjamin Bishara asked.

"It looks as if he and a policeman shot each other."

"I'll come right over."

"It isn't safe here," Jahmshidi said. "Meet me at my hotel."

"I'll be there within the hour."

WHEN CAPT. JEFFREY Robison entered his Midtown South office, he found a plain white envelope on his desk. It contained a letter from Lt. Frank Santini.

Jeff,

I want you to go into my e-mail—I know you can access all our accounts—and download an attachment from someone called Mongo. Watch the video, and you'll see that Stuyvesant Hall is in great danger. I believe terrorists are going to make an attack at tonight's session, using sarin gas, which is what killed those people on the train in Chicago. That was a test; tonight's the real thing.

You must prevent it, otherwise hundreds of people

*could die. I don't know what kind of delivery system
they'll be using, but look for some type of atomizer, possibly as small as a container of nose spray. Check with the
authorities in Chicago; it may be the same method of attack as on the train.*

*I hope to be there with you, but I may not make it. I have
some personal business to take care of this morning, and it
may just be that I'm biting off more than I can chew.*

Frank

"Personal business?" Robison said aloud. "What the hell
kind of personal business could be so important that he
can't follow up on something like this?"

The captain quickly logged into Santini's office account,
using the administrator password that he thought none of
his subordinates knew about. The e-mail from Mongo was
near the top, and he downloaded and launched the attached
video file. He sat transfixed as two known terrorists and a
former Vatican official discussed their planned attack on the
People of the Book symposium.

After watching the video a second time, Robison picked
up the phone and called Santini's office and then his cell
phone. When he got no answer, he stepped out into the squad
room and called out, "Has anyone seen Santini?"

"He left about forty-five minutes ago," one of the officers
replied.

"Did he say where he was going?"

"Nope."

"As soon as he returns, send him to my office."

"Yes, sir."

"On second thought, have him meet me at Stuyvesant
Hall."

"Will do, Captain."

* * *

"WHERE DID YOU get this?" Benjamin Bishara asked as he examined the Masada scroll, which was partly un-rolled on the coffee table in Mehdi Jahmshidi's hotel room.

"I found it clutched in Sangremano's hand."

"You have no right to this," Bishara said. "Neither did Sangremano. It's a Jewish antiquity."

"I care nothing about your antiquities," Jahmshidi said. "You are welcome to it—a gift from Arkaan."

"I . . . thank you. I didn't think you'd part with it so eas-ily." He leaned over the table for a closer inspection. "This is odd. It's in Greek, but this part is in Hebrew."

"Where," Jahmshidi asked as he sat down on the couch beside Bishara.

"Right here," Bishara said, pointing to the scroll.

He felt a little sting, as if a pin had been left in the front of his shirt, but it quickly grew to a deep, penetrating pain. Looking down, he saw that Jahmshidi was holding a knife that had gone in under his rib cage.

"Why?" he asked in confusion and shock.

"For the same reason I killed Sangremano—because you have served your purpose."

Jahmshidi gave the knife a downward twist, opening the wound wide enough for some intestines to spill out. Bishara slipped forward off the couch, dead before he hit the floor.

Jahmshidi stared down at the body. "Shalom, Benjamin. And if you see Sangremano, tell him I knew he was trying to double-cross us both. It seems Lieutenant Santini was a member of Via Dei."

CHAPTER 37

ORONTES VALLEY

By the time al-Aarif and three of Sultan Barkiyaruq's soldiers reached Antioch, the city had already fallen to the Christian army. He sent two of the men back to Jerusalem with a report for the sultan, while he and the remaining soldier followed the army, which had already set off across the Orontes Valley, capturing and destroying towns and fortresses along the way.

The Christians bypassed Tripoli after receiving a substantial payment from the local emir. Beirut, Tyre, and Acre offered no resistance, so they did not attack but instead turned inland at Jaffa and passed through Ramleh. It was there that al-Aarif and his comrade caught up to them. Seeking better intelligence as to their plans, al-Aarif went alone into the city, posing as a tradesman looking to sell olives and dates to the invading army. It was a fairly simple matter to overhear their strategy for attacking Jerusalem, since the soldiers spoke freely in front of him, having no idea he understood their language.

As soon as al-Aarif could slip away from Ramleh, he and his comrade hurried back to Jerusalem, bearing news of the approaching army.

JERUSALEM

"Have no fear, my friend," Sultan Barkiyaruq said after receiving al-Aarif's report. "We will destroy the infidels here, as we did at Xerigordon."

Al-Aarif shook his head. "No, Your Highness, I don't think we will. For your own safety, I urge you to leave."

"Never," Barkiyaruq replied. "This is my city. My army and my loyal subjects will protect me. I am safe here."

"I pray Allah will protect you," al-Aarif replied.

Al-Aarif carried the same message back to Tobias Garlande, who was more receptive but reluctant to leave until he had completed his work.

"How much longer will it take you?" al-Aarif asked.

"A few more days. The work is very exacting. I must be absolutely precise in what I'm doing."

Al-Aarif shook his head. "We may not have a few more days."

"God will give me the time I need to complete my work."

"What if you finish but are killed in the battle that is sure to come? What good will the completed work do for you then?"

"I am not doing it for me," Tobias replied.

Al-Aarif shrugged in frustration, then went in search of Rachel, hoping she might be able to convince Tobias to leave the city. He doubted she would succeed, and he knew she would not leave Jerusalem without Tobias.

PHILIPPE GUISCHARD WAITED until al-Aarif had left the scriptorium; then he slipped inside. Quietly approaching the table where Tobias was working, he stood watching for a few minutes. Finally the old man glanced up and saw him.

"You startled me," Tobias said with a smile.

"I didn't want to disturb your work." He moved closer to the table. "I confess, I overheard what al-Aarif told you. Is it wise to remain in Jerusalem?"

"That is for God to decide."

"And how will you know when the Lord thinks it the right time to go?"

"I already know." Tobias saw Philippe's confused expression and added, "He wants me to remain in Jerusalem until this transcription is complete."

"But can't you finish in Toledo?"

"Toledo?" Tobias shook his head ruefully. "That is not to be."

Philippe came a few steps closer. "Might I ask you something about this scroll?"

"Of course."

"You have kept your work a private matter, and I respect that. But I've noticed that you aren't doing a translation or even a simple copy, but instead an exact duplicate."

Tobias nodded. "Which is why I was so grateful for your assistance in finding papyrus that matched."

"Wouldn't it make more sense to do a translation into a language more can read? I, myself, know Greek, but not this Greek of the first century."

Tobias put down the quill and straightened in his chair. He massaged the back of his neck as he gazed at the two scrolls on the table, one written in Dismas's own hand, the other a perfect match in his own. So skillful was Tobias's transcription that the only way to tell them apart was that the copy was not yet finished.

"I'm sorry if I've spoken out of turn," Philippe continued, "but a treasure such as this . . . won't the followers of Dismas be eager to know precisely what he proclaims in his gospel? Why not provide a translation rather than a duplicate that can be read by only a few?"

"I'm not sure I can answer that," Tobias replied. "But I believe that this is what the Lord wants me to do."

Philippe nodded but spoke no more as he left the chamber. He suspected that when the old man first read the gospel, he realized that Dismas had spoken of Via Dei, the one path to

God, and not Trevia Dei, the three paths that are one. And he feared that Tobias's copy was not as perfect as he led them to believe—that a few words were being changed to support the heretical "three path" interpretation that Via Dei had unmasked and rejected.

Philippe did not intend to let anyone, Tobias included, pervert the true message of Dismas and Via Dei. When the moment was right, he would carry off the original and bring it to Grand Master Jean Fournier in Lourdes, thus assuring his own position in the church and Via Dei.

Yes, Philippe was going back, not in humiliation as a slave who had renounced Jesus, but in glory as the protector of the Gospel of Dismas and one of the architects of the fall of Jerusalem. Already, Philippe had drawn maps of the city's defenses, which he intended to deliver to the approaching army.

FROM AL-AARIF'S POSITION on the walls surrounding the city of Jerusalem, he could look down upon the ranks of the Christians. They were spread out for many rods in each direction, a well-armed force consisting of thousands of soldiers seasoned by battle. Dozens of tents rose from the desert, with colorful flags and pennants identifying the various commanders.

A constant cloud of dust hung over the area as horses and men moved about, shifting positions and preparing for battle. Often the clarion call of trumpets could be heard, accompanied by the beating of drums.

Al-Aarif considered the fate of the inhabitants of Jerusalem. As at Xerigordon, the contrast in the size of the two armies was dramatically evident, only here the numbers were reversed. The Christians had the upper hand, with the sultan's force spread across the Holy Land and only a small number inside the walls of the city.

Suddenly al-Aarif felt a tingling sensation, similar to

what he had experienced when he had had a vision of Dismas. Now, looking around, he saw a powerfully built black man standing on the wall beside him.

"Who are you?" al-Aarif asked.

"I am a friend to Tobias, and to you," the man said. "I am Simon."

"You shouldn't be on the wall unarmed. You place yourself in danger."

"I am in no danger," Simon replied. "Come, there's something I must show you."

Without knowing how he got there, al-Aarif found himself standing outside the largest tent on the battlefield. He looked around, but the strange black man was nowhere in sight.

"Simon!" he called. "Where are you?"

Seeing a Christian soldier nearby, al-Aarif expected to be taken into custody. But it quickly became apparent that the soldier had not heard him.

I must be asleep, al-Aarif thought, then said aloud, "Is this a vision?"

When the soldier walked past without seeing him, al-Aarif followed him into the tent. Inside, one of the principal commanders was seated at a table laid with food and wine. Raising a joint of meat, he waggled it toward what appeared to be a lowly mendicant. As al-Aarif moved closer to look at the monk's face, he realized with a start that it was Peter the Hermit, whom he had last seen at the encampment outside Constantinople.

"Peter, my friend, seat yourself and eat with me."

"Thank you, Godfrey." Peter took the offered seat, picked up a knife, and began cutting an apple.

"What have your spies seen?" Godfrey of Bouillon asked as he bit into the joint of meat.

"Jerusalem is well defended, and the walls are thick and impenetrable."

Godfrey used the back of his hand to wipe the juice of

the meat from his beardless chin. "How many defenders do they have?"

"More than twice our number."

"You lie," al-Aarif said aloud, confident he could not be heard or seen. "Yours is the larger army."

Godfrey picked up a goblet and took a swallow of wine to wash down his food. "Are you saying we cannot take the city?"

"Not at all. But it is my duty to provide the information you will need when considering your actions."

"Peter, do you know the story of Rainald and Xerigordon?" Godfrey asked. Without awaiting a reply, he continued, "When the city fell, the infidels demanded that the Christian defenders renounce their faith and convert to Islam or be beheaded. Some did convert, but most were inspired by Rainald's sacrifice and remained true to their faith unto death."

"They truly are saints," Peter said.

"I am Christian, and I want to lead my army in the way of Jesus the Christ. If faced with the same choice as Rainald, I, too, would give my life for my Lord."

"Godfrey, you aren't suggesting we present ourselves for execution, are you?" Peter asked.

Godfrey laughed. "No. What I'm saying is simple: We must fight and defeat the infidels who occupy Jerusalem."

"And that we shall do, for God will be with us in such a fight," Peter declared.

"I know that's true, because the ghost of Adhemar of Monteil visited me last night and assured me of victory."

"May God rest his soul," Peter said of the recently deceased bishop of Le Puy, who had been accompanying the army.

"He said that if we would have victory, we must fast for the entire day this Sunday. On that day, too, we must march in solemn procession around the walls of Jerusalem. Afterwards, we will assemble the army on the Mount of Olives, where you will preach a sermon. I shall also address them, and Arnulf Malecorne, as well. If we do precisely as directed, Bishop Adhemar assures me that we cannot fail."

"By the grace of God, we shall not," Peter replied.

Al-Aarif took a step toward the table where Peter the Hermit and Godfrey of Bouillon were seated. Suddenly he felt very dizzy, as if he were falling, and he realized with a start that he was no longer in the tent but standing precariously at the edge of Jerusalem's west wall, near the Valley Gate.

"Tobias," he said aloud. The old man had experienced many visions and had even shared one with al-Aarif. Surely he would know what this one was about.

CHAPTER 38

JERUSALEM

Philippe Guischard slipped quietly down the hall to the scriptorium where Tobias worked on the Dismas scroll. He was about to enter when a voice said, "You cannot go in there." He turned to see one of the palace servants standing on guard in the shadows.

"I work for Tobias Garlande," Philippe said authoritatively.

"No one may enter without permission of Tobias, and he is not yet here."

"Who are you, a mere servant, to stop me?" Philippe challenged.

"I am a paid servant, you are but a slave," the man said, turning away. "I shall inform Tobias. If he wishes to let you in, then—"

The servant got no farther before Philippe stepped up behind him and stabbed him in the back. The man fell dead, and Philippe pulled his knife out, wiped it on the hem of the servant's robe, and dragged the body into an antechamber where it would not be found for some time.

Inside the scriptorium, Philippe set about going through the stack of manuscripts and jerking open drawers. In the bottom one, he found what he was seeking. He rolled open both scrolls and saw that the two ended with the same verse and that Tobias had finished his work. He could tell from the smell which was the newer version, but he rolled them up together, intent on taking both with him.

"Have you seen Rashid?" a voice asked, and Philippe spun around to see Tobias in the dimly lit doorway. "He was supposed to wake me, but he's not in the hall."

Philippe tucked the scrolls under his left arm and started from the room.

"What happened?" Tobias asked as he took a step closer and saw the open drawers and manuscripts strewn about. His gaze fixed on the documents the younger man was carrying. "What are you doing?"

"The Gospel of Dismas belongs to Via Dei, by right," Philippe proclaimed, halting in front of the old man.

"It is Trevia Dei, not Via Dei. And the scroll belongs to all of Christianity. Certainly you wouldn't steal it, would you?"

"This is no theft," Philippe said. "I take only what rightly belongs to Via Dei. This is your last chance. I leave at once to join the Christians, and then to bring the scroll to France. Will you come with me or not?"

"No, I will not join you." Tobias reached for the rolled-up papyrus under Philippe's arm. "And I will not let you have that."

Surprisingly, Philippe made no effort to stop the old man from retrieving the scrolls. But as Tobias carried them back to the table and rolled them open to confirm they were un-damaged, Philippe drew the knife from his robe and came up behind him. Reaching around Tobias, he plunged the knife deep into his belly.

Tobias gasped in surprise and shock as he sank to his knees in front of the table. Withdrawing the knife, Philippe grabbed him by the hair and pulled his head back, baring his throat to the blade.

"No!" a voice shouted, and Philippe jerked his head around to see al-Aarif racing into the room, his scimitar held high.

Releasing Tobias, Philippe jumped to his side, but not before the thin, curved blade of the scimitar sliced through the air, opening a wide gash across Philippe's stomach. He clutched at his belly, trying to keep his guts from spilling out. As he dropped to the floor, he took a final longing glance in the direction of the Dismas scroll, then landed on the cold stone, his eyes staring lifelessly into the distance.

"Tobias!" al-Aarif shouted as he dropped to his knees beside the old man, who was coughing and sputtering as he tried to catch his breath.

Rachel came into the chamber just then, and she screamed as she ran over to Tobias. Kneeling beside him, she lifted his head onto her lap and stroked his cheek.

"Th-the scroll," he stammered, raising his hand toward the table above. "I-I must f-finish."

"Rest easy," Rachel soothed. "Don't try to talk."

Tobias's eyes widened, and he reached out and clutched the sleeve of al-Aarif's robe. "Now! G-get me the scroll. Th-there is one more thing I m-must do."

Al-Aarif looked deeply into the old man's eyes, then nodded. Standing, he retrieved the copy of the scroll and started to kneel back down.

"And the quill," Tobias ordered.

Al-Aarif complied. Handing him the quill, he unrolled the beginning of the scroll and held it open in front of Tobias. The old man took a few deep breaths, then dipped the end of the quill in his own blood. Lifting the quill to the papyrus, he took another breath and carefully drew the symbol of Trevia Dei in two places, matching the versions written in Dismas's blood.

The quill slipped from Tobias's fingers. With the faintest of smiles, he whispered, "This one . . . you must t-take to Masada. Place it in the urn and r-return it to the ground."

"But, why?" Rachel asked. "You worked so hard to make a perfect copy, only to have us bury it?"

"Yes," Tobias said. He reached up and grasped Rachel's hand. "You must," he whispered. "You must."

"I will," Rachel replied weakly.

"And what of the original?" al-Aarif asked.

Tobias grimaced against the pain, then calmed his breathing and tried to speak.

"When the time comes, you will know what to do."

For a moment al-Aarif thought the dying man had spoken, but it was a different though familiar voice. He looked up and saw the black man named Simon standing just beyond where Tobias lay. He was not alone; several others were gathered around him.

"You have come to honor Tobias," al-Aarif said. "*Assalamu alaikum.*"

"*Wa alaikum assalam,*" Simon replied.

"Al-Aarif," Rachel said. "With whom are you speaking?"

"With Simon and the others." He gestured across the room.

"But there's no one there." She looked in puzzlement at al-Aarif and then down at Tobias.

The old man was resting calmly now, his breath slowing, his expression peaceful. He turned his head slightly and looked where al-Aarif had pointed. "Yes, I see them. Do you know their names?" he asked al-Aarif.

"Bishlam, Elihu, Ephraim," al-Aarif began, looking surprised as the names came to his lips. "Jacob, Esther, Mary, James, Miriam, Joseph, Nicholas, Judith, Demetrius, Ahmad, Moshe." He shook his head in wonder. "Tobias, how is it that I know their names?"

"Because you are one of us now," Tobias said, his voice gaining strength despite his mortal wound. Reaching up, he removed the necklace from around his neck and held it forth. "You are now Keeper of the Sign."

"No," al-Aarif said, pushing away the necklace. "Rachel is like a daughter to you. It should go to her."

"No, she has not had the visions," Tobias said, pressing it into al-Aarif's hand. "I once thought it might be Rachel, but her role was to bring you to me . . . and to walk by your side. The necklace and its treasure are your destiny. Accept this in service to the Lord, and in the knowledge that God loves the children of all three paths that lead to him."

As al-Aarif lifted the necklace around his neck, the breath went out of Tobias's body, and Rachel held him close and wept.

"Let your vision expand," the voice of Tobias said, and al-Aarif looked up to see the old man standing in the company of Simon and the other Keepers, his body glowing with the same inner light.

Closing his eyes, al-Aarif gazed deep into the darkness, until it awakened like the break of dawn. He saw Rachel standing beside him and knew she was his wife. And around them were children and grandchildren, extending far into the future. He also caught a glimpse of someone approaching; he could not be sure if it was a young man or woman, but he knew this person would carry the symbol when his own time was at an end.

When al-Aarif opened his eyes again, Tobias and the others were gone. With them went all his doubts, and he knew that he had been given and had accepted this great commission. Al-Aarif of al-Andalus, a Muslim prince, was the new Keeper of Trevia Dei.

"TURN OUT! TURN out! Rally the men!" a man shouted from somewhere in the sultan's palace. "Our battle begins!"

Al-Aarif and Rachel had just finished lifting Tobias's body onto the table where he had spent months working on his manuscripts. Hearing the call to arms, al-Aarif crossed the room and covered Philippe's body with a rug. Returning to Rachel, he gripped her shoulders and said, "Lock yourself in your room until I return."

"What about these bodies?" Rachel said, shuddering.

"Before this is over, blood will run in the streets of Jerusalem as deep as a horse's bridle, and there will be thousands of bodies. You must stay hidden so that you are not one of them."

"I—I will," Rachel promised.

"Come quickly."

He led her out of the chamber and down the hall to her room, where he showed her the best place to hide should the Christians breach the walls and storm the palace. Then they shared a long embrace, and with a final kiss, he left her in the locked room and headed outside the palace.

Al-Aarif saw a great deal of commotion in the streets of Jerusalem as the sultan's soldiers hurried to the city walls to defend them against the Christians. The new Keeper took his place among their ranks, ascending the west wall and looking out across the valley where the invading army had made camp. A force of at least twenty thousand was on the move, marching in disciplined ranks across the field toward the largest of the city gates.

Behind al-Aarif, a long line of Muslim archers had their bows drawn, the arrows nocked and pointed upward.

"Launch arrows!" an officer shouted, and hundreds of arrows sailed through the bright blue sky, arcing over the walls and plunging into the ranks of the attacking army.

Even from inside the wall, al-Aarif could hear the cries of pain from soldiers who were struck. Within moments the barrage was answered by one twice as intense, and al-Aarif had to move quickly to avoid being hit.

The battle raged for hours as the Christians brought up tall ladders to scale the walls and open the gates from within. When at last one of the gates was breached, the fighting moved into the city streets, with many of the sultan's men regrouping at the massive Muslim fortress on the site of the Tower of David.

The two forces came together beneath the fortress's tall Phasael Tower, named after King Herod's brother. Swords and battle axes crashed, and soldiers screamed in fear and fury. For the first hour, the defenders looked as if they might beat back the invading army, but as more and more Christians slipped through the gates, the balance tipped. They pushed farther into the city, forming a powerful wedge against the sultan's army, splitting the defenders into two groups.

"We are defeated!" one of the defenders shouted, and others took up his cry. "Save yourselves! We are defeated!"

As the remnants of the sultan's army scrambled toward safety inside the fortress walls, al-Aarif and other officers tried to rally the troops for a final stand. With his scimitar raised high, he and a few brave souls ran forward against the Christians, shouting the name of Allah as they cut a swath through the enemy ranks.

Suddenly al-Aarif saw a burst of color and light as something crashed into the back of his head. The scimitar went clattering across the ground as he landed among the bodies that littered the roadway.

WHEN AL-AARIF REGAINED consciousness, his head throbbed and the smell of death filled his nostrils. Opening his eyes, he found himself surrounded by bodies of attackers and defenders alike. He wondered how he had survived, then realized he must have been taken for dead.

He heard a man scream, then a loud cackling laugh as someone shouted, "Where is your Allah now? Pray to Muhammad, it will do you no good!"

Al-Aarif remained motionless as he watched marauding soldiers move among the bodies, thrusting spears into dead and living alike. Spying his scimitar a few feet away, he managed to grab hold of it, wrapping his hands around the hilt as he prepared to defend himself to the death.

"Come! All come!" someone shouted. "Godfrey of Bouillon is to be named ruler of Jerusalem!"

The soldiers put up their spears and swords and hurried off to the ceremony.

Rising slowly, al-Aarif moved cautiously through

Jerusalem. A pall of smoke filled the sky from the burning houses, many of which had been set afire by their Muslim occupants in order to deny the fruits of victory to the Christians, who were terrorizing the city with unrestrained looting, butchery, and rape. The streets were awash with blood and lined on both sides with bodies.

As Al-Aarif made his way back to the sultan's palace, a roving band passed by without taking notice of him. He turned toward them, wondering why he had not been challenged, when a voice said, "They cannot see you." He knew at once it was Simon of Cyrene, the first Keeper of the Sign.

"Then this is all a vision, and Jerusalem has not yet fallen?" al-Aarif asked as he looked at Simon, who stood beside him. He touched the back of his head and felt the painful lump. "I didn't know I could be hurt in a vision."

"I am part of your vision," Simon said, then with a wave of his hand took in the devastation all around them. "But this is not."

"Then why didn't they see me?"

"Put your hand on the necklace and the sacred cloth it contains," Simon said.

Al-Aarif lifted the necklace and gripped the locket that bore the Trevia Dei symbol.

"With this cloth, you shall have powers heretofore unknown to you," Simon explained.

"What sort of powers?"

"Power for good, which will be revealed in time. For now, go find Rachel. You have a great task before you."

"AL-AARIF!" RACHEL CRIED out in joy and relief when he entered her room. "I feared you were dead!" She ran into his arms.

"And I feared the same of you," he replied.

"It's terrible," Rachel whispered. "They are sacking the city and killing everyone."

"Yes, and they will soon be here at the palace. We must escape the city."

"I think I know a way," Rachel said as she smiled up at him.

A HALF HOUR later, al-Aarif and Rachel approached the Dung Gate in the southeast corner of the wall. Both were on horseback, but Rachel had her hands tied before her and al-Aarif was leading her horse. He no longer wore his Moorish robes but instead a mantle emblazoned with a red cross. His scimitar had been replaced with a broadsword taken from one of the fallen invaders.

One of the soldiers guarding the gate held up his hand and asked, "Where are you going?"

Al-Aarif heard Simon whisper a name, which he repeated as he greeted the man. "Good day to you, Laurence of Bastille. Would you stop me from delivering this bounty to the tent of our commander?"

"You know me?" the guard asked, surprised at being called by name.

Al-Aarif laughed. "Friend Laurence, did you tip so many tankards of ale as we waited outside Constantinople that you have lost your memory?"

"Ha!" one of the other guards said, pointing to Laurence. "He knows you well, for you were often drunk."

"Suppose I deliver this girl, then return with some wine," al-Aarif suggested. "It's odious enough having to stand guard while others enjoy their spoils. You should not have to stand here with nothing to wet your tongue."

"Yes," Laurence said. "You may pass. But don't forget to bring some wine."

"And so I shall." Al-Aarif kicked his horse forward, and as he passed through the gate, he looked back at Rachel and said gruffly, "Keep up, girl, or I shall dump you from your horse and let these men take their pleasure."

CHAPTER 39

NEW YORK CITY

F r. Michael Flannery sat on the couch in the safe-house apartment, his head back and his eyes closed. He appeared to be taking a nap but was actually back at Masada in the underground chamber where the Gospel of Dismas had been discovered the year before.

As in past visions, he saw a man and woman digging a hole large enough to contain an urn, which sat beside them on the ground. But these two were not Tibro bar-Dismas and his wife, Marcella, who had carried his brother's scroll from Rome to Jerusalem and finally to Masada, where they buried it when the fortress was about to fall to the Romans. They were two different people, burying the urn at the same place but in a different time.

"I STILL DON'T understand why we're burying this," the woman says as she hands the urn to her companion, who lowers it into the hole. "It's such a perfect copy. One can scarcely tell it from the original. Even the papyrus is a perfect match, from the same era a millennium ago."

"It was Tobias's dying wish," the man replies. "There is much I still don't understand, but I know we must fulfill his mission by burying the copy and carrying the original to safety."

"That's a copy?" Flannery says.

Neither of them respond, and he realizes they cannot see or hear him. It's a wonder he even understood what they said, for he can tell they speak an archaic form of Spanish, yet he perceives the words in modern English.

"Then the scroll I held in my hands last year must have been a copy," he muses aloud.

"Yes, it was my copy," Tobias replies as he materializes beside Flannery.

"Who are these people?" Flannery asks, not surprised at the old Keeper's arrival.

"Rachel Benyuli was my assistant. Her future husband is al-Aarif, the new Keeper." Tobias smiles. "He is new to me, but very old to you. And their marriage, while yet to come, took place a thousand years before your time."

"Why are they burying your copy and not the original?"

"So that the true scroll of Dismas will not be stolen by Via Dei," Tobias replies.

"Then, if they have the copy, where's the original?"

"It lies hidden, awaiting you in—"

"FATHER FLANNERY! MICHAEL!"

Opening his eyes, Flannery saw he was back in the living room of the safe-house apartment with Sarah Arad standing over him.

"What is it?" he asked, frustrated at being summoned prematurely from the vision.

"You were in such a deep sleep, I was beginning to worry about you," she said.

"I'm sorry. I must be more tired than I realized." He rubbed his temples to clear his head. The vision had disappeared so abruptly that he felt as if he had been moved violently from one era to another.

"There's something else," Sarah said. "It's Lieutenant Santini. He's dead."

"Dead? When? How?"

"The police found him in an apartment being used by Antonio Sangremano. They're both dead, and the police think they shot each other."

Flannery crossed himself, then breathed a quick prayer: *"Aufer a nobis, quaesumus, Domine, iniquitates nostras ut ad Sancta sanctorum puris mereamur mentibus introire. Per Christum Dominum nostrum. Amen."*

"But they didn't kill each other," David Meyers said as he and Preston Lewkis came into the living room. "Mehdi Jahmshidi killed them both."

"Why would he do that?" Flannery asked. "Santini, maybe, but Jahmshidi and Sangremano were working together."

"He was also working with Benjamin Bishara and killed him," David said.

"Bishara's also dead?"

"Show him," Sarah said.

Nodding, David retrieved his laptop and opened it in front of Flannery. When the video-capture program started running, Flannery recognized Jahmshidi's hotel room from the earlier recording. The Arkaan leader was unrolling a scroll on the coffee table and showing it to Bishara.

"That's the Masada scroll," Flannery said.

"I knew you'd find that interesting," Sarah replied.

Flannery watched and listened as Jahmshidi described finding the bodies of Sangremano and the police lieutenant. The two men argued briefly over who should get the scroll, and then with cold efficiency Jahmshidi stabbed Bishara.

Jahmshidi then said that he killed Bishara "for the same reason I killed Sangremano—because you have served your purpose." After this confession to the earlier murder, he added a startling revelation: "Shalom, Benjamin. And if you see Sangremano, tell him I knew he was trying to double-cross us both. It seems Lieutenant Santini was a member of Via Dei."

"Santini?" Flannery said in disbelief. "I had no idea."

"It's clear, now, who killed Sangremano," Preston said. "And I don't think there's any question what he's planning to do at Stuyvesant Hall. We need to get tonight's session canceled."

"I hate to let him stop me from presenting the Dismas gospel. He'll have won, even without an attack."

"We saw what happened on that commuter train in Chicago," Preston reminded them. "It's far too dangerous to risk anything like that here."

"Maybe not as dangerous as you think," David put in.

"What do you mean?" Sarah asked.

David glanced at his watch. "We have almost three hours until tonight's session." He turned to Flannery and Preston. "You two get down to Stuyvesant Hall. If you don't hear from me in an hour, do what you can to cancel tonight's session and evacuate the building."

"What about me?" Sarah asked.

"I need you with me." He gave an enigmatic smile. "Let's see if you've got the heart of a hacker."

STUYVESANT HALL WAS crowded with delegates and members of the press. Because the final session featured the presentation of a newly discovered first-century Gospel, it was being held in the large auditorium, with half the seats open to the public on a first-come, first-served basis.

"What's the count, now?" Capt. Jeffrey Robison asked the event director.

"A full house—just over seven thousand," the woman replied.

"Lord help us if something happens tonight," Robison said. "It could make the World Trade Center look like child's play."

"Captain, we haven't had this many officers in one place since 9/11," one of his men said. He gestured toward the lobby. "It's like an airport out there. Folks are annoyed we're taking away their eye drops, nose spray, mouthwash, what have you. But better safe than sorry."

"Spread the men out across the floor," Robison said. "Look for anything suspicious. And don't be afraid to profile."

"Profile? Damn, Captain, at least a third of the delegates look Middle Eastern. How do we profile?"

"Just do it!" Robison snapped, running his hand through his thinning hair in frustration.

ACROSS THE CONVENTION floor, two men in jumpsuits with the words EVENT STAFF on the back were pushing a large steel coffee cart. They set up at the back of the auditorium and almost immediately had customers for the free coffee they were offering delegates and attendees.

When the session was gaveled to order, the crowd around the coffee cart thinned. As the opening speakers took to the stage, one of the men at the cart lifted the cover off an unused coffee urn, reached inside, and removed a metal thermos. Unscrewing the top, he took out five Binaca breath sprays. He pocketed one and handed a second to his partner. Then he nodded to a nearby delegate, who brought two companions over for coffee.

"Are you enjoying the symposium?"

"Yes, very much, Mehdi—" The delegate caught himself midsentence, realizing he had spoken the leader's name. He started to apologize, but Mehdi Jahmshidi smiled broadly.

"You'll especially want to hear the presentation by Father Michael Flannery," Jahmshidi said, signaling that they were to wait until that portion of the program.

Jahmshidi served coffee to the three men, and his partner, Ahmad Faruk, handed each a napkin that concealed a small canister of sarin disguised as Binaca spray. As the three men walked back toward their seats, one of them dropped his napkin, and the others halted as the breath spray rolled across the floor.

A nearby police officer had paid only scant attention to the men at the coffee cart, deciding their conversation was innocuous enough. But when he was the small bottle of spray, he moved closer. The man seemed quite nervous as he picked it up, and then the officer noticed that one of the other men was clutching a similar-looking bottle.

Drawing his revolver on the three men, the officer shouted, "Hold it right there! Put those canisters on the floor!"

Some of the delegates seated nearby realized something was wrong, and they began to scatter from their seats toward the exit doors. As the panic spread, people at a distance began to scream, not knowing what was going on. Someone shouted that there was a bomb, and others took up the cry.

Captain Robison ran onto the stage and grabbed the microphone. "Please remain calm," he said. "The situation is under control."

The area around the three suspects emptied out as the other delegates continued to move off into the aisles and through the exits. Realizing the auditorium would soon be empty, one of the men nodded to the others, and all three jerked the caps off their canisters and pointed them out in different directions.

The police captain's voice came booming over the PA: "Put down those canisters! Our snipers have you in their sights. Put them down now, before anyone is hurt!"

The three men hesitated a moment; then they looked at each other as if passing some sort of signal between them.

"Allahu Akbar!" they yelled as one.

Each man pressed the button atop his canister, and it released a small minty spray. They pressed again and again, looking surprised as the bottles discharged only small spurts rather than the steady stream they had been designed to release. One by one, the suspects turned the bottles and sprayed into their own mouths. They stood smacking their lips, tasting the peppermint as they looked at one another in confusion.

"Everyone stay calm!" the captain told the crowd, which was still scrambling for the exits. "The suspects are in custody." He nodded toward his officers, who had already moved in and were putting the three men in handcuffs.

AS THE STANDOFF came to an end, Mehdi Jahmshidi and Ahmad Faruk managed to slip through the nearest exit door and into the lobby. A few delegates were still coming out of the auditorium, heading for the street doors, and Jahmshidi gestured for his friend to follow them out of the building.

"Hold it right there!" a woman shouted, and Jahmshidi turned to see Sarah Arad standing ten feet away, her Beretta trained on his chest. "Clear the area!" she called to the other delegates, who quickly complied.

Faruk, trembling with fear, fumbled with his spray bottle, trying to remove the cap.

"Squirt that thing all you want. We broke into your apartment two hours ago and switched the sarin with real bottles of Binaca."

Jahmshidi looked confused, then began to smile as he recalled how he had been called down to the lobby of the Hotel Musée to clear up a problem with his bill.

"That was me at the front desk," she explained.

"While I snuck into your room," David said, coming up beside her. "The same way I snuck in the other day and planted some cameras, which is how I figured out you were using that breath spray."

"Get the police," Sarah told David, motioning for him to go back into the auditorium.

"Wait," Jahmshidi said. Dropping his canister, he jerked open the top of his jumpsuit. Underneath was a thin bomb vest, and tucked behind it was a scroll of papyrus.

"How the hell did he get in here with that?" Captain Robison called out as he appeared in the open doorway to the auditorium.

Jahmshidi held up the scroll. "You know what this is, don't you?" he asked as he looked beyond the police captain to where Fr. Michael Flannery was now standing.

"Yes," Flannery said. "I know what it is."

"You Christians have waited two thousand years for this," Jahmshidi continued. "If I press this button, the scroll is lost forever." He showed that he was holding a small detonator.

"What do you want?" Robison asked.

"Safe passage out of here for Faruk and me. If not, I'll blow myself up and take your treasure with me."

"I can't bargain with you, Jahmshidi," Robison said.

"Then get someone down here who can."

"Take me instead," Sarah said.

"What do you mean?" Jahmshidi asked.

Sarah put down her gun and raised her hands. "Take me as your hostage instead of the scroll."

"You're a Jew," Jahmshidi said. "What does the scroll mean to you?"

"When our work here is fulfilled, what is sacred to one religion will be sacred to all," she replied.

"Never!" Jahmshidi shouted. "I will never let that happen!"

"Get down!" Robison shouted as Jahmshidi pressed the detonator.

Even as they were diving for the ground, there was a flash of light and a burst of smoke. They felt the heat and the concussion of the blast, but fortunately the vest did not contain any shrapnel.

When they rose a few minutes later, they saw a blackened area and the bloody, charred body parts that once were Ahmad Faruk and Mehdi Jahmshidi. A confetti of papyrus hung suspended in the air and slowly settled to the floor.

CHAPTER 40

TOLEDO

The Hotel San Juan de los Reyes was in the old Jewish quarter of Toledo, close to such important monuments as El Monasterio San Juan de los Reyes, La Sinagoga de Santa María la Blanca, and La Casa de Biblioteca, the former home of Tobias el Transcriptor.

Fr. Michael Flannery sat in his hotel room, sipping a cup of heavily creamed and sweetened coffee as he watched the English broadcast of World Cable News.

"Although it is too early to tell if the effects of the People of the Book symposium will last, the results so far have been remarkable," the newscaster was saying.

"Muslims around the world have embraced their religion's message of peace and are calling for an end to the extremism that has brought so much suffering, not only to the rest of the world, but to their own people.

"Christians and Jews are holding combined services to explore the commonality of their religions.

"The organizers of the People of the Book symposium are setting up a World Faith Organization, similar to the United Nations, to explore peace and understanding through the one God of all."

Hearing a knock on the door, Flannery turned off the TV and went to greet Preston Lewkis and Sarah Arad.

"What a beautiful place this is!" Sarah said as she swept

into the room. "And what a wonderful idea to come here for our wedding."

"I knew you'd like it," Flannery said.

"Did you have any trouble arranging to perform the ceremony?" Preston asked.

"Well, yes and no," Flannery said. "You'll need to have a civil ceremony first, then I can celebrate the rites of marriage."

"A Catholic priest marrying a Protestant to a Jew," Preston said. "That's the People of the Book in operation."

Flannery smiled. "Shall I find an imam to assist?"

"That's not a bad idea," Sarah said. "I heard that an imam, a rabbi, and a minister held a joint service in Israel the other day."

"I pray that what we've started will grow into lasting universal brotherhood. After all, Jesus said we should love the Lord and we should love each other as we love ourselves. Upon those two commandments hang all the rest. And they apply equally to all three religions."

"I just wish. . . ." Sarah let the words hang, incomplete.

"You wish what?"

She sighed. "I wish we hadn't lost the Masada scroll."

Flannery smiled broadly. "When something is lost, something else is often found. I want you to come with me to the Casa de Biblioteca."

"Where?" Preston asked.

"It's called Library House in English. It was the home of many scholars, including Tobias the Transcriber."

"You've mentioned him before," Preston said. "Twelfth— no, eleventh century, right? He copied hundreds of manuscripts that otherwise would have been lost."

"Yes, that's the one," Flannery said without elaboration.

"Wonderful, a field trip," Sarah said with enthusiasm. "When shall we go?"

"How about now?"

* * *

LA CASA DE Biblioteca had already closed for the day, but Flannery gave the night watchman fifty euros to give them a private tour. The man led them through the house, showing them the living and dining quarters and finally the basement, which had served as a storage room and now held a display of kitchen items. When he was ready to lead them back upstairs, Flannery offered him another twenty euros to allow them some private time "so we may discuss what we've seen," he explained.

The guard looked around and shrugged, probably thinking to himself, "Crazy foreigners." But since there was nothing of worth in the basement, he pocketed the money and told them to take as long as they desired.

"What did you want to show us?" Preston asked when they were alone. "This lovely *cuenco*?" He picked up a dusty wooden bowl.

"Not here. It's down below."

Sarah and Preston looked at him questioningly but said nothing as he led them past a set of shelves to a small, half-height door at the back of the basement. He gave it a push, and it creaked open. Reaching in, he flipped a switch, and some lights turned on, revealing an exceedingly narrow stone stairway that led down to a sub-basement.

"You want us to go down there?" Sarah said dubiously.

"It's fine. Just bend low and be careful on the steps. They're slippery."

At the bottom, they found themselves in a long, narrow stone chamber lit by a pair of naked bulbs that hung from electric cords.

"What did Tobias use this for?" Preston asked, looking around the empty room.

"He didn't. He may never have come down here."

"Good. Those stairs and this stale air might have killed him."

"What killed him was a knife, and not here in Toledo. He joined the First Crusade and died in Jerusalem."

"But he left something down here you want us to see, right?" Sarah asked.

"No, he didn't. But two of his companions did," Flannery said mysteriously. "Something they brought back from the Holy Land."

"Okay, you've got us filled with curiosity," Preston admitted. "What's down here?"

"Shh," Flannery said, holding up his hand.

"Do you hear something?"

Sarah jabbed Preston in the side. "He said be quiet, so be quiet."

"We're not even married yet," Preston teased, only to receive a second jab.

As they stood in silence, Flannery stared down the long corridor. A bubble of light appeared near the far end of the chamber, and he recognized a woman and a man.

"Rachel . . . Al-Aarif," he whispered.

Al-Aarif pulled a stone away from the wall, and Rachel slid something into a secret compartment behind the wall. As al-Aarif replaced the stone, the vision faded.

"It's right here, behind this stone," Flannery said, leading them over to the far wall. "And it has been here for nine hundred years."

"Whoa, if this stone has set that long, we're going to need some tools to get it out," Preston pointed out.

"I was here yesterday. I've already loosened it."

"Then you've seen what's in there?"

Flannery shook his head. "I wanted us to do that together."

"But you know what it is, don't you?"

"Yes."

"Preston, will you stop asking so many questions and remove the stone?" Sarah said in exasperation.

"Is that a hint of married life to come?" Preston asked, softening the comment with a broad smile.

He slid his fingers along the edge of the stone until he found a grip. Flannery and Sarah did likewise, and together they managed to slide the stone out of the wall.

They tried to peer into the dark opening, but the light didn't reach within.

"Go on," Sarah told Flannery. "You found it; you should be the one to pull it out, whatever it is."

Nodding, Flannery reached both hands into the opening.

"Watch out for snakes," Preston teased.

Flannery jerked his hands back, then frowned at Preston and reached back in. His fingers touched something cold and smooth, and he took hold and drew it out.

"An urn!" Sarah exclaimed as he held it against his chest.

"And look at this," Preston said, pulling Flannery over to the nearest lightbulb. "The entire urn is sealed in a thick layer of wax, not just the cover."

"They knew it was too damp here to survive the centuries until we found it."

"They?" Sarah asked. "Those names you said before?"

"Rachel Benyuli was a Jew who worked for Tobias. Al-Aarif was a Muslim prince and her husband. They were with Tobias on Masada when he discovered the scroll."

"What are you talking about?" Preston said.

"The scroll we found last year—the one that got blown to smithereens in New York—it wasn't the real scroll. It was a perfect copy transcribed by Tobias onto a sheet of first-century papyrus."

"And this?" Sarah asked, placing her hand on the urn.

"The Gospel of Dismas bar-Dismas, written in his own hand and carried by his brother, Tibro, to Masada, where it lay for a thousand years until Tobias switched it for a copy and had the original buried here."

"But why?"

"Because he was a member of a society called Trevia Dei when it took the wrong path and became Via Dei, and he knew they would not give up until they possessed the scroll and kept its secrets hidden for all time."

"This is the real scroll?" Sarah said in awe. "Via Dei never even had it . . .?"

"And won't be hunting it down," Preston continued, "for they believe it was blown up by a Muslim fanatic." He shook his head in wonder. "Someday you're going to have to tell us exactly how you figured out all of that."

"Come, let's get this back to the hotel and see what a real first-century gospel looks like." Flannery turned to Preston. "Can you spare another fifty euros for the guard?"

"You won't need any money," Sarah told them. "I'll take care of the guard. You just keep that urn out of sight when we get upstairs."

"You're not gonna hurt him?" Preston asked.

"I'm a woman—I can distract a man without hurting him," she said with a smile.

"Yes, but—"

"We're not married yet, remember?"

TWO DAYS LATER, Fr. Michael Flannery stood in his vestments at the altar in a small chapel of San Tomé, once a mosque but rebuilt as a church in the fifteenth century. Preston and Sarah stood before him, already married in the civil service that morning, but now consecrating their union with the ancient blessings of God.

"I now pronounce you man and wife," Flannery concluded. "The bride and groom may kiss."

Flannery thought their kiss lasted a bit longer than at a typical Catholic ceremony, and he fought the temptation to pull them apart. With the ceremony finished, they accepted the good wishes of a dozen or so friends and family who had flown to Spain for the event.

One guest waited in the back of the chapel, biding his time. Seeing him, Flannery waved him over.

"David!" Sarah exclaimed, giving David Meyers a big hug. "You made it."

"Miss your wedding? Never." He turned and pumped Preston's hand enthusiastically. "So, where are you off to for your honeymoon?"

"As far away as we could find," Preston told him. "We fly to New Zealand in the morning."

"Here," David said, removing an envelope from his pocket and handing it to Preston.

"You didn't need to—"

"It was nothing . . . really." He turned to leave.

"You're coming to the reception at the hotel, aren't you?" Sarah called after him.

David merely waved as he headed from the chapel.

"Aren't you going to open that?" Flannery asked as Preston tucked the envelope into his coat pocket.

"I'll put it with the other gifts."

"I think you ought to open it now."

Shrugging, Preston took the envelope back out and slit it open. He read the note inside and began to laugh.

"What is it?" Sarah asked.

"A first-class upgrade on tomorrow's flight to New Zealand." Preston looked at Flannery suspiciously. "Did you tell him our itinerary?"

"I had nothing to do with it."

"Then how did you know what he gave us? Another one of your visions?"

Flannery grinned broadly. "Nothing so mystical. It was merely a hunch. I've flown with David before, remember?"

He wrapped his arms around Preston and Sarah and led the newly married couple up the aisle.